ONE WEALTHY HUSBAND

Daniel Sellington is a desperate man—every woman around wants to be his blushing bride, but do they want him . . . or his money? The only way to find out is for him to give his wealth away. And when he meets Kathryn Jordan, the one gal in town who doesn't seem to know who he is, Daniel thinks he's found his dream woman. Suddenly he's pursuing the spirited beauty with the same hungry determination he's run from in the past.

FOUND:
ONE DETERMINED BRIDE

Kathryn's goal is to marry Daniel by any means possible, even if she must deceive him. After all, his fortune will save her family and avenge her father's name. But Kathryn soon realizes that the passion she's found in his arms is worth far more than the cash in his bank account. Now, Kathryn must convince Daniel that she's married the most wanted bachelor for love—before she loses him forever.

"A SINFUL INDULGENCE
OF THE BEST KIND."
Christina Dodd

Susan Kay Law

The Most Wanted Bachelor

An Avon Romantic Treasure

AVON BOOKS
An Imprint of HarperCollins*Publishers*

This is a work of fiction. Names, characters, places, and incidents are products of the author's imagination or are used fictitiously and are not to be construed as real. Any resemblance to actual events, locales, organizations, or persons, living or dead, is entirely coincidental.

AVON BOOKS
An Imprint of HarperCollins*Publishers*
10 East 53rd Street
New York, New York 10022-5299

First Avon Books paperback printing: June 2000

Avon Trademark Reg. U.S. Pat. Off. and in Other Countries, Marca Registrada, Hecho en U.S.A.
HarperCollins® is a trademark of HarperCollins Publishers Inc.

Printed in the U.S.A.

WCD 10 9 8 7 6 5 4 3 2 1

For Matthew

Because I got tired of waiting to write
the one that was good enough
to dedicate to you,
and so decided all that matters
is that *you're* the one, always.

All my love.

Chapter 1

Denver, 1887

Daniel Sellington was a rich man. A very, *very* rich man.

Kathryn Jordan knew little more about him than that. It didn't matter. It was all she needed to know.

She had every intention of marrying him.

Her sweat-dampened fingers clenching, she wrinkled the grimy newspaper she'd clutched ever since she'd found it blown against the soot-streaked back wall of the Schatz House Billiard Hall and Saloon. Never one to overlook the slightest boon, she'd snatched it up. Another crack in the thin walls of her home could be pitifully armored against the winds roaring off the mountains next winter, she figured. But as she considered uses for the paper, the name *Sellington,* in huge letters black as Satan's heart, had screamed out at her from the front page of the *Rocky Mountain News.*

She forced her tight grip to relax and studied the face that claimed a full quarter of the page. Edward

1

Sellington, whose name she'd heard her mother curse every single day of the last fifteen years, stared coolly back at her. He'd been a handsome man, she thought dispassionately; she'd always imagined him as monstrously disfigured, as if his outer husk must reveal the evil harbored within. Instead, if the artist could be trusted, he'd owned patrician features. Only his eyes, beautifully shaped and framed by elegantly arched brows, hinted at something else; he had mean eyes. She couldn't have said what made them mean, but anyone who grew up in her neighborhood would understand exactly what she meant, and know enough to steer clear of them.

Pity her father hadn't known.

"Sure were a handsome one, weren't he?" The woman to her left nudged a bare, plump elbow into Kathryn's ribs. "Think this one looks anythin' like him?"

Kathryn eyed her. Cheap red satin, as shiny in the August heat as the woman's lavishly exposed skin, erupted above and below her tightly cinched waist. Though the dress was aggressively improper, Kathryn couldn't help envying the ventilation as she sweated in her heavy black mourning dress, handed down from a generous employer. *Former* employer, she amended bitterly, and formerly generous, for Mrs. Chivington had been anything but generous when she fired her after her son, Richard, claimed Kathryn's behavior was improper—when it had been her emphatic *lack* of impropriety to which he'd truly objected. Mrs. Chivington had made certain that no other of Denver's leading matrons would ever hire Kathryn for anything, either.

The gloomy, stifling dress had been the best Kathryn could dredge up on short notice. She'd hoped the mourning garb might engender a bit of sympathy. She could use every advantage she could get.

"I imagine," Kathryn said, "that this one's very much like his father." Edward Sellington looked like the type that would breed true.

"Oooh," the woman cooed, a grin of anticipation curving her red-glossed lips. "Seems hardly fair, does it? Rich as that, and looks, too?"

"Hardly fair," Kathryn murmured, her fingers crushing the paper again.

There was little doubt why the woman, and three dozen others, had turned up here at two o'clock on a steaming Tuesday afternoon. They clustered in front of a great iron gate, the solid black bars as sturdy as any that caged a fierce zoo creature. Except these bars, of course, were meant to keep the animals out.

She recognized old Blind Willie, bent over his twisted oak cane, who was no more blind than she was. And Mrs. O'Neill, painfully thin and pale, whose husband had died of a lung hemorrhage three months ago, leaving her with five children under the age of six—and, by the looks of things, one more to arrive any day. Though Kathryn didn't know the names of any of the others, she recognized them, too, the residents of tent villages and tenements and vermin-infested boardinghouses, equally split between confidence men—and women—thieves, and the honestly desperate. Oh yes, she recognized them.

She was one of them.

And, just like every one of them, she wanted a piece of the Sellington millions.

Up by the gate, a man with the cadaverous look of a lung patient whacked a stick across the bars, keeping up a steady clang. "Let us in!" he shouted. "We just wants to talk to the bloke!"

The red-clad woman curled a plump lip. "Oh, yeah, *that's* gonna get them to let us in." She peered at the paper in Kathryn's hand. "Say anything in there about him? What this one's like?"

"It doesn't say much about him." But the *News* had plenty else to say. Though she already knew much of what the paper had printed, she'd read every word twice.

The article had gone back to the beginning, to the mysterious disappearance of Edward Sellington. One of the richest men in New York, his mining interests in Colorado had only expanded that unimaginable wealth. But nearly fifteen years ago, he, along with his wife and young son, had vanished without a trace.

His mother had spent years searching the West for him. Finally, she'd gone into the monolithic mansion Edward had built on Arapahoe Street and never come out again. Rumor had it grief had finally driven her mad.

There was no fresh news for years. Children avoided the looming house, telling stories of the crazed woman and restless ghosts. The newspapers moved on to more timely topics. But then, five years ago, Edward Sellington's long-lost son, Daniel, had suddenly reappeared to claim his heritage.

Just as they had this week, the newsmen had descended immediately, but he'd been unwilling to talk, steadfastly refusing to explain what happened to him or his father all those years ago. He hadn't stayed in town more than a few months before disappearing back from where he came . . . or so they'd all believed.

Except that he'd been here all along. In Denver, in an ordinary house in Curtis Park, living under the name of Daniel Hall. It was as mysterious and intriguing as the rest of his story.

Here, where she could gain access to him, and to his fortune. And to discover it now, this very week, when the rope she'd been clinging to for years had finally unraveled to one thin, fraying thread. When she'd lost her job and her sister in the space of a day.

It was almost as if Fate were finally taking a hand, giving her a chance to reclaim all that they'd lost.

And all she had to do now was figure out how the hell to manage it.

The mob pressed around her, the smell and heat and worry unsettling her stomach. "Excuse me," she said, and squeezed by a well-dressed young man with the sharp-eyed look of a gambler. She gave wide berth to an old man with the stooped posture of one who'd spent years hunched over a gold pan, praying for a nugget—she'd caught a whiff of him when she'd first arrived, and once was more than enough.

"Givin' up?" the woman called after her, grinning. "Good! That's all the more for the rest of us!"

But she couldn't give up. Kathryn stopped at the edge of the throng, where the air was clearer, her mind whirling with possibilities and half-formed plans as she watched a young, straw-haired boy work his way through the crowd as well, his nimble fingers dipping into pockets and handbags, coming back out empty. As he edged by her, she tapped him on the shoulder.

"If you hope to make a profit," she said, "you'd do well to pick a richer crowd than this."

He looked up at her, surprise in his brown eyes. Then a gap-toothed smile split his narrow face. "You saw, huh? Damn. See why I gotta practice on someone?" he asked. "Ain't no one here likely to bother to drag me off to the station, even if'n they catch me. They don' like the cops any better'n me."

"I see," she said. "Still, I'd make sure you didn't pinch so much as a penny, should you find one. The police would be the least of your problem, if any of these people happened to catch you."

"Naw, ain't nobody 'round here quick enough to nab me."

It was true that a good share of his intended victims were either old, infirm, drunk, or some combination of the three. Still, he reminded her too much of her younger brother Thomas a few years ago for her to want to see him beaten for thievery.

"*I* could," she informed him. "Besides, it never hurts to be careful." She jabbed a finger in the direction of a tall, lean figure clad in brown-flecked tweed who appeared deep in conversation with Blind Willie. "He looks like he might be able to keep up with you, too."

Speculation leapt into the boy's eyes. "Nice suit."

"I wouldn't try it if I were you."

"But you ain't me." He cocked his head. "You gonna cry me out?"

She debated only briefly. The child's moral development was hardly her concern, and she'd learned long ago that worrying about her *own* family was all she could manage. Not to mention that, from the looks of him, the boy could use the contents of Willie's new friend's pockets far more than he could. Ethics and legalities were trivialities when measured against survival. "Who am I to interfere with free enterprise?"

His smile grew cheeky, then submerged to a frown of concentration. He eased behind an enormous woman in green calico, brushed against the back of the man.

Kathryn suppressed a twinge of guilt. Now where had that come from? She thought she'd rid herself of that inconvenient and useless emotion years ago.

The man's head snapped up, and Kathryn tensed in preparation. Despite all her good intentions about staying out of others' business, she couldn't let the boy be captured.

The thief froze, but when his target didn't move again, he took a slow step backward. Kathryn caught a glimpse of a thick black leather wallet before it disappeared into the depths of the kid's pocket. He flashed her a quick thumbs-up before speeding off down the street.

Well, at least the boy knew when to take his winnings and run, she thought, watching him scurry around the corner.

"And how about you, ma'am?"

Her heart startled into an uneven rhythm as she looked back to find the thief's victim had managed to slip up beside her. Raised in a place where inatten-

tiveness could mean death, she was seldom caught un-
aware.

"Excuse me?" she asked carefully, grateful that the
swath of black veil falling from her hat brim shielded
her expression.

"And what's your story? What do you want from
Daniel Sellington?"

His waistcoat matched his jacket, an autumn-hued
tweed of decent quality, baggily cut. Ink smudged his
otherwise crisply white collar. He hunched over a thin
pad of paper, pencil in hand, the brim of his black felt
bowler hiding his face.

A reporter, she thought in disgust. Every six months
or so one of that species ventured to the right bank of
the Platte, made earnest speeches about the power of
the press to facilitate change, and wrote heart-rending
stories about the pitiable conditions to be found in
Denver's poorest neighborhoods. Stories that also
managed to hint subtly that if those poor souls who
survived there—lived was too optimistic a word for
it—had only worked harder, been smarter, made better
choices, they wouldn't be in such a deplorable state in
the first place.

Nothing ever changed.

"Ma'am?" he repeated without so much as glancing
at her, all the while scribbling away furiously.

How dare he? How dare he use their misery, their
fragile hopes, to sell his newspapers?

She'd not actually expected to meet Daniel Sellington that day. Her mission had been more investigative
in nature, although, just in case, she'd formulated a
weak story about the Ladies' Assistance Committee

and a new orphanage. Now, however, her overactive imagination sprang to the ready.

"I don't want anything from Daniel Sellington," she said softly.

"Of course not." He flipped to a new page.

She allowed a distinct quaver to enter her voice. "I'm here to see Daniel *Hall*."

"Oh?" His pencil lead was worn to a nub. He glared at it for a moment, swore, and tossed it away before pulling another from behind his left ear.

The *least* he could do, she thought resentfully, was look at the person he was interviewing. But then she doubted she was a person to him; she was simply a possible story.

"I'm here to"—one pitiful sob should do, she judged—"to *beg* him to support his children."

"*What?*" The fresh lead splintered against the page. His head whipped up, gaze arrowing to her at last.

Oh, unfair! He was younger than she'd thought, his hard, aristocratic features saved from being too grimly severe by the thick fringe of dark hair curling from beneath the brim of his hat. But it was his eyes that caught her, the hot and brutal blue of the August sky, undiminished by the thin barrier of his gold-framed spectacles. Eyes that had no doubt caused too many women to spill far too many stories to this man.

It would do him good, she decided, to waste his time running all over town in a futile attempt to verify her story. Or to print something wildly inaccurate and be called on the carpet by Daniel Sellington himself. Not to mention it would hardly make her unhappy to see a Sellington publicly portrayed in a less than flattering light.

"His children," she repeated.

"Children," he said flatly.

"Yes." She warmed to her role. "Three in four years." She gripped her handbag in both hands and pulled it snug against her belly. "So far," she added in a shy whisper.

"His . . . children."

Clearly not the quickest fellow in the profession, for all his fine looks. Perhaps it was just as well he was so handsome; it was Fate's compensation for his other deficiencies.

"His . . . *our* children," she said slowly, to make certain he caught it all.

"Daniel . . . *Hall's.*"

"That's what he *told* me his name was." She groped in her handbag and pulled out a graying, wrinkled handkerchief. "He said he l . . . he . . . *loved* me. But his wife—his wife, she . . ." Sticking the kerchief beneath her veil, she wailed into it.

"His wife."

"That was what he told me." She looked pointedly at his hand, hovering motionless over the pad. "Shouldn't you be writing this down?"

"Oh. Of course."

"What paper did you say you worked for again?"

"Oh . . . whoever. Whoever pays me." He waved the pencil in a vague circle.

Yes, it was a very good thing the man at least had looks.

"Yes, his wife. I know it was wrong of me, but, but—"

"But you loved him," he said without inflection, those outrageous blue eyes sharpening in a way that made her wonder if she'd underestimated him after all.

Too much wailing, she concluded, retreating into an occasional watery sniff. "She had all the money, he said. That's why he couldn't support us the way he wanted to, the way he promised he *would* when he could figure out a way to divorce her and marry me without losing everything."

He contemplated her as a sprinkler cart, pulled by a pair of massive draft horses, rumbled by in the street behind him, spraying the road to keep down the dust. The cascade of fine droplets captured the sunlight and shimmered, the suggestion of a rainbow arching behind the reporter.

The city never watered *her* street. There, passing vehicles and wandering drunks stirred up the road until you tasted the dust in your mouth every time you stepped outside.

"I don't suppose," he said, "that it's occurred to you that someone else was simply appropriating Mr. Sellington's—Hall's name, and that it wasn't him at all that . . . ?" His gaze dropped to her stomach, and a flush of red that might have been the heat colored his strong neck.

"Oh, no, it's him, all right." She dabbed at her eyes. "I followed him home once, you see—"

"Had your suspicions even then, did you?"

"I did not! I was only . . . I could not bear to say good-bye to him that night, you understand, and I wanted to see where he lived with my own eyes, so I could have that image of him to comfort me when we were apart."

"Hmm." He inspected her from the ragged, feather-tufted crown of her hat to the scuffed boots peeking beneath the accordion-pleated hem of her skirt. "And the mourning gear is because . . . ?"

"It is symbolic of the death of my dreams!" she cried, wondering why, despite her best efforts, she'd never been able to make her living on the stage. Horace Steck, the philistine who cast the plays at the Palace Theater, obviously had no taste, or he would have cast her despite her refusal to demonstrate her skills in a more private venue. "He *lied* to me, all these years! The children and I lived in a hovel, when all this time he could have married me, kept us in the style that his children deserve!"

"Ah." He nodded sympathetically.

"You are so very understanding."

"So I've been told." He tapped his pencil against the pad, a steady rhythm in time with the consumptive's banging on Daniel Sellington's front gate. "And your name is?"

"Lavina Thrush. L-A-V-I-"

"I believe I can manage to spell it."

"Oh, of course you can! Clever man like you, writing all those words every day."

"It is very taxing. Few people appreciate that."

She sniffled. "That . . . that was what Daniel always said! That I knew how to *appreciate* things."

"I'm sure." He flipped his notebook shut and stepped back, jamming his pencil back behind his ear where one of those disobedient waves embraced it. Perhaps, Kathryn thought irrelevantly, he'd tip his hat at her as he left, and she could see if the rest of his hair was just as gorgeous. "I'd best be going. There's much work to be done if I want to get my story finished before the next issue goes to press."

She stretched an entreating hand toward him. "You will . . . you will help us, then? In your article? Encourage Daniel to live up to his responsibilities and properly care for his family?"

"I'm sure you'll be very pleased with the results, ma'am." He disappeared into the crowd, and Kathryn sighed. He hadn't once doffed that hat.

Still, he'd proved to be an effective distraction from her problems. She only wished she'd be able to witness the results of the seed she'd just planted. She'd almost be sorry if the handsome young reporter got into *too* much trouble.

Her own problems, however, could no longer be ignored.

A scuffle broke out on the far side of the crowd when a young man refused to relinquish his prized spot near the gate to a more recent, and much larger, arrival. Shouts went up, and a small circle cleared as the two combatants tumbled to the ground.

"I'll take the blue-shirted fella!" Blind Willie hollered. "Even odds!"

"You've got it!" another replied, and the enthusiastic spectators closed in to obscure her view.

Standing around here was doing her no good at all. She'd make one circle of Sellington's house and go home to ponder the dilemma out of the sun.

It was not at all the kind of place in which one would expect to find a rich man living, a far cry from the stone castle where his crazed grandmother resided. Though the neighborhood was decent, it was hardly fashionable. The house itself was much like its neighbors: simple, sturdy, charming, solidly built of brick the color of the sunrise, faced with rows of small, identical windows. It looked like any one of a dozen boardinghouses in this part of the city; perhaps it had been one once, though she couldn't imagine why a man of Sellington's wealth and position would want to live in rooms formerly inhabited by middle-class bachelors.

But the other houses on the street had low, white-painted fences, easily climbed, easily overlooked. Here the iron barrier, at least seven feet tall and tipped with evil-looking spikes, marched all the way around the property. The area it enclosed was as modest as the house, no more than two standard lots, perhaps fifty by one hundred and twenty-five feet.

It was a place that its owner could easily maintain with a few hours of effort on Sunday afternoon. But here, too, Sellington's house differed from its neighbors, for no less than three men worked steadily, pulling weeds from the meticulous flower beds and shearing a uniform eighth of an inch from the neatly clipped grass. Riotous banks of flowers curved shaggy rainbows at the base of the fence and curled lovingly along the house; bright butterflies swooped over the heads of the workers, who paid no more attention to them than they did to the people who hollered to them through the fence.

What a waste! Her fingers trailed slowly over black

bars gleaming with fresh paint. She could have cared well for her entire family with the money that Sellington spent caring for his lawn. It only served to prove how careless the rich were with their wealth—which, she supposed, suited her purpose well. It should be all the easier to separate him from some of it, one way or the other.

The house sat on a corner lot, and Kathryn turned, happy to leave the mob at the front gate behind. Trees had been planted there two decades ago; now twin lines of oaks reached above, casting blessed shade over the street. There was another gate on that side, guarding a graveled drive that led into stables nearly as large as the house. A young man slumped against the gate, shoulders drooping, cap low. A familiar man, she realized as she drew closer.

"Joey?" she ventured.

"Yeah. Whaddya want?" he snarled.

"Is that any way to speak to your elders, Joey? Especially one who *didn't* force you to return the nickel you swindled from her brother throwing dice when you were ten?"

He tried to peer under the black netting. "Miz Jordan? Is that you?"

"It's me." She rolled the veil up, tucking it firmly beneath a band of ribbon. "Whew, that's better."

His eyes widened. "Who died?"

"Nobody died, Joey."

"Why ya rigged out in that getup, then?"

"It's a long story."

"I've got plenty of time," he said glumly.

"Oh?"

"I'm gonna lose my job." Disconsolate, he slid down to sit with his heels against his skinny rump, hands drooping between his spread knees.

"You had a job?" Joey Gibson had been one of a dozen adolescents who, along with her younger brother Tommy, had roamed the streets like a pack of jackals, looking for all the world like each one of them would either be behind bars or dead by the age of twenty. "So that's why I haven't seen you around in a while."

"Yup," he said proudly. "I was running a game over on Larimar last summer, and a guy offered me a whole dollar to watch his horse for an hour. Did such a good job he hired me right on to help with his horses, permanent-like."

Kathryn's gaze moved from Joey to the white-washed stables just beyond the gate. "Mr. Sellington?"

"Mr. *Hall*," he clarified. "If'n that's what he wants to be called, that's what I'm gonna call him."

"Did you know who he really was?"

"Never told me, but it weren't no secret among the help. But *I* never woulda ratted him out. Hell—beg pardon—he paid us all three times the going rate, for half the work! I ain't dumb enough to chance messin' that up!"

"I'm sure you're not."

"It was that stupid Gracie." He swiped a thin, bare forearm under his nose. "Thinkin' she should have a different, uh, *position* than downstairs maid, if ya know what I mean." He reddened.

"I believe I do."

"Got all huffy when Mr. Hall kept turning her down, went runnin' to the papers with the real story. And now she's messed it up for all of us!" he wailed.

"You don't think he'll fire all of you over Gracie's mistake, do you?"

"But he's leavin'! What'll he need with all of us when he's gone?"

"Leaving?" He couldn't *leave*. How could she marry him if he left?

"Yeah." Joey ripped the cap off his head and crushed it between his outsize, growing-puppy hands. "Heard the cook tell the head groom. He ain't stayin' here, now that he's been found out."

"Did you hear where he was goin'?"

"Minnesota, they said. He's got people there, they all trooped down here last Christmas. Nice people. Brought us all beaver hats."

"Minnesota." That far away, he'd be no good to her at all. She had to get to him first, and quickly. "On the train, I suppose?"

"Naw, he figures the reporters'll be watching for him there. Gonna take the stage north first thing tomorrow." His eyes narrowed suspiciously. "Say, you ain't figurin' you might succeed where Gracie failed, are ya? I mean, you're a lot prettier and all, but I'd hate to be the one that sicced *another* problem on Mr. Hall."

"Of course not," she assured him, while her thoughts raced. It didn't give her much time, and it was an enormous, and maybe ridiculous, gamble any way you looked at it. But what choice did she have? It wasn't as if she had many other options. How much more did she have to lose? "But Joey? You take a quarter off Tommy anytime you want, and I promise I won't say a word."

Led by hope, chased by desperation, she raced down the street at a speed far too fast for decorum.

Perhaps it was too late to save her sister's soul.

But surely it was not too late to ransom her body.

In the dim, malodorous shadow of the Swansea Smelter, a pregnant young widow named Moira O'Neill, a toddler slung over her left hip, stepped outside her ragged tent, in a small, squalid city of equally ragged tents, to call her brood for what promised to be an inadequate dinner. Just beyond her door, she nearly stumbled across a paper-wrapped package. Too weary to be curious, she opened it without hope and stared at the thick wad of bills inside for a full minute before her brain comprehended what her eyes saw.

"Sweet Jesus," she repeated over and over, as she kissed her baby's cheeks, his nose, his precious mouth. "Sweet Jesus, we're saved!"

Six blocks away, in a bare room on the top floor of a crowded tenement building, a young man with old lungs who'd come to Denver for the air and stayed to die, wept over a pile of gleaming coins.

And, across town, on a corner where the gas streetlight hadn't worked for six months, a man lurked in the darkened doorway of an abandoned saloon and spied on the gloomy shack across the street. He watched the thin young pickpocket who claimed the place warily approach the black-robed priest who'd taken up residence in front of the shanty an hour ago.

He continued to watch as the priest handed the boy a sack that held two pairs of pants, three new shirts, boots, and a good wool coat, and informed him that he should report to St. Peter's School Monday morning, for his tuition, room, and ample board had been paid for the next four years. And when he saw disbelief on the boy's face change to hope, and the thief who'd plucked his pocket that afternoon leap into the air, fist pumping in exultation, Daniel Sellington smiled.

He was pleased with the day's work. His only failure had been his inability to locate his . . . "lover." Though what he planned to do with the lying wench once he found her, he hadn't been sure. Still, not a bad day's work at all.

Thirteen thousand down, he thought.

Only forty-one million to go.

Chapter 2

It was either truly brave, or outright stupid, for an unaccompanied woman to venture onto Blake Street at any time, and after dark it was doubly so.

Kathryn was neither. She simply had no other choice.

She'd spent the day in a headlong, impulsive rush of preparation and planning, so that it was an hour past sunset by the time she made her way there. She'd sold everything she could, including the mourning dress, and now twenty-three dollars resided in the bottom of her handbag. Twenty-three dollars, and the rent was due in two days, which meant her mother would have to pay Herman Schatz with something other than money.

It was not the first time. Pray God it would be the last.

Light shimmered from rows of windows in the big brick building, its facade diced into light and dark squares like a checkerboard. But darkness discreetly cloaked the doorway, since far too many of those who visited there didn't care to be seen.

All day long, she had tried very hard not to think too deeply about what she planned, for fear that she would not be able to go through with it. She was imaginative by nature, not impulsive, and the same imagination that had been her solace and escape and had conjured up this wild scheme in the first place, insisted on envisioning all the things that could go terribly wrong.

Why did she persist in believing that she could get Daniel Sellington to marry her?

She was a beautiful woman. Kathryn couldn't afford modesty any more than she could afford vanity; a woman who lived life on the edge of destitution must know her worth to the penny. She could cook passably but had real talent with a needle; she bore up well under hard work and spoke like an educated, well-bred woman, the legacy of a mother who never forgot she'd been born to a station far better than the one in which she now lived; she was poor with numbers, except when they involved money, at which point she was scrupulously accurate; and she was prettier than most. That was the sum total of her worth.

However, Sellington had no doubt known many beautiful women of his own circle. So far he'd evidently evaded marriage with any of them. But their efforts were no doubt hampered by the social rules and graces they'd been brought up to adhere to, while she—*she* would do anything to get him to wed her.

It disturbed her a little that she was so set on marrying him. Her conscience had long ago bowed to the demands of survival. Thievery was hardly beneath her. And it wasn't as if a healthy portion of the wealth

Sellington enjoyed hadn't been swindled from her father in the first place.

Undoubtedly Sellington would much prefer she simply stole from him and left him to go on his merry way. It wasn't as if he would *miss* a few dollars here and there. Even a few thousand. And she wouldn't be bound for life to the devil's spawn, who no doubt had been well spoiled with all the power and delusions that money could buy, thoroughly corrupting him in his father's image.

There was the crux of it. She didn't *want* him to go blithely on. Surely, surely, he was overdue a little suffering. And no simple burglary would bring her the kind of money her family had lost; it would stave off the wolf for a while, but what then? They'd be right back at the threshold of the poorhouse again. Whereas if she actually *married* him . . . piles and piles of gleaming coins sprouted in her mind, erupted and grew like a glorious golden volcano.

Then she'd be rich. Then she'd be safe.

Not to mention there was the added advantage that she couldn't be *hung* for marrying him.

So she'd try, as outrageous and unlikely as it seemed on the face of it. And if she couldn't marry him, at least she'd be close enough to him to steal something of real value.

Because it wasn't as if she had many other options. There was only one, really. One last thing left to sell.

Either way, first she had to enter that building.

So, armored with clean, shining dreams of security and safety, she headed for the door to hell.

It was said that in one of Simon Moore's houses

one could buy anything for the right price—Chinese opium and Irish whiskey, frantic entertainment or oblivion, men and women of all ages and races. Even life and death. He owned five establishments, spread throughout the city, because there were customers who could not be lured to that section of town even by the extraordinary temptations he offered. But he lived and ran his unholy empire from there, in a building larger and far finer than any of its neighbors at the edge of the colored district.

There was only one thing Simon sold that interested Kathryn.

Her younger sister, Isabelle.

Before she could knock, she heard the scrape of a bolt, and the door cracked open. A thin sliver of light escaped and fell on her. Though hardly bright, after the deep dark of the entrance, it made her squint.

"What do you want?" a voice from within growled.

"I need to talk to Mr. Moore," she said.

"No."

Afraid the door would close before she had a chance to speak her piece, she flew forward and wedged her toe in the narrow opening. "Please sir! I must. It's very important."

"To who?" he jeered. "Missy, d'ya know how many people tell me that?"

"Please." She thought frantically. "I would—it would be worth his while, I promise."

"So? It's Miz Evie you want to be talkin' to, then. She picks all the new girls. An' selective enough she is, too."

"No! I only want to talk to Mr. Moore. Nobody else."

"Guess that's your problem." The opening narrowed, pinching her toes.

"Wait!" she called again, and reached up to sweep her hat off, turning her face up to meager light. "If I can't talk to Mr. Moore himself, I'll go someplace else. Maybe Ruby Dee's, or the Cat House. Can't you just *ask* him if he wants to see me?" And perhaps while the door guard went to speak to his employer, she could find her own way inside.

The door yawned opened, revealing a hulking giant of a man with skin as dark as the night. He studied her for a moment, then nodded. "Guess he might want to see you at that."

He turned and, as if expecting her simply to follow, plodded off down a hallway that gave the impression of narrowness only because his shoulders clogged its width. There were dozens of doors; from behind them she could hear the distant tinkle of music, a spray of laughter, a tortured moan that could have been pleasure or pain.

Dark, vine-patterned wallpaper covered the walls. The gaslights gave off faint light and a stronger, serpentine hiss. It seemed as if, at any moment, cobras might untwine from the vines and strike.

The hall ended at another door, sturdier than the rest, a thick slab of solid wood padded with nail-studded velvet. The massive doorman yanked it open and plunged up a dark, narrow stairway, Kathryn hard on his heels; she would *not* get caught downstairs alone. The staircase turned in on itself twice, disorienting her, before emerging into a bright, well-lit space.

Offices. So ordinary that Kathryn blinked in surprise at the pristine white walls, wood floors, and plain cabinets. It could have belonged to any legitimate, prosperous business. A man dressed as inconspicuously as a clerk, his age as difficult to determine as his race, leaned over a desk, scratching a gleaming gold pen over a thick sheaf of papers.

Her guide stomped over to the man and bent, murmuring to him. The clerk glanced her way, unhooked a pair of spectacles, and laid them aside. He inspected her from head to foot as if she were a piece of merchandise—and a substandard one, at that.

"Luther says you wish to speak to Mr. Moore." He frowned. "You really should have an appointment."

"Well, I don't." She resisted the urge to bow her head like a disobedient pupil. "I apologize."

He stared at her for a moment longer. "Wait here."

He disappeared through another door at the back of the offices. Luther took up a position in front of the door, his huge fists clasped in front of him, ensuring that there was no way Kathryn would get through uninvited. She clamped down hard on her impatience; there was so much to do, so little time, but she had no options except to wait.

The clerk returned, his face tense with disapproval. "Mr. Moore will see you." He held the door wide and gestured for her to come. "These are his private apartments. You may wait for him in the parlor."

Kathryn took a deep breath and walked right in.

She'd expected blood-red draperies and flocked

wallpaper, gilded statues of naked people in lewd positions. Instead, she entered a room that could have fit comfortably in the grandest, most respectable houses in Denver, the likes of which she hadn't entered, except through the servants' entrance, in fifteen years.

Her feet sank deeply into the Brussels carpet. A grand chandelier tossed shimmers of gold over glossy wood and rich fabrics and dazzled off a diamond-dust mirror taller than she was. Folding lace shutters over the windows barred any glimpse of the world outside and the dirty, dangerous streets that seemed as if they had no connection with this place—even though she knew they'd paid for it.

Kathryn stood frozen just inside the entrance. She heard the clerk close the door behind her, but she didn't dare move, unwilling to risk any action that might annoy Simon Moore.

"You may sit down, you know." Soft-voiced words, soundless footsteps, and he appeared from behind a fall of thick, deep green velvet that curtained off the rear of the room. She'd heard the man described a hundred times, in hushed, fearful whispers, and still his appearance was a surprise. Taller than any man she'd ever seen, almost painfully thin, all long bones and ropey muscle and skin that gleamed shades darker than the black walnut of his desk. His suit was deep gray and beautiful, his cheekbones sharp as a razor. "Albert should have shown you a chair."

"No." She cleared her throat. "No, I'll stand." All the better to run.

He folded his great length into an oxblood-leather chair.

She waited in vain for him to say something. Did he expect her to talk? Would he consider it insulting if she spoke first? She didn't dare make a mistake, and couldn't read the answer in his black, expressionless eyes.

"Thank you for agreeing to see me," she said finally.

He nodded, accepting, but said nothing.

"I want to buy my sister back," she ventured.

"Your sister?"

"Isabelle. Isabelle Jordan."

"Ah." He nodded. "I do see the resemblance."

"Yes." She swallowed hard. But he hadn't called for her head yet. "She shouldn't be here."

"She was not kidnapped, Miss Jordan. Nor forced. It was her own choice to come to work for me."

It only hurt all the more to know that he was right. Isabelle had gotten tired of the hunger, and the work, and looked for an easier way.

"You cannot believe that it was a free choice. You know where she comes from, the life she was fleeing."

"It is as much of a choice as most of us are fortunate enough to have, Miss Jordan."

She couldn't argue that, either. "Which is why I don't expect you to give her up without recompense."

"Oh? What do you have to offer me?"

"I'll pay you."

He pressed a long finger to his lips, considering. "How much do you have?"

"I have twenty-three dollars," she admitted. Then, as his laughter, rich, dark, terrifying, filled the room, she hurried to explain. "It's just the beginning! I'll get more, I've got plans—"

"Wait." Teeth flashing white, he held up a hand to stop her outburst. "Thank you for the amusement, if nothing else. But I don't believe we have anything further to discuss."

"How much will you take for her?"

He shrugged. "I'd have to give it some thought. A thousand, perhaps two, at the minimum. She's a very lovely girl, your sister. We've only had her a week. The novelty has yet to wear off, despite her lack of . . . enthusiasm for her customers. And there are those who prefer that, as I'm sure you are aware."

A thousand dollars. She could work her entire life, sew and clean and cook until her fingers were worn to nubs, and never see that much money. "I'll get it."

"Fine," he said, but she could tell he didn't believe her for a moment. "I'll speak to you when you do."

"No!" Isabelle would never survive here that long. "I want to take her with me now."

"And why would I allow that?"

"I'll pay you extra if you let her go now . . . how much interest do you usually charge? I'll double it."

"My usual fee is one percent a day—"

She closed her eyes briefly and numbers wheeled behind her lids. How much did that add up to?

"But I still don't believe that is adequate to get me to release Isabelle to you now," he went on, undisturbed by her gasp. "I'd have to insist she leave us, as she was the one who initially came to me. And keep watch, to make certain she doesn't attempt to work for anyone else. No, when you have the money, *if* you have the money, we will speak again." He levered out of the chair, rising until she thought his head might touch the ceiling.

She had to make it worth his while. "*If* I fail, then you can have me instead."

"You?" He tilted his head in consideration. "You are a lovely woman, there is no doubt about that. But I already have her, and she is younger than you."

"She may be younger than I, but I'm stronger." Dear God, what was she saying? The words kept spurting out of her mouth of their own volition, disconnected from thought, lost to any reality. "She's far too fragile for this life. You'd have me much longer, and I'd work harder."

"Still—"

"And I am a virgin."

That laughter again, rich amusement that speared fear up her spine. "Please, Miss Jordan! So far you have not insulted me. Surely you do not expect me to believe that you have remained untouched in all these years. Whyever *would* you?"

"Because," she said simply, "it is the last thing I had left of any value. Thus far, I have not been forced to pawn it."

"Ah, I *do* understand." He nodded. "Very well, then. Our terms will be my usual arrangements. I will supply the rooms, the clothes, the customers—"

She did not want to know. She could not think of it. "It's not necessary to go into this now—"

"And we will split your fees precisely in half," he went on, ignoring her protests, supremely confident that she would, indeed, soon be employed under this agreement. "I'm fairer than most, as I'm sure you realize."

"All right." What else could she do? "You will release Isabelle tonight?"

"If you wish, she can be in your home within an hour." Her sigh of relief choked off abruptly at his next words. "However, if you fail to bring me the payment, I will have *both* of you."

"No, I don't think—"

"Fine. Then Isabelle remains here." Clearly dismissing the topic, he moved to escort her out.

Panic left her breathless, stabbing hard behind her ribs. "But—"

"There really is no room for negotiation here, Miss Jordan."

It had never been the poverty of her life that she hated so much as the powerlessness. She had never felt it more keenly.

"I'll need at least six months," she whispered.

"Three."

"You're sure that she'll—" The look on his face was lethal, and she abruptly shut up. Simon Moore did not like to have his word questioned. There was no honor in the man, but there was pride, and one of the reasons for his unchallenged position in a lawless world was that his word could be relied upon. If he said he would protect you, you could walk through the meanest alleys without worry.

And if he said you were dead, you died.

"I'm pleased that you have the wisdom to trust me," he said. "I will return the favor, and refrain from warning you not to try to run, for I'm certain you realize that I would find you." She had no doubt that he would. "I believe we shall deal well together."

She walked to the door on legs that had gone numb. Dear God, what had she just done?

But what else could she have done? Isabelle would be home, tonight, and safe for at least three months. She clung to that thought, and to the comforting image of Daniel Sellington's money. This time, as she raced through the house and down the stairs, she didn't notice the bright office, or Albert, or Luther, or the wicked, empty laughter resonating through closed doors.

She would marry Sellington.

She had to.

Chapter 3

⌒⌒ⒼⒸ⌒⌒

This was it.

Clasping the battered valise and old string handbag that held everything she still owned in the world, Kathryn stood on the boardwalk in Monroe City, six miles north of Denver, and watched as her future pulled up to the stage stop.

The coach was old and small, its glossy sides painted a rich maroon chipped in a dozen spots. The faded gilt letters above the door were a faint shadow of their former glory, like the coaching business itself. The coaches were now reserved for customers too poor to scrape together the price of a train ticket and towns too insignificant to command a rail stop. A fortunate occurrence for Kathryn, for her ticket had cost only half her stash.

Luck had been with her thus far. After waiting until Isabelle's safe return—safe, but drugged nearly insensate, her painfully thin body draped over Luther's giant shoulder, alternately swearing and sobbing at Kathryn for her unwanted interference—Kathryn managed to catch a ride with a farmer and his wife. After a day's excursion into Denver, they were returning to Monroe City, which saved her from having to rent—or steal—a horse to get there. She'd been afraid it might take days to catch up with Sellington's coach. Instead, she'd beaten him there! After reluctantly giving up the idea of taking a room in the small inn she'd bedded down in the stables instead. That morning, she'd dressed and washed hurriedly in a trough of freezing water and was now fully prepared to meet her fate.

The driver, a man as thin as he was old, arced a dark stream of tobacco juice into the road and squinted down at her. "You waitin' for the northbound stage?"

"Yes," she said quickly, before she could surrender to all the doubts and *what-ifs* that, along with the restless kicking of the horse occupying the stall next to the one she'd hidden in, had kept her from getting any sleep at all.

She handed up her valise. The driver chomped down on his bolus of tobacco and carelessly tossed her luggage onto the small, haphazard pile atop the coach.

"Don't you think you should tie that down better?"

This time, the tobacco juice stream came within inches of her hem. But he grudgingly fashioned a couple of quick knots around her case.

"Ticket?"

She handed it up. Clearly, if he ever had any intention of assisting her up into the high coach, she'd forfeited that courtesy with her inordinate demands.

Making a graceful entrance was out of the question. Oh well, maybe Sellington was an ankle man. She grabbed her skirts in her left hand, took a firm grip on the door with her right, and heaved herself upward.

The low top edge of the doorway dislodged her hat, leaving it hanging from limp ribbons around her throat.

She hovered in the doorway, bent over as if she were decades older than her age, and peered into the dusky interior.

Was that him? Two narrow seats, covered in dark red velvet that had lost its nap years ago, faced each other. A matched pair of very large, middle-aged people with identical poufs of silver hair occupied the front one. Married? Brother and sister?

The man occupying the rear seat sat ramrod stiff, staring out the window. His shoulders were angled toward the outer wall as if he could close himself off from the other passengers. His clothes were plain; his hair, dark and rich and riotously wavy.

It had to be him; there was no one else in the coach. His hands rested on his knees. Big hands, sun-darkened, with long fingers and broad knuckles and scrupulously clean, well-clipped nails. The men she knew had hands with dirt and grease ground in, dark crescents under thick, ridged nails.

If all went as planned, sometime soon—perhaps very soon—he would touch her intimately with those strong-looking hands. Her heart surrendered a beat, started again in double time.

"S'pose I should let you ladies sit together." The big man grunted and began to rise from his seat.

"Oh, no," she said quickly, "I wouldn't dream of asking you to give up your place for me. I'm sure we all understand that some of the proprieties must be bent during the inconveniences of travel."

He grunted again, which Kathryn took to be an expression of gratitude. She breathed a sigh of relief when he plopped back down. Untying her hat to hold it in her lap, she slid into the empty space. The man glanced her way at last, and she felt the shock of bold, familiar blue.

She knew those eyes. There were no spectacles shielding them now, and no hat wedged over the thick, shining hair. No ink-stained collar, no pencil, no baggy tweed suit, but there was nevertheless no doubt about the identity of her new seatmate.

Kathryn tensed, awaiting his accusation. Surely he'd checked out the ridiculous story she'd fed him, and he couldn't be happy with her for sending him out on such a wild hare. But he said nothing, merely gave a nod so brief as to be more impolite than none at all, and returned his attention to the window.

He'd no idea who she was. Kathryn blessed the mourning veil worn yesterday, even as she scrambled to think through the complications his presence presented. He must have bribed one of Sellington's employees and tracked his quarry here, much as she had. How was she going to attract Sellington's interest if some nosy reporter was poking his nose—even such a handsome nose—into things, digging for a story?

There was a shout outside, followed by the wicked snap of a whip. The coach lurched forward, jerking her head back against the hard seat.

"Wait!" she burst out.

"Excuse me?" the big man opposite her asked.

"Isn't there someone else? I mean . . . I thought there was another passenger."

That brilliant blue gaze turned her way again. "No," he said. "There's no one else."

Her simmering worry abruptly burst into dread.

"But there has to be—" His eyebrow arched up in question, and she shut up.

What could have gone wrong? Joey had no reason to lie to her. Probably Sellington had stumbled onto this damned reporter's pursuit and changed his plans. She took a moment to indulge a vivid image of beating the reporter around his gorgeous head. She just *knew* it was all his fault.

What was she going to do? Get off the stage at the first opportunity, go back to Denver, and start all over? Maybe she could talk to Joey again, somehow track Sellington down. If not, it was time to move on to an alternate plan, one that didn't revolve around Daniel Sellington.

Too bad she didn't *have* an alternate plan.

Glumly, she stared down at her hands, encased in worn white gloves. She'd worried about them. Her clothes, rescued from Mrs. Chivington's trash bin over the past year and remade, while not the first stare of fashion, could pass for at least comfortable circumstances. Her gloves, though, were grayed, mended visibly across two fingers. But her hands were worse; one look at her hands and anyone would know she worked for a living.

Now, however, none of that mattered. Not if she couldn't find Daniel Sellington.

"Well." The woman slapped her ample thighs and addressed Kathryn. "Seein' as how we're going to be cooped up here for a while, might as well introduce ourselves. I'm Evelyn Thatcher, and this"—she jerked a stubby thumb over her right shoulder—"is my husband, Frank. We was in Denver visiting our daughter, and now we're headin' back to our place in Julesburg. Own the restaurant there, we do."

"I'm Kathryn Jordan," she offered. "Off to visit my sister in Minneapolis." The lie came easily; she'd rehearsed her story dozens of times. It would have been suspicious, she'd decided, to get on the stage in Denver, headed for Minneapolis, when she so easily could have ridden a train the entire way. So she'd chosen to begin her charade in Monroe City instead. "I know it would have been easier to go into Denver and take the train from there, but it seemed like more of an adventure this way. And my father is always in favor of a plan that saves him a few dollars."

"He allowed you to travel alone?"

"Oh, well." She tried to look abashed. "There was little choice. My mother could not come with me, and my sister is soon to be blessed with her third child. She needs my help."

All three of them turned their attention to the silent man at the window, waiting for him to do the polite thing: introduce himself and join the conversation.

Kathryn could have told the Thatchers that *politeness* was not a particularly cherished quality in a reporter.

"And you, sir?" Frank prompted.

The coach picked up speed. Yellow dust boiled through the small window, hazing the interior of the

coach. Evelyn coughed significantly. The reporter
sighed and pulled the leather shade down over the window, trapping dust and darkness inside the coach.

"I'm Daniel Smith," he said flatly.

Daniel. Daniel Sellington, Daniel Hall . . . Daniel
Smith? Could he be that cruel, to anonymously work
his way through a crowd come to beg his aid, entertaining himself with their stories of misery?

Stupid question. He was Edward Sellington's son;
he'd been spoiled and indulged his entire life. Of
course he could be that cruel.

"What a . . . unique name," she said.

He frowned, his brows slashing into a line.

Kathryn could have bit her tongue off. If he *was*
Daniel Sellington in truth, she could hardly afford to
antagonize him.

She searched for signs of familial resemblance between the man beside her and the face she'd seen on
the front page of the *Rocky Mountain News*. This
man's coloring was far darker than Edward's golden
good looks. Still, there was the same cool superiority
in the elegant shape of his eyes, aristocratic arrogance
in the high-bridged nose.

She couldn't afford to make a mistake. It *had* to be
him, and somehow she must find out for sure.

And in the meantime, she would proceed as if he
were indeed Sellington—Daniel, she amended
quickly; better to think of him in warmer, more familiar terms, if she intended to entice the man.
Otherwise, some of her true feelings toward him might
show.

And if it turned out that he was simply the reporter after all, his name merely a coincidence, then perhaps he could still be of use to her. His experience and resources might be useful in locating the real Daniel Sellington.

"Where you headed?" Frank asked, obviously having had his fill of waiting for Daniel to initiate a friendly conversation. Not a neighborly sort at all, this "Smith."

"I'm not entirely sure." He spoke quietly, with little inflection, his focus on the outer wall of the coach rather than his enforced companions, as if he would have vastly preferred to have the stage to himself.

"Doesn't seem too efficient a way to travel, if you don't mind my saying so," Frank said gruffly. "Taking coaches here and there without knowing where you're going. Make a lot of wrong turns, if you ask me."

Daniel shrugged. With a lean forefinger, he edged open the side of the leather shade so he could peer out. "And a few unexpected right ones, as well."

An adventurer, then, she concluded. Bored, aimless, looking for something to hold his interest. How could she use that? What would catch the attention of a man who'd seen and experienced far too much?

Frank snorted, unimpressed. "Make a good living doing that, d'ya?"

Daniel gave him a long look. "I manage."

"Sure. That's why you're crammed into this old coach with us, 'stead of in one of those fancy private cars on the Kansas Pacific."

"Perhaps I like it this way." He released the shade,

and his gaze slid to Kathryn, met her own briefly, an intense glitter of hot blue. "Never know what you might find."

Hope and nerves fluttered in her stomach. She lowered her lashes and tried to summon a becoming blush. He'd want the woman he married to be naive, she decided, but overwhelmingly, irresistibly drawn to him. An untouched woman whose deep passions had been saved only for him, ready to explode at his slightest touch. All men wanted that, didn't they?

Cold sweat slicked her palms. This would never do. She looked at his strong hands again, envisioned them on her breasts, and her cheeks obligingly heated.

Better. But it disturbed her how quickly just the thought of his touch could warm her. It would make her task much easier, but it shouldn't happen. Revulsion was a more justifiable response than attraction, for the devil's son was surely a devil himself.

But such a handsome one.

"Besides," Daniel said, "there are so many stories to be found unexpectedly."

"Stories?" Evelyn perked up. "You a writer?"

"Yes."

"What kind? I'm right fond of adventure novels, myself."

"No novels, I'm afraid. Just collections of the places I go and the people I meet along the way. Whatever is of interest."

"Oh." Evelyn was only slightly disappointed. "You know, how me 'n' Frank got first hitched up, that's a right interestin' story. I was working at the . . . well, never mind, I was workin', and once, when I was, uh, engaged for the entire evenin', and Frank strolled on in, and . . ."

Kathryn let Evelyn's words fade into the background. Too bad she couldn't do the same to the Thatchers themselves. While they were surely pleasant enough companions, whose company she would otherwise appreciate, there was a limit to what she could do to attract Daniel with them all crammed into the stage together.

Evelyn's voice droned on, a distant buzz like a friendly fly. Kathryn swayed in rhythm with the coach, the soothing motion of a grandmother's rocker, the air almost too warm, and she suddenly remembered she'd gotten very little sleep the previous night.

She allowed her head to sag. Daniel's legs were long, encased in somber gray wool, his knees nearly bumping into Frank's melon-sized ones each time the stage shimmied over a rock. His shoulders, too, took up more than their fair share of the space; they'd improperly rub her own with every corner if she wasn't careful.

But she wasn't supposed to be careful anymore, was she? Not about that. She slowly edged in his direction, let her shoulder slip behind his and her eyelids droop. He jumped, just a little, and she froze, waiting to see if he'd nudge her away. But instead he stilled, too, barely breathing.

No more than a few square inches of their shoulders met, and there were at least three layers of fabric between them. Kathryn knew that. But she felt his heat just the same, the solid presence of muscle and bone.

Sensation burst in her shoulder, showered through her arm and torso like a torch shedding sparks.

He smelled nice, she thought dimly. So *clean*. Of starched collars and shaving soap and good wool. And then she felt his shoulder move forward a bare inch, causing her to slide more firmly against him, and her breath caught.

"I think," Frank said, "that the lady doesn't find our company particularly stimulating."

"I suppose we should be insulted," Daniel murmured, a low, soothing rumble in her ear.

". . . and then we moved to Whitetail, to try our hand at farming . . ." Evelyn's steady monologue apparently didn't require anyone else's participation.

"You don't have to put up with it," her husband went on. "The rules are clearly posted: no sleeping on your fellow travelers."

"Would *you* mind?" Daniel asked, a hint of a smile in his voice.

"Don't suppose I would." Frank expelled a blast of air when Evelyn's elbow found his ribs.

Kathryn dropped her head all the way to Daniel's shoulder, and her eyes drifted completely shut. Her head fit there like the curve of his neck had been made just for that purpose.

It had so been many years since she'd had a shoulder to lean on.

It shouldn't feel right. He was Edward Sellington's son. She needed to use him, to *take* from him, or a life that had been lived on the edge of despair nearly as long as she could remember would catapult right over the cliff.

But he was warm and strong and handsome, and he liked her head on his shoulder.

And so, snuggled up against the side of a man she meant to hurt, she fell beautifully, safely asleep.

Chapter 4

Daniel Hall stood in the kitchen garden outside an old stage inn, wrapped in heat and the smell of herbs and fresh-turned earth, and thought about her.

She'd slept on his shoulder for over two hours that afternoon, and he'd scarcely dared breathe in case she might wake up and move properly away. Now and then, as the coach jostled over a bump, she'd snuggle in closer. Her hand had fallen to his left hip, lying loose and relaxed against his thigh, and, though he knew a gentleman would have gallantly moved it away, he let it stay. Thank God the Thatchers were dozing, too. He'd had to grab his hat and hold it in his lap to ensure that they wouldn't wake up and notice just how much he liked her sleeping against his side.

How long since the last time he'd had a woman that close to him? Four years, nearly five? And, though he knew it was taking shameless advantage, he enjoyed it to the fullest.

She smelled like soap and sunshine, with a surprising hint of fresh-cut hay. A farm girl, then, like the ones he'd grown up with, hardworking and fun-loving and unimpressed by his name. Her hair against his neck was softer than any silk he'd ever touched. The faint weight of her breast against his upper arm had burned itself into his memory, and he doubted he'd ever evict it. Or if he'd ever want to.

He knew the instant she awoke, heard her breath quicken and felt her stiffen slightly against him, and he almost swore. He'd half hoped she'd never wake up, just stay there against him forever.

But she hadn't jumped away immediately, as he'd expected. She'd looked up at him, eyes the color of the sea beneath a thick fringe of lashes many shades darker than her hair, slumberous and innocently seductive in her slow awakening. Her mouth had curved up, a perfect, intimate smile, and she slid away with a reluctance he was almost certain he hadn't imagined.

And he'd spent the rest of the day plotting how he could ruin her sleep tonight, so that she'd be exhausted enough tomorrow to nap on his shoulder again.

"Hello."

She spoke from behind him and, in the moment before he turned, he thought he was dreaming, had conjured her up out of years of vague fantasies and hopes that had finally coalesced, taking real and beautiful form.

Jesus, she was pretty. The thin sliver of a moon was surprisingly bright, shedding silver radiance over her as if specifically designed to show her to best advantage. Her pale hair shimmered, capturing the moonlight and making it its own. Her face glowed, a purity of line and skin that stole his breath and gave it back again, quicker and uneven.

He was dazzled. He knew it, knew it was shallow and precipitous. Knew full well that he'd been alone a long time, and so was susceptible to a pretty face and soft hair. But it didn't feel that way, deep down in his gut. It felt tantalizingly real, and because he'd never experienced the like before, he let it stay for a moment and savored it.

Her mouth moved; her teeth flashed, sparkled, and disappeared again behind her sweetly curved lips, but he didn't register a word. She looked at him in question, one startlingly dark brow lifting, and he realized she'd spoken to him.

"I'm sorry," he said, feeling awkward and untried, as if he were a decade younger. "I wasn't—" He stopped; even *he* remembered that admitting he wasn't paying attention to a woman's conversation was a bad idea. "I was lost in thought. Sometimes it takes me a moment to come back."

"Writing in your head, were you?"

"Something like that."

"Well, as I was saying, I didn't realize anyone else was out here." She stepped closer, and, as she moved her skirts brushed the densely packed beds of herbs, releasing clouds of scent, mint, thyme, savory. "I don't mean to intrude. I could leave you to your . . . writing."

"You're not! It's not *my* garden, after—" He snapped his mouth shut and tried again. "I'd be pleased to have your company."

Her smile reappeared, a quicksilver brilliance. "I suppose I shouldn't," she said. "It's most improper, isn't it? The two of us out here all alone."

Alone. It could not have hit him harder if the roof shingles had all suddenly let go and come crashing down on him at once. She was only an arm's length away. He could reach out and touch her in an instant. "Who would know?"

She pondered a moment, and then her grin widened. "Yes, who's to know?" And the breath he'd been holding released in a heady rush.

"Besides, it's much too close in there to go back inside," she said. "I was desperately in need of some air, after spending all day shut up in the coach."

With her hand against his hip, her fingers trailing over his thigh. "Yes."

He could kiss her. All he'd need to do was take one step, lean down, and press his mouth to hers. At which point she, shocked by the liberty he'd stolen, would no doubt run shrieking back into the inn, after she slapped him for his impertinence.

Though it would surely be worth the price.

Since he was eighteen, when he'd shouldered the Sellington millions, he'd never known if a woman wanted him or his money. Or he'd known, and not liked the answer. He'd decided that, if he couldn't separate commerce from affection, he'd rather have neither, and so he'd resigned himself to solitude until he discharged his duty. It was, he admitted to himself, lonely. But much simpler. Now, however, he wondered if he'd left it too long.

"So," she ventured. "You're a writer."

"Yes." He waited while a hot breeze rustled the grass beyond the stables. From an open window he heard the clink of dishes, a burst of bright laughter—

the innkeeper and his wife cleaning up after their late supper, no doubt. A night bird screeched in the distance, and still she said nothing.

It was why he'd finally settled on calling himself a writer, though he wrote nothing but an occasional note to his mother. Whether he claimed he penned stories or books or newspaper articles, all he had to do was mention his profession and people rushed to tell him their own tales. It relieved him of the necessity of making conversation, allowed him to escape being peppered with questions he must answer with lies. And, sometimes, as they told him their stories, he'd discover someone who could really use part of the fortune he'd inherited from Edward. Someone whose real need would transform something evil into something good.

Would that he could convert the rest of his legacy the same way.

But Kathryn Jordan seemed in no hurry to spill her story. She just gazed at him with bright interest, waiting politely for him to hold up his end of the conversation. And his tongue felt swollen to twice its normal size.

"Where are you from?" she finally asked.

"Hard to say." Then, because he couldn't see the harm in telling her, he said: "New York, Minnesota, Denver. Take your pick."

"How lucky!" she said, and for the first time in years he felt like he was. After all, he was here with her, wasn't he? "To have lived in so many places. Do you get to travel much?"

"Not as much as I'd like."

"Oh, me either. I mean, not ever, really. That's why

I wanted to stretch out this trip as long as I could. And what did I do? I slept through most of the first day." Her gaze slid to his shoulder, as if she'd suddenly recalled exactly where she'd slept, and her lashes lowered demurely. "Will you be gone long this time?"

"Probably not." Only until he received word to hurry home. If he went more than a few days without visiting his grandmother, her fragile hold on sanity loosened rapidly, which kept him tied tightly to Denver. But she'd seemed to have drawn even further inside herself recently, doing little but sifting through the tangle of heavily bejeweled chains she always kept in her lap. Maybe, he thought with a hopeful, guilty pang, she'd hardly notice he was gone this time, and he'd be able to travel for a while.

"Oh, that's too bad." Somehow, he'd gotten closer to her. Had she moved? Had he? Or was it simply a trick of his moon-fogged brain? "Unless you're in a hurry to get home?"

"No. No hurry." No hurry to return to the mess that awaited him back in the city. It would be no different than when he'd first arrived there, only six months after gaining control of his inheritance, hordes of avid-eyed, too-eager people descending with sad stories, brilliant business propositions, and tragic debts.

Then, he hadn't been a good judge of people; he'd had trouble sifting through the petitions presented him to find those who truly needed what he could give and would use it wisely.

It would be so much simpler if he could just indiscriminately give it all away, casting fistfuls of cash out amongst all those who came to beg at his door, scattering a fortune willy-nilly to fall where it would and be done with it. But he felt a terrible responsibility to choose well, to make some good out of what had already done such harm. And he was determined to distribute it in the proper amounts as well, enough to help and ease, but not enough to spoil and corrupt.

"How long will you be on the stage, then?" she asked.

"All the way to Julesburg, I hope, before I catch the train to Minneapolis. If I'm not called home."

"Oh!" she said with flattering eagerness. "That's where I'm going, too!"

How fortunate for him.

Their conversation lurched on. Kathryn didn't seem to notice his hard-earned reticence, or mind it if she did. She just kept talking, asking questions, seemingly interested and charmed every time he managed to dredge up a vaguely amusing story about the people he'd met. And each time she smiled up at him, his heart took another jolt.

"I'd love to see some of the city while I'm there. Are you familiar with it, Daniel?" Her lids swept down. "Excuse me. I meant Mr. Smith, of course. Forgive me?"

His name on her lips was as intimate as a kiss. He savored the sound, tried to think of a way to get her to speak it again. And finally he couldn't resist any longer. He laid his hands on her shoulders. They were firm and narrow, warm beneath wash-softened cotton. He knew she'd pull away; he was sure of it. She was a properly raised woman and he was a stranger. Still he couldn't stop himself. Didn't want to stop himself.

Her eyes went wide, dark as if they'd swallowed up their own piece of the sky, stars dancing deep in the pupils, and he bent his head.

Because he wanted to savor, to memorize each instant, he went slow. He brushed his mouth against hers, once, twice, again. At the first touch, he felt her shoulders stiffen under his hands, her breath catch. Then air sighed out of her and into his own mouth, her posture easing into welcoming pliancy.

It was almost enough; her breath was sweet, her lips soft and warm as body-heated satin. He meant it to be just the one kiss. More would be taking dishonorable advantage of her solitude, her eagerness for adventure. But when he drew back and gazed down at her, a shimmering glaze of moonlight spilling over her purely beautiful features, he had to have more. His hands tightened their grasp on her shoulders, holding her in place. His mouth came down hard this time, her lips opening and fitting beneath his as if they'd done so a hundred times before. But the feeling was dazzlingly new.

This was no girl he kissed, he discovered. The tips of her breasts brushed his chest with each shallow breath she took. Her hand came up, touched the center of his back. He slid his tongue inside her mouth, found the clean, sharp edge of her teeth, touched the very tip of her own tongue. Miraculously, amazingly, he felt her lift up to her tiptoes, press her mouth more firmly against his own.

Oh, Lord, how had he managed alone so long? Passion rose swiftly, hard and demanding and impossible, and he knew it had only been lying in wait for him to give it the slightest opportunity. His hands flexed, tempted to go further, to explore beyond the hard curve of her shoulders, for there were more curves, more swells to discover, ones that he suspected were far softer, and far more interesting.

His mind whirled as his blood heated and roared until he thought he might burst from his own skin. Her mouth, dark and sweet, was his without reservation, offered up for him to plunder as he would. And finally there were only two choices left: to take her down to the soft garden earth, among the heady scents of herbs and night-blooming flowers, and lose himself in her.

Or put her away from himself.

And because he was sure she wasn't the kind of woman to say yes, and because he couldn't bear to hear her say no, he gently grasped her upper arms and pushed her away.

"Oh!" She lifted her hand, pressed three fingers to her lips. Shock? Embarrassment? Undoubtedly. But his foolish heart also read *wonder* there, because he recognized it in himself. He fisted his hands at his side, welcoming the slice of his nails against his palms, hoping it would help to cool his head if not his body. But it didn't work; it only made him remember how much better his hands felt on her, and how much better yet it would be if there were no cloth between his palms and her skin.

"You'd better go," he said. Control had always been easy for him. But that was only, he knew now, because he'd never allowed anyone close. He'd never tested himself, never let temptation near enough to take a firm hold.

Or perhaps it was just this particular woman who could threaten his resolve.

"I—" Moonlit skin, moon-glossed hair, eyes like the sea at midnight. She had to leave!

"Go!" he ordered, harsher than he wanted, the only way he could.

Her hand still held to her mouth, as if she would preserve the feel of his kiss there, she whirled and fled.

The dim interior of the coach swirled with road dust and snores. They'd pulled out of the inn's barren yard shortly after five, as the rising sun burned low over the horizon, heat already simmering over the plains. Mountains peaked far to the west, a cool, distant memory.

The Thatchers had propped themselves up against each other and gone promptly back to sleep, earning Kathryn's envy. Though her bed had been the most comfortable she could remember lying on—it should be, considering the price, which she'd been unable to figure a way out of paying—she'd wasted it, incapable of quieting her mind long enough to fall asleep.

For she'd discovered that her hastily formed plan had one huge, fat, obvious hole, right in the center of it.

Find Daniel Sellington. Marry Daniel Sellington.

What she'd overlooked completely was exactly *how* she was going to get the man to marry her.

There weren't a whole lot of proper society ladies out here to be appalled if he compromised her reputation and demand that he make appropriate reparation. And somehow, he didn't strike her as the type of man to bow to the opinion of a bunch of self-satisfied matrons in any case.

She didn't have the convenience of a father or a handful of burly brothers to force him to a preacher at the business end of a shotgun, either. No suitors to vie for her affections, spurring his jealousy and forcing his hand.

No reason for him to marry her at all.

She sneaked a peek at him. Ever since they'd climbed aboard, he'd been absorbed in whatever he'd been scribbling in his leather-bound notebook; she didn't think he'd so much as glanced her way. His hair was a mess, thick brown waves curving whichever way they wanted, falling over his broad forehead. She was sorry she hadn't touched it the night before when she'd had the chance. But then, she'd been a bit distracted.

He focused intently on the page, as if inscribing the secrets of the world. The coach hit a rut, the right side plummeted six inches, and his pen shot off the paper. He just kept on writing.

The road had steadily deteriorated all morning, and she didn't see how he could possibly read his scrawl. Or what he could be writing, for that matter. Maybe, she thought hopefully, he was figuring his next year's income, or adding up all his investments. She'd give a lot to finagle a look at that. At least she'd be closer to proving that he was, indeed, Sellington.

Her gaze traveled up, snagged on the curve of his mouth.

All night, all morning, she'd been valiantly trying to think *around* their kiss. The simple fact that he'd

kissed her mattered, and she should be trying to inter-
pret what it meant and portended, searching for a way
to use it to her advantage. But the kiss *itself* shouldn't
have mattered at all.

Except she kept getting all tangled up in it, 'til she
could barely think about anything else.

The man kissed like a dream, like he'd spent years
studying the art and earned an expert's education in it.
Hot and smooth and deadly tempting. Never too much,
nor too little. Not too fast, not too slow. Where she
would have expected selfishness, there was instead
heady generosity. But she supposed that he'd acquired
that skill as well, perfecting the illusion of a shared
experience because that got him what he wanted more
expediently than did revealing his greed.

Most of all, though, she'd never, ever expected her
own reaction to it. She'd always believed she was not
a woman of strong passions; she'd never been able to
afford the luxury. Oh, she knew many who spent their
lust freely, looking for something, anything to mute
their harsh existence for a while, grabbing what little
pleasure they could wherever they found it. She understood that. But she also understood what small cur-
rency she owned, and her body was a good part of it.
She hadn't dared squander it on an hour's pleasure.

So where had that desire that had swelled and burst
inside her last night come from? She would have
sworn that it had never existed before. He lured it out
with the ease that his whole life had undoubtedly been.
Whatever Daniel Sellington wanted was simply
handed over to him without a struggle. She hated that
rousing her passion was just as effortless for him.

She wondered if he liked her.

Wanted her? Yes, she thought so; the evidence had burned within his hungry embrace.

But liked her? Who could tell?

He was so cool. Remote, unreachable, uncommunicative, as he had been ever since she'd entered the coach this morning and found him already hunched over that blasted notebook. As he'd been since she'd met him . . . except when he'd drawn her to him in a moon-shadowed garden.

Oh, damn, why couldn't she stop thinking about that stupid kiss?

She was watching him. Had been watching him all day.

Daniel stared down at the paper, scrawled another meaningless line across it. He'd drawn thirty-two square block houses, which were the upper limit of his artistic abilities; practiced his penmanship for three pages; plotted a meandering route through the United States, which would take at least two years to follow, and which he fully intended to pursue at the first opportunity; and invented eighteen pseudonyms that began with *D*. Through it all, he'd felt the weight of her regard, steady and unsettling.

He didn't dare look at her. God only knew what he might do if he did so. Throw open the coach door and pitch the Thatchers out, so he'd finally be closeted alone with her—yeah, that seemed like an appropriate start. Drag her off to the nearest abandoned cabin and lock her up for the next decade or two; now there was a distinct possibility. Throw her over his shoulder and howl at the moon? At the very least.

Would she protest if he did? And why did the suspicion, the persistently burgeoning hope that she might not argue at all, not terrify him? It should scare the hell out of him.

"Mr. Smith?" she said softly.

His fingers tightened around the pen, threatening to snap it like a dry twig. The scribbles on the paper blurred before his eyes.

With a terrible anticipation that bordered on dread, he lifted his head.

Nothing awful happened. He didn't stutter, didn't pass out, didn't rip off her clothes, didn't ravish the woman in the middle of the coach.

He just damn near drowned in those beautiful, sea-colored eyes.

Wisps of hair, pale as last night's moonlight, curled along her cheek and jawline and held there, as if reluctant to give up their claim. Not that he blamed the gleaming strands. He wouldn't let go, either.

"Miss Jordan, I—"

A sharp crack stopped him cold. "Yaw!" The coachman's cry shrieked overhead, echoed by the snap of a whip. The coach lurched forward, then rumbled and shivered with increasing speed.

Her eyes widened. "What's happening?"

"Well, hell," he said. "I believe we're being robbed."

Chapter 5

~～◯◯◯◯～~

Daniel nudged Frank Thatcher's shin with his booted toe. "You're probably going to want to wake up now."

Frank discharged a snort like a bull blowing out mucus. "Huh?"

Two more shots rang out, closer this time, and then a louder report, just over their head, which finally startled Evelyn awake.

"I believe," Daniel said mildly, "that someone's holding up the stage."

"Not again." Evelyn crossed her arms firmly over her sturdy chest. "They're not getting my good corset, Frank. Not this time."

"This . . . happens often?" Kathryn was not unaccustomed to danger; she expected it in the streets of Denver, was alert and prepared. For some reason, she'd not been looking for it out here. She should have known better.

Frank shrugged. "Now and then. Depends how good a shot the coachman is, and how fast the horses are, whether they'll catch us or not."

58

Daniel edged open the window shade and peered out. "Two on this side." There was another report, and twin holes appeared in the shade and its opposite companion. "You'd better get down," he told Kathryn, and she obediently sprawled across the seat. He leaned over her, reaching for the other shade, trying not to register the feel of horizontal female beneath him— *Not now*, he scolded himself, *not now!*—and peered out the brand-new eye hole that the bullet had conveniently punched. "Nobody over here."

It was a man's duty to protect a defenseless woman, wasn't it? And so he curled his body over hers. She was delicate and small beneath him, temptingly feminine. "So there's just two of them out there, unless there's someone behind the coach that I couldn't see."

Frank, who'd wedged Evelyn into the far corner, shielding her completely with his bulk, cocked his head and listened to the cruel pop of gunfire. "Sounds like just two to me, too."

"That's good. Maybe we won't have to stop and—"

The wicked, metallic shriek of protesting brakes slapped over the rest of his words. The coach slowed and jerked to an abrupt stop. "I never was good at predictions," Daniel murmured.

The door flew open and banged against the side of the coach. A shaking hand, holding a very large gun, appeared in the open doorway first, followed by a quick glimpse of a bandanna-wrapped face shadowed by a crushed black hat.

"You all come out of there, now," he drawled. "Hands up. And only two of you at a time!"

The occupants of the coach stared glumly at each other in the vain hope that some brave soul, some *other* brave soul, would volunteer to be the first person to surrender to the outlaws.

"Oh, all right," Daniel said at last. "Come on, Miss Jordan. We might as well get it over with."

"Why should *we* have to be the first ones out?" she blurted. "They're obviously experienced in such matters!" And it would give her a few moments to come up with . . . something.

But Daniel, hands jammed in the air, was already halfway out the door. "Stay behind me," he ordered over his shoulder, and Kathryn hurried to obey. *Obey* wasn't something she generally did all that well, but this was clearly a good time to make an exception.

Her hands on Daniel's shoulders to steady herself, she jumped down. Huddling up behind him, Kathryn peered cautiously around him, deciding there was more than one reason to be grateful the man had such fine shoulders. They did a really marvelous job of shielding her.

There were three men after all, each one tall and thin, all dressed in their best bandit black. Dark blue handkerchiefs covered their faces from the nose down, and hats pulled low concealed the rest. One stood beside the stage, his gun pointed up at the driver, whose right sleeve was bright red with blood. Another, a few yards away, sat a big gray horse that stamped impatiently, the reins of two more expensive-looking animals curled into his fist. The third, the one that currently captured most of Kathryn's attention, aimed the barrel of his revolver not more than eight inches from the center of Daniel's chest.

The outlaw mumbled something, his words muffled by the tightly wrapped handkerchief.

"Excuse me?" Daniel asked.

"Stan' an' deliver!" he shouted.

"What a surprise," Daniel said companionably. "You know, you might want to try it without the mask next time. Kinda hard to follow directions when you can't make them out."

The would-be robber growled and jabbed his gun at Daniel's midsection.

"I don't think he appreciated your suggestion," Kathryn whispered.

"True. Just trying to be helpful, and you see what happens? Not very polite, is he?"

"Now!" the man shouted.

"And just how do you expect me to do that," Daniel asked, "with my hands sticking up here over my head?"

"You can take them down," the outlaw mumbled. "But slow!"

"Slow. Got it." Daniel's hands crept down at a pace that would have made a snail look like a racehorse, and Kathryn decided she could attempt inching into her own handbag. If Daniel could just keep delaying . . .

Something thudded hard to Kathryn's left. The stage driver, his one-handed movements awkward, untied the ropes that held their luggage to the top of the coach. He released a large black case and gave it a shove with his foot. It cartwheeled off the roof and landed next to the one whose descent had caught Kathryn's attention in the first place.

"Hey," shouted the man standing guard over the driver. "Some of these are kind of big. How're we gonna get 'em all out of here?"

She could hear the rider's exasperated sigh from where she stood. He nudged his horse forward and dismounted, leaving all three sets of reins to trail on the ground. "Jes' pick the ones that look good. You pitch 'em over my way and I'll tie 'em on the back of our saddles."

"Do your holdups always go this efficiently?" Daniel put in, trying to keep his voice light. It was a dangerous line to walk, attempting to keep the man's attention off Kathryn while still probing for an opening. All without antagonizing him so much he'd decide to start firing.

From the narrow shadow wedged between his nose and his hat, their personal guard glared at them, eyes glowing like a hungry coyote's. "Hey, Harlan," he shouted to the man by the horses. "This'un's real annoying. Can't I just shoot him and get it over with?"

"Not yet."

"How disappointing for you," Daniel said.

The gun was now nudging Daniel's chest, so close that Kathryn's heart speared into her throat. If Daniel got himself shot, she wondered frantically, could the bullet go all the way through him and into her? And why, oh *why*, did he seem so intent on irritating a man holding a gun on him?

"So," he went on, "is Harlan his real name?"

Damn! The string that held closed the top of her bag

resisted her numb fingers. She'd been so determined it would not open of its own accord!

"What do you think?" the thief snarled. "And would you hurry up!"

Daniel had inched his hands all the way down to shoulder level. "You told me to go slow," he reminded him reasonably.

"Not that slow!"

Kathryn's nerves were nearly shredded. "Would you just do as you're told and shut up!" she whispered fiercely.

"All right."

Daniel dug in his pockets. He pulled out a roll of bills and a handful of coins, which he dropped one by one into the bandit's outstretched hand.

"And you back there, missy," the man said, stuffing his bounty into the deep pockets of his grease-streaked pants. "You can just hand over your pocketbook, too."

"Me?" Kathryn had half hoped that he'd been so busy with Daniel he'd forgotten all about her. She'd finally gotten one hand stuffed into her bag, groping in the bottom, and now she froze with it well hidden behind Daniel's back. "What pocketbook?"

"Oh, jeez, don't do that." The thief rolled his eyes. "The one you're holding."

"I don't have a bag," she insisted, as she stealthily lifted the back of Daniel's coat and tried to stuff her bag into his pants at the small of his back. Now as long as Daniel didn't turn around . . .

His hand came back and swatted at hers. *Well!* she thought. *Not exactly cooperative of him.*

"The one you're trying to hide," the outlaw said wearily.

"No."

"No?" At her denial, the thief perked up a little, as if the prospect of having to enforce his commands physically spiked his interest.

"For God's sake," Daniel said, "just give him the damn thing and get it over with."

Easy for him to say, Kathryn thought. He wasn't being forced to hand over everything he owned in the entire world.

"It's only money," Daniel went on.

And only a man who'd always had enough would consider it *only* money.

"He can't have it."

"Oh, you don't think so?" The bandit sidled to one side, swinging the gaping maw of his gun from Daniel to her. "Well now, we'll just see about that, won't we?"

"Damn it, Kathryn, now see what you've done?" You really had to admire the woman's courage, Daniel thought. Even if she wasn't too bright about it. "Really, it's best just to go along with him."

Kathryn brought her handbag to her chest and folded her arms protectively over it. She knew it was foolish; she knew she'd probably lose. But she'd had enough stolen from her in her life, been forced to surrender her meager treasures so often, that she just couldn't compel her arms to hand it over.

"Well, now." The stiff fabric of his bandanna wrinkled, betraying his smile. "You can't say I din't give you a fair chance." He started in her direction.

"You're not going to make this easy, are you?" Daniel asked her.

Kathryn remained stubbornly silent.

Daniel heaved a sigh. "Well, hell."

His left arm lashed out, knocked the gunman's arm and sent the weapon flying. At the same instant, his right fist connected with the outlaw's chin with a solid *chunk*.

Shouts burst behind Kathryn, a scattering of gunfire. She paid them no mind, but scrambled for the gun that glittered dangerously on the scrub-studded ground ten feet away. A bullet kicked up a small geyser of dirt a few steps to her left; she ducked and lunged.

Got it. Gun clenched in her numb hand, she spun, leveling it in the direction of Daniel and his opponent. The two circled each other slowly, Daniel balanced lightly on his toes, his body angled, fists held loose and easy in front of him. His expression was intent, but he looked amazingly relaxed, all things considered. A most unpredictable man, she decided.

"Don't shoot!" The shout broke from her right. She looked over to find to her dismay that the robber on the horse had his own gun trained on her. "Or I will."

Damn. She cocked her head. "What now?" she asked him.

He pondered a moment, then shrugged. "We wait, I guess."

The gun was a repulsive weight in her hand, the stock still warm from the outlaw's grip. Whom to cover? Could she shoot first, quick enough, straight enough, before he could return fire? Her thoughts wavered, swirled like the heated air shimmering on the horizon.

Not being in any immediate danger, she decided it was best to wait, and tried to keep her attention on the man who aimed at her. Except she kept getting distracted by the combat. She'd assumed Daniel would end up flat in the dirt inside of a minute; she didn't guess he was the type of man who'd spent a lot of time in barroom brawls or street fights, hardly a worthy opponent for a ruthless outlaw.

But somewhere, somehow, the man had learned to fight. And not at all the way she expected.

The thief hauled back and let loose with a roundhouse punch that, had it connected, would have blasted Daniel into the next county. Except Daniel merely jerked his head back so quickly that it seemed he'd never been there at all, so the punch whistled through thin air. He returned with a quick left-handed jab to the chin that shot the man's head back with a vicious snap.

Daniel moved like summer lightning, there and gone and back again before his opponent could even register the motion. Two quick punches to the body, another that connected solidly with his nose. Kathryn sucked in a breath in admiration.

Commotion erupted by the stage. Kathryn noted it vaguely, but couldn't spare her attention. The outlaw had the constitution of a lumbering bull, slow, stupid, tough. She couldn't believe he hadn't gone down already, but he was apparently too dumb to know when he was outclassed. He kept throwing wild punches, looking shocked when they met nothing but air.

Finally, Daniel dropped his hands, leaving his head and body exposed and tempting. The thief bellowed and charged, throwing his entire weight behind one desperate attack. Daniel sidestepped and brought his right fist up hard, clipping the man neatly beneath his chin.

The outlaw wavered for a moment, then toppled like a felled tree.

Daniel stood over the fallen outlaw like an ancient hunter claiming his prize. His jacket was ripped at the shoulder, his knuckles bloody. A thick shock of hair had fallen over his right eye, and he shot her a cocky grin, one that clearly said: *Hey, you see that? Betcha didn't think I could do* that.

And she hadn't. He looked male and messy, a thousand times more approachable than usual, and damned if she didn't feel like cheering.

Then Daniel looked behind her and his smile vanished.

"Damn," he said.

Alarmed, Kathryn spun around. Oh, she *knew* she should have paid more attention to the other bandits, shouldn't have gotten so caught up in watching Daniel's fight. But he'd been so efficient, so darn good at it, she hadn't been able to help herself.

The good news was the horseman's gun was no longer pointed at her head. The bad news was the outlaws had apparently opted to chase more tempting prey, for the two that remained conscious were riding hell for leather after the fleeing coach, already a good half mile down the road.

"Wait!" she hollered, and sprinted after it.

She damned the skirts that slowed her down, and
the high-heeled boots that she'd chosen to prove she
was a lady and therefore not required to walk too far.
Her petticoats tangled about her legs. She stumbled
into a rut, wrenching her ankle painfully. And still the
coach faded into a cloud of trail dust. A single black
valise, apparently dislodged by the rough ride, cata-
pulted off the back of the stage and rammed into the
ground.

Of course, *she'd* had to insist the coachman tie her
luggage down securely.

Panting heavily, she gave up and, resting her hands
on her knees, she bent over and tried to gulp a decent
lungful of air. When she could stand straight again,
she shaded her eyes with her hand and squinted back
at Daniel.

"Why didn't you stop them?" she shouted at him.

"Well, at first I was kind of busy. Also, I've never
suffered from the delusion that I could outrun a team
of horses." He nudged the unconscious outlaw with
his toe, none too gently. Satisfied the man wouldn't be
waking up anytime soon, he ambled toward her.

"But they *left* us," she cried, still unable to credit it.
"After we paid for our fare and everything!"

"So we'll get our money back."

Which wasn't the point at all, and the infernal man
should know it. "But why would they leave us?"

He shrugged. If he was the slightest bit disconcerted
by recent events, it certainly didn't show. "Are the
Thatchers all right? Did you see what happened to
them?"

"I don't think they ever poked their noses out of the stage."

"Must have all decided to get out while the getting was good," he said. "And maybe the driver was trying to lead the outlaws away from us."

Her dark look clearly told him she was not pleased with his suggestion. For the life of him, Daniel couldn't seem to work up an appropriate anger about the situation. He'd gotten a bit of good exercise, for one thing. For the second thing—the one which, he admitted to himself, was mostly responsible for his good mood—he was out here in the middle of nowhere, *alone*, with one of the most delectable women he'd ever met in his life.

"Besides," he pointed out, "at least you got to keep your handbag."

She expelled a frustrated breath and pointed toward the still figure of the fallen outlaw.

"What are we going to do with him?"

"I hadn't planned on doing anything with him."

"You're just going to leave him there?"

"That was the general idea. He'll wake up in an hour or two. Either his buddies'll come back for him or he'll just have to find his own way home."

She swept her gaze around, looking for a way out, and sighed. "I don't suppose you saw what happened to his horse, did you?"

He jerked his thumb over his shoulder. "Figure it's a mile toward home by now. Wherever that is." He glanced at her hand. "Are you going to hang on to that gun?"

She'd forgotten all about it. It gleamed hot silver,

ugly and beautiful at once. "I'd kind of thought I would," she said. "Unless you want it?"

"Depends. Are you any good with it?"

Actually, she was quite competent. But she doubted he was the kind of man who would consider that an asset in a potential wife. More than a few would, she supposed, but good aim wasn't the kind of feminine accomplishment likely to impress a millionaire. Hosting glamorous parties, speaking several languages, playing piano—those seemed much more the type of skills he'd admire.

Better she'd set her sights on one of the outlaws than him.

"I'd rather you took it. Please." She handed it over, both relieved and frightened to have it gone. He quickly checked the loading.

"How many bullets left?"

"Two." Only two, which weren't going to stretch very far if they got in a situation that required a serious defense. He spun the chamber, tucked the gun in the small of his back where she'd tried to hide her bag.

"If you had just let me stick my handbag there, none of this would have happened."

Actually, Daniel's only regret was that he'd been too occupied at the time to appreciate properly her hands' finding their way inside his clothes. "Yeah, I'm sure they would never have noticed the bulge. New fashion, men's bustles. All the rage."

She smiled at that, unwillingly amused, and his temperature notched up twenty degrees in less than a second.

With any luck, he thought, it would be a very, very long way to the nearest town.

"So?" At some time during the commotion, her hair had loosened, pale, fine strands waving in the breeze. He wondered what she'd do if he reached up and tucked one of those soft-looking tendrils away. "What do we do now?"

In answer, he snapped his heels together and formally presented his arm, as if requesting a dance at the most formal of balls. "Now," he said cheerfully, "we walk."

Chapter 6

⌒♾⌒

The valise that tumbled from the back of the stage as it sped away was Daniel's, of course. Daniel, who she suspected could have shed possessions from there to the Atlantic and never noticed their loss. Kathryn could do nothing but shake her head when they discovered it; wasn't that just how it always went?

"I don't suppose," she ventured, "that you happen to have a nice cache of bullets in there, do you?"

He'd just smiled and hefted the case to his shoulder. She couldn't help but admire that, even after what had to have been a rather strenuous bout with the still-unconscious bandit—just how hard *had* he hit him?—Daniel lifted his good-sized burden with complete ease. Like a man who worked for a living, whose muscles were strong and accustomed to heavy use, rather than one who lived off his father's ill-gotten fortune.

They'd walked all day, keeping to the edge of the rutted road. For all Kathryn could tell, they might not have gone a mile, for the scenery they trekked by hardly changed: flat expanses of land, all brown and dusty green, pocked with sage and brush and prairie-dog

72

mounds. And, far to their left, the mountains rose, both unchanging and constantly varied. Their bulk and shape were familiar and immutable, but their color, the angles of light and shadow, flickered restlessly. They hadn't passed a single sign of human habitation, much less civilization.

Kathryn was hot. The inconsiderate sun, unmoved by the fact that her hat had disappeared with the coach, burned down on her head and shoulders. Sweat dampened her back and arms—oh, she was sure Daniel was going to find *that* enormously attractive! Not to mention that, from the feel of things, right nasty blisters had erupted on one heel and both ankles.

And it was all she could do to keep from grinning like a giddy fool, for she had finally, *finally*, smartened up two hours ago.

Try as she might, she could not have arranged this better herself. She was utterly and completely alone with Daniel Sellington. No Thatchers to peer, interrupt, snore, or otherwise function as inconvenient, if unintentional, chaperones. No innkeepers, no private room for Daniel to retreat to, no notebook for him to hide behind. For one night, at least, and maybe for a few more days as well, he couldn't escape her.

Also, she'd finally realized what a blessing it really was that her luggage *hadn't* fallen off the coach. Now she needn't worry about making excuses for her meager wardrobe. The fact that she had no money was easily explained by implying that she'd only kept a small amount in her pocketbook, feeling it safer to lock the rest away in her valise. If she had nothing, it was only because it had been lost, not because Edward

Sellington had swindled every penny her father had ever made.

And, as they'd sweated through what had to be one of the emptiest, dustiest stretches of Colorado, Daniel had finally begun to unbend toward her. He'd lost a bit of his rigid stiffness, eased that arrogant detachment. She caught him looking at her now and then, with admiration—and perhaps something else—glowing in those astounding blue eyes. When she'd caught him at it, he hadn't even looked away, just grinned reassuringly. Their misfortune had afforded her the perfect opportunity to prove how cheerfully brave and uncomplaining she was.

Though she was admittedly getting awfully tired of walking, and remaining *un*complaining was fast becoming a real challenge.

"Shouldn't we stop soon?"

"Stop?" he asked, as if the thought had never occurred to him.

"Yes, stop. You didn't really plan to keep going the entire night through, did you? I have to tell you that, though I'm trying awfully hard to demonstrate my valiant good nature about this entire episode, I'm afraid that would be more than I could manage."

"You *have* been valiant." And a lot more than that, he reflected. Amazingly, she hadn't complained once, hadn't fussed over the deteriorating condition of her feet, her hair, or her clothes. Hadn't shrieked at insects or rodents or even the sleek, disgruntled hognose snake they'd stumbled across.

So yes, he had sort of planned to keep walking all night. Because stopping, being alone with her miles and miles from any other human, sounded like the best damn idea he'd ever heard in his life. Which made it far too tempting by half.

"Thank you," she said, brushing a damp swath of hair from her forehead. The sun had colored her skin, lured out a few freckles across the narrow bridge of her nose. A fine layer of dust clung to her clothes, and her shoulders drooped as low as the limp ruffles at her neck. But he would have sworn she was prettier now than when he'd first laid eyes on her.

"What do you think?" she asked. "Here's as good a place as any."

A small stream had burbled alongside the road for the last two miles, cottonwoods studding the banks at irregular intervals, thickening into a grove where the river curved east. Yeah, it was as good a place as any. And maybe, if he stuck her on one side of the river and himself on the other, there was a remote chance of him getting through the night without touching her.

"If we go a little farther, we might come across a ranch or something. Even an abandoned line shack would be better than nothing." Someplace—anyplace— where there'd be a door she could lock against him.

"Oh," she said softly, disappointment turning down the corners of her fine mouth in a most delectable manner.

"Why?" he asked. "Are you tired?"

"Yes," she admitted.

"And there's no sign that we're going to come upon anyplace soon."

"Yes."

"And it'll be dark before long."

"That it will," she said, and each of her agreements rang another death knell for his good intentions.

He lowered the valise to the ground. "All right, we'll stay here." His shoulder had stiffened under the weight of his burden, and he rolled it, trying to work out the kinks. She contemplated him a moment, and, before he could stop her—for surely he would have been smart enough to stop her—she'd stepped to his side and put her hands right there.

"Tell me if I hurt you." Her thumbs dug into his flesh, finding the exact spot between his neck and his shoulders where his tendons had tied themselves up into a knot.

"You shouldn't . . . I mean, you don't have to . . ." *Please don't stop. Ever.*

"Yes, I do," she said briskly. "This shoulder has been a fair amount of use to me over the last couple of days. I'd hate to see anything happen to it."

For such a small, delicate-looking woman, she had surprisingly strong hands. She kneaded his aching muscles, her palms rubbing over the ball of his shoulder, the firm pressure just one degree shy of painful and utterly wonderful. He groaned aloud in pleasure. Her hands stilled, and he almost moaned again, this time in disappointment.

"Are you all right?" she asked.

He felt himself flush. Okay, maybe the sound he'd made resembled one made in the grip of a different kind of pleasure entirely, but really, what could she expect of him? He was only human.

"I was fine," he said, twisting to look over his shoulder at her, "until you stopped."

She ducked her chin as if his comment embarrassed her, but a smile flirted with the corners of her mouth, and she went back to doing those wonderful things to his shoulder.

Nope, he thought, the stream wasn't going to do it.

A full-blown, raging, drown-an-entire-city flood wouldn't be enough.

Night and a chill had dropped without warning, fast and hard. There was no moon, so the bright stars spangling the sky shone without competition.

Kathryn wiggled to her side, the ground hard beneath her hip, and tugged Daniel's coat more firmly around her. Shortly after they stopped, he'd pulled it from his valise, surprising her with his thoughtfulness. But after that kindness, he'd ignored her as he'd moved around the small clearing, removing the worst of the rocks and brush from the ground and building a small fire.

Perhaps, she reflected, he'd always disregarded the common courtesies, and that was why he ignored her so totally. For he didn't have to work to make friends; he could simply buy them. No doubt he spent more time fending off all the people trying to find a place in his affections than he did developing friendships.

She looked through the flickering orange flames to where he lay across from her, to all appearances fast asleep. The firelight honed the angles of his face to sharp, regal edges, making him look like an ancient, pagan lord conjured up out of the blaze. The wool of his jacket, a finely woven fabric like she'd sewn a hundred times for others but never been able to afford for herself, cocooned rich and soft around her. While she worked she'd endeavored to ignore the cloth she used. What use was there in tempting herself with things she could never have? But now she reveled in it, snuggling her cheek up against the collar. It smelled of him, rare and warm. She hadn't realized she'd noted his scent, but obviously it had crept into her senses, her memories, as she'd slumbered on his shoulder, for she recognized it now as if she'd always known it.

"I'm hungry," she said.

In his uncomfortable bed on the far side of the flames where he'd valiantly struggled to maintain the illusion of being fast asleep, Daniel opened his eyes to find that Kathryn looked every bit as lovely by fire-light as he'd expected.

"Didn't believe I was really asleep for a moment, did you? I should have known better."

"Yes," she said, smiling. "You should have."

"I suppose," he said slowly, "that I could try and hunt something. Shoot a rabbit, maybe."

She thought for a moment, then shook her head. "We should probably conserve our ammunition, shouldn't we? In case we really need it."

"That's true," he agreed.

"Will it be much farther, do you think?" she asked in a very small voice. It was the first hint of fear he'd seen in her and his heart, which was fast becoming all too susceptible to her, squeezed a little. He longed to comfort her, to go to her and put his arms around her, but he was pretty sure that would present far more danger to her than any of the worries she currently entertained.

"I'm sure it won't be," he said, for that was the only reassurance he dared give her. "The coach can only travel so far before they have to change the horses, or at least rest them. So there must be a stage stop before too much farther. We're probably almost there already."

She nodded, accepting, then winced. "I think you somehow overlooked a boulder or two when you picked this campsite. And I am quite certain one is lodged directly under my right hip."

He laughed, and she frowned at him. "I'm glad my pain amuses you," she groused.

"No, it's just—so you *do* complain after all. I was beginning to wonder. It was unnatural."

"Oh, you noticed that, did you?" She brightened. "I was trying so very hard to restrain myself. I wanted you to be properly impressed with my forbearance."

"I am," he assured her. "And you certainly have a right to be a little put out. This is not exactly the trip you had planned."

"Ah, well, I *did* hope for an adventure, didn't I?"

"That you did." He rolled up to prop himself on his elbow, and winced. "And this *isn't* exactly the best mattress I've ever had the privilege of resting on. I swear, when I used to go camping with Nic when we were kids, I don't recall it *ever* feeling like this. Maybe the ground's softer back home than here."

"Nic?"

"My brother."

"You have a brother?" She didn't remember ever hearing anything about a brother. She'd been going along secure in the assumption that this man was, indeed, Daniel Sellington. But the slight possibility she was wrong still existed. Somehow, and soon, she was going to have to confirm his identity one way or the other.

"Well, sort of." He shoved a hand through his hair, and, despite everything, Kathryn couldn't help but wish she was the one privileged to do that. "His uncle married my mother—well, my stepmother—and . . . it's complicated. Suffice it to say I consider him my brother, and I imagine he does the same." His grin was full of fond exasperation. "He certainly takes advantage of me often enough."

"Families tend to do that," she agreed. Not really his brother, then. His answer neither verified nor disproved his identity, and she tried to think of a way to steer the conversation into something that would. Maybe, if she could just keep him talking . . .

"Does yours?" he asked, catching her up short. People did not generally ask about her life. Her customers didn't care, as long as she did her work, and her neighbors had plenty of their own worries without asking after hers.

"I suppose," she said.

"Do you have a lot of family? Besides your sister, of course?"

Her sister? What did he know of her sister?

"You won't miss the bi—um, you won't be too late, will you? Since we took this little detour."

Of course. The fictional sister she'd claimed to be traveling to assist. She was going to have to watch her step more closely, if she intended to keep all her lies straight. And she did.

Still, he'd remembered a passing comment she'd made. That had to be a good sign.

"I'm sure she'll be fine."

"Do you have others?"

And, unexpectedly, she felt the burn of tears at the back of her eyes. She blinked, grateful that the darkness would cover her expression.

Pete. Ah, Pete.

She thought she'd used up all her tears a long time ago. How much could one person cry? How much could one afford to, when life just kept flooding right at you, unpredictable and relentless? Life didn't wait for you to stop and mourn.

It had been a long time since she'd cried over her family, *any* of her family. Even when Isabelle had run to Simon Moore's, there'd been worry and anger and fear, but she hadn't indulged in tears. So why now?

Perhaps it'd had been the warm, exasperated fondness in Daniel's voice when he'd talked about his "brother." She hadn't expected his emotion, this sign of his humanity, and couldn't afford to heed the thought that he might not be completely his father's son. His tone reminded her a little of Pete's, that same mix of irritation and love that often shaded her older brother's voice when he'd talked about Tommy. And she rarely permitted herself to think about Pete; of all the things that had happened to her, his loss was still the one that, if she allowed it, would cripple her. The one that made her think, what was the use of fighting so hard? He'd fought, too, battled like a boxing champion, and look at what it had got him.

"So do you?" Daniel repeated. "Have other brothers and sisters?"

"I'm cold," she said, by way of changing the topic.

"Oh, so we're back to the complaints?" But he didn't seem annoyed. "Saved them up to use all at once, did you?"

"Perhaps I just couldn't hold them in any longer."

He rolled up to a sitting position. "Let me see what I have in my case."

He poked at the fire, inciting it to flare up, birthing sparks that spiraled up into the darkness and died an instant later. He dug deep in his valise, coming up with two white shirts and another suit jacket.

She'd watched him the whole time he worked. Daniel felt her eyes upon him, tried to ignore them, but couldn't help that they warmed him far more effectively than the fire. He should just toss the clothes to her; it would be the smartest thing. But he came around the fire toward her anyway. The firelight danced in her eyes, flickered lovingly over her skin as he knelt by her side, and yearning lumped in his throat.

He carefully spread the shirts over her, laid the coat over it all until her figure was a small, delectable form beneath the pile of fabric. *His* clothes, which seemed somehow forbidden and intimate. They'd covered him, and now they covered her.

He tried not to touch her, he truly did, but as he tugged the coat up around her neck his hands lingered of their own accord, drawing a slow line down her throat, and he felt her shudder.

"You're still cold?"

"Maybe a little," she said, then gave a breathless

laugh. "Even though I must look as if I decided to take a rest in the bottom of the laundry basket."

She was chilled. It would be the gentlemanly thing, the thoughtful thing, to lie down beside her and keep her warm.

And completely improper, and totally dangerous, and heart-poundingly tempting.

"I suppose," he said slowly, "keeping you warm by any means necessary would be only considerate of me."

Her eyes searched his gravely. "Anything else would be almost rude, now that I think about it."

Just how was he supposed to do this? Lie down beside her without touching anyplace he shouldn't, that he really, really *wanted* to touch? Easing down beside her, he edged up behind her back, angling his lower regions away because he was afraid that, even through her petticoats, she'd discover right quickly just how, ah, *considerate* he was.

"Is that better?" he whispered. Because he couldn't capture enough air to speak normally.

"Well . . . it's getting there."

"More complaints, hmm?" He moved forward another inch, until his chest bumped up firm behind her back. Heat seeped into him—*her* heat—evaporating whatever logic he'd previously possessed into the cool summer night.

Sighing, she pressed back against him. "Oh, you're so *warm*."

No kidding, he thought.

It had all been going so well thus far that he decided to chance slipping his arm around her waist. Her torso dipped abruptly from her rib cage, creating a deep valley where his forearm settled as though it was supposed to be there all along.

Oh, he should have gotten married years ago, if this was what it was like.

The thought brought him up abruptly, for he'd not thought of marriage for years. Once he'd claimed his heritage—his burden—he'd quickly discovered he couldn't marry any of the women introduced to him, those smiling, lovely women, their desperation not quite hidden beneath a thin veneer of well-groomed beauty. For it hadn't taken him long to discern that it was primarily his bank account that attracted them. It was simply too easy to "accidentally" end up alone and unchaperoned with them, their improper attempts at seduction too blatant. Thank God he figured out what they were up to before it went any further than it had, or he would have ended up honor-bound to marry a woman who loved his father's fortune more than she loved him.

He'd even thought of going back home to Minnesota, taking up again with Meribel, the girl he'd left behind. He'd never felt more than mild affection for her, paired with a healthy lust that even then they'd both understood had more to do with their ages than each other, and so which they'd explored but never fully indulged because neither had been willing to risk a hasty adolescent wedding. But at least with her, he'd known it wasn't his money she wanted, for they'd kept company before anyone in New Ulm had an inkling who he really was.

But, on his one brief visit home, he'd found her

already happily married to a strapping young farmer named Schultz, her first child on the way. He'd wished her well with only a twinge of regret, and resigned himself to a resolutely solitary, and quite probably celibate, existence for many years to come.

It was only one of the many prices he'd paid for being Edward Sellington's son.

And now he held a woman in his arms, a fragrant, glorious, soft woman. Soft hair, soft skin, soft sighs when he tightened his arm around her narrow waist. A woman he wanted far more than he'd ever wanted Meribel, with a man's passion, and years of solitude to give it power.

If he were married, he'd have a wife in his bed every night. And if he were married, his body reminded him with cruel insistence, he'd have the right to do far more than simply hold her through the dark hours.

Leaning back against him, Kathryn turned her face up to look into his. "Daniel?"

Her tongue slid quickly over her bottom lip, leaving a shiny glaze of moisture and starlight behind. His gaze was drawn inevitably there. And he suspected that if he bent his head to kiss her, she would welcome him as she had the previous night, and oh, he wanted to do that. Wanted to do it with every wish and dream and desire that had been denied and ignored inside him for years, all dammed up behind a wall of responsibility and regret.

"Go to sleep," he said gruffly, summoning all his will to drop his head to the crook formed of his folded right arm.

So he'd hold her, sleep with the wonder of her cradled in his embrace. But not kiss her.

For he knew that, if he started to kiss her again, there was no way in hell he was ever going to stop.

Chapter 7

The fire dwindled to a thick bed of gray ashes, a hint of red embers glowing bright in its depths. Twice in the night, Daniel had gotten up from beside her and fed a few more thin branches to the blaze. He'd obviously tried to be quiet, easing away and tip-toeing around the campsite. But his absence had snapped Kathryn awake, and, try as she might, as exhausted as she was, she'd been unable to drop back off until he'd returned to his place. Only then had she fallen asleep again.

It was only because she was accustomed to sleeping wedged between her mother and Isabelle, she told herself; that was the only reason she couldn't sleep without the hard comfort of his body close behind her. It had nothing to do with *him*, specifically.

He was certainly close behind her now. One long leg looped over hers, his foot hooked around her ankle. His face was buried against the nape of her neck. Each time he exhaled, she could feel the warmth of his breath over her skin. His hips were snugged up against . . . she preferred not to consider exactly *what* was tucked exactly *where* in that particular instance, because it tended to spur an almost uncontrollable urge to wriggle her own hips. Whether *toward* or *away*, she was afraid to guess.

The morning was a promise on the verge of becoming real. Faint gray light sifted through the small clearing, and the sky overhead was the color of the ashes. A breeze shuffled between the cottonwoods, nipped at the tip of her nose—the one part of her entire body that wasn't thoroughly warmed by Daniel Sellington. It prodded the fire's coals to a brief instant of brilliance, then abandoned them to die back to darkness.

There were a dozen reasons to stay exactly where she was. She was warm. She was safe. And, she hoped, Daniel was growing accustomed to, *attached* to, the feeling of her in his arms.

However, there was one very good, unignorable reason to move: Once and for all, she had to find out if it really was Daniel Sellington's arms warming her so well, and not those of an attractive reporter with a coincidental name.

Oh, why hadn't the man kissed her last night? She'd practically delivered him an engraved invitation. He *should* have kissed her. And she would have allowed it, and perhaps a delicious bit more before she, with impassioned but appropriately maidenly reluctance, ended the interlude.

Had she been too forward? Not forward enough? Frustration gnawed at her, more worrisome than the hunger that growled in her stomach. It seemed more drastic measures might well be called for, if she meant to inflame him into the necessary rash act. And, if they were, she had to be absolutely certain that those same drastic measures were aimed at the correct man.

Slowly, holding her breath for fear of startling him, she eased his arm from around her waist and wiggled her foot out from beneath his. He mumbled something, rolled a little in her direction. But he didn't move any farther, and she inched forward, slipping out from the warm shelter created by his body. He frowned in his sleep for a moment, then his expression softened. The faint lines bracketing his mouth and spearing between his brows disappeared, and he looked young and carefree and handsome. Her hand reached out of its own volition, smoothed back a disobedient wave of rich dark hair, admiring the healthy shine.

Wishing she could crawl back into her nest, she shivered in the predawn chill. But how he'd felt beside her, how he looked in sleep, were things that shouldn't matter at all. Only his identity mattered.

After assuring herself that he was still fast asleep, she hurried over to where his black-leather case sat next to a deep, cracked gray boulder and a clump of mule's ears. She reached for the latch, noting with surprise that her hand shook.

The latch opened with a soft click. She inhaled sharply and flipped open the lid.

She wasn't entirely sure what she expected to find. Bars of gold? A cache of jewels, bankbooks containing entries with lots and lots of zeroes? Instead she found things that might have belonged to any traveler: a few shirts, some socks, three pairs of pants. A couple of more notebooks, a stash of stubby-tipped pencils. She flipped through the notebooks and found them mostly empty. One held more than a dozen drawings—hastily made, not very good. The subjects seemed entirely random: a lopsided house, a wilted flower, a badly proportioned bowl of fruit. Nothing that looked as though they were quick sketches intended to remind him of things he might describe in an article. If he truly was a writer, he was certainly not a very prolific one. Her heart sank further with each item she examined and set aside without learning anything of importance.

But the last notebook, bound in battered black leather and tied with a piece of twine, its spine loose and curling up like an apple peel, was stuffed with names and addresses. Often followed by a few indecipherable notes, each entry ended with a string of numbers, sometimes running into six digits. *There*, she thought. People who owed him money, most likely. She wondered if he charged rates as exorbitant as Simon Moore's. And if he enforced them just as emphatically.

She slid the notebook back in its place, wedged between a thickly knit sweater the color of midnight and a wadded-up pair of drawers. At the very bottom of the valise, beneath a layer of cotton undershirts and two spare collars, she found a large, bulky package wrapped in plain brown paper.

She shot a glance at Daniel, relieved to find him still fast asleep. The pile of clothing that served as her blankets the night before were all jumbled together and his arms wrapped tightly around them, as if in sleep he believed he was still holding her close. She tried very hard not to be sorry he wasn't.

The paper wrapping fell apart in her hands, and at the first dull twinkle of coins her breath caught. There had to be hundreds—thousands—maybe tens of thousands of dollars there, all spilling out of the thin, crinkly paper and into her palms. Banded stacks of ten- and fifty-dollar bills, plain cloth bags bulging with dollar coins. The abundance overwhelmed her, shocked her, excited her.

How could the man simply walk around with such riches stuffed in his case like they were spare socks? Wasn't he afraid he'd lose them? Maybe he had so much that this was only an insignificant portion. The idea that this huge fortune was simply his walking-around money boggled her.

She wanted to run her fingers through it, learn the smell and feel. It was only money, she told herself, paper and ink and metal. But she knew better; the lack of it had killed her father, her brother, and nearly destroyed what remained of her family. It *wasn't* just money. It was safety and power and security, everything she'd never had and always craved.

She could take it and just go, she thought. Grab the whole bundle and run off into the plains. How much cash was there? More than she'd ever thought she'd see in her life, that was for certain. But enough to provide for every eventuality, all the disasters life might hurl her way? Enough to cover expensive illnesses, to support an entire family through depressions and unexpected expenses and natural disasters?

How much was enough? For most of her life, a hundred dollars had seemed like unimaginable wealth. But to make absolutely sure that she, and those she loved, would always be well protected, it seemed as if there could never be enough.

Not to mention that it wasn't likely she'd get too far before he woke up and discovered her crime. He was faster than she was, stronger; he'd run her down in the grasslands like a hunter scenting prey. Or simply turn her name over to the police and let them chase her. The odds of her getting away with it seemed longer than she wanted to take.

No, her original plan still seemed the best approach. *If* she could pull it off.

If not, and here she had to admit that the odds were not in her favor, well, at least she knew where he kept his stash. If not enough to insulate them forever, at least it was enough to free them from Simon.

Hurriedly, she scraped the pile of money together, foldeded the paper around it again. How had it all fit together? She should have paid more attention before she'd unwrapped it, memorized how he'd knotted the string and where the lumps were. Would he know that she'd invaded his personal belongings? That she'd had her hands on his wealth?

In the midst of shoving the entire mess back into the bottom of his valise, she glanced his way again.

And met the shock of fierce blue.

Instinctively she reacted like a doe who'd scented a wolf, freezing in place. Except freezing in place with her hands deep within his case was hardly the most productive response, she realized belatedly.

His eyes, cool and expressionless, held hers as she slowly removed her hands and folded them in her lap.

"May I help you with something?" he asked formally, his words as chiseled as cut granite.

"Ah . . ." Unable to hold his gaze, she pulled hers away. "I . . . needed . . . something. You were sleeping so well, and heaven knows you earned a rest, and well, I just didn't want to wake you."

"How thoughtful of you." She heard the swish of fabric as he unfolded himself from the ground, the snap of a twig as he made his way around the dying fire to stand beside her, his shadow falling over her like a shroud.

"But I'm sure it would be more expedient if you asked my assistance, rather than rummaging around in unfamiliar areas on your own," he murmured, dragging the case across the sandy ground to rest out of her reach at his side. "What do you need?"

"I—" Thankfully, her brain, which had frozen when her hands had, suddenly decided to function again. "It's a private matter," she whispered.

"Private, hmm? Well, as you said, certainly some of the proprieties must bow to the inconveniences of travel. And surely there is little more inconvenient than *this*." His tone was edged with knife points of suspicion.

"I need some—" Swallowing hard, she dragged her gaze up to meet his eyes. "Some cloth," she finished in a hushed tone, as if speaking of the dead.

"Cloth."

"I—" She didn't have to force this blush. Heat poured into her cheeks, her neck. "I had some in my bag, of course, but I used them all yesterday, and I must have more."

"Cloths," he repeated flatly.

"I'm bleeding," she said, with a reluctance that was only slightly enhanced, for she discovered it was harder to lie to him than she expected.

"Bleeding?" Skepticism warred with concern. "You're injured? Why didn't you say—"

"Not that kind of bleeding."

He looked thunderstruck, as if one of the cottonwoods had just up and talked to him. Comprehension and color flooded him at once, turning his complexion the color of the sunrise pinkening the sky behind him.

He dived for his valise and his arms disappeared up to his elbows. Items flew out at random. A woolen suit jacket ended up hanging over the sharp branches of a stunted chokecherry. A pair of socks fluttered in the breeze like black butterflies before settling to rest on a patch of dead buffalo grass. He yanked out the sweater, held it triumphantly aloft before, frowning, he balled it up and hurled it over his shoulder. He plunged in again and came up with a fine white shirt. The sound of tearing cloth rent the air before Kathryn could say a word of protest.

A pile of white strips began growing at her feet. Kathryn bit down on her lip and mourned the waste. Surely she could have gotten at least a dollar for that shirt! It had been a very nice one.

Still, it was very convenient that men were so predictable about certain things. Even the most worldly man would rather face a dozen maddened bulls than be confronted with a woman's more intimate complaints.

The pile of fabric at her feet outgrew even a large

prairie-dog mound. Panting, Daniel paused, another shirt clutched in his hand, long enough to ask her, "Do you think that's enough?"

Kathryn swallowed a smile. He was really quite . . . adorable, so flustered, all his forbidding, arrogant-aristocrat demeanor submerged beneath blind male panic. "I'm sure that's sufficient." If she'd been a battlefield casualty, it'd still be sufficient.

"Because I could—"

She rushed in to forestall the demise of any more perfectly good shirts. "No, it's absolutely fine. Ah . . . thank you."

"Of course. Happy to—" He focused on something far over her shoulder as if to ensure there was no chance of accidentally meeting her eyes. "I mean, you're welcome. Obviously."

Belatedly it occurred to her that in doing a brilliant job at deflecting his suspicions, she'd probably been equally effective in dousing his carnal urges toward her.

"Besides, it's almost over," she said hastily. "By this evening, at the latest. The *very* latest. I just wanted to be prepared."

He swallowed hard. "If you need any more—"

"I won't," she assured him, inwardly chastising herself for her oh-so-clever foolishness. Oh, she'd confirmed his identity to her satisfaction, and wriggled out of being caught red-handed, but she'd nearly damned her entire plan in the process. He certainly wasn't thinking about seducing her at that precise moment.

Luckily, in her experience, men showed a remarkable ability to recover from any dampening effect on their male drives. She'd done everything but vomit on Robert Chivington's shoes—and she would have tried that, too, had she been able to get her stomach to co-operate—and it had never dissuaded him for more than an hour or two.

Daniel knelt and began jamming all his belongings back into his valise. He bent his head over his work, and an inch of tanned, strong neck showed between his white collar and the shaggy edge of his hair. Idly, she wondered what he'd do if she reached down and kissed him, right there on that lovely spot. Just up and kissing a man for no other reason than that she wanted to was certainly not a notion that had ever occurred to her before, and she wondered what had sparked it. Though it was most assuredly a very nice neck.

"Are you, ah, well enough to continue?" he asked, his head still down. "I'm sure we'll find a town soon."

Kathryn sighed for the lost opportunities of the pre-vious night. Perhaps she should turn an ankle this morning, forcing them to spend a few more days and nights alone. But her empty stomach rumbled in pro-test.

"I'm fine," she said firmly. Surely Daniel would be in a much more amorous frame of mind after a good meal, too. To show she was made of good and opti-mistic stock, she squared her shoulders and turned to the trail. "Perfect morning for a walk, don't you think? I'm quite looking forward to it."

Less than two hours down the road, they stumbled across a young ranch hand headed to town for sup-plies. While Kathryn knew it would have been much more productive to remain alone with Daniel, drawing him into conversation, and maybe a bit more, her feet were nonetheless very grateful for the ride.

It took less than an hour, bumping along in the back of the buckboard, to reach Porterville, a city that proudly boasted a dozen dilapidated buildings and a full cemetery. Porterville's grasp on prosperity looked every bit as tenuous as Kathryn's own.

They went first to a small, unpainted frame building carrying a sign half as big as the building itself. The sign read simply Harry's, which was apparently enough of an explanation for this store/post office/inn/ stage stop/everything-else-its-owner-could-think-of.

"Hello," Daniel said to the small man, his skin and hair the flat gray of a gloomy sky, holding court behind a glass-fronted case jammed with an array of dry goods that would have done a tinker proud. "I'm Daniel Smith—"

"You the two who jumped the stage?" he barked. A massively fat cat the color of orange marmalade rested on a deep blue pillow on the case in front of the man, and he ran his hand over it, his fingers leaving deep furrows like garden rows in the rusty fur.

Jumped the stage? As if they'd had a choice? If Kathryn ever got her hands on that stage driver, she thought with malicious glee, he'd wish he'd let those outlaws murder him instead.

"I wouldn't exactly put it that way," Daniel said. "More like, we're the two who were *abandoned*."

The storekeeper chuckled. "Yeah, that Jerome Sisty. Don't know why they gave him his own route. He's got a yellow streak wider'n his ass. Swear he loses more freight than he brings in."

"Yes, well, I don't suppose they're still here, are they?"

The shopkeeper's lined forehead folded up like an accordion. " 'Course not. It'd make the stage late for the next stop, if he waited around for passengers who tweren't on board when he's ready to pull out. Jerome prides hisself on being on time."

"Of course," Daniel murmured, more quietly, completely without expression, while Kathryn battled the urge to shake another answer out of the man. It wasn't his fault that Jerome had fled, but he was the one within arm's reach. "When's the next stage come through?"

"Four days," the storekeeper told him.

Heat flickered briefly in Daniel's eyes, quickly extinguished, and Kathryn held back a cheer. Four whole days! Then a couple more on the stage, and two, maybe three, on the train. At least eight more nights with him. Eight more opportunities to seduce Daniel Sellington into marrying her.

"But don't worry," the storekeeper continued. "I got a couple rooms over the store where's you can stay. I'm sure you'll find somethin' to do to occupy yourself until the next coach comes through." He winked a cloudy brown eye in Kathryn's direction.

She should have been insulted, she supposed. Except that slightly ribald comment was milder and more amiable than what she'd been exposed to dozens of times before.

However, Daniel scowled at the gray little man and

slid her way as if to shield her from such offenses. *Hmm.* Perhaps she could find a way to spur his protective instincts.

"If you'll just tell me where he left our luggage, we'd like to clean up."

"And get something to eat," Kathryn added quickly.

Daniel's quick, understanding smile, filled with the intimacy of having been through—well, it wasn't exactly an *ordeal*, she admitted. A potentially dangerous adventure?—together, caused a slow warmth to simmer in her stomach. Reporter; itinerant writer; wealthy, distant heir; in all his guises, that smile was the most potent weapon the man owned. How fortunate that he wielded it so rarely, or there'd be rows of slain women left behind him.

"And get something to eat," he affirmed.

" 'Fraid I can't give you your stuff," the storekeeper said.

"Look, Harry—"

"Ain't Harry, either." He rested his hand on the cat's broad head, and its purr rumbled through the room. "This is."

"Nice cat."

"Yup, he is." Unbent by Daniel's admiration of his cat, he offered, "I'm Mouse. But I still can't give you your stuff, 'cause I don't got it."

"You don't have it," Daniel repeated flatly.

"Nope. Stage company won't store freight at a minor stop like this one. Not secure, they say, though I'd like to see anyone try and hold *me* up. Said to tell you, if you came in, that they'd keep it at Julesberg for ya."

"Now let me get this straight." Kathryn elbowed

Daniel out of her way and slapped her hands on the top of the counter. The glass rattled wickedly. Harry hissed at her, and it was all she could do not to hiss back. "He abandoned us to the whims of those outlaws, taking all our things with him, and he didn't even *leave* them here for us so we can get our possessions as soon as possible? And I don't suppose he even sent someone back to check on us, did he, just to see if we were bleeding in the dust?"

"Well . . . nah." Mouse scooped up his cat, held him protectively against his chest, though Kathryn wasn't sure if he intended to protect the cat or the cat was supposed to guard him. If she had to pick one to tangle with, it certainly wouldn't be the cat. "Jerome said that you looked like you were doing okay, ma'am. That *he*"—Mouse pointed at Daniel—"was doing better'n okay. Figured you'd make out all right."

"That we did. And thank you," Daniel said. Irritated that he seemed so easily to accept the wrong the stage company had done them, she whirled on Daniel. Didn't he *ever* get upset? Didn't he care about anything enough? Even when he was beating the stuffing out of the outlaw, nothing had pierced his cool, collected mien. But then he touched her shoulder, and just that brief contact defused her anger in an instant. She feared that her own display of temper might have disturbed him, but there was warmth, and perhaps even amusement, in his eyes.

"I'll take care of it," he told her. "It's not Mouse's fault. But I'll get your things back for you. Trust me."

And, God help her, she did.

"Oh, by the way," Mouse said, fishing in a bag on the far end of the counter. He came up with a piece of paper, waved it around. "I got a telegraph for Mr. Daniel—"

"I'll take that!" With the speed he'd shown when fighting the outlaw, Daniel dived across the case and snatched the paper. He unfolded it and scanned its contents, and the distant, unemotional mask he'd worn when she'd first seen him in the coach snapped over his features.

"Is something wrong?"

He ignored her, addressing Mouse instead. "When's the coach back to Denver?"

"Day after tomorrow."

"Fine."

He spun away, leaving Kathryn to stare at the broad, forbidding wall of his shoulders. Those shoulders had been so comfortable, so welcoming, when they cushioned her sleep. So sturdy, when she'd needed them to lean on during their trek. Now they separated him from her, closed him off as surely as if he'd slammed a door.

She could not allow it.

She scurried around him, laid a hand on his arm as he reached to grab his valise. He looked down at her hand on his arm, then up at her, the bright blue of his eyes darkening to stormy indigo.

"Daniel, what's the matter?" she asked, finding, to her surprise, that she really wanted to know. Only because it would further her cause, she told herself; she could not afford any real emotion, good or bad, toward this man. Emotion might make her waver, and would interfere with clear thinking.

He swallowed hard, as if it were hard to force the words out. "I have to go back."

Chapter 8

◠◡◠◡◠

The one thing that Harry's was *not*, apparently, was a restaurant. Mouse directed them next door, to a shack that at first glance they'd took to be abandoned long ago. Certainly it *should* have been abandoned years ago.

But it belonged to an elderly widow named Mrs. Mills, her family and money long gone, who stubbornly clung to what remained of her life, meager and joyless as it might seem to others. She assured them she'd be delighted to serve them tonight, managed to give the impression she welcomed them but certainly didn't *need* their business, and ushered them into her shabby front room. After seating them at a single, battered square table, she disappeared out the back. Daniel suspected that she'd gone next door to get Harry to advance her enough supplies to prepare them a meal.

And so, while they waited, he'd simply stared at Kathryn over the bare table set with a pair of chipped plates and bent forks and tried to find his tongue.

Their small adventure had pushed them into a precipitous intimacy, had broken down the barrier that he normally erected between himself and everyone he met. With their return to civilization, that wall had sprung back into place, something for which he should be grateful. He was comfortable with his barriers, knew they protected him from enormous disaster.

But he'd never realized how much he hated it.

He admired her. Admired her practicality, her ready humor. The way annoyance brought a higher set to her shoulders, as if she were fully prepared to shoulder the world, and how it firmed that soft mouth into a determined line. And, he admitted, he admired how very fine she looked when she was being practical and serious and determined. He idly wondered if he'd ever met a prettier woman. He certainly couldn't recall one.

Oh, he knew very well the folly of being drawn to someone, of judging someone, by their appearance. What a truly inconsequential attribute beauty was in the long run. But he didn't think there was a man alive who could look at her and *not* be nearly overwhelmed.

"So," he said, "tell me about your family."

Kathryn shifted her fork an inch to the left as she sighed inwardly. They'd been attempting a conversation for a good twenty minutes and had yet to manage one. It was difficult to conduct a sparkling, seductive interaction while both parties carefully hoarded their secrets, guarding every word to prevent giving too much away. It was not a good sign, she thought, that he was so intent on guarding his secrets. He did not trust her yet.

Perhaps she must give him a little of herself to encourage him to do the same in return.

"There are four of us," she began. "My youngest brother, Tommy, who's nearly sixteen. More than a head taller than me, ten pounds lighter, and convinced he's got life all figured out."

"And does he annoy you?" he asked.

"Of course. But somewhat less than I annoy him, I expect. He is ever convinced he is far older than I persist in treating him to be." Daniel's rare, quicksilver smile flashed. "You look as if you are familiar with brothers."

He hesitated before answering. His family was a difficult thing to describe to an acquaintance—though acquaintance was a term he was having a harder and harder time applying to Kathryn.

"Stepbrothers, technically," he admitted. "The one I mentioned last night, plus another. A sister, too. But I'm willing to match their efforts at fraternal annoyance with anyone's."

"Oh really? Did he ever use your petticoats to build a tent? Right in the middle of the front yard?"

"Well, no. But the first time I kissed a girl, Nic spied on me and then told everyone there was spit dribbling down my chin afterward."

"Oh, my." Laughter bubbled. "You've certainly outgrown that tendency, haven't you?" The tentative ease between them vanished, supplanted by a simmering awareness. Her gaze slid from his, fastened on a deep scar on the tabletop, and color touched the high curves of her cheekbones. The thought that she remembered his kiss, and that it could make her blush, brought a heady spurt of pride and pleasure to him. An unfamiliar feeling, one almost as seductive as kissing her had been.

"And the rest of your family . . ."

The part of Daniel that had heard too many leading questions, and suspected all of them, automatically recoiled. He shifted back in his chair, folding his arms across his chest. "I'd much rather hear about yours."

Lost opportunities. Patience came hard to her in any case, but it was even more difficult when the specter of Simon Moore's whorehouse loomed over her shoulder. "There's my sister. There are three years between us, but it always felt like more. Like I had a certain responsibility to her—"

"I thought she was your older sister," he broke in.

Kathryn sucked in a breath. Wiser to keep close to the truth, or make the lies so outrageous there was no chance of getting lost in them, she thought. This narrow ledge between the two was far too easy to fall off. "She is. But, as she spent so much time helping care for me and Tommy when we were younger, I feel an obligation to return the favor now."

"Understandable. And admirable."

And too close, she thought. "Then there was Peter." She never, ever indulged in tears. They took too much time, too much energy, and solved too little. But for some reason Daniel's warm sympathy kept encouraging them, inconvenient but unstoppable. "My oldest brother. He . . . we lost him when he was but nineteen."

"I'm sorry." He bent toward her, dropping his forearms to the tabletop, and covered her hands with his own. "I'm so sorry, Kathryn. Was it an accident?"

An accident. An accident of fate, an accident Daniel's father had caused that forced Peter to labor in the smelters, where the poisonous lead could invade his lungs, steal his precious life.

Daniel's hand covering hers was warm, comforting. And something more, which made her wish she dared remove her gloves, learn the texture of his palms without that thin barrier between them. He'd called her *Kathryn*, the first time he'd used her given name, and he'd done so thoughtlessly; she doubted he'd even noticed.

But she had.

He thinks of me as Kathryn. "Yes. A riding accident." The lies again. But now she remembered why she gave them, and that the only thing she could do for Peter now was free Tommy from the same fate.

She rarely allowed herself to dwell on memories of Peter. But he came back to her now, that stiff pride and unbendable determination, qualities that, had her father possessed them, might have saved them all years ago. And there was a surprising amount of comfort in the remembrance. Peter's lungs had betrayed him before he could rescue the rest of his family; now she would manage what he had not.

"I'm so sorry," Daniel repeated. Words were so inadequate, he thought bleakly. The only comfort he knew to give was to go around the table and take her in his arms. But this was hardly the place, and he doubted his motives were entirely unselfish.

"Here we are!" Mrs. Mills shuffled through the doorway, bent under the weight of the blackened kettle she carried in her thin, veined hands.

"Let me help you with that." Daniel came half out of his chair before she jammed the kettle in his direction.

"No, sit," she said with a frown that brooked no disobedience. "I ain't so old I don't remember how to treat a guest. Nor a customer, neither." She plopped the kettle in the middle of the table and lifted the lid. Steam curled up to the water-stained ceiling. "It's just beans and salt pork. Nothing fancy. But then, I didn't know you was coming, did I?"

"I'm sure it's wonderful," Kathryn said, watching the vapor waver and dance because she found it difficult to look at Mrs. Mills. Her life, her struggles, were too familiar to her. Kathryn feared that, if she didn't do something drastic, either here or soon, her life in sixty years would be little different than Mrs. Mills's. She felt the dark, insistent press of panic. Oh, there was so little time! She'd racked her brain trying to think up a clever excuse for returning to Denver with him and come up empty.

Food heaped Daniel's plate by the time Mrs. Mills shambled from the room. He ladled two big scoops onto hers and then snatched his fork.

Trying to remember the etiquette that her mother had drilled into her head and she'd never before found a use for, Kathryn stared down at her hands. Her gloved hands. If she removed them, as manners dictated . . . surely he would notice. Her hands were simply not those of a gently reared woman.

"Umm, not to rush you or anything, but could we *please* eat?"

She looked at him blankly. His fork hovered over

his meal. Her brothers always dived into their food even before the plate hit the table. A man had never delayed his appetite for her.

Smiling, she lifted her own fork. The man was clearly far too hungry to worry about trivialities such as her gloves. And there were no women around to judge her manners.

"Please, go right ahead. Far be it from me to get between a hungry man and his food. After all the hard work you did yesterday and all."

"I did, didn't I?"

"You certainly did."

Her eyes, her smile, were full of admiration. Admiration for *him*. Daniel didn't trust it, could hardly believe it; he was far too accustomed to looking into eyes filled with avaricious speculation.

But then, Kathryn had no idea who he really was. An idea had been resting in the back of his brain, prodding him, warming him; now it pushed forward, full-blown, bright, enormously tempting. It was every bit as alluring as those lovely eyes and smile were themselves. Maybe more so.

She likes me, and she doesn't know who I am.

It was something he hadn't dared hope for. Didn't have the slightest idea what to do about. If only the time wasn't so short, if he didn't have to return to Denver so soon. If they had the wonderful, lazy length of the trip to Minnesota to discover each other.

Maybe when she returned from her sister's. Perhaps, before he got on that stage back to Denver, he'd ask where she lived. He could pay a call on her when she got back, court her favor.

Unfortunately, Monroe City was only six miles from Denver. His grandmother's mansion would undoubtedly be watched by reporters; his arrival would be emblazoned across the front page of the newspaper. But as long as they didn't get a good picture, or her family didn't take the paper, maybe she wouldn't discover who he was. Not until he was more certain she was attracted to who he was instead of what he owned.

One would never guess from the way Daniel devoured the plain food Mrs. Mills had prepared that he was surely much more accustomed to delicacies like creamed sweetbreads and French pastries. Real hunger, Kathryn mused, probably had a broadening effect on one's taste buds.

"Can I get you anything else?" Mrs. Mills asked. She'd brought them crackers and coffee and a dish of stewed apples, and now hovered beside the table with her hands folded before the stained apron covering her concave stomach.

Daniel wiped his mouth with a napkin and smiled up at her. "It was wonderful, thank you. I knew you were unprepared for guests, but we'd not eaten in some time and certainly appreciate your hospitality."

"Good." She nodded, accepting her due. She *had* been most accommodating. "That'll be two bits." Her gaze slid to Kathryn, who'd found it a challenge to eat her fill—a luxury she'd not had in some time—without *appearing* to devour as much as Daniel. "*Apiece.*"

She reached for her handbag, but Daniel forestalled her. "Why don't you let me get this? I know that most of your funds must have gone the way of your trunk."

"Thank you." He dug in his pockets, and Kathryn envisioned all those piles and piles of money snuggled safely in the bottom of his valise. All those unnecessary gardeners at his house in Denver, and Joey Gibson's words, indicated that he was lavish, or just plain careless, with his wealth. To slip Mrs. Mills an extra ten or twenty would mean *nothing* to him, and would mean so much to her.

She held her breath until Daniel came up with a dollar and tucked it into Mrs. Mills's hand. "There," he said without meeting her eyes, "a bit extra for your trouble." And all the air in Kathryn's lungs expelled in a disappointed rush.

Mrs. Mills, happy with her tip, smiled broadly. "Thank you kindly, sir."

But Mrs. Mills didn't know what she'd just missed out on. She didn't *know*.

Why should it matter to her, Kathryn wondered? It might not have been thoughtlessly cruel; Daniel, having never known want, might simply not have noticed nor recognized it in another. And, even if he had, she'd suspected it all along, hadn't she? That a man who'd been raised with excess was probably thoughtless, uncaring toward those less fortunate. Likely he believed that they, through their own choices and inadequacies, had somehow earned their suffering.

His selfishness should be unimportant to her. The only thing that mattered was that he had plenty of money and she was going to get a lot of it.

But the disillusionment was still there, a vague, gray ache in her chest. Foolishly, unreasonably, she'd hoped for better from him.

It didn't matter. She couldn't let it matter.

* * *

The next afternoon he had to get on that stage and head back to Denver. Saturday had fled too quickly. First, he'd had to wait until Mrs. Mills went to the necessary to sneak into her kitchen and bury a bag of dollar bills in the bottom of her flour barrel. He worried that it would take her too long to find it; he didn't want her to struggle any longer than necessary. But he needed to be long gone by the time she unearthed the tidy sum.

Then, there was the visit to a failing rancher he'd backed years ago who lived no more than three miles west. Daniel hadn't seen the man in nearly two years. So he'd gone to the Bar Z. He found it—of course, flourishing beyond its owner's wildest dreams and showing every indication of increasing Daniel's wealth yet again.

It was another example of why ridding himself of the Sellington millions had turned out to be far more difficult than he'd expected. His was a Midas touch, and he looked forward with great anticipation to the day he could test it freely, to the challenge of building his own business from nothing, one that he could take pride in and would support not only his family but many others with honest dignity.

Now he lay on the bed in the room that Mouse had assigned him over the store, though *room* was perhaps an inflated term for it. Scarcely large enough to be a dressing room, it held only a narrow, thin-mattressed bed, bordered by no more than a foot of bare space on each side, and a wall shelf for his personal items. A kerosene lantern hung on a hook over the bed. Its flickering light cast an outsize shadow of his booted feet on the opposite wall.

Gaps as wide as the one between Mouse's front teeth studded the thin board walls. Through them Daniel could occasionally hear Kathryn moving around in her cell, the creak of her bed ropes and the thunk of her boots when she pulled them off and dropped them to the floor. Once, last night, she'd cried out in her sleep, the wrenching sound jerking him awake, and he'd had to fight the compulsion to run to her and assure himself of her safety.

He was feeling quite noble that he'd resisted the temptation. He was far less successful in resisting the visions of what might have happened if he had.

He'd hardly spent any time with Kathryn that day. Too little, too much. Far, far too little to satisfy what was quickly becoming an unmanageable craving to spend time in her company. He recognized the danger there, the fact that he was nearly drunk on her beauty and charm and her unpurchased interest in him. So it was better, he'd decided, to do nothing rash immediately. To allow the chaos that the newspaper article had spawned in his life to settle, and then seek a relationship with her if he still felt this strong attraction to her. When the Bar Z's owner had invited him to stay for a meal, he'd accepted and returned after Kathryn had retired for the evening. The only time he'd rested his eyes upon her had been quite early, when she, blurry-eyed, sleep-mussed, had waved at him from Harry's front porch before he'd ridden off to the ranch.

And yet it had been too much. Because even that

brief glance had almost been enough to keep him there. It had given him more than enough fuel for an entire day's fantasies, and was fast showing evidence of filling an entire night's as well.

He tapped his boots together, watched the giant shadows repeat the gesture on the knot-studded wall. What was she doing over there? Ears straining, he listened for a hint of heavy breathing, the soft rumble of a snore. He was sure that, if she snored, it was in a ravishingly delectable way, and he grinned at his own fancy.

A knock shot him to his feet. He yanked open the door to find her standing on the other side, every fantasy he'd ever owned spun to magical life. His heart thudded hard, and all his good intentions shattered, like a wineglass crushed beneath a bootheel.

And he knew that if this was a test of his will, his gentlemanly restraint, he was about to fail miserably.

Chapter 9

She was still dressed in the same blouse and skirt she'd worn when he met her, though they were now rumpled and stiff from having been washed but not ironed. Her jacket was gone, and she looked fragile and wan in the weak light that spilled through the door. His shadow fell on her, angling across her torso, over the peak of one breast, as if his body covered hers. Her brow was furrowed, her soft mouth tense.

"Is something wrong?" he asked.

She glanced beyond him, into his tiny room, her gaze settling on the bed with its worn sheets and thin pillow before skittering away.

"Ah . . . could I come in for a moment?"

As if there was a man alive who would refuse her. "Of course." He stepped aside, waved his hand to allow her entrance, and tried not to think of how small the room was. And how late it was, and the fact that Mouse was surely fast asleep in his rooms at the back of the store.

"Thank you." It had taken all her courage to get this far. She'd spent the entire day worrying over it, decided there was nothing to do but come to him tonight and . . . something. She still wasn't sure exactly what. Something that will make him unwilling to get on that stage tomorrow and leave her. But still, her heart knocked high against her throat, threatened to beat out of her chest, and she had to summon the image of her family and their needs to find the will to enter his room.

Her skirts brushed Daniel's shins as she passed. Her scent, something new and floral and feminine—he'd seen her buying a few items in the store—filled his nose, clouded his head. It suited her, but he missed the fragrance that was pure Kathryn.

At the foot of the bed she turned to face him, leaving no more than two feet separating them. The door had creaked shut behind her, leaving them to share a space that seemed half again as big as it had a moment ago.

"I—" Her fingers, still encased in graying cotton, twined together, linking tightly as overgrown grapevines. He was developing an inordinate wish to see her naked hands, which now seemed as intimate to him as viewing other parts of her bare, simply because he'd never seen her without those gloves.

She lifted her chin, allowing him to glimpse the curve of her neck, skin as white and fine as moonglow. "I wanted to say good-bye," she said with clear determination.

He recognized the danger here, even if she did not, but he still snagged one of those worrying hands, linked it with his own. "Who says it's good-bye?"

Her shoulders lifted and fell. Her hair was loose, a

cloud of spun silver over her shoulders. Something dark shadowed her eyes, and he could tell she didn't believe him. That she thought he would go away the following day and forget her, that she would never see him again.

He couldn't promise they would ever see each other again. But he knew he would never forget her.

Her breath stuttered in, expelled just as raggedly.

"What is it?"

The corner of her mouth turned up wryly. "I believe I'm afraid."

"Afraid?" Afraid of what? Of losing him? Her next words dashed his selfish, budding hope.

"Yes. When I get on the next stage without you. What if there's another holdup? Or an accident, or . . . what will I do?"

He squeezed her hands, and her eyes shimmered in the lamplight.

"What will I do without you there?"

Her plaintive words tore straight into his heart. He groaned, tugged her forward by her hands, and pulled her up against him. With one palm, he cradled the back of her head and tucked it up against his neck where it belonged.

"You're afraid?" he murmured. "You? Who would have dropped that outlaw in his tracks if I hadn't grabbed all the fun for myself? You, who slept on the ground where all sorts of insects and snakes and who knows what else could have gotten you, and didn't whimper once?"

"I hadn't really thought about the bugs that night. Thank you *so* much for reminding me. Can I whimper now?" His shirt was open at the collar; in that small naked wedge of skin, he felt her mouth curve up in a smile against him. It could just as easily have been a kiss, and blood pulsed in his groin.

"Whimper away," he said roughly. Please whimper, he thought, completely caught by the idea of hearing that sound released from her throat. And having far too many ideas of how he could incite it.

"I did stand up to that outlaw, didn't I?"

"You certainly did."

"But I rather had the impression that you considered that stupidity, not bravery."

He chuckled. "Stupidity, bravery. That's almost always a matter of opinion, isn't it?"

She slapped lightly at his back in reproach, and then, blessedly, her hand apparently decided to stay, flattening itself in the hollow of his lower back.

"What do you call your little skirmish, then?"

"Temporary insanity," he admitted, but didn't tell her that any madness he claimed could be laid entirely at her feet and was expanding by the moment. "But next time," he went on, "just give the man what he wants, okay?"

Oh, Lord, had he really just said that? He waited for her, finally realizing what she risked by coming to his room, to launch herself out of his arms and flee for the door. Instead, she merely leaned back and turned her face up, so her mouth was inches from his. "I could do that," she murmured. "Maybe. Depending on who the man was, of course."

What remained of his sanity evaporated; control abandoned him. Only *she* remained, a light, warm weight in his arms, the faint gleam of moisture on her mouth. His hand slid up the firm, narrow slope of her back, into the heavy mass of her hair, and took a fistful of it. It filled his palm, soft, springy, warm, as if it had a life of its own. He bent his head and covered her mouth with his.

She was everything female, everything he'd wanted, everything that was missing in his life, had given up hope of having. Yielding and strong, sweet and tender and determined. *Woman*.

He could kiss her forever. Maybe he would. He couldn't think of a single good reason to stop.

Her mouth opened beneath his. Her tongue hesitantly touched his, retreated. When he groaned in disappointment, her mouth opened wider, and she drew him inside. He ventured deep, filling her mouth, drowning himself in the taste of her, the scent of her, the feel of her. He knew he gave her no room for retreat; his left arm vised her back, his right hand gripped her hair, wound it around his fingers like a silken rope, making it impossible for her to move away. He didn't care. Maybe he should have, but he didn't; she wasn't going anywhere, not if he could stop it.

At the first touch of his lips, Kathryn's thoughts scattered. She gathered them with effort, knowing she could not afford to keep less than a clear head. This had to be handled carefully; each step along the path weighed, each decision made with due consideration. But oh, it was hard. She felt his fingertips on her scalp, the tug on her hair as he brought her mouth closer, took the kiss deeper, and she wondered how much she deceived herself. She'd told herself she did this to further her cause, to enchant him, to make him burn for her. But niggling at the back of her brain was the suspicion that perhaps she'd come to his room tonight only because she so badly wanted to kiss him again.

How could a man so fundamentally selfish be so generous in this? He luxuriated in her, made her feel like there was nothing on earth he wanted except to kiss her. She *knew* his kiss lied, but she couldn't seem to hold on to the knowledge.

His tongue teased the tip of hers, lured her into the play, retreated and returned in a way that seemed designed to drive her mad. In frustration, she finally grabbed his head in both hands and *made* him kiss her hard.

Maybe he chuckled, maybe he moaned. It didn't matter which, as long as he didn't stop.

His tongue found sensitive places in her mouth she'd have sworn didn't exist. Who would have thought that the inside of her lip was so vulnerable to the slightest stroke? That the roof of her mouth, the inside of her cheek, had nerve receptors that had obviously been made for his touch alone?

She fought hard for the logic she felt—no, not slipping, *rushing* away. She'd planned to lead him right up to the edge before, with maidenly propriety but clear reluctance, delaying the interlude until the legalities were served. But now she wondered just how far she dared go, uncertain of her ability to handle his response . . . and her own.

The edge of the bed bumped against her legs, and her knees buckled. It would be so much easier to kiss him properly, she thought dimly, if she were relieved of the burden of standing up.

Daniel had no idea how much time passed. Ten minutes? Twenty? Or twenty hours? Surfacing from a hazy, heated fog of passion, he found that somehow, some way, they'd ended up lying on the bed. He was angled a bit to one side, propped on one elbow while his other hand still had its vise grip on her hair. The bed was too narrow to allow them much room, and the curve of her hip pressed against his groin, and he thought: Well, isn't that convenient? Now and then his hips would pulse forward, seemingly of their own accord, the added pressure rewarding him with a lightning strike of pleasure spearing up his belly and spine.

"Kathryn," he murmured into her mouth. He had a vague notion that there was something not entirely correct about their abandoned behavior, couldn't decide if he cared. And then she threw her arms around his neck, kissing him deeply, and he forgot how to think.

Her mouth bewitched him. Her hair was satin threaded through his fingers. But greed gripped him; he wanted to taste more, touch more, sure in the knowledge that there were ever more wondrous things to discover.

He eased the pressure of his kiss, moved his mouth to the corner of hers, found the tip of her chin, the angle of her jaw, the hollow beneath her hairline. Such a luxury of choices! So astoundingly beneficent of her to share them with him. When he pressed his lips to the curve of her neck, he felt her pulse, fragile, steady under her delicate skin.

His hand released her hair with reluctance but felt

her head press back into his grasp and warmth flooded him, different from the heat that burned in his belly. No less wonderful.

His mouth met the edge of her collar, the abrasion of old lace harsh after the fineness of her skin. Only a few layers of cotton separated him from what he sought, and he wanted them gone. He thumbed open the top button of her blouse. It separated easily, as if it had only been waiting for him to part, and he dived into the slight gap, slicked his tongue over the sharp angle of her collarbone, settled into the hollow at the base of her throat.

Oh, but she'd been arrogant, Kathryn discovered. Looked with such disdain on those who'd risked so much for a few brief moments of pleasure. But she hadn't suspected, not at all, how that pleasure could grip you, rule you, make all those goals and priorities seem like flimsy, unimportant conceits in the wake of such sensations. How easy to drown in it all, to surrender completely to the feelings. Letting them swell and overcome all worries and troubles, if only for a while. And she simply couldn't permit it.

But she wanted to. Oh, but she wanted to.

All the other round, pearled buttons gave way as easily as the first. The hem of her blouse remained in the waistline of her skirt, and Daniel tucked the opened panels around the swell of her bosom, leaving her breasts clad in thin, worn linen that allowed the dusky shadow of her nipples to show through, like sweet summer berries under the veiling of a fine napkin.

He drew back a moment to admire the view.

Her hair, a froth of pale silk, lay in abandoned

waves around her. A dusky flush colored her cheeks, like the mark of ripeness on a sun-warmed peach. Every bit as sweet. The startling darkness of her brows served to point up those beautiful eyes, hazy with passion, her lids slumberous and drooping low. It was as if the world's most talented artist had called on all his skills, all his most heated desires, to create this masterpiece: *Impassioned Woman.*

And it was his touch, his kiss, *he*, that had brought her to this. Fierce pride surged, carried along on a tidal wave of want.

With each quick breath she took, the upper curves of her breasts rose above the ragged boundary of her shift. He hooked his finger in the edge, slowly inched it down, revealing in breathless increments perfect skin, burnished to a fine gold in the lanternlight. And then her nipple sprang free, deep-colored, gathered tight, and his heart pounded. She was real, and near, and *Kathryn*. Awed, he touched a finger to the very tip, amazed when she arched into that slight touch, as if she craved more.

She had not known. It was the one thought that Kathryn managed to keep firm hold on, for it resurfaced anew with each new touch.

She had not known.

Hers was not a life bounded by the inconveniences of morality. That she'd not found pleasure with another was due entirely to practicality, not virtue. And so she had occasionally, when not completely sapped by exhaustion, explored her own body, discovered those little spasms of momentary gratification that could give her a very temporary respite from her immediate worries.

But those faint, distant indulgences were no closer to this than the whiff of a baking pie in a neighbor's kitchen was like the sweet, intense burst of fruit when you actually bit in. The difference when it was another's hands that touched her staggered Kathryn.

When it was Daniel's hands.

And then he bent his head and put his mouth to her breast. She nearly came off the bed. Her back arched. The breath snagged in her throat, and a cry tore free.

There had to be a price for this, Daniel thought. Life did not give so freely. But he could not imagine a cost that he'd regret. Her nipple was hard against his tongue, and the scent of her rose from her skin. He grew drunk on the smell and taste of her, more potent than any wine he'd ever swallowed. He pushed her shift below her other breast and cupped it in his hand. The sounds she made pierced whatever meager control he still owned, found their way into his memories like they meant to stay.

Kathryn was dancing on the edge of danger as surely as if she tiptoed along the rim of a canyon. The sane part of her, the tiny corner not completely in the thrall of this astounding wonder, knew it. Knew she should stop him now, before it was too late. But a bigger part, the wild, carnal part that had been released with his first kiss, urged her on. Just a little more. A bit more delight, another rush of wild joy, before she would end it.

I have to be certain, she told herself. Take Daniel

to the absolute brink of insanity so that he would drag her to a preacher before his head cleared.

But those reasons rang hollow even as she ignored the prodding of her conscience. And perhaps the risk itself, that narrow instant between perfection and disaster, was an incitement of its own.

She did not halt it now because she could not bear to. Instead, she burrowed her hands in that glorious mass of hair to hold him in place, his mouth hot and wet and tugging hard on her breast.

The hand that gently kneaded her other breast let go, to glide over the rumpled mass of her blouse, her rib cage. A low sound of complaint hummed in her throat; how was he to touch her everywhere at once? So she pulled at his shoulders, bringing the weight of him upon her, freeing the hand he'd used to prop himself up. Ah, that was better, to have his belly pressed against hers. She spread her legs wide, allowing the hammock of her skirts—and him, oh yes, *him*—to fall between them, the sudden, heavy weight of him there sparking an abrupt, glowing spurt of pleasure.

Her hands slid down his back, suddenly dissatisfied with the texture of his shirt, hungry for bare skin. She tugged his shirt from his pants, shoved it up, and spread her hands wide on his back, touching as much as she could at once. Ah, there, smooth hot skin over heavy muscle and bone. She could feel the strength he'd used to such good advantage against the outlaw in the broad planes of his muscle, and she wanted to touch it all. She ventured farther, dipped the tips of her fingers beneath his waistband, and her own daring astonished her. Surely it was not a decision she made;

her body simply seemed to seek what it craved of its own accord.

He reared back. "Oh God, I have to do this." Then, before she realized what he was about, he grabbed her hands and yanked the gloves from them. He shoved them under his shirt, holding her palms flat against his hard chest, and he closed his eyes in pleasure.

She'd worried for nothing. The man didn't care at all about the condition of her hands. He didn't even notice. All he cared about was feeling them naked on him. And she liked it very much better that way herself.

Had he been starved for her all his life? Daniel wondered. Even before he'd known she existed? The feast was before him, and he had no thought but to sate himself. Too many places to touch, to explore, to kiss; he roamed quickly, greedy and relentless, filling his hands and his mouth with her. The glowing curve of her shoulder was heaven. The slope of her ribs into her belly invited a lifetime's exploration.

His legs tangled in her skirts, and he damned them for their interference. There was nothing for it but to get them out of the way. He reached down and grabbed a wadded handful, levering a slight space between his body and hers—he hated doing it, but it was only for a moment—and yanked them up, the thin wool and a flurry of petticoats, until they pooled around her waist before he settled back into the place she'd made for him between her legs.

She lifted her knees and tilted her hips, bringing her most intimate parts in full contact with the hard length of his arousal. Instinctively he rocked his hips against her, and she jerked in response, her head rolling back against that poor pillow, her neck arching like a bow.

More. She had to have more. Each time he pressed himself against her, pleasure speared, and she pushed upward against him, urging him on with her body, silently begging harder, more, faster. She did not know if the sobs she made were joy or lamentation; she only knew that if he stopped, left her at this precipice, she would be utterly bereft.

What had seemed like such a luxury at first, to press himself between her legs without her skirts between them, now seemed completely inadequate to Daniel. There were hints of heat, the promise of moisture, but no matter how he strained closer, he knew it was as much imagination as real sensation. So, with one hand—one hand was all he could bear to take from her—he reached down, jerked open his pants, and shoved them and his drawers down a few inches. Far enough; his sex sprang free, and immediately he pressed himself against her again.

There. She cried out instantly, her hips taking up the rhythm as he rubbed against her, the dampened cloth of her drawers only a slight barrier. The slit in them shifted with their straining movements, rewarding him with brief, tantalizing moments when his erection touched slick, hot female skin.

"Daniel," he dimly heard her say, his name a plea, and entreaty. He must help her, and himself, for surely neither could long survive this feeling, this bursting, straining need that burned in every nerve, every cell. "Please," she whispered.

He angled back; she followed, the motion of her

hips as much a supplication as her words. He reached between them, widened the slit in her drawers, exposing her most intimate parts, and pressed himself against her again. She was wet and hot, and he slid against her easily; she writhed against him, whimpering, her face drawn with strain.

Oh, God. He *had* to complete this; he just had to. He could no more control it than he could govern the beat of his heart. He positioned himself at the entrance to her body and touched heaven. Teeth clenched, body damp, muscles rigid, he inched forward.

He had drawn back; the contact between them was less than it had been, and Kathryn could not endure it to be so. She clamped her arms around him to hold him close and surged upward. He thrust inside her in response, driving deep, and she cried out, inarticulate, at the sudden, unanticipated dart of pain that pierced her glorious haze, gave her a glimmer of sanity.

God no! They could not do this, she should never have let it get this far. Hampered by the crumpled encumbrance of her clothes, she struggled to wedge her arms between them and push him away, fought to find her voice to tell him no.

But it was too late. He plunged forward again and shouted her name, his body convulsing.

And then he collapsed on top of her wounded body, her lacerated dreams.

Chapter 10

Surprisingly, they slept, entwined in each other's limbs and loosened clothes on the narrow bed. He, replete, deeply satisfied, his dreams shimmering with images of silky skin and welcoming arms and rounded breasts. She, the dreamless, motionless sleep of the wholly exhausted, her consciousness sapped by the events of the last days and months and years, escaping from what she'd just done in the blessed, temporary haven of slumber.

She awoke with an abrupt start, her heart thumping, to discover Daniel still half on top of her, one heavy leg across her thighs, a claiming arm angled across her body, his hand cupping one breast. Gasping, she scrambled away, curling up at the head of the bed, her back against the rough-plastered wall. With shaking hands she shoved her skirts down, over the drawers she knew were stained with her blood and his seed, and drew her blouse over her shoulders. She tried to rebutton it, couldn't get her fingers to work, and finally gave up. Wrapping her arms around her updrawn knees, she stared at him—the repository of all her plans, the ruination of all her hopes. For he had no reason to marry her now.

He did not look dangerous in sleep. He hadn't awoken when she'd moved, merely turned farther on his side and grabbed a fistful of the threadbare linen sheet. His shirt was rumpled, loose and open, exposing one side of his ridged abdomen. His pants were still around his hips, his sex lying soft, unthreatening, in a nest of dark hair. His expression was completely relaxed, the corners of his mouth turning up slightly, the dark shadow of a new beard shading the clean line of his jaw.

Dear God, what had she done?

There was no window in Daniel's small chamber, so she'd no idea of the time. How long had her future been gone? Five minutes or five hours? Was it a new day, or the same one? Somehow it seemed terribly important to know.

What should she, *could* she, do now? How to salvage something from this disaster that she'd allowed— no, she thought with unsparing honesty, this disaster that she'd encouraged, even embraced? Her mind raced, searched, clutched at meager straws.

She had no father, no brothers of an age to be intimidating, to arrive with guns cocked and fists raised to enforce her virtue. Tommy, should he ever discover what had happened, would try, valiant and outraged. Daniel, who'd dealt so competently with a ruthless thief, could brush him aside as easily as a housefly, no more than a mild annoyance.

Could she manufacture protectors? Hire someone to portray her family long enough to force Daniel into marriage? But the big, meaty, bribeable men she knew had no more chance of passing themselves off as her well-bred, concerned relatives than they did of living their life without having personal traffic with Denver's Finest. The few men who could portray more gently raised man—because they were—had no need of her meager incentives.

Given enough time, perhaps she could come up with someone. But could she find Daniel then? He could be anywhere in the United States by the time she groomed, say, the bouncer at Herman Schatz's or his like to be her father.

Revulsion rose, clogging her throat at the thought that she might have to force a man she'd held in her arms, taken into her body, to marry her at the end of a hired gun.

A wry, bitter smile curled her upper lip. She was bemused by the unpredictable twists and turns of her conscience. Oh, she was ready to seduce Daniel into marriage, to trick and beg him into it, but balked at the idea of pressing the issue with a death threat.

Still, she knew that, if it came to it, she would find a way to force herself through that as well, for death *did* hang over the heads of herself and her family should she fail.

Daniel stirred, rolling toward his belly. His up-drawn knee now hid her view of his sex, and relief washed her, for his nakedness accused her as much as her own doubts.

But there was no easy redress for the mistake she'd just made. She knew the ways of rich men with poor women. To be used and abandoned was the expected fate. She'd avoided it thus far only through constant vigilance and quick feet.

But now she'd thrown herself headlong into it simply by her own foolishness, her ridiculous lack of control. She'd been so sure, so *sure*, that she was not prey to weaknesses of the flesh. How wrong she'd been.

Her hand crept to her belly. Last night he'd kissed her there, stroked her as if he'd discovered a new, fine texture the likes of which he'd never touched before and couldn't get enough of now.

Perhaps, in a few weeks, she could claim to be with child. Would he marry her then? She didn't want to believe him the kind of man who'd abandon his own flesh and blood. But nothing had been beyond Edward Sellington; her father's blood on his hands had proved no more than a momentary inconvenience to him. Was it something she'd learned of Daniel's character that led her to believe he'd do right by his offspring, or her own wishful thinking? And surely he was wise enough in the ways of husband-hunting women to wait to see her belly swell before he made a decision in the matter.

And what . . . dear God, what if she'd conceived a child in truth? It was only the one time. Many a girl she'd grown up with had insisted they'd been caught when "it was the first time, I swear it!" She'd always been skeptical of their claims. But she was not so naive not to realize there was always that possibility. And, considering the mess she'd made of things thus far, wouldn't it serve her right if she'd fallen right into that trap, as well?

Fear iced her nerve endings, tingled at the back of her brain, threatened to suck her right into hysteria.

She could scarcely feed the family she had now! There was no money for doctors or schools, or any one of a hundred things she would want to give to a child of her own. Had she, thoughtlessly caught in the spell his magic hands and mouth had cast, condemned her own child to a life as dreary and hopeless as her own?

Maybe she should just go ahead and steal the money hidden in the bottom of Daniel's valise after all. There were horses in Mouse's stable, more ways for her to— possibly—escape.

Perhaps what she could filch wouldn't be nearly enough to support them all in safety and comfort for the rest of their lives. But it was better than nothing.

She choked back a sob. Too late; his eyes blinked open, swung around to fasten on her, and a lazy, satisfied smile lit his handsome face.

"Good morning," he rumbled in a voice rough with sleep and sex, and reached for her.

Cringing away from his touch, Kathryn huddled up against the wall as if it could protect her from him.

Daniel frowned, curled the offending hand into a fist, and pulled it back, rolling up to sit crosswise on the narrow bed, which protested his movement with a pained squeak. Anger washed over him, that she would reject his touch now, and he yanked his pants together and fastened them, leaving his shirt hanging open.

Her skin shone unnaturally pale, the arch of her brows a slash of dark on white. Her lips were bloodless, her arms wrapped around herself as if she felt the need to hold herself together physically.

Was she wounded? Had he somehow, in his rough passion, injured her untried body? Remorse clutched at him, threatened to overwhelm the lingering after-glow of pleasure.

"Did I hurt you?" he ventured. "You must let me help, I . . ." His words trailed off as he reached for the hem of her skirt, steeling himself for the sight of blood and bruises that he—*he*, who only wanted to have her share in the joy he'd experienced—had put on that flawless flesh.

"No!" Her voice was high, thready, sounding noth-ing like her usual rich tones. She brought her hand to her mouth, bit down on the heel of her palm. Her eyes were wide, darker, the stormy color born when a calm bay pours into the depths of a turbulent ocean.

"If you are in pain," he said carefully, around the stone lodged in his throat, "however you feel about me now, you must allow my assistance."

He thought he had harmed her! Kathryn felt hysteria threaten, ridiculous laughter blended with tears. As if those strong, wonderful, gentle hands could cause her pain. The guilt she saw on his handsome face disturbed her, when it was she, herself, who'd caused her own ruination.

"It is not a physical wound."

His posture relaxed. "What is it then?"

It was so simple for him, she thought bitterly. For a man. Either there was an injury, or everything was fine. None of the other, far more complicated, worri-some outcomes concerned him. "I—we—" Peter's image flooded her mind. *Oh, Peter, I am so sorry!* "My family!" she cried.

Of course, Daniel thought. He should have realized. She was a gently reared woman of good family. To have given her virginity before marriage was surely of grave concern for her.

"They do not have to know," he pointed out reasonably.

Jaw dropping, she stared at him. And then, surprising them both, she burst into tears.

"Aw, damn." Unsure whether she would shrink from him again, he inched over to sit beside her and patted her awkwardly on her shoulder. "It'll be all right."

"No, it won't!" The tears washed out of her, tears she'd been storing up for a decade. She knew it was frivolous, a waste of time and energy that solved nothing. But oh, it felt good just to surrender to it for a change, let it sweep over her. So much less tiring than the constant battle for control. "We shouldn't have done that!"

Well, okay, maybe they shouldn't have. Though he could hardly find it in himself to regret it, not when the tingle and heat and memories were so vivid. He *was* sorry, though, that she was so upset about it. But they were hardly the first couple to indulge without benefit of vows.

She dropped her head to her knees and wailed. He winced, wondering if it would bring Mouse running to see exactly what wild creature had invaded the rooms over his store.

The next thought, awful, inconceivable, blindsided

him. Had he been so lost, so overwhelmed, that somewhere in the proceedings she'd tried to push him away,
attempted to tell him *no*, and he hadn't realized it? Or
worse yet, clutched in the grip of that overpowering
drive, he'd chosen to ignore her without conscious
thought?

"Kathryn." He touched her back with awkward hesitation. "I did not . . . you did not want . . ." He had to
know. He swallowed hard, made the awful words
come out. "Did you ask me to stop?"

His question shocked her enough to break the tears,
bring her head up with a snap.

He thought that he had forced her? Here was an
opportunity she'd not expected. All she had to do was
say yes to play on his guilt and conscience. He would
owe her.

"No," she said, appalled at her foolish honesty. "It
was only folly on my part. Not a crime on yours."

Kathryn Jordan wanted me that much.

Not Daniel Sellington. Him, Daniel Hall . . . Smith . . .
whatever. Not Sellington, which was the crucial part.
Him. So much so that she'd thrown caution to the
winds, forgotten a lifetime of propriety, and allowed
him to take unthinkable liberties. Marvelous liberties,
he thought with heated nostalgia. Even now, he felt
the pull, the urge to take her in his arms and push her
back down on that bed, bringing them both back to
that blinding madness.

He couldn't help it. She was still upset, it solved
nothing, but he grinned anyway. How many men could
say that a woman like Kathryn Jordan had wanted
them like that? Gamely, she attempted to smile back,

her eyes watery and puffy, her hair a silken tangle around her shoulders.

Oh, yes, she deserved better. What could he do for her?

Automatically the thought of his fortune sprang to mind, and immediately he recoiled, as repulsed as if he'd stumbled on a rotting corpse. He could not, would not, bring the corruption of money into the shining purity of last night. Nor would he put the burden of great wealth on her narrow, perfect shoulders.

He'd taken her virginity.

In recompense, he really should marry her.

He waited for his saner side, his cautious, practical side, to holler halt. And waited. And all he found inside was a jitter of excitement.

The lamplight sputtered, danced loving shadows over the glorious lines of her face, the rich tumble of her hair. Her eyes held secrets and pain and promises. She was studying him seriously, dark brows pinched in concentration, as if she were trying to look through his eyes and read the soul of this man to whom she'd given herself.

He didn't know her. Only three days, though it seemed like so much more. Knew so little about her. Not what she dreamed of when she closed her eyes, or how old she was when she received her first kiss, nor what frightened her most in the dark hours of the night.

But he knew what her skin tasted like. The feel of her breast in his mouth. How her flesh opened and then gripped him when he slid into her body.

He knew it was precipitous and rash, two things which he'd never been.

But knowing someone was no guarantee of a good union. His mother had thought she'd known Edward when she married him, and what a disaster that marriage had turned out to be.

Hundreds of men throughout the West had taken mail-order brides, wedding women they knew only through a few scrawled lines in a letter. Was this, then, such an outrageous risk?

He knew, too, that he was rationalizing. Because there was one overwhelming thought front and center in his mind, pushing out all the good and logical reasons not to leap: If he married her, then she'd be his.

What they'd done last night, he could do every night, every day. More than once, if he wanted. That, and a thousand other things. He'd have every right. *Every night*.

His flesh hardened abruptly in anticipation, threatened to burst just at the thought. And if that wouldn't be the most embarrassing moment of his life, he thought wryly, he didn't want to know what would be.

"Kathryn." Deliberately, he took her hands in his, waited until she gave him her full attention. "We should get married."

She stared at him for so long he wondered if she'd heard, or understood, a word he'd said, while all the while his heart pumped like a piston. Finally, she asked on a squeak: "Married? To *you*?"

"Who else?" he asked with an awkward laugh that was all he had the air for. It felt as if, for this moment, the world was balanced on a pin, and when she answered him it would topple over, one direction or the other, and there'd be no pushing it back into the place it had held before.

Her jaw sagged low. Her eyes, dark-lashed, beautiful, gleamed with shock. And then she launched herself at him, shrieking, and tumbled him back on the bed. The hard mattress drove the breath from his lungs. She dropped smacking kisses on his cheek, his throat, his mouth, his chest, and he thought: this has to be right, this *has* to be. Nothing that felt so good could be wrong. Could it?

He ducked his head to snare one of her quick kisses, capturing her mouth with his own. She relaxed on him immediately, her lips softening, her breath sighing into him, blending with his own. He smoothed his hand down her back, pressed her rump forward so that her belly cradled the hard ridge of his erection. She remained for one delicious moment pushing herself back. Her hair fell around her face, tickling his cheek, and her smile was broad, purely happy.

"Oh, no," she told him. "You're going to have to wait."

"But we're getting married anyway!" he protested, impatient. He'd gone his entire life without sex; he had a lot of catching up to do. "What difference would one more time make?"

"But we're not married yet." Kathryn was suspicious of believing too soon, of counting her chickens before they were wed. But his frown worried her; should she allow it to assure his compliance? Or would he, having gotten what he wanted—*again*—have more reason to duck out before following through on his proposal? "I'll make it up you," she promised with what she hoped was a seductive smile. A little more incentive couldn't hurt. "I *promise*." And she lowered her head to kiss him, long and heated, until she was reluctant to pull away and he was even harder pressed to allow it. "When?"

He'd already made the decision to marry her. What good would it do to ponder it? The last thing he wanted was second thoughts. Not to mention that the sooner they got married, the sooner they got to the wedding night. And right now, with the taste of her still on his tongue, the light weight of her breasts just touching his chest, his sex-scrambled brain was having a hard time thinking about much else.

Well, he was hardly the first man who rushed into marriage because he was in a fever to get to the wedding night. "How about right now?"

Chapter 11

Eight hours later, hardly anything had changed outwardly from four days earlier. A stagecoach rumbled down the same rutted, barren road, only in a southwesterly direction. This time Kathryn and Daniel were the only two passengers, but there was still a wiry, profane coachman up top, driving a weary, sturdy team of trail-hardened horses out front. The seats were covered in that same worn napped velvet. Only the color, a faded royal blue, differed.

Except now they were married. *Married*, Kathryn marveled. It was hard to credit, to believe. No ring circled her finger, and the ceremony had been anything but ceremonial.

When they'd poked their heads of out that tiny room in which everything had changed, they'd discovered it was still early—very early. Daniel had waited, chafing at the delay, although he did have an idea or two about how to pass the time, which Kathryn turned aside with a reluctance that, to her surprise, was hardly feigned at all. While the end of the previous night's interlude hadn't been satisfying physically, after only a few of his expert, delicious kisses, any lurking dissatisfaction quickly transformed into potent, simmering desire. No doubt about it, the man had the mouth of a magician.

When the sun had finally deigned to peek over the horizon, burning weakly through a low, gray haze, Daniel pounded on Mouse's door, the thudding loud enough to wake the dead. And when a grumbling Mouse poked his head out, his gray complexion so resembled the stiff, dead color of his hair that Kathryn thought perhaps Daniel had done just that.

Daniel demanded the name of the nearest preacher; Kathryn supposed they shouldn't have been surprised to find Mouse proudly offering himself for the task.

While Mouse went in search of his Bible and the appropriate papers, Daniel pulled Kathryn aside, whispering he had something to tell her first.

"Smith is not my real name," he informed her.

Kathryn stifled her rising excitement. It would not do to reveal too much, not when she was so close. "Oh?"

"It's really Hall."

"Hall." Her mood plummeted. So he still didn't dare entrust her with his true identity. "But why did you tell us it was Smith, then?"

"Oh." He jammed his hands in his pockets and studied a knot on the bare wood wall. "Call it a whim."

"That's a rather unusual whim."

He shrugged. "I suppose it was."

"Hall, you said?" A new concern surfaced. If he signed their license Hall, not Sellington, would their marriage be legal? "You mentioned a stepfather? Is that his name?"

"He's my father in every way that counts. We changed my name to his legally when I was eleven."

"I see." She nodded. "Mrs. Kathryn Hall, hmm? What do you think?"

"I could get used to it."

"You'd better," she told him sternly.

"Found it!" Mouse reappeared waving a thick black Bible. Three dollars, a few repeated vows, and a couple of scribbled signatures later, Mouse pronounced them man and wife.

The rain had started an hour before they left town. The sky outside the coach was the dull gray of tarnished silver; raindrops pelted the roof, gusted against the closed window shades. Not an auspicious day to begin her marriage.

Daniel had taken the seat opposite her, his long legs stretched across the space between them. He made a very fine groom, the kind any woman would be proud to marry. His white shirt was only slightly wrinkled from being folded in his valise, the crisp white collar nicely setting off the deepened color he'd acquired during their day tramping across the plains. His pants were deep gray, elegantly draped. He'd polished his boots for the occasion, and they winked at her in the dim light when he crossed his ankles.

She wished that she'd been a bride worthy of him. All she'd had to wear was the traveling suit she'd had on for three days, hastily washed the previous afternoon while Daniel had been absent, the blouse and skirt thoroughly crumpled from being slept—and *not* slept—in the night before. But when he'd smiled at her during the wedding, she'd felt like she'd been clothed in satin.

Daniel had been contemplating his feet since they climbed into the stage. Perhaps he was having second thoughts, worrying over the rash marriage into which he'd plunged. It wouldn't be surprising, she supposed.

But she didn't want him to be sorry. Kathryn felt a rush of fervent gratitude for him. Oh, certainly she still had a few concerns herself. He'd mentioned nothing to her about an allowance, or anything whatsoever about money for that matter. But surely that would come once they returned to Denver. She would think of it later.

But oh, he had done the honorable thing and married her! After she'd botched her plan so badly, he'd offered salvation readily, without her having to trick or threaten him, and she felt an extraordinary warmth toward him for his honorableness. She owed him for that.

"You did not seem happy to have to return to Denver," she said.

"No," he said, quick and flat.

"Would you . . . would you like to tell me about it," she ventured.

"My grandmother is ill. In my absence, she took a turn for the worse."

"Oh!" The crazed grandmother, of course. "I am very sorry."

He shrugged. "It is not a new condition. I had expected the summons, but I had hoped . . ." Sighing, he leaned forward, bridging the space between them, and took one of her hands. The damp air had coaxed his hair into deeper waves, and it gleamed softly in the dim light. "I have not been very good company to you this afternoon, have I?"

She smiled at him. "It's all right."

"No." Daniel was unaccustomed to sharing his thoughts and emotions. But Kathryn was his wife now. He would have to learn to do so—some of them, anyway. Not the parts of him he inherited from his father. No, never that.

She looked tired. Shadows purpled the thin skin beneath her eyes, hollowed out her cheekbones. Tendrils of pale hair curled around her cheek and her gently curved jaw. Surely she was feeling confused, disoriented. She'd been bedded and married in less than a day by a man she scarcely knew. She deserved his comfort, his assurances. And he'd been too much in shock himself to reassure her.

His gaze moved from her face, touched the bare sweep of her neck into the froth of pale lace at her collar. In the stuffy confines of the closed coach she'd removed her jacket, and the fabric of her bodice lay limp against the high curves of her breasts. She wore no gloves—finally—and her hands were folded in her lap. He had vague, delicious memories of those hands on his back, stroking the top of his butt.

Kathryn Hall. Mrs. Daniel Hall. His bride. *His wife.*

She shrieked as he swooped, scooping from her seat and settling back into his own with her on his lap. "Daniel!"

He loved the sound of his name on her tongue.

"Yes?"

"What are you doing?"

"Being a thoughtful husband." There, he'd said it aloud. *Husband.* "These seats are a bit hard, haven't you noticed? And you must be a bit, ah, tender today. I'm just trying to ensure your comfort."

Her cheeks bloomed pink. She peered at him through the thick, dark fringe of her lashes. Hesitantly, she looped her arms around his neck, giving him the perfect opportunity to kiss her. Her arms tightened immediately; her mouth opened without any urging.

His flesh rose hard and eager. Last night's activities had clearly not sated his body in any way. Instead it apparently had only made him all the more eager, now that he knew what he'd been missing all those years.

The sway and dip of the coach caused her weight to keep shifting on his lap, pressing a little harder here, a bit more there, unpredictable and exciting. He found himself holding his breath, waiting, praying, for the next bump in the road.

"All day long, that first day in the coach," he murmured against the suede-plush skin beneath her ear, "I imagined I was doing this. God, how often I wished the Thatchers gone!"

"Did you?" She let her head drop back, giving him better access. His tongue flicked her earlobe and she shivered. "Would you have done this, then?"

"Probably not," he admitted. Thank God he no longer had to worry about her virtue!

"Well, I'm glad we're alone this time."

"Me too." His hand came up, dealt with the buttons at her neckline, and slid inside, discovering warm flesh and soft skin.

"Daniel . . . what are you doing?"

"I would think that would be obvious." He met the edge of her shift, traced it with his thumb. "You know what I regret most about last night?"

His fingers skated over the surface of her shift, found the tight bud of her nipple and stroked it through the thin fabric. She just barely managed a "hmm?"

"That I was in so much of a hurry I hardly got any of your clothes off. I wanted you naked."

That brought her eyes open. "You're not taking my clothes off *here*!"

His mouth was on the upper swell of her breast, and she felt his laughter as hot puffs of air against her skin. "Not all of them," he promised.

He tongued her through the cloth of her shift, easing her back until she was half-lying in the corner of the seat. "I'm so glad," he said, "that you don't wear all those layers and corsets and . . . things . . . to get in the way."

She didn't wear them, Kathryn thought with amusement, because she couldn't afford them. And because corsets were a hindrance to those who scrubbed things for a living. "You're welcome."

He looked up at her, a hot, mischievous light in his eyes. "How much do you like this shift?"

"Don't you dare!" she told him sternly, trying to ignore the tingle of excitement his words spurred. It was so *wicked*. "It's the only one I've got!"

"Good." He tore it in half as easily as a cobweb, leaving her breasts completely bare in the half-light of the coach's interior.

They could be married for sixty years, he thought with the corner of his brain that still worked, and he would not get enough of her. When he died—hopefully as an old, old man, preferably in her bed—the first thing he was going to thank God for was inventing such glorious things as breasts.

He should have done better by her last night. But now—ah, thank God he'd thought to marry her—he was going to have years and years to make it up to her. And, while he was inexperienced, practically speaking, he had, once upon a time, made a rather thorough intellectual study of the subject. So he'd be prepared when he had need of the information. He found himself as eager to try out that knowledge as he'd been to enter her for the first time.

He stroked down her side, over the sharp dip of her waistline, the narrow slope of her hip, the angle of her thigh. He lifted her off his lap, wincing at the release of the delicious pressure on his groin and he thought: Patience, patience. One could not have *all* the good stuff at once.

"What are you doing?" she asked, as he set her down on the seat next to him, her legs over his lap.

"Do you really want to know?" he asked. "Or would you rather be surprised?"

"I—" Which did she want? She hated surprises, didn't she? But the promise in his eyes was so tempting, the surprises thus far so sweet.

"You have five seconds to make up your mind."

"I—" His hand was on her ankle, wandering up her calf, lifting her dress out of the way. And then he kissed her knee, and whatever she'd planned to say scattered.

"Time's up." His mouth brushed a little higher, on

the inside of her thigh, and she didn't know whether to damn the thinness of her drawers' cotton or to be thankful for it. "I'll describe every step of the way next time. You'll like that too, I promise. But this time—" He reared up, his eyes hot, determined. "This time, I want you to wonder, every moment, every step, what I'm going to do next."

He rolled her dress all the way up to her waist, leaving her sprawled on the seat, and leaned back to look at her. She looked the wildest wanton, breasts spilling free of the froth of opened blouse and torn shift; skirt shoved out of the way so his gaze could trace the long, lean length of her legs. Drooping strings tied her drawers tight around her waist but failed to hold the slit completely closed. A few curls the color of antique gold peeked through, tempting him away from his plans. Later, he abjured himself. This time was for her.

Her face was serious, beautiful, maybe just a little apprehensive. "You, right now, right here, are the most amazing thing I've ever seen in my life," he told her, and her expression cleared.

He reached forward, ran his fingers along the opening of her drawers, widening the space, exposing her to his view. He heard her gasp, color flooding her neck and cheeks. But she didn't move to cover herself, or hide in any way, and blood and power thundered in him.

She was his bride.

He bent, began to kiss his way up her leg. Her ankle, her calf, the inside of her knee. Higher, higher. She kept making little hiccups of sound, surprise and pleasure, faster, louder, with each increment he advanced.

He kissed the inside of her thigh, high above her knee, and her flesh quivered. "You can't!" she gasped, scandalized.

"Why not?" he murmured, finding the valley where her leg met her torso. He was almost enveloped in her. Her skirts spilled around his head; her thigh pressed his cheek; and the smell of her, the scent of an aroused and ready woman, swam in his head. Soon, he thought. Soon, he would know the taste of her, too. He could hardly wait.

"Because . . . because . . ." He kissed her *there*. One brief instant, and it shot through Kathryn's entire body, tingling in her toes, warming her fingers, muddling her brain.

He was her husband. He had every right to do this to her, this and anything else he wanted. She had to allow it.

Not to mention that, if he quit now, she was damn well going to scream. "No reason," she said breathlessly. "Carry on."

He was so close to her that she felt his smile against her thigh, felt his hot breath stirring the curls that shielded her sex. "But what happens next is supposed to be a surprise."

His lips just brushed her as his mouth moved; unable to stop herself, she lifted her hips, trying to get closer. "I'll be surprised," she told him. "I promise."

"Well, as long as you promise."

And then his mouth was there fully at last and she arched, her whole back bowing up. Her high, keening cry bounced through the confines of the small coach.

He was careful at first. A gentle kiss, the slightest

stroke of his tongue, each of which sent sensation careening through her body. And at last he settled his mouth flat against her, his tongue stroking evenly, deeply, and her hips began to circle, taking up the rhythm and urging him faster.

She'd had a vague notion that such a thing existed. The more earthy parts of life were not a secret in her neighborhood, not the way they would be if she'd been gently reared in truth. But, had she given it a passing thought, she would have considered it a relatively odd practice. Embarrassing, certainly; vulgar; and quite probably repulsive.

Instead, she soared on the heat of his mouth, the generosity of his gift. Her thighs tightened around his head. Her hands burrowed in his hair, clutching tight to hold him close. She pressed up against his mouth, seeking more . . . more pressure, more strokes, more glory.

Daniel had been planning this since the morning, since he'd proposed their wedding. He knew he'd mostly taken last night, giving too little in return. His starved body had simply not been able to hold out against the feel of her flesh closing tight around him. And so this—not in the coach, that had been a sudden burst of inspiration and impatience—but the pleasuring of her, he'd been plotting that for hours.

But he hadn't counted on Kathryn. Hadn't thought of how the taste of her, rich and salty and sweet, would flood his mouth. How the sound of her, lost to the sensation he caused, would prove as potent an incitement as sinking into her had been.

He was fully clothed. But, as he half lay on the

coach seat, and his stiff arousal rubbed against it as he worked on her, as every one of his senses was overwhelmed with the feast, the splendor, that was this woman, he found himself edging close to completion himself, and he clamped down hard on his relentless passions.

This was supposed to be just for her, he reminded himself. But it felt as much for himself, as selfish as his taking of her last night had been. For the pleasure was just as strong, as insistent. Maybe even more satisfying.

Light spangled behind Kathryn's closed lids, and she strained for it. She knew that Daniel could not have stopped if he'd wanted to, her grip on him was so strong, her inarticulate demands too insistent. She didn't care. She had to finish this, had to find that peak that hovered just out of her reach, promising heaven, taunting her with its nearness.

And then it was all hers, all of it, a starburst of pleasure that seized her muscles, stormed her nerves, simultaneously sapped all her strength and returned it stronger.

She was shaking beneath his mouth, crying out, and Daniel thought, I don't know if I'm going to make it. And he didn't care anymore. This was the most glorious moment of his life, that he could do this for his wife. Could return to her some portion of the gift she'd given him.

When she collapsed beneath him, her body limp and still, he rested there, his cheek on her thigh, chest-thumping proud, astounded that he had given her this.

Her hand lay on his head, still and limp, as if it had

taken all her strength to put it there and now she had to gather her energies before moving it farther. And then her fingers burrowed deep in his hair, back and forth, back and forth over his skull.

He felt her struggle to sit up. "Stay," he murmured, placing a hand on her belly to hold her still, marveling again that he had the right to do so. "Rest for a while."

"That would be lovely," she said, "but my back is not in agreement."

He sprang up immediately, reached out a hand to pull her up to a more comfortable position. "My apologies."

"It is not your fault." Her smile was lit with impish glee. "Until a moment ago, I hadn't noticed at all. But, once I was less, umm, distracted, it decided to protest being bent into that corner."

"I hope there is no lasting damage," he said sincerely. Not, he admitted ruefully, entirely due to a husband's appropriate concern for his wife's health. But also because he did not want to wait days and days for her full recovery before exploring his marital rights again.

Her grin broadened, as if she'd clearly read his concern. "Oh, I don't believe you have anything to worry about. In fact, it is probably best if I get some further exercise right now. Work out the kinks before it stiffens up on me."

She was quick and limber. She was in his lap facing him, straddling his hips, pinning his shoulders against the back of the carriage, before he thought to protest. He admitted that perhaps a certain reluctance to object slowed his response, though he knew it was the gentlemanly thing to do.

Her blouse was still open. The ruins of her shift fluttered around her breasts, and he couldn't help but notice the delectable splendor that was no more than five inches from his mouth.

"It occurs to me," she said, seduction purring through every syllable, "that I have not been a particularly active participant in our encounters thus far. Most unfair of me, don't you think?"

One of her hands meandered down his chest, fingers dipping in and out of the gaps between his buttons, tickling skin and then retreating. Over his chest, down his belly, before he could gather his thoughts enough to realize that she seemed to have no intention of halting.

Damned if gentlemanly plans weren't sometimes a real pain in the ass.

He caught her hand, though he couldn't bring himself to pluck it away completely. He merely halted its progress, flattening her hand against him as two of her fingers continued to stroke a patch of skin right beneath his navel. If only, he thought, she'd gotten a bit farther before he'd remembered he was supposed to be stopping her.

Her eyes, deep and as warmly aqua as the Caribbean he'd once visited on a trip with his father, met his. "Don't you want me to? I mean, *you* didn't . . . at least I don't *think* you . . ."

His pained laughter rumbled through the coach. "No, I didn't. And whether I want to—well, I'm certain that is perfectly obvious to you."

"Well, then . . ." Her hand wandered lower.

"But this time was supposed to be just for you," he said around his gasp. He'd been feeling so gallant about giving her pleasure while resisting his own. But his resolve was fading rapidly. Why had he thought that seemed like a good idea? "I know that for you last night was not as pleasurable as it was for me. So today will be your turn, and then we'll be even." He grinned. "Tonight will be for us both. And from now on."

It hardly seemed possible to Kathryn that this was to be her life from this day forward. She had thought only of the absolute freedom that the security of marrying Daniel would bring; the ability no longer to have to worry over every penny, every meal, every day.

But this was entirely unexpected. The wonders of the flesh to be found with him, the right to revel in this handsome man daily.

He was not a selfish man, she admitted to herself. Perhaps she'd tried to cast him in that light to make her pursuit more palatable; it was not so terrible to wrong a bad man. Perhaps, raised in plenty, he was just utterly oblivious to the lack of it in others. But no truly selfish man would have said what he'd just said, done what he'd just done, seeing to her pleasure while eschewing his own due to some odd sense of fair play.

The disordered waves of his hair lay loose over his forehead, a disarray caused by her seeking fingers. The gleam in his eyes, the bright contrast between brilliant blue iris and deep black pupil, was startling. His mouth glistened—evidence of her excitement still on his lips. It was shocking, utterly erotic, and blood tingled low.

"I've never," she told him, "cared that much about being fair." And her hand skated down, traced the outline of his erection through his pants, thumb on one side, fingers on the other, learning his size, his response.

"I surrender," he said quickly.

"And well you should. A man should always listen to his wife's opinions about such matters, don't you think?"

Her hand molded him through his trousers. He was so hard, she marveled. And so much larger than he'd appeared that morning in a relaxed state. "This is so fascinating," she said without thinking.

His head was back, against the curve of the seat, and he cracked one eye open. "Fascinating?" he asked, not entirely sure whether he liked the description.

"I do not . . . well, you must admit the change is quite amazing. Nothing on me does anything like *that*."

With a lazy smile, he reached up to cup one breast in his palm, squeezing the nipple between his thumb and forefinger, and it puckered up immediately. "Oh, you have a few rather interesting parts yourself."

She had not, until then, watched anything he'd done to her. But the sight of his large, sun-browned hand on her white flesh, the deep rose tip of her breast peeking between his fingers, made her gasp.

She wiggled against him, trying to ease the ache growing between her thighs. The air rushed out of him, a hiss through his clenched teeth. "You're welcome to explore further," he said with some difficulty. "I mean, since you're so fascinated and all."

"That's very considerate of you."

Her impatient fingers scrambled at his buttons and fastenings, freeing his erection into her palms. So hard, but the skin covering him so very soft, like the finest velvet. Blood pulsed in him, *life* beat in him.

Further investigation would have to wait. Curiosity gave way to the stronger demand of desire. She lifted herself up to move her skirts aside, positioned his cock at her entrance, and sank down. "Oh!" Her skirts billowed out, settled back down to hide their joining.

Without the diversion of pain, she could concentrate on the sensation of having him deep within her. That gratifying fullness, a hot tingling pleasure where they joined, and something more, deep inside where . . . perhaps he touched her womb, she thought with a delicious shiver.

Experimentally, she slid up once, until he almost left her body, and then sank back down, gasping at her body's violent response. Daniel grimaced and gripped her hips in both hands.

She began to move, Daniel greeting each stroke that she made with an upthrust of his own. She had not believed it possible that he could go so deeply inside her. Nor had she known that the delight could be even richer and stronger than last time, she thought, recognizing the rising spiral of ecstasy. Despite the fact that she set the rhythm of their joining, her own response seemed less controlled than when Daniel had loved her with his mouth. The pleasure was less concentrated, wilder, spread more widely throughout her body.

Suddenly he pushed up inside her hard, holding her

in place against him. She could feel the heat of his seed flooding deep inside her, and it propelled her to her own climax. She shuddered against him, again and again, before collapsing into his arms. The gasping, harsh sounds of their labored respiration filled the coach, sparring with the rumble of the wheels.

"Do you think," she murmured, "that we will ever be able to move again?"

"We'd better." He hugged her, and a softer warmth, no less joyous, filled her. "Because I swear, one of these times, I really, *really*, want to get you completely naked."

They laughed together, and she felt joy and relief bubble up, a light, lifting sensation until she thought she might simply rise and float away. She'd been weighed down by worry and struggle for so long, she hadn't remembered what it was like to feel any other way.

But if she did float away, she thought fancifully, surely Daniel would catch her.

A sharp sound cracked the air. One side of the coach pitched down, and the vehicle lurched to an uneven stop.

"Well, hell," Daniel said. "What now?"

Chapter 12

They'd broken an axle. Hit a good-sized rock smack in the road, which the coachman swore hadn't been there the week before and snapped the front one completely in two.

The sun had apparently chased away the clouds sometime while they'd been . . . distracted . . . in the coach. So now they stood broiling while the coachman clanged and swore and rummaged beneath the coach.

This trip, his flight from Denver, had been cursed from the start. First the ambush, then the stage driver's defection. The note from his assistant calling him back to Denver, and then his forced marriage.

Not that a forced marriage was necessarily a bad thing.

Kathryn was at his side, her sturdy hand firmly in his. She'd wrapped her fair hair in some complicated arrangement of braids, but it was too fine to remain demurely tucked away. Little wisps kept springing free, making it look as if she were surrounded by a corona of sunlight. Her skin gleamed delicately with perspiration—not, he thought with a certain amount of

159

masculine satisfaction, entirely due to the heat of the
sun, but also to their exertions in the coach. They'd
just managed to cover themselves before the coachman
flung the door open, and Kathryn hadn't been able to
look at Daniel since without color springing into her
cheeks.

And he could not dislodge the realization that, beneath her blouse, her shift was shredded to ribbons—
had his hands, he marveled, really *done* that?—and her
breasts were bare against the thin lawn of her blouse.
Aroused by the thought—his passions were proving
much quicker to recover than he'd ever suspected—
he shifted and squeezed her hand. She smiled in response, and he couldn't bring himself to regret the unexpected turn of his journey that led him to her.

By this point in his life, he should have known the
folly of trying to run away from his past. It always
caught up with him. Even as a child, when he and his
mother had run from Edward and buried themselves
in a sheltered, unimportant town in the middle of the
country, as far from Edward's gilded world as they
could get, he'd still found them.

Reflexively, he shuddered away from the memory
of what came next. Any normal man would feel great
remorse and guilt at witnessing his sire's death. All
he'd felt—all he'd *ever* felt—was relief.

"Well." The coachman crawled out from beneath
the coach. Wrench in hand, he swiped a blue-clad forearm across his dripping forehead. "It's done for. Nothing for it but to get a new one."

"I thought you were required to carry spare parts."

"Well, yeah." He shoved his wrench into a back

pocket and rested his hands on his skinny hips. "But I used one when I broke down outside of Julesberg a month ago. Ain't replaced it yet."

Daniel sighed deeply. Beside him, Kathryn smothered a spurt of laughter, and he cocked a brow at her in question.

"Am I the one who is cursed, do you suppose?" she asked. "Or is this your fault?"

"Oh, of course it is mine," he said with a gallant bow. "It would be most ungentlemanly of me to lay our troubles at your dainty feet, wouldn't it?" Unable to resist, he fingered one of the stray wisps that waved along her temple. The hair was soft and light as feather down. It curled around his finger, twining and clinging like it meant to stay. He had a growing suspicion that his new wife was doing the very same thing to his heart.

"Nothing for it," the coachman said, "but to walk on into the next town and get a new one. You can stay here. Or you can come with me. Your choice, but I ain't promising how long it's gonna take."

Daniel sighed. He eyed the coach, his mind filling with arousing memories of Kathryn sprawled in passion-hazed abandon on the old blue-velvet seats. It was terribly tempting. He was convinced that they could find . . . productive . . . things to do with their time.

However—he was not at all liking this *however*—without the breeze provided by the coach's motion the temperature inside would spike rapidly. He supposed expiring from heat exhaustion would likely put a damper on their love play. They had no food, and only a little water. Not to mention that they had rather convincing evidence that there were criminals along this road.

"How far is it to the next town?" Kathryn asked without a hint of petulance or accusation in her voice.

The coachman shrugged, popped his wad of tobacco from one cheek into the other. "Two miles, tops."

Daniel's sigh this time was one of resignation. And not a little disappointment.

"At least we can ride this time," Kathryn suggested.

The coachman shook his head, spewing droplets of tobacco juice. "Naw. They ain't riding horses. Wouldn't be likely to keep you on their backs. Can't leave 'em out here, though. We'll have to lead 'em along."

"Well, my dear," Daniel said as he grabbed his valise, "it looks like we're in for another stroll."

"You do know how to show a girl a good time."

After Porterville, Pine River looked like a bustling city. There were three—*three*—hotels, plus an additional restaurant from which the most delicious smell of baking biscuits curled out the open front door and drifted down the town's central street. Kathryn counted two dry goods stores, a stable, three very successful-looking saloons and one very much less-than-prosperous-appearing church.

The coachman deposited them at the restaurant while he went to check on the availability of parts. Over antelope and the fresh biscuits that proved to be every bit as delicious as they smelled, Kathryn was immensely relieved to discover she and her new husband were at last far more at ease with each other than they'd been during the previous meals they'd shared.

She'd heard of the phenomenon, that sexual gratification often turned the most intractable man amenable and content. But she had not suspected that she herself was susceptible.

However, it was soon quite clear that Daniel had far from reached the satiation point. For all they were in a bustling restaurant, it seemed at times as if they were alone in the world. The air between them was charged with heated expectation, far more potent for being built on memories rather than anticipation. His eyes, the blue of a hotly burning flame, never left her. They looked deeply into her own eyes, studied her mouth, contemplated her neck, and settled for long moments on her bodice. And Kathryn found herself tingling, in her newly sensitized breasts and nether regions, feelings which she was certain no real lady would experience in such public surroundings. And perhaps not even in private ones.

Maybe, she thought, boldly returning his regard, in some ways she could make Daniel *happy* that he had not married a real lady. He ran a finger under his collar, as though it had suddenly grown too tight.

"You all still eatin'?" The coachman strolled up to their table, streaks of grease bisecting his shirtfront. "Wish I could say the same, but some of us got jobs to do, you know." He snatched a biscuit from a cloth-lined basket, tore it in half, and stuffed a piece into his mouth.

"Please, help yourself," Daniel said, amused.

"Thanks." He chewed briefly, mouth open, and

swallowed hard. "They ain't got exactly the right axle, but I can make it work. Figure an hour or two for adjustments, and a couple more for me to get back to the coach, make the repairs, get the horses hitched up, and get back here."

"Thank you."

While the driver left, Daniel considered his options. The most delightful of which was simply to engage a room at one of the nearby hotels, sweep his bride into it, and finally strip her of every single stitch of clothing covering her lovely frame. The fact that it was bright daylight held an added appeal; he could study every inch to his heart's content. Though he suspected it would take far more than one afternoon to fulfill his heart's content where viewing her naked body was concerned.

However, renting a room for only a few hours was really a bit obvious, he supposed. Not to mention that after two rather, uh, energetic encounters in the space of less than twenty-four hours . . . well, a third, and probably a fourth, was rather a lot to ask of a previously virginal new bride.

Damn it.

What he *should* do was take advantage of the unexpected stopover and attend to a bit of business. He had holdings in the area, only a few miles east of town. He'd been promising Hans Peterson, his manager, that he would come and survey some recent improvements for months.

It certainly did not have the appeal of secluding himself in a bedroom with Kathryn for a few hours.

Her head bent, she addressed the cherry pie with

delicate precision. He saw the clean line of her part, the skin pink from all her recent exposure to the sun, the shining swoop of her hair on either side.

She could stay in town, rest or shop or relax as she chose, while he made his visit. Surely she could use a few hours of privacy to accustom herself to the rapid and unexpected changes in her life.

It was a considerate plan. It was also an excuse, and he knew it as soon as the thought formed.

He did not want to take Kathryn along.

The realization was not a happy one. She was his wife, a new partner in his life and any future endeavors. Surely she had a right to know about his business interests.

But he loved that she knew and wanted and married him as an unknown writer—not penniless, perhaps, but certainly with no outward indications of great wealth. He feared her reaction to finding out differently. He did not want to see that light of avarice in her eyes that he was so familiar with in the women who had known him as Daniel Sellington.

But she would know before long anyway, as soon as they returned to Denver and his grandmother's mansion. He was not giving her enough credit. She was his wife, and she'd given no indication—beyond that extreme reluctance to surrender her purse, he admitted—that material things held an inordinate value for her.

It was his duty as her husband to trust her.

"Kathryn," he said, his clipped tone enough to quickly snag her attention. "I have some . . . business to attend to this afternoon. You are welcome to join me. I can engage a horse and team, if you'd like. Or, if you have had enough of bouncing up and down on a seat, you may stay here and recuperate from our adventures." *Coward*, to give her the choice.

"I have no need of recuperation." Her smile was intimate, softly suggestive. "And I would like nothing better than to spend the afternoon with you."

Despite her carefully worded questions, Daniel had not been forthcoming about exactly what business he had outside of Pine River that afternoon. His closed expression clearly warned her off probing further, and she did not feel comfortable forcing the issue. She didn't know how he would react. And now that they were safely married, she had some time.

Not a lot, she thought, shuddering at the memory of Simon Moore's confident assumptions that both she and Isabelle would soon be in his . . . employ. But some.

"Is it much farther?" she finally asked.

"No. See that next curve, way down beyond that copse of trees? It is just around the bend from there."

Excitement made it difficult for her to remain properly still in her seat. What could it be? A silver mine? A large and prosperous ranch?

It would be the first of Daniel's business interests she would glimpse. And, as his wife, it was in some ways *hers*. It would help provide for her and her family for years to come. Her children, *their* children, would no doubt take over its management one day, ensuring they would never have to do distasteful and dangerous things in order to survive. She had an unaccountable urge to throw herself from the buggy and kiss the ground in front of the . . . whatever it turned out to be.

"I wish I'd something better to wear. I would have liked to make a good impression on your—" She had almost said employees. But he'd said nothing of the precise nature of his business; for all she was supposed to know, it could have easily been *Daniel's* employers they were going to meet. Or partners, or even potential investors. She couldn't give Daniel even an inkling that she might know something of his circumstances.

Nervously, she smoothed a hand down her rumpled shirt front, checked the buttoning of her close-cut jacket. It had not been in great condition to begin with and was now definitely the worse for the wear.

"What will they think of me?"

He glanced over at her, belatedly realizing she still wore the same clothes she'd had when he met her, and he could have whacked himself on the skull for his stupidity. Of *course* she had on the same clothes; everything she owned was in Julesberg by now. He should have sent her off to the store in Pine River, but he'd been too damn inattentive to notice. Not to mention that it was what was *inside* the clothes that interested him.

He never really thought about clothes. Every once in a while, he'd find some comfortable old shirt had disappeared and been replaced by a crisp new one, because Libeus, his assistant, had decided it was required. And that was as much attention as he'd ever paid them.

It was different for women. Even he knew that. She

fiddled with a button, tried to smooth her travel-
crushed skirts into better condition.

"This is the first of your . . . well, anyone you knew
before our marriage that I've met," she said.

She wanted him to be proud of her, he thought
warmly. He wasn't used to having someone else's actions reflect on him, or the other way around. But her
future, her actions, were entwined with his, and his
with hers.

"You could be wearing rags, and Mr. Peterson will
be dazzled," he told her. "As I would be."

And that smile, he thought, did far more than dazzle
him, every single time she bestowed it. He wondered
if that sizzle of heat would ever fade.

As they grew closer, Kathryn heard the sounds of
industry—the brutal clash of metal on metal, the banging of hammers on wood. A plume of dark smoke
spiraled up above the trees. Daniel turned the buggy
off the main road and guided the team through an
opening in the trees.

Immediately, the ride smoothed, the road far better
maintained than the one they'd just left. In a few more
moments, the trees fell away, and there it was.

A smelter.

Revulsion curled in her stomach. Smelters were the
bane, and the inescapable king, of the Platte River district. The dead ash and harsh smoke they belched forth
at all hours of the day continually dimmed the sky and
settled a gray film over all exposed surfaces—tables,
clothing, skin. It came almost as relief when it clogged
your nostrils to the point that you no longer could
smell, for no one who dwelled in its shadows could

breathe in that odor without knowing it was the scent of death.

It was the only resort for most of her neighbors, the only place where they could earn a day's wages without sacrificing their souls in the process. But the price they paid for its being honest labor was a high one. Accidents killed quickly. Lead poisoning killed far more insidiously. Both were nearly inescapable.

The large, brick main building sprawled over a broad patch of bare, beaten earth. Outbuildings clustered around it like chickens around a coop. Piles of wood and ore claimed their own ground. Three wagons lined up along one side of the building, awaiting their cargo, while a filled one rumbled by, heading for the main road. Beyond, she could see more buildings, these small, identical, and widely spaced, grouped behind the stables.

A blond man, big and gorgeous and hearty, bounded down the front steps. He extended his right arm in greeting, his empty left sleeve knotted and swinging free.

"Hans!" Daniel sprang down from his seat, pumped the outstretched hand in what seemed to be genuine pleasure. "You're looking well."

"We are well. My Amelia will soon to give me another child, you know. And you have not been to see us since Nathan was a baby!"

"You do not have to feel obligated to produce an entire next generation of managers for me, you know."

Hans chuckled heartily. "Ah, but I would not allow you to go to the trouble of searching them out." His

speculative gaze lit on Kathryn, took in her clothing
and stiff posture. "You have another worker for me?"

"No." He reached up a hand to assist her descent.
"This is my wife, Kathryn."

"*Wife?*"

Speculation turned to open suspicion. Kathryn attempted to lift her chin and return his glare with pride
and confidence, but guilt nagged her, for she *was*
everything that Mr. Peterson obviously suspected of
her. Despite herself, she sidled closer to Daniel. But
then his hand was there, wrapping hers in warm support, and she straightened.

"You had not told me," Hans said slowly, "that you
were thinking of marriage."

"I'm not sure either of us were exactly *thinking*,"
she admitted, flashing a grin at her husband, gratified
to see humor and surprise light his eyes. "We rather
swept each other off our feet."

"That we did," he murmured, lifting her hand to
kiss. At the bare brush of his mouth, she remembered
the touch of his mouth other times, other places, and
her stomach fluttered like an intoxicated butterfly.

"Hmm." Hans contemplated them for a moment
longer, then shrugged, reserving judgment. "Do you
want to look around? Or I suppose we could find you
an empty cottage somewhere."

Daniel's neck reddened, but he laughed with more
than a little pride. "Just a quick report on your progress
will do," he said with some reluctance at turning down
the empty cottage and its empty bed. "Then we'll be
on our way."

"I'd like a tour," Kathryn put in.

He'd always been careful to keep his ownership a secret from everyone but Hans, who he'd found years ago outside of a run-down saloon and installed in the position. What a stroke of luck that had been, for the man turned out to be an enormously capable manager, not to mention a good friend. However, a tour couldn't hurt, could it? None of the employees would know who he was unless told. And he wasn't inclined to refuse anything Kathryn asked of him.

He took his wife's elbow to steer her up the steep brick stairs. "*Your* managers?" she asked, looking at him out of the corner of her eye.

She'd picked up on Hans's passing comment. Daniel quashed a ripple of disquiet. She'd not married him for his money, he reminded himself. But it wasn't going to be a disappointment to her to find out he had some. "Yes."

Her head lifted as she looked up at the sheer broad face of the building towering over her. The curve of her chin into her neck was clean and beautiful. "You own this?"

"Yes."

Her "hmm" was every bit as noncommittal as Hans's had been. One brow lifted in elegant question. "A writer?"

"I *am* that." A terrible one, but there were only so many things he was willing to confess. "Among other things."

"Are you going to tell me about the other things?"

"Eventually."

He waited for her questions, probing into the life of this stranger she'd married. She had to be curious. He

was. But she merely lifted her skirts and followed
Hans.

The slums Kathryn had dwelled in for most of her
life slammed hard against Denver's industrial area, the
two entwined and merging like malignant growths
feeding off each other. Factories, mills, smelters—she
knew them well, the blank, ugly shells housing darkness and danger, spewing smoke and cinders, sucking
in fresh, healthy young men and spitting out old, dying
ones. Along the way, her vision of the inside of one
of those awful places and hell had merged into one:
heat and fire and agony.

So she felt a distinct shiver of apprehension as she
went inside, which immediately transformed into awed
amazement.

Rows and rows of big windows admitted light and
ventilation; Kathryn could only guess at the expense
of all that clear, broad glass. The machinery was
widely spaced, the floor between them sanded smooth
and golden. Healthy-looking employees bent industriously to their work. Her fingers fiddled with the pleats
of wool at her waist; most of the workers were far
better dressed than she was.

The room clashed with noise; there was little to be
done about that. But the soaring ceilings let the ca-
cophony drift up and made it bearable, the sound of
industry and honest labor. Along the far wall she
glimpsed an oilcloth-covered table, piled with plates
of cookies, loaves of bread, a wheel of cheese, and an
entire ham. Two big metal canisters dripping conden-
sation stood beside a collection of mugs. Two broad
doors, thrown wide, framed a scattering of tables out-

side, a dozen workers sitting and laughing, downing sandwiches as if they had all the time and food in the world.

Factory owners cut corners wherever they could, earning their dollars by pinching pennies off the backs of their workers. But Daniel—Daniel obviously coddled his. She tried to feel pride at his generosity, but all she could think of was that the cost of one of those windows would have fed her family for a month. Was it really necessary to have so many?

Her hand tucked firmly in the crook of his arm, Daniel seemed to have no intention of letting her stray beyond reach, which pleased and flattered her to a surprising degree. As they trailed after Hans, her surprise grew. The employees greeted Hans with jovial and fearless respect, seeming to have no idea at all of Daniel's identity. Nor did Daniel appear inclined to enlighten them.

After half the tour, she was ready to move her entire neighborhood into the mill. There were comfortably cushioned chairs, out of the way but within easy reach of any tired worker. There was even a room which appeared to serve no other purpose but a place for employees to rest if they did not choose to take their break outside, the fat black stoves it contained attesting to the fact that it would be as cozily warm in winter as it was breezy and light now. And, at any time, fully one quarter of the workers appeared to be doing just that!

Heavens, if this whole marriage plan didn't work out, she was going to move here, get down on her hands and knees, and *beg* Hans to let her work at Daniel's smelter.

After an exhaustive tour of the place in which he clearly took great pride, Hans led them out the back doors, into the shade of a great cottonwood tree. The low rumble from inside was punctuated by the bright chatter of the men and women who sat at the tables, appearing as if they were enjoying a picnic rather than taking a break from their labors.

"That's the infirmary over there." Hans jabbed a thick finger in the direction of a neat brick building a hundred yards from any others, bright flowers blooming merrily on either side of the front door. "We have a nurse on staff, and the doctor comes twice a week. More if he's needed, of course."

"Just for the people who work here?" Peter's pale, devastated face, his handsome features distorted into his death mask, shot up from the deep pit of memories where she'd tried to bury it. An echo of the awful panic she'd felt when she'd been unable to find a doctor willing to treat him for the few coins she had tightened her stomach. And here there was a nurse and a doctor, just waiting around whether someone needed them or not. The unfairness hit her in the sternum, a physical blow that knocked the breath from her lungs.

"The revenue projections?" Daniel prompted.

Hans's smile beamed. "Up twenty percent from last quarter."

Daniel frowned. "You're sure?"

"Daniel, when have you ever known me to make a mistake where profits are concerned?"

His frown became a forbidding scowl. What kind of

growth would have made him happy? Kathryn wondered. It seemed like a lot to her.

"All right." Daniel sighed. "Double the wages again."

"What?" Kathryn's exclamation was lost in the explosion of Hans's laughter.

"We can't do that, Daniel," Hans told him.

"Of course we can."

"Daniel, we're already paying them five dollars a day!"

Five dollars a day. Tommy made five dollars a week for double the work. If Daniel—if *they*—paid these workers an extra twenty-five dollars a week . . . that money, saved and squirreled safely away, would armor them against so many disasters. She felt security, her family's *future*, slipping through her grasp like gold turned to slick, glittering sand.

"So?"

"So the same thing will happen that happened the last time you did that. They'll all be so damn grateful they'll work twice as hard. The last thing they want is for the smelter to lose money and close down."

"Did you tell them they won't lose their jobs no matter what?"

"Daniel, if you'd lived their life, would *you* believe that? Hell, it took years for me to trust it."

"But we keep making a profit!"

Confusion whirled, spun wildly with fear. She couldn't have heard right. Daniel didn't *want* to make money? What kind of careless irresponsibility was that?

"If they keep pushing themselves to work any harder, you're going to have people keeling over at their machines. You don't want that, do you?"

"Of course not." His gaze traced the yard, the rows of comfortable cottages. "Let's build them some new houses, then. These are kind of small."

"They're only two years old! And there's no way I want all the wives after me because they've got *more* floors to polish and windows to wash and furniture to dust." Hans smiled indulgently. "Leave it alone, Daniel. There's no sin in making money."

Little do you know, Daniel thought in frustration. He'd vowed five years ago to rid himself of his corrupt and corrupting inheritance, and he was richer now than he'd been on the day he'd made that pledge.

"How about—"

"Daniel." Kathryn's fingers tightened around his arm. "Perhaps Mr. Peterson is right."

Something dark shadowed Kathryn's beautiful features. Disapproval? Fear? He couldn't read her well enough to decipher it, and suspected that deep inside he didn't want to.

She just doesn't understand, he promised himself.

"Kathryn, it's none of your concern."

He saw her swallow hard, her brow clearing. "You're already paying them more than generously," she said evenly.

But it's Edward's money. He bit back the words before they could spill out. It was not greed but practicality that had spawned her comments.

It was unrealistic to expect perfection in a brand-new marriage, that they would be as perfectly attuned in opinion and thought as they were in bed. It would be ridiculous of him to be disappointed.

"All right," he agreed reluctantly. "We'll leave things alone for the time being."

Until he could come up with something better. And preferably much more expensive.

Daniel spent that night, in a cozy, clean inn fifteen miles from Denver, in a fever of exploration. Running his hands, his mouth, his gaze over Kathryn again and again, burying them both in sexual pleasure. Assuring himself that, yes, he knew the woman he married. Knew the important things, the deep, easy way she shared her passion, the tenderness of her gaze and touch. The joy that sprang up and took flight when their bodies joined.

At four o'clock the next afternoon, he stood on the diamond-cut marble walk in front of the mansion Edward Sellington had built and watched her gaze lift up, and up, to the turreted roof sheathed in charcoal gray slate that swallowed light and life, studded with the ugly square protrusions of a dozen chimneys. He watched her awe rise as well, the bright sheen of excitement in her eyes. Her lips parted the exact same way they did when he kissed her.

He'd considered taking her to the house he'd lived in the last five years, the refuge that was no longer a refuge. Or at least preparing her for what awaited. But he'd done neither. He wasn't sure why. There was so much yet to tell her, so much to discover, and he liked things the way they were. Shouldn't they have a little while to indulge in honeymoon bliss before beginning the challenge of building a marriage between strangers? And facing the complexities and challenges of the inheritance he decried?

So he'd grabbed her hand and hustled her past the single reporter loitering outside, brushing aside Kathryn's questions until the massive gate clanged shut behind them with a ringing sound like a death knell. The oppression swamped him, just as always, like having a prison door close behind him for the last time. He had a pang of regret for his comfortable, modest place in Curtis Park, luxurious only in the number of people he employed. But the fence here was higher, the facilities to house a score of guards available, and the buffer of thick vegetation between the house and the world much wider.

"This is yours?" she asked, pulling her gaze away from the massive structure at last.

"Yes."

"Daniel?" Sunlight showered her hair as if it had been sprinkled with gold dust. "How rich *are* you?"

"Very."

Her head tilted, her expression betraying no emotion. "Why didn't you tell me?"

"Because it has nothing to do with you."

Her head jerked back. "Daniel, I'm your wife."

"It doesn't matter how much money I have now. Because I'm giving it all away."

Chapter 13

What could Daniel have meant?

Confusion and dread spiked her wonder as Daniel, his face drawn with tension, ushered her into his house . . . though house hardly seemed the appropriate appellation. The rooms delivered on what the massive, elegant facade had promised. Soaring ceilings swirled with ornate plaster vines and curving ornaments. Floors of rich wood and dark marble gleamed as if a layer of glass had been laid over them. Enormous arches guarded the entrance to rooms paneled in dark, shining carved wood.

The rooms were as ostentatious as they were beautiful. No hint of merry sunlight dared interrupt the brooding grandness. Now and then, she saw people scurry by, lifting a hand in acknowledgment of Daniel before they hurried off again. No doubt they accounted for the impeccable condition of the house, their intentness of purpose marking their duties despite the fact that none wore a servant's uniform.

But there her expectations ended. For while the rooms had obviously been dusted and polished with

179

ruthless energy, most were otherwise completely empty. No jewel-toned rugs softened the hard floors. Darker rectangles marked where paintings had once hung on walls covered with sun-streaked moiré.

What could have happened? Kathryn wondered. Could he have given so much money away already? Panic knocked in her chest. But the ubiquitous staff belied that notion. And he *had* told her he was very rich.

Just before he'd told her he was going to get rid of it all.

The plan that had seemed so simple, if ridiculously improbable, when she'd conceived it was twisting and turning into complexities she could barely guess at. But Daniel's hand was solid in hers. She clung to it, and the knowledge that, if there was far more—and less—here than she'd expected, at least Isabelle would not be returning to Simon Moore's.

Daniel stopped on the landing at the top of a long, winding staircase that emptied into a hallway where the red-and-blue-striped silk on the walls had faded to weak pastels.

"There's a good deal more to tell you," Daniel said, brows drawn into a harsh slash. "I know it's confusing, and it's a lot all at once. I'll explain later, but now I need to—"

"It's all right."

"You don't have to come," he said. His grandmother was not to be inflicted on the unprepared. Much less on a young woman whose life had changed radically in the last few days. "Are you hungry? I could take you to the kitchen, get you something."

She was so lovely, he reflected. Even now, after looking at little else but her for days, the shock of her beauty hadn't even begun to wear off. Just the sight of her still gave him a little jolt.

But she hadn't wanted him to raise the smelter workers' wages. And she'd gazed at this ridiculous mansion like it was the grandest thing she'd ever seen, an answer to all her dreams.

"I'm going with you."

"She's not well at all," he warned her.

"All the more reason for me to come along," she said firmly, and he felt a rush of warmth, the kind that had nothing to do with sex and everything to do with the fact that, for once, he didn't have to do this alone.

A man waddled down the hall toward them, feet softly slapping the floor in quick, short steps. His round face gleamed with sweat and what appeared to be genuine pleasure. "Daniel! You're home."

"Don't I always do as you tell me?"

"Only when it's what you're planning to do anyway."

The man was nearly as broad as he was tall, his bulk clothed in perfectly cut gray wool. Kathryn thought that if someone tipped the man on his side, he might roll down the hall as easily as a ten-pin ball. His grin faded as soon as he turned his attention to her.

"Ah, Daniel, what did you bring home this time?" he asked with a mix of exasperation and indulgence.

Daniel drew Kathryn to his side. "This is Kathryn, Libeus. My wife."

Libeus's round, eloquent face was wiped clean of

expression, as if a damp cloth had been drawn over a slate. "Pardon me, ma'am. Daniel did not inform me of your . . . he did not inform me of *you*."

"Kathryn, I'd like you to meet Libeus Hungate. We work together."

"Work together?" Libeus bowed formally toward Kathryn, a gesture that seemed curiously natural to his rotund bulk. "I am his assistant, Mrs. Hall."

"My assistant? Doesn't being my assistant imply that you follow *my* orders?"

"Being your assistant specifies that I assist in whatever way is most helpful. If that requires a creative interpretation of your instructions, so be it."

Daniel chuckled. "Oh, so that's your excuse? And here I just thought you had a natural talent for insubordination."

"One must always be aware of one's strengths and use them accordingly." He turned from Daniel to Kathryn, his warmth cooling to absolutely correct formality. "If there's anything I can do for you in the future, I would be pleased to be at your assistance as well."

"Thank you."

"How is she?" Daniel asked, the pleasantries having delayed the query as long as they could.

"Not well." Libeus shook his head, jowls jiggling like unmolded gelatin.

"How long since she's eaten?" They started down the broad hallway, and Kathryn fell into step behind them.

"Two days."

"Water?"

"No."

Guilt weighed on Daniel like an overcoat fashioned of inch-thick lead. "I shouldn't have left."

"And if I thought there was a chance in the world that you wouldn't torture yourself for years if I hadn't, I would never have telegraphed you."

"She's my grandmother," Daniel said, as if that was the only explanation necessary.

Libeus sighed deeply. "I know."

As they wound deeper and deeper into the mansion, Daniel questioned Libeus about the details of his grandmother's condition. Despite her best efforts, Kathryn completely lost track of the twists and turns, of the echoing hallways and the empty rooms they passed. She knew she'd never find her way out by herself.

Finally, they stepped through a massive set of double doors and into a room that looked exactly as the entire mansion must once have. Dark portraits of forbidding, bejeweled women, their gilded frames as elaborate as the silk-upholstered furnishings, glowered down on rugs so thick an earring lost in one would surely never be found again. Velvet shadowed the windows and covered tasseled pillows. Kathryn wondered about her vague sense of recognition until she realized that the rich elegance of the decor reminded her of Simon Moore's apartments. One of the silk-covered settees was, she was sure, identical, something which probably would have caused no small amount of horror to the room's owner.

The air was heavy with the scent of roses, which was unable to hide a strong, medicinal odor and the faint smell of urine. Another pair of broad double doors opened off a small alcove at the back of the room. A high, mournful cry, too stripped of energy to be a wail, drained through them.

Daniel took a breath, squaring his shoulders, and his grip on Kathryn's hand tightened. But he said: "Would you like to wait here?"

She studied him, trying to decipher whether he actually preferred to face his grandmother alone. Any curiosity she might have had was well drowned by the dread engendered by that eerie, unremitting sound.

"Do you *want* me to leave you alone?" she finally asked, though she figured a good wife would have known without being told.

It was on the tip of Daniel's tongue to say yes. He wanted to protect her from unhappy encounters such as this. But there was importance in the truth, too, wasn't there? Especially when their marriage still suffered so many sins of omission on his part. How would they ever learn each other if they hid behind *shoulds*?

"No," he said finally.

"Then my place is with you."

He leaned down and stamped a hard kiss on her mouth, right there in front of Libeus, leaving her pink and flustered despite all the kisses they'd shared.

"All right, then."

The doors swung open at a touch, and the volume of the crying increased. The room was as elegantly furnished as the one they'd just left, dominated by a gorgeously carved mahogany four-poster. At their entrance, a pretty, dark-haired young woman dressed as a nurse sprang up from a small chair stationed beside the bed.

"Oh, Mr. Hall, you're back!"

"Yes." There was a slight ripple underneath the bed-clothes, the only hint—besides that unearthly cry—that there was someone in the bed.

"Dr. Wynkoop was here this morning," the nurse reported, stepping aside to allow Daniel access to the bed.

"And?"

"She's the same, sir. I'm sorry."

"Did he give her anything?"

"Yes. It's wearing off now, obviously, but I daren't give her another dose for another two hours."

He stared down at the bed, a muscle going tight in his jaw, the set of his shoulders rigid and weary. This was a different man, Kathryn thought, than the breezy, confident one who'd played the reporter, and the distant, controlled one who she'd met upon entering the stage. And far different from the deeply passionate one she knew best. Another side to her husband and, even in her concern, she filed it away.

"Has she slept?" he asked quietly, barely audible over the lament.

"A few hours, after the first dosage."

The cries echoed strangely as he just kept looking at her, an eerie enough sound to make Kathryn shudder a little. If an echo of that sob could be heard on the street, it was no surprise that the children thought the Sellington Mansion haunted.

"She's been so confused lately," Daniel said at last. "I'd hoped . . . well, I thought perhaps she wouldn't take note of the days. That she wouldn't know if I were gone for a while. Was it very long before she began crying?"

The nurse pursed her lips and gave a slight shake to her head—reluctantly, Kathryn thought, as if she knew her answer would add to Daniel's burden and she didn't wish to do that.

"Would you go down to the kitchen, ask Mrs. Hughes to send up some broth? Perhaps she'll eat now that I'm here."

"I'm sure she will." She scurried to comply with his request.

"Oh, and Julia?" he called after her, halting her departure just as she reached the doors. "Thank you for everything. I know it is not easy."

Her smile was brilliant. "I don't mind."

She doesn't mind as long as it's Daniel who asks her, Kathryn thought. The little twinge of venom surprised her. Was that jealousy, then? Of a man she barely knew, just because a pretty young thing smiled at his appreciation?

It was not something of which to be proud.

He took no notice of Julia's departure. He merely sucked in a deep breath, then sank carefully down on the edge of the bed.

"Shhh," he said softly. "It's all right. I'm here."

Her crying halted immediately. "Edward?"

"I'm here," Daniel repeated.

Her sigh of relief was a long, sliding note. "I looked for you," she said, in a voice that quavered and broke. "I waited for you to come home, and then I looked, and I looked, and I couldn't—" Her breath caught on a sob.

"I'm home."

Kathryn didn't want to startle the woman. But the compulsion to touch him, to lay her hand on his shoulder in pride and comfort, drove her forward.

The woman's skin lay loose over her bones; her hair was gray and coarse, fashioned into a complex, dated arrangement on the top of her head. Around her on the bed were—

Kathryn felt her eyes pop wide. They couldn't be real, could they? Ropes of pearl, glittering chains of gold studded with gems, a snaking loop of what seemed to be one diamond strung right after another, lay twisted and ignored as if they were the leftover threads from a morning's darning. Mrs. Sellington clutched an egg-sized red stone set into a swirl of gold in her decimated hand. More stones glittered at her slack earlobes and encrusted a ring around her thin, wrinkled neck.

"They're real," Daniel said over his shoulder, matter-of-fact, a little amused, as if he'd gotten used to them long ago.

As if anyone ever could! Even her imagination, extreme as it was, had never conjured up wealth such as this.

"But Daniel—"

"I know. It's absurd, isn't it? But they're the only thing that comforts her, other than me."

Mrs. Sellington's eyes, hazel gone pale and milky long ago, sharpened on Kathryn, her lips disappearing into a fierce frown. Kathryn had to work not to quail under that hostile glare.

"Edward, you know I don't like it when you bring those sluts near me."

Not wanting to upset the old woman further, Kathryn made to move away. But Daniel's hand came up to cover hers on his shoulder, holding her in place.

"No, this is Kathryn. We married yesterday."

"Married?" She sighed deeply. "Heavens, not another one," she said and glared at Kathryn. "I hope that *you*, at least, are worthy of him."

"I . . ."

Daniel looked over his shoulder at his wife. There was some of the pity he'd expected to find in her expression; how could there not be? But not revulsion, or fear, or even shock. As if the cruelties of life, the ravages caused by illness and madness, were not entirely strangers to her. Instead, he saw kindness, and patience, and compassion.

How lucky he was to have found her; how strange the sequence of events that had led them to one another. Fate, he reminded himself once again, was an unpredictable and ungovernable creature.

Her uncertain gaze fell to his. He smiled at her, and her expression softened, warmth welling in her bluegreen eyes.

"I promise I shall do my very, very best to be worthy of him," she said softly.

Chapter 14

By the time Daniel had sat by his grandmother's bedside for a full half hour, patiently spooning a thin beef broth into her mouth, cajoling her into swallowing it, Kathryn finally admitted to herself what she should have suspected from the start.

Daniel Sellington was not his father's son.

Oh, there'd been hints all along. She'd ignored them, set on the idea that a man raised with indulgence and privilege and power would necessarily be spoiled by them. And secure in the conviction that a man as wicked as Edward Sellington had naturally passed his unconscionable qualities on to his only son.

And just maybe, she realized, she'd ignored the idea that Daniel was a different kind of man because that distance, that contempt, allowed her to execute her plans without undue pangs of conscience. The Daniel she'd imagined *deserved* to be married for his money, *owed* her family that much. It seemed somehow less of a crime to use so blatantly for her own purposes a bad man than a good one.

But that Daniel did not exist. Would it have changed

anything? she wondered. His goodness did not miti-
gate her own desperation in any way. It only made her
feel a great deal more guilty about the steps she'd
taken.

If she'd known the kind of man he truly was, perhaps, *perhaps*, she'd only have had to go to him and
ask him to return the money his father had swindled.
Maybe he would have done so. Could she have taken
that chance? And would it have been enough money
to support them all through the terrible blows that fate
had a way of handing to those who didn't deserve
them?

Well, it was too late. There was only one thing she
could do about it at this late date, and it was exactly
what she'd told Mrs. Sellington.

Perhaps she'd married him for all the wrong reasons. But she was going to try mightily to be a wife
to him for all the right ones.

Mrs. Sellington had slipped into sleep at last, the
coverlet over her skeletal torso rising and falling
faintly. Daniel set the soup bowl on a bedside table,
dropped the spoon into it, and expelled a weary sigh.
He kneaded the back of his neck as if it pained him,
and she immediately went to him, pushed his hands
away, and took up the massage.

"Ahhh." Her fingers dug into muscles drawn into
knots, soothed away the stiffness of tension that had
settled right into the base of his neck. "Kathryn, I need
to tell you—"

"It can wait."

He savored that temptation for a moment. He'd love
to wait, surrendering to the magic her hands worked

on his muscles, and maybe encouraging it to turn into magic of another sort as well. It would give him time to deliberate, allowing him to carefully select the correct things to tell her and the best way to do it. For he couldn't tell her everything. There were things buried deep that he would rather not remember himself. He wasn't dragging those malignant memories and scalding emotions up to soil her shining presence.

"It's already waited longer than it should have," he said. She was his wife. She had a right to know something of the man she'd married.

Where to go posed a problem. Libeus had hovered in the sitting room for quite some time, poking his head in at regular intervals to inquire if he could be of assistance, his small, dark eyes bright with curiosity and disapproving suspicion. Daniel had finally set him off on an item of business that they both knew was simply an excuse. And there would certainly be others, hovering in the halls, dusting in whatever room they tried, their curiosity the reason and their work the excuse, who would be avidly listening for a hint of the identity of the woman that Mr. Hall had brought home.

He did keep a bedroom in the mansion for the rare occasions when he deemed it necessary to stay overnight. On the top floor, in the far southwestern corner, it was close enough to his grandmother's apartments that he could be summoned quickly, but well away from most of the activity in the house. A small room, intended for an unimportant scullery maid, tucked up and away. But, four stories up, looking out on the neat roll of lawn and the sweep of mountains in the dis-

tance, it reminded him a little of the tree house he and
Nic had built when they were twelve.

It was the only room in the whole damn mausoleum
where he could breathe.

And so the room that Daniel took Kathryn to was
about as different from his grandmother's suite as a
prison cell to a room at Brown's Palace. The walls
were starkly whitewashed, the floors bare. Hooks on
the wall held one single change of clothing. No curtains shielded his view, for that was why he'd chosen
this room in the first place. The lone drawback was
the low, slanted ceiling. He had to duck as he entered
to avoid banging his head, which he'd done a few too
many times for comfort.

Which, Libeus claimed, explained a lot.

The room contained no chairs. It caught him by surprise that, after all the unabashed intimacies they'd
shared, he felt somewhat awkward bringing her to his
bedroom and asking her to sit on his bed. It seemed
so . . . blatant.

But she sat down without hesitation, the springs
barely squeaking beneath her light weight, her back
straight and feet politely on the floor. He took a place
at the foot of the bed and the whole mattress dipped
his way, so she had to put down a hand to keep from
tipping over.

"Kathryn, I . . ." Lord, he had no idea where to start!
There was so much of it, some that he hardly remembered, some that he remembered only too well.

Late-afternoon sun slanted through the lone window. The walls glowed rose, a beautiful, clear color

that was completely eclipsed by the lovely hues of her skin.

So much for awkwardness. He bounded across the bed, settled himself with his back against the wall. Then he tugged her to his side so she leaned against him, the back of her head tucked comfortably against his shoulder, his arm wrapped around her. "There. That's better."

"It's perfect," she agreed.

Where to begin? Nowhere but the beginning, he supposed, or at least the beginning he knew.

"I was born Daniel Sellington."

She started, and he looked down to find her eyes wide and swirling with emotion but her face carefully blank. "Ah, you know the name."

"I . . . well . . . who doesn't?" she admitted.

"That's true. Well, I—"

"Daniel . . . if you're really Daniel Sellington, are we really married? You told me your name was Hall—"

"Of course we are," he assured her. "I've been a Hall since I was ten. It is my legal name, just as I told you."

Thank God. And it had been an unexpected bonus, not to have to carry the hated name of Sellington. *Mrs. Hall.* She rather thought she could grow very fond of that name.

"Edward—well, I'm sure you've heard some about him, if you know enough to recognize the name. I don't how much you know—"

"Why don't you tell me it all?" she suggested. "The

papers are hardly the most reliable source of the story."

"True." One of his hands was stroking her arm, an automatic gesture, as if he'd already accustomed himself to having her beside him, as if his hands moved to touch her without there needing to be conscious thought behind the caress.

She, however, might never accustom herself to his touch, as a shimmer of warmth glowed behind each stroke.

"Well, he was a rich man. I imagine you know that much, at least. Obscenely rich. I don't really know how he earned it all. A variety of businesses, some mining, a few other things that weren't obvious by the time I was old enough to take a look at the books. Or were well hidden by then."

I could tell him about some of that, she thought. More than most men would want to know about their fathers.

"His father was rich, too, and a fair amount came from him, though Edward multiplied it many times over. What a lot of people don't know, however, is that Edward was not a nice man at all."

But she knew that, too. As had her father, only too well.

"Having all that money . . . I don't think it's good for a person. I don't suppose anyone ever told him 'no' his whole life. I know damn well his mother didn't. The money, and the power that went with it—okay, I was young, I only remember a little. But I always had the sense that he was certain that he was the very center of the whole damn world, and woe to anyone who didn't bow to that. That he believed that the petty little rules that applied to the rest of the world did not apply to him."

There was surprisingly little emotion in his voice. A tremor there, a suggestion of tightness breaking through. As though he'd gone over this so many times already in his mind that he'd muted the powerful emotions that must accompany it.

"My mother, the woman who gave birth to me, died shortly after." Daniel paused, swallowed hard. This part was difficult. And not something he could tell her yet. Maybe not ever. He'd spent far too much time trying to forget it. He did not want his wife to know that the blood of a man who could do such terrible things ran in his veins. And maybe had left a hidden mark somewhere which would rise and seize him if he wasn't very, very careful.

"Edward married again shortly afterward. My stepmother—she's always been my mother to me, loved me as much as anyone could. But he wasn't any . . . kinder, and we finally left when I was nine. Disappeared to the middle of Minnesota."

And then came another memory best left buried deep and unexamined. He paused a moment, struggling to keep it where he'd locked it long ago, for his own response to what happened was as difficult to remember as the event itself.

Her form was relaxed against him. As if she'd found the one place on earth where she was always meant to be. Her arm came around, looped across his stomach, and he caught his breath. Damn, but it was such a luxury, to be able to hold her anytime he wanted!

"Is that when your father disappeared?" she prodded.

"That's when Edward disappeared." *Edward*, she thought. He did not even give him the honor of calling him father. "My mother remarried, to a very fine man. They're my parents now, the only ones that matter. He was raising a nephew—that's Nic—and they adopted two more. No one could have had a better family."

Perhaps that explained something of who he'd become. How he could have grown into such a fine man despite being born of Edward Sellington. Because he'd been raised by another man, obviously a much better man.

"When I was eighteen, though, I decided it was time to claim what Edward had left. I guess even then I had a vague notion of doing something good with it. I went to New York first, found that damn mansion I'd been born in still maintained as if they expected him to come home any day!"

He'd walked into that dark palace and the memories tumbled down on him like a black avalanche. He'd hardly been able to breathe the whole time he'd been there.

"The trustees were a bunch of rich, powerful, old men, and they didn't much like the idea of turning control of all that money over to an eighteen-year-old stripling who'd appeared from the middle of nowhere. We fought for four months before they had to relinquish it." He'd taken bitter pleasure in that. He couldn't beat his father—Edward's death had robbed him of that satisfaction—but he'd beaten a half dozen men just like him.

But if he'd had a notion that, in returning to that house, he'd be able to exorcise a few demons, he'd been quickly disabused of it. He'd fled the cursed place as soon as he'd concluded his business.

"What'd you do with the house?"

"Hmm?"

"Well, I don't imagine you just left it there to molder away, did you?"

"What a wise wife you are." To reward her, he kissed her, lingering over it longer than he intended because her mouth responded so sweetly to his while his heart lifted with the possibilities for this marriage, hopes that seemed to be growing every day. Somehow, in their impulsiveness, it seemed he'd had the extreme good fortune to stumble into something greater than he'd ever hoped to have. "It's a maternity hospital now." He grinned, for that *had* exorcised a good share of the demons, far more effectively than he had been able to on his own. "A charity one, no less. I can't imagine the neighbors are too pleased with me, but what the hell."

He looked so pleased with himself for that, Kathryn thought, his eyes glowing, an easy smile washing away the lines of tension that often gathered between his brows. She tried to be just as proud. It *was* a good thing he'd done, a wonderful thing. And she, more than anyone, understood full well how difficult it was for those who couldn't pay to get competent doctoring. But the cold reality of poverty still shivered up her spine. If Daniel truly meant to rid himself of all his wealth, and they, or one of their children, grew seriously ill, would someone extend the same charity to *them*?

"So you left," she prompted, not wanting to settle into that train of thought.

"Yes. The lawyers said Grandmother was here, she'd gone looking for my father after he disappeared and never came back. I wanted . . ." Beneath the arm she'd draped over his waist, she felt his renewed anxiety, the jump of muscles responding to his mind's pain. "Wanted to confront her, I guess, like I'd never be able to my father. My memories of her were . . . difficult. She had a lot to do with the man he became, as much as the money in some ways. Always insisting that whatever he thought, whatever he wanted, was more important than what anyone else did. And she never once did a thing to gainsay him when . . ." His hand on her waist clenched, released. "Not even for me."

What had his father done? A lot more than she knew. As terrible as Edward had been to others, to her father, that cruelty clearly hadn't spared his own family. She was not unfamiliar with the pain that humans could wreak on their own flesh and blood. Was it better to draw Daniel's out, face it, and then put it away? Or to let it remain buried in the dark?

"The vast majority of the estate was left to me. I had every intention of kicking her out on the streets. Making her learn what it was like without this." His gesture encompassed the entire mansion and all that went with it. "Find out what life is like for most people. I figured maybe she'd come to regret what she'd done. And what she didn't do."

"But you let her stay. You ensure she's cared for."

He shrugged. "She was pretty much already like that when I found her. Confused, broken, desperate. Who can be angry with someone like that? She's not the woman I hated all those years anymore. There'd be no point in pretending she was."

"She calls you Edward."

"That started as soon as she saw me again. I'm not entirely sure why. I've always been told I favor my mother more, at least in coloring. But there must be something in my features that her ruined mind latched on to. And what good would it serve to disabuse her? I tried briefly but it only upset her. And, as drawn as she looks now, she was worse then. I couldn't imagine how she'd managed to stay alive so long. As soon as she decided I was Edward returned to her, she began to improve a little. Seemed to me that doing anything else was just cruel."

"But you're so careful with her, Daniel, the way you made sure she was fed. That is more than just not being cruel."

He ran a finger along the clean line of her jaw, enjoying the softness, the fine texture. The admiration in her voice made him feel like the world's most famous hero. Half of him wanted to leave her with her illusions so she kept looking at him like that. But it was not a good idea to build a marriage on illusion. "That's so easy to do, Kathryn. Because you know what? I don't feel a damn thing for her."

"Nothing?"

"A little pity. And a devout hope that I never, ever end up like that."

She wasn't shocked at his admission, like he'd expected. Instead, she shocked him, by lifting her chin to give him a firm kiss, one that almost made him forget about his past and his family and fortune.

"I am so proud," she said when she pulled back, "to call you husband."

"Well." He cleared his throat, not knowing what to do next. Who would have thought?

But he quickly figured out what to do next after all. He skimmed his free hand up her waist to cup the firm curve of her breast. "Do you know, I don't think we've made love for at least, oh, ten hours or so. That's a record for our marriage. I don't figure we should let it go much longer," he said soberly. "Why take any chances?"

She tried to frown at him, but her eyes sparkled. "Tell me the rest of the story first," she said.

"Aww . . ." He reluctantly released her, and she looked pointedly down at his empty hand, a mischievous smile flirting with the corners of her mouth.

"I didn't say you had to move that."

"Oh." Quickly, just in case she changed her mind, he settled his hand back over her breast, his fingers wide. He felt the thump of her heartbeat beneath his thumb. "I could get to like this."

"I should hope so," she said archly.

"But I'm not sure I can talk coherently."

"Well, then . . ." She pretended as if she were going to move away.

"Too late. I've got you now," he said, and gave her breast a gentle squeeze that left them both short of breath. "Okay, I'll talk fast.

"Anyway, considering her condition, I was stuck in Denver for a while. I tried living here, but it's—well, you'll see, it's like living in a mausoleum. And, as soon as word got out that I was here, I was . . . Kathryn, you can't imagine how bad it was! The papers, people who wanted money for some surefire scheme or another, heartbreaking stories that were, I finally figured out, at least three-quarters lies, women who"— a hint of red colored the tips of his ears—"wanted to meet me, either to show me off at some charity ball or another, or to, well . . ."

Or to marry him. Or get their hands on his money one way or another. Guilt and jealousy were an acid mix, burning their way through her.

"I could have dealt with it better, I guess. But I wasn't nineteen yet, and, well—" He shrugged. "Nobody knew me as Daniel Hall. I *am* Daniel Hall. So I just made Daniel Sellington disappear."

"And nobody ever discovered you?"

"No. It's a big house, lots of people in and out. Dressed like a servant, or a deliveryman—nobody ever looked at me twice. Who'd expect a Sellington to go around looking like that?"

This was so nice. Curled up on his bed, his hand upon her with a husband's possession and warmth, a simmer of desire running beneath it all, waiting for its chance to burst into full life, and knowing it would come. Listening to him talk, learning something of a man who was so much more than she'd ever expected. As bad as her luck had run for sixteen years, this was almost worth it all. She could hardly believe that she was there with him.

Perhaps, she thought, she could tell him the truth. He was an understanding man, a man with a deep compulsion to help others. Surely he could forgive her.

But this contentment seemed so fragile. So easily gained, so easily lost. Nothing good in her life had ever lasted. How could she risk this now?

And, while he might have forgiven his grandmother, he didn't *love* her. And Kathryn suddenly, desperately, wanted her husband to love her.

Well there, Kathryn, aren't you a greedy wench? her conscience jeered. *You got the money you were after, and now you want him, too?*

But how could she not? She wasn't strong enough not to want him. She doubted any woman would be.

"And it's so much easier to give the money away," he continued, "when nobody knows who I am. I can sort through the stories I hear and find the people who are truly in want, rather than trying to unearth the one real need among two dozen people clamoring for cash."

"Daniel." She laid her hand on his chest, over that big, wonderful, hurting heart. "I admire your generosity. But did you mean what you said, about giving it *all* away?"

"Of course I did."

"But Daniel—"

He knew it was not something most people would understand. Why had he expected his wife to immediately see the necessity of it?

"That money is—I know it must seem strange to attribute this power to an inanimate thing. But it's *evil*, Kathryn. It corrupted him, and everyone else who had it, and let him get away with the immorality for his whole life. I *hate* that money. I don't want it, don't want anything to do with it." The emotions, cold and hot at the same time, churned inside him, all the anger that had been so painfully birthed so many years ago. His father. His money. They were the same, couldn't she see that?

"But Daniel," she said carefully, "it's just money. It can't make people do things, or not do things—"

"But it's not just money! It's *too much* money. Wealth on that scale means power, the kind that encouraged a man, maybe *any* man, to believe that he's *more* than just a man. And that's a dangerous, dangerous thing."

"But you've still got some left, right? Why haven't you gotten rid of it all already, given that's how you feel about it?"

"Oh, I've tried." He shook his head in exasperation. "But it's not that simple. I want it to go to people who need it, who can use it well. And it can't be too much at once. Enough to spur incentive, not kill it. To help, not hurt. Because I know how it can hurt. I can't do that to someone else."

He meant it, she saw, and an icicle of terror pierced her warm comfort. He wanted to rid himself of that money every bit as much as she craved its security.

"But Daniel . . . what will you do, once it's all gone? How will you live?"

"I'll work just like everyone else."

He'd work? Only a man who'd never known what it was like to lie in his bed at night doubled over with hunger pains, to watch someone he loved die without a doctor's care, to lose his sister to a desperate gamble, would say that so easily. Assume it so simply.

She had to make him understand. "Daniel, you're— we're a family now. We'll have children, they'll be our *responsibility* to make sure they're cared for. We have to consider them, too."

Family. Children. Everything had happened so quickly, been in such a whirl . . . the thought blind- sided Daniel, left him reeling as if he'd just been spun like a child's top. *Children.* A little boy, maybe, who he'd teach to play baseball, just as his father had him. Or a girl, a girl who looked like her mother—oh, God, he'd be beating boys off with a bat!

He slid his hand down, over her narrow ribs, to the flat, small plane of her belly.

"Kathryn?" he asked with a mix of hope and terror.

Her eyes shimmered with that same mix. "I don't know. It's too soon."

"Oh." The world stopped reeling, settled back on its axis, tilted a few degrees from where it had rested before. "I'd always take care of you, Kathryn, and our children."

"But—"

"You're my wife." And she should trust him on this. Believe that he would always make sure she had what she needed. "I really am quite competent in most ways, Kathryn. I promise I'll always take care of you," he repeated.

Her father, she suspected, had made those exact same promises to her mother.

"But why take a chance we don't have to?"

She didn't understand, he thought. But she would. Someday she would.

"It's not my money," he told her. "It's *his*." The bitterness contained in that single syllable, *his*, told her more about his father than his words had. "And it's theirs, all the people that he took it from."

"But it is yours now," she argued. "Isn't it better to get *something* good from him? To use that wealth to secure your family's future?"

"I have to do this," he said, in a tone that warned her to drop the topic, immediatly, or risk something she had no intention of risking. "I *have* to."

"But what," she persisted, knowing she was stepping onto thin ice but unable to do anything else. She had to make him *see*. "What if, God forbid, something happens to you? What do we do then?"

He simply stared at her, immovable in his determination.

Okay, she thought. There was nothing else she could do right now. Given time, he'd understand. She had to believe that.

And so she moved closer to him instead, hearing with gratification the way his breath caught as she pressed her body to his, feeling her own senses leap to dazzling life the moment his mouth met hers. Because his touch had the power to chase fear in an instant, and his kiss filled her with a faith that she felt at no other moment.

Because there, that moment, in Daniel's arms, she was safe.

Chapter 15

$\sim\!\!\sim\!\!\mathcal{O}\mathcal{O}\!\!\sim$

Kathryn moved through the next few days in a shifting haze, as if she couldn't quite reconcile the information her senses provided with the things she knew to be true deep inside.

She appeared to be warm and safe. For the first time in her recollection she pushed away from the table completely full, without feeling compelled to gobble up every crumb in case she'd never get another chance. Without the necessity of working, she found herself somewhat at loose ends. She tried to pitch in with the care of the house—here was something, at least, she knew well—but the staff, if not openly suspicious of Daniel's interloping new wife, did not appreciate her encroaching on their duties. And, as Daniel moved all the employees from his Curtis Park house to the mansion, there were plenty of hands already. So she had the immense luxury of having no pressing duties, something that she quickly discovered afforded far too much time for her mind to spin.

Unable to shake the bone-deep certainty that she did not belong there, she hadn't earned it, she feared that soon it would all disappear like the wisp of imagination that it simply must be.

She'd had to do some quick talking to Daniel around the topic of her family, and found her previously glib tongue had lost its nimble flair. No, they didn't have to run out to meet her family; she'd telegraphed them about their marriage, they were thrilled for them, but wouldn't dream of taking him away from his grandmother and duties now. They'd meet soon, once things calmed down. And yes, her sister had managed to find someone to help her during her confinement. And no, he really did not need to wire them personally.

Those explanations would only satisfy him for a few weeks. What then? Invent some sudden, horrible tragedy that would end any discussion of her family once and for all? It was the only answer she could come up with, and it was distasteful enough to give her sharp pains in her stomach anytime she contemplated it.

She felt as if she were threading her way through a maze studded with trapdoors and quicksand, each step threatening to send her hurtling down. She had to go see her real family, but she couldn't figure out a way to do it. Reporters still hovered outside the front gates, leaving them effectively imprisoned. What excuse could she give Daniel for venturing out without his company that would not raise his suspicions?

It was as if they were bound together by spider threads, thin and glittering, too fragile to be tested. Daniel didn't demand more information about her family, which made her alternately grateful and a little bewildered. Perhaps he felt the fragility of their bonds, too, and had no more wish to stretch those threads than she did.

The only time her fearful haze thinned was when Daniel took her to bed. There, lost in the wonder that they created together, in the pleasure that pierced deep and sweet each time he sank into her, she felt those spiderwebs thicken and strengthen, felt hope swell and rise with her rapture. Then, she wasn't playacting at all. It was the only thing in her life that felt completely real.

Three days after their return to Denver, they sat down to a luncheon of roast duck and creamed potatoes in a dining room of grand proportions furnished with nothing but an extremely ordinary, and cheap, pine table. Libeus, already seated at the far end, plucked a ripe olive from a crockery bowl, popped it in his mouth, and nodded at her without expression. When they were in the same room, his usually merry eyes focused on her with patient precision, as if he'd yet to make up his mind about her and was just waiting for her to do or say something that would reveal her true colors either way. She struggled not to allow his unrelenting scrutiny to unsettle her nerves and failed miserably.

"Thank you." Daniel accepted a composed salad from one of the servers and sighed. "I keep telling Mrs. Hughes that all this fancy food isn't necessary."

"Daniel, you must allow the woman to have her fun," Kathryn said.

He smiled at her across the table, an intimate smile that instantly recalled the morning, when they'd come down for breakfast a full two hours after they'd intended. She'd not seen him since, for he'd been closeted with Libeus all morning. Now a slow heat kindled in her belly, making her instantly wonder just how long luncheon would take. And how many times a woman could demand her wifely privileges in one day without ill-using her husband. There were *supposed* to be limits to a man's endurance, weren't there? But she'd yet to find the boundaries of Daniel's.

His gaze dropped to her mouth, traced down her neck and farther yet. Each place he looked tingled, as if he'd touched her physically, just as she knew he was in his imagination.

And then his regard moved down again and he frowned.

Frowned? The sight of her bosom had certainly never provoked a frown from Daniel before. She really doubted she could have completely lost her shape between sunup and now.

"Clothes," he said.

"Clothes?" she repeated in confusion.

"Those are the same clothes you were wearing when I met you, aren't they? All the rest of your things are probably still in Julesberg. Kathryn, my apologies. I forgot all about it."

"That's all right." And it was, mostly because she figured he hadn't been noticing her clothes because he was so fully occupied with what she looked like *out* of them. And that was hardly a bad thing for a new husband to be distracted by.

"No, it's not." His frown deepened. "You should have said something."

"Oh. Well . . ." She made a vague gesture. "I guess I forgot, too."

"If you forgot, ma'am, then I must say you are the most singular woman I've ever met," Libeus interjected smoothly. Kathryn eyed him, trying to guess whether he meant that in admiration or insult.

"Why didn't you ask me?"

Silent, Kathryn folded her hands in her lap. She hadn't been able to bring herself to ask him for anything. Not when she'd already taken so much from him without his knowledge or permission.

"As soon as we're done, I'll take you shopping," he decided. "We'll buy you a whole wardrobe. Lots and lots of clothes, in fact. How much money can we get rid of today, do you think?"

"Daniel, the very last thing in the world you want to spend your afternoon doing is buying *clothes*, and we both know it. Not to mention, if I were wasteful, you would sit there thinking of all the people you could have given it to."

"I won't mind. Because we'll be shopping for *you*."

"They won't let you follow me into the dressing room," she told him.

"Well, shoot," he said. "What's the fun in that?"

Libeus coughed to cover his chuckle. "We have a meeting with the Gilberts this afternoon as well," he told Daniel.

"So we'll reschedule."

"There's no reason to rearrange your plans for me," she said firmly. "I'm quite capable of buying a dress or two by myself."

Daniel looked torn, caught between what was

clearly his duty, to accompany and protect his wife on her outing, and the fact that he would probably rather march outside and surrender to the reporters' inquisition than spend an afternoon shopping. Especially if he couldn't hold out hope of catching a clandestine glimpse of bare skin now and again.

"You don't know Denver that well," he objected. "There are areas that simply aren't safe."

Like where I lived for fifteen years? she thought. "I won't go to those areas, then."

Daniel shook his head. "If something happened to you . . ."

Warmth rushed over her, unexpected, achingly sweet. "Nothing's going to happen to me," she said, and, for the first time, she almost believed it. "I'll take Joey with me, if it would make you feel better."

"Joey Gibson?"

"Isn't that his name? I met him when you showed me the stables. I got the impression that the young man likely had rather good knowledge of which parts of town to avoid." And, despite his obvious loyalty to his employer, he hadn't given her away when Daniel had introduced them, for who was he to interfere with another's good fortune, so long as it didn't threaten his own? For which consideration she'd been immensely grateful.

"That's true. All right then, you can go as long as Joey accompanies you."

Relief flooded her, marred by just a twinge of guilt. She forced a light laugh. "You look like a boy who just got let out of school for the afternoon."

"I do not. I'm devastated that I'm not going to spend

all afternoon debating the advantages of twill over sateen."

"Well, *I* am thoroughly impressed that you even know there are such things."

"I've got a couple of textile mills," he admitted. "Couldn't pick out which was which if you laid them over my stomach, though." He stabbed a potato with his fork. "Libeus, give her some money."

Libeus hefted his bulk from the chair and wiggled his fingers into his vest pocket. "How much?"

"How should I know? Kathryn, how much can you spend?"

"I—" How much would be appropriate? The last thing she wanted was to appear greedy in Daniel's eyes. Even though, she thought sadly, that was the truth. "I don't know."

"Libeus, I know you know," Daniel said. "So stop pretending you don't."

"It is not usually considered a matter for masculine pride to know the price of a lady's dress," Libeus replied gravely.

"You know the price of everything."

Libeus walked over to Kathryn, all the while peeling bills off a sturdy stack. "Well, most of the things you'll want will have to be made up especially for you," he mused. "You'll pay for most of that work on delivery. I suppose a hundred dollars should be sufficient to get you started." His gaze sharpened on her. "Unless you don't think that's enough."

Not enough? A bubble of hysteria threatened to rise and break free. A hundred dollars for *clothes*? He put a nice thick bundle of well-worn bills in her hand, and her fingers curled around them of their own accord, as if they knew exactly what they held and had every intention of hanging on—more money than she'd ever called her own in her entire life.

And it wasn't nearly enough. Not to pay off Simon Moore. She pushed that unwelcome thought away; she still had some time, and this, while it might not immediately get her family out of that rathole over the saloon, was a very good start.

Simon Moore would simply have to wait.

There wasn't any way out of buying a few clothes, she supposed. While Daniel might not notice, Libeus assuredly would. But she took one glance at the prices in the small, elegant shop that Joey first led her to, winced, and headed for the nearest dry goods store. Her needlework had been good enough for more than one of Denver's richest matrons; surely it would serve for her as well. She purchased two simple, ready-made cotton dresses—not the cheapest in the store, but nearly so—plus the fabric for three more. Then she informed Joey she was going to visit her mother. He'd hemmed and hawed for a good five minutes, digging his toe into the churned-up mud that bordered the street, because he'd promised Mr. Hall he'd keep her to the safe parts of town.

But the rules that applied to the sheltered, fragile young woman that Daniel thought he'd married surely didn't apply to her, and they both knew it. And so Joey finally agreed, allowing he rather looked forward to seeing the old gang, anyway. Kathryn knew she'd tested the limits of his loyalty to an old friend. She wouldn't dare ask him to help her again.

She'd wondered how it would feel to go back into that hellish maze of tenements and squalid boarding-houses and tar-paper shacks that crowded along the right bank of the South Platte, all the way from the Omaha and Grant Smelter down to Colfax.

She was going home.

But this confused jumble of factories and dwellings hard on the edges of noisy railroad yards, the crumbling warehouses sheltering as many rodents as commercial goods, was not her home. Shouldn't have to be *anybody's* home.

The stench hit her like a wave of nausea, all the worse for having been away from it for over a week. The river was too handy a place to dump inconvenient carcasses, dead horses, mules, swine, and probably more she'd rather not think about. A group of five young boys skittered by, shotguns in hand, on the hunt for the packs of feral dogs that would bring them a precious twenty-five cents a head from the city.

"Remember when me 'n' Tommy used to go dog huntin'?" Joey asked with no small amount of nostalgia. " 'Course, none of us was ever as good as Petey was with a gun."

"You miss it, Joey?"

"Naw," he said quickly. "Well, maybe the boys, now 'n' then. But a body gets accustomed to eatin' regular, don't it?"

"That it does."

They turned a corner, carefully skirting the shattered glass from a broken streetlight, and there it was, The

THE MOST WANTED BACHELOR 215

Schatz House Billiard Hall and Saloon. Built of cheap pinkish brick, two of the four front windows had been broken out, a poster advertising shots of Taos Lightning for two bits failing to completely cover one. A scrubby pine struggled for life in a small patch of bare dirt, right next to a mounted human skull and a sign that read: *Died from asking too many questions,* a sentiment with which many of the Schatz House's patrons heartily agreed.

"Miz Jordan—I mean, Miz Hall? You all right?"

"Yeah." She searched herself for fear, for hatred, and found instead only immense relief. *I don't live here anymore.* "Yeah, Joey, I'm better than I've been in a long time."

"Tommy off workin' at the smelter, d'ya think?"

"I imagine he will be." But not for much longer, if Kathryn had anything to say about it.

"Yeah, I figured." Joey squinted off down the street, where a couple of tall, lanky young men leaned against a lamppost, smoking. "I'll leave you to your visit, then. If you're sure you're okay alone, that is."

"I'm sure."

" 'Kay. An hour?"

"That's plenty," she agreed, finding herself anxious to get home. To her husband, she thought, grinning.

The staircase leading to the upper floor was wedged in the dank, narrow space between Schatz's saloon and the equally disreputable one next door, although Flaherty's catered to the Irish immigrants, rather than the Germans, a distinction discernible only by the accents of its customers and the fact that they were more likely to burst into "The Wearing of the Green" than "Yodel Hi Lee Hi Loo."

The door's paint had peeled off years ago, leaving only a few scrapes of deep red like ancient bloodstains. It yielded an old, dull sound when Kathryn rapped on it.

"Who is it?"

"It's me."

There was a long pause; it took some time to unwrap the heavy looped and tied rope that substituted for the lock that had rusted through. And then the door eased open with a wicked shriek.

"Mother."

The daughter of a prosperous shopkeeper, Eudora Jordan was born into comfort, raised to be a lady, and married into what she thought to be solid affluence. When her husband's seemingly sturdy nest egg disappeared into the depths of Edward Sellington's fortune, never to be seen again, she'd been stunned. But when Kathryn's father had taken his own life rather than face his mistakes, leaving Eudora with three young children and another on the way, she'd been furious at his cowardly abandonment.

A person couldn't live on anger. But it provided damn-fine incentive for survival, and that monstrous rage had sustained her mother for over fifteen years and showed no signs of letting her down yet. It bolstered Eudora when she turned her meager supper portion over to her children; it kept her alive when her eldest son died in her arms; and it gave her courage when she submitted to the rutting of the piggish Herman Schatz so that he wouldn't turn her and her children out on the streets on a cold January day.

It was a hell of a lot more than she'd been able to say about her husband.

And now, over the threshold, looking into the bright, fiery eyes of her mother, Kathryn knew all that fierce anger was focused directly on her.

"Where have you been?" Eudora demanded.

"I sent you a note."

Kathryn slipped into the tiny room, one of two the Jordans called their own. This one held only a table salvaged from a scrap heap and a sagging, metal-framed bed where her brother slept, the box where he kept his things shoved underneath.

"A note! What did that tell me? All it said was not to worry. I always worry the most when someone tells me not to worry!"

Her mother was a small woman, all softness pared away years ago. The hair swirled into a high knot was thick, though dulled. She looked ten years older than her forty-three years, but it was still easy to see who her daughters favored. Her cheekbones were cleanly sculpted, her jaw uncompromising.

"And when that man delivered your sister—I thought that—I thought—" She stopped.

"You thought that I'd traded myself for her." Kathryn took her mother's hand, feeling the delicate bones shift under the loose skin. "I would have, if it came to that. And you know it would be better me than it were Isabelle."

Eudora's eyes lowered, as if she knew what she was about to say was a lie. "She's not your responsibility."

Eudora, with whatever help her children could give, had managed to keep them alive. But, since Peter's death, Kathryn had always known that anything more was up to her. Her mother was too lost to her anger, too worn down by her life, to do any more than she was.

"Sit down." They plopped on the bed, on the striped ticking that had lost most of its straw. "Here." She'd kept ten dollars back in reserve—imagine having something tucked away for emergencies!—and now she put the rest of her clothing allowance, plus what remained of the hoard she'd carried when she'd left Denver chasing Daniel, into her mother's hands. A coin spilled off the side of her palm, rolled across the floor, and spun to a stop beneath the table. "Seventy-eight dollars, sixty-three cents," she said triumphantly.

Eudora's eyes grew as round as one of the coins she clutched. "Kathryn, what have you *done*?"

"Not what you think." This happiness was an amazing feeling; she thought if any more bubbled up inside her she was going to float right up to the ceiling. "I got married."

"Married." Her mouth popped open. "Married? To *whom*?"

"His name's Daniel." She hesitated, unwilling to sully this bright moment with the name *Sellington*. "Daniel Hall. Mama, he's rich."

"Rich." Concern pulled at the corners of her mouth. "But what kind of a man is he?" She didn't have to say the rest. *Did you marry someone cruel and mean? Will he lose his money as your father did?*

"He's a good man, Mother," she said with absolute confidence. As to his ability to keep his money . . . better not to get into that right now. Daniel had been trying for almost six years and hadn't managed to get rid of it yet. Maybe, she thought hopefully, he never would.

"Mother, I thought I heard—" Isabelle stopped in the doorway from the room where she'd obviously been sleeping. Her loose hair tangled around her narrow shoulders, and a pillow crease marred her cheek. At the sight of her sister, welcome flashed briefly across her face before she rearranged her features in sulky lines. "Damn. It's you."

"Isabelle," her mother said warningly.

"As if there aren't a hundred worse things I've done than swear a little now and then."

So that was how it was going to be, Kathryn thought tiredly. Isabelle would insist on playing the wounded party. She'd always hated being told what to do, no matter how much she needed the advice.

She moved into the room, wearing an old, loose nightgown that had been washed so much the cotton was thin as gauze. Even in the dimly lit room, her breasts and the dark patch of her pubic hair were clearly visible. Embarrassed, Kathryn looked away.

"Offended?" Isabelle's brittle laughter sounded more sad than defiant. "It's nothing that plenty of people haven't seen."

"Oh, Isabelle." Kathryn squeezed her eyes shut to pinch off the threatening tears.

"Simon made Luther take me home, said I couldn't come back no matter what. I tried to go to Mattie Silks's, and Jennie Rogers's place, too, but no one else would take me on. How the hell did you talk him into giving me the boot?"

Had she really no right to interfere in her sister's life? Kathryn opened her eyes to study Isabelle. She'd always been thin, but now she looked as if a strong wind would snap her in two. Her unnaturally pale skin clung to her cheekbones, the purple shadows beneath her eyes so dark they looked like old bruises.

"Does it matter how I convinced him?" she asked. "It only matters that I did, and there's no changing it now."

Isabelle crumpled into the nearest chair, as if she lacked the energy to stand up any longer. "I suppose it doesn't." Her shoulders drooped, and she plucked at a fold of cotton over her knees. "I was making money," she said. "And all I had to do was lie there." Her lower lip trembled, like a child denied a favored toy.

Only three when their father left, Isabelle had been too young to remember when they weren't poor. Their situation, which had angered her mother and worried Kathryn, had always terrified Isabelle. There'd been more than one time that Kathryn had feared Isabelle would take their father's escape rather than face the uncertainty and struggle of another day. It was as if the fear she could neither live with nor shake had stolen pieces of Isabelle over the years, leaving her with less of herself. There was no way she could sell bits of her soul to a hundred strangers and have anything left.

"You can't mean that." Kathryn leaned forward intently. "Can you really, honestly tell me that you could lie beneath those men and believe it to be *easy*?"

"Easier than starving," Isabelle insisted without any conviction behind it.

"You're not going to starve. And you're not going back there."

"You won't tell Simon he can take me back?"

"No."

Isabelle stared at her, tears rising and hovering at the rim of her eyes before spilling over.

"Thank you."

Chapter 16

H is opponent was huge, four inches taller, out-
weighing him by over fifty pounds, an ugly
giant of Irish descent known throughout eight states as
Big John McCauly. He hadn't been defeated in forty-
two bouts, and thirty-six of those opponents had been
unconscious when they'd been dragged from the ring.
Legend held one hadn't awakened for ten days.

They circled slowly. Out of the corner of his eye
Daniel caught the twitch of muscle in Big John's
shoulder. He pulled left, feeling the whistle of that
massive fist as it just missed his right cheek. But the
next thing he knew he was flat on his back on the thick
mat on the floor, staring up at bright golden ceiling
overhead.

"Ah, damn," he swore, gingerly waggling his chin
back and forth, relieved to find it still worked.

A shadow fell across him, thoroughly blocking out
the sunlight from a bank of windows on the far side
of the room. It used to be a ballroom. He'd stripped it
of most of its fancy trappings before he'd strung rope
around posts to fashion a good-sized boxing ring, sus-

pended a punching bag from the high ceiling, the hanging of which had damn near killed him, and lugged in a dozen sandbags of various weights to serve as exercise equipment. Still, the gymnasium at his old house was much better suited than this one; gold gilt just didn't seem an appropriate background for blood and sweat, and the parquet floors didn't hold up worth a damn.

"What'd I do wrong this time?" he mumbled.

Big John shrugged his massive shoulders. "The same. Weren't looking for the second punch from the other side."

Daniel stuck out his hand. John grabbed it, pulled him to his feet in a clean, fast yank as sure as his jab.

"Much more of this, and I'm gonna have to find myself a new sparring partner," John said. "Can't even pretend you're givin' me a good fight anymore."

"Sorry." Daniel eyed his friend, debating the wisdom of a surprise attack.

"Seems to me that you just ain't got the incentive you used to. Working out all your frustrations in another venue, you might say."

Daniel felt the blush creep up his neck, but he grinned and looked over to where Kathryn perched on a rickety stool. Her answering smile was game, if a little sickly. "There is that," he said as he untied his gloves and tugged them off. "How bad did she scream this time?"

"Just the one," Big John answered. "A really *loud* one, but I have to say she's getting better. Didn't even come close to fainting this time."

"Why do you suppose she insists on watching?"

"Don't you know?" He flashed the grin that had enchanted nearly as many women as the size of the purses he'd won. "She can't resist the sight of us without our shirts." His playful punch to Daniel's midsection nearly doubled him over. "Even if you are a little puny."

"Not all of us can be the size of a mountain." Daniel scooped up a towel and looped it around his neck. Now that he mentioned it, it *did* seem like Kathryn spent an inordinate amount of time staring at his chest. And she did *not* pay equal attention to Big John's. His grin widened, until he saw the smug expression on John's face. "You want something to drink?"

"Yeah, I'll take a beer."

Despite his recent reacquaintance with the floor, there was a swagger in Daniel's step as he sauntered over to his wife. Oblivious to John's close attention and ill-disguised amusement, he bent down and pressed a pretty healthy smack on her lips, enough to make her eyes linger on him as he walked away.

John went over to Kathryn and plopped unceremoniously on the floor next to her stool. "By damn, ma'am, but it's fine to see him so happy."

She looked startled. "You think he's happy?" She gazed off at the doorway through which Daniel had just disappeared, her eyes soft and warm enough to make any man a bit jealous that that expression wasn't for him.

"Thank you," Big John said. "For doing that for him."

"Oh." She gave a small, embarrassed laugh, a becoming blush prettying up her cheeks. "I'm the one who should be thankful."

It had shocked Big John to discover Daniel had up and gotten married without a word to anyone. Daniel had never struck him as the type to do something on impulse. And he'd never been one to be led by his dick, either. He couldn't believe that Daniel hadn't even hinted that he'd met somebody special; John had been a little hurt about that. He'd always sort of fancied himself as best man, even if he had to fight Daniel's brother for the honor.

But then he'd met the girl. Oh, my, but she was a pretty thing. Maybe the fairest he'd ever seen, with that great pile of shining hair and those big blue-green eyes. Still, he'd never known Daniel to be all that susceptible to a pretty face.

But the way the two looked at each other . . . well, there was no faking that look. It gave him a little pang sometimes, wondering if he'd ever have that. Oh, women eyed him plenty, but they were all impressed by Big John, the fierce and famous prizefighter. None of them ever showed much interest in finding out about the Johnny McCauly that lived deep inside his bulk, the one who had to work not to cry when he held a baby and who'd stick needles in his own eye before he'd see a puppy hurt.

"How long have you two known each other?" she asked.

"Ah, now there's a story." He leaned back, reminiscing. "I was in New York, scrabbling to make a living on the challenge bare-knuckle circuit, working at a—" He stopped, thought better of mentioning to such a fine lady exactly where he'd been working. "Working at a particular establishment, escorting out the customers when they got too rough."

He leaned back and slapped his hard belly. "Weighed about forty pounds more then—"

"You were *bigger*?"

"Oh, yeah. All of it in my belly, too. Made me slow, and I lost a damn sight more than I won. Plus I was way too fond of drinking my profits."

She was a good listener, and he warmed to his story. "Daniel stumbled across me one morning—okay, he tripped across me, 'cause I was lying on the sidewalk where I'd been since Wild Bill Wootten laid me out with a left hook the night before. He woke me up— he was a skinny thing he was, back then, a pretty boy, looked like he was maybe fourteen. I came up swinging, and he didn't even flinch. He dragged me home— never seen a place like *that* before, I can tell you that—and cleaned me up."

"That sounds like him."

He raised a thick black eyebrow at her. "Ah, so you've discovered that about him, huh?"

"It's sort of hard to overlook."

"Guess it is at that."

Big John was oddly attractive in his own unusual way, Kathryn thought. In a mountainous, rough-featured, obey-me-or-I'll-kill-you sort of way. His hair was coal black and thick, his nose angled to one side where it had probably once been punched and decided to stay, his eyes clear and blue beneath low, prominent brows. Not handsome like Daniel, of course, but the man was sort of growing on her. Especially since he would so clearly throw himself in front of the Kansas Pacific for Daniel.

"So then what?" she prodded, intrigued by this glimpse into Daniel's past.

"He offered to back me, of course. Hired a trainer, staked me to some real good fights, told me to keep going when I damn near got myself killed the first couple times." His chuckle rattled the walls. "Think he figured to lose a bundle on me, truth, but I fooled him on that one."

Her eyes twinkled. "Has he taken to betting against you yet?"

"Naw. Much as he wants to get rid of that money, the man just hasn't got it in him to be purposely foolish about anything."

"No," she murmured, a shadow edging into her bright happiness. She didn't want to be the one thing Daniel had been foolish about.

Three weeks. Three weeks they'd been married, and for three weeks she'd been living in a glorious, golden, earthbound version of heaven. Any threats to that heaven, any hints of a more earthly world, she'd ignored, even as she knew the current happiness was only a temporary respite. But it was *her* respite, one she'd earned. Simon could wait, if only for a week; her family had enough money to eat and soon, she was certain, a much better life all around; and the temporary lifting of her responsibilities had left her giddy.

And she was terribly afraid she was falling wildly, deeply in love with her husband. Who could *not* love him? If there was a man on this earth who deserved to be loved, it was Daniel.

Perhaps he merited better than she. And if she knew, deep down, that her house of cards would come tumbling down someday soon, well, she'd deal with that when it came. For even if this was temporary, it was far, far more than she'd ever dared dream of. If she had to live on the memories for the rest of her life, it was worth it.

Her world was still bounded by the gates of the Sellington Mansion. Not much longer, and she'd have to move beyond that protective enclosure again. Kathryn found herself dreading the day. Out there was her past, and a host of problems she'd rather not face.

In here, she was Daniel's bride. And Daniel Hall's bride was, she was sure, the very best thing in the entire world to be.

Except when he insisted on sparring with Big John. She nearly died every time he got hit. The first time she'd rushed to his side, and got snarled at—by both of them—for her trouble. Now she stayed on the sidelines, biting back the cry that tried to burst out with each punch, and prayed that her husband would come to his senses before they got knocked out of him permanently. Although she had to admit to a certain surprise, despite having seen him drop that outlaw so easily, at how well he sparred with a man whose arms were a half foot longer than his and whose record was unmatched.

She'd heard of Big John. Who hadn't? His exploits were legend, and more than one patron of Herman Schatz's had won a bundle on one of his fights—or lost an even greater amount betting against him. But Daniel was quick, even quicker than John, who possessed amazing reflexes for such a large man, and she thought the fierce fire that burned in Daniel's eyes when he fought would make any man quail. It would make *her* quail if she hadn't been so certain that he'd never, ever use it against her.

"He's good, isn't he?" she asked.

"Hmm?" John swiped at his forehead with an arm the size of a locomotive piston.

"Daniel. At boxing. The first time I saw him—I didn't expect it, but he is."

"Yeah, he's good. The first time he asked me to teach him I thought he was crazy. But he's fast, and he's tough, and he takes a punch better'n I do."

"Why'd he want to learn?"

John shrugged shoulders that could have moved a mountain. "He wouldn't tell me. But I was hardly gonna say no to him, was I?"

"No." She smiled. "He's hard to say no to."

"Yeah. But he's good enough to make a fair livin' at it, should he ever have to." He laughed. "Not that he'd ever have to."

"Here we go." Daniel strolled back in, two beers in one hand, a tall glass of lemonade in the other. He stopped just inside the door and eyed them suspiciously. "You've been talking about me."

" 'Course we have," John said. "What'd you expect?"

"Do I still have a wife? And a best friend?"

"Only because I couldn't convince her to run away with me."

"You turned Big John McCauly down for me? I'm honored." Daniel handed John one bottle, then gave the glass to Kathryn. His hand hovered for a moment, then found a stray strand of hair and tucked it away behind her ear. His fingers were very warm, and he drew them along the length of her jaw, a gentle possession. "This one, John," he said softly, "I might really fight you for."

"Well, all I can say is—" He tipped his beer toward them in salute, then took a big slug. "It's about damn time."

Daniel laughed. "That it is, John."

He flopped down next to Kathryn and put a hand on her knee with obvious familiarity. Sweat gleamed on his chest, slicked his muscled shoulders. A faint bruise marked where John's fist had connected with his jaw, and she wanted to kiss it, soothing away the sting. Yet she had to admit to a certain pride as well. Her man had taken a punch from the toughest man in the state and come out whole.

Odd, how Big John's bare chest, which was far more improper for her to view than her husband's, hadn't embarrassed her at all. Hadn't affected her in any way, except a vague sort of feminine appreciation. But Daniel, bare-chested, looking so carefree and happy, made her heart flop over, her stomach quiver. Made her wish that John wasn't there, so that she could tip Daniel back on the floor and have her wicked way with him.

"All right, now, you two gotta stop looking at each other like that in public. It's downright embarrassing to witness. Plus it's kinda depressing for a single man."

The way their gazes immediately skittered away

from each other had John rolling on the floor in laughter like a six-year-old. "Oh, Lordie, look at the both of you! It's a dead tie whose color is closer to an August tomato. You look like a coupla kids who got caught out behind the barn by the preacher!"

"Heavens, what's all the hilarity?" Libeus strolled in, as impeccably dressed as if he were headed for lunch at the Denver Club. He wrinkled his nose and waved a hand in front of his face. "My, my, it's beyond me how the two of you can stink up a room this size so quickly."

"Everyone's gotta have his talents," John said.

"True."

"What's that?" Daniel asked, pointing with his beer bottle to the brown-wrapped package Libeus held.

"Ah, this." He lifted the parcel up like an offering. "It just arrived. From Minnesota."

"Really?" Daniel sprang to his feet and reached for the package.

"Nope, it's not for you." Libeus deftly pulled the small box from Daniel's reach and laid it in Kathryn's lap. "It's for her."

"But—" Bewildered, Kathryn looked from Libeus to Daniel. "What is it?"

"I think, love," Daniel said, "that it's a wedding present."

Love. She savored the word for a moment, then stored it away in her heart.

"A wedding present? You . . . you told your family? About me?"

"Of course I did." He poked at the parcel. "Actually,

I'm kind of surprised that they didn't bring it themselves."

Libeus handed Daniel a stiff, square envelope. "I
believe you'll find the answer to that in there."

He stuck his finger under the envelope's flap and
tore it open with one quick jab. He yanked out the
letter and scanned it quickly. "Oh. Dad's brewmaster
broke his leg. He'll be fine, but my father doesn't feel
like he can leave until after the harvest."

"Thought your pop made beer," John put in.

"He does." Daniel nodded at the dark amber bottle
in John's hand. "Made that."

"And a very fine beer it is. And heaven knows I've
tasted more than a few."

"I know. But that's why he's got to oversee them
bringing in the hops and the barley, and then . . . well,
it'll be a while before they can get away." After
quickly skimming the rest of the letter, he looked up
at Kathryn, smiling. "They'll come for Christmas. And
they can't wait to meet you."

"I . . . and I can't wait to meet them," she finally
managed. Would they like her? His family was obviously extremely important to him. And by Christmas
. . . by Christmas, Daniel might not want to have anything to do with her. She swallowed hard, struggled to
present a calm mien.

She couldn't lose him. But dear God, however was
she going to keep him?

Daniel nudged the package in her lap with his
knuckle. "Not too heavy," he commented, and reached
for it.

"Tut-tut!" Libeus said. "I have my instructions. And

I will certainly *not* be the one to let Mrs. Hall down. The letter is for you, but the package is *hers*, and you are not to touch it."

"Oh come now—"

"Do you really want to accept the consequences if you don't do as you were told?"

Daniel snatched his hand back. "Lord, no!"

His mother must be a fearsome woman indeed, Kathryn thought, her unease multiplying. "What would she do?"

"She might *cook*," Daniel said with a shudder. "Oh, I know it doesn't sound such a terrible punishment, but really, you have no idea."

"Well, open it!" Big John demanded, scooting forward for a good view. "I love presents."

"Oh." Kathryn's hands hovered over the package. A present. She knew nothing of presents, either giving or receiving. It was a luxury her life had not allowed. She had a vague memory of a Christmas doll when she was perhaps four, and that was it.

The wrapping paper was thick and sturdy, neatly squared at the corners, but it was smudged and worn from its journey. Thin twine crisscrossed the package, holding it secure.

She found herself strangely reluctant to open it. The anticipation was too new, too enjoyable; she wanted to draw it out for a little longer.

"Go on," Daniel urged, and she bent to her task.

Layers of paper fell away, exposing a simple, sturdy wooden box. She unlatched it and opened the lid, finding spirals of cotton batting that unfurled in one long length, revealing a deep blue velvet pouch tied with a gold cord.

She picked it up. What in the world? It felt as if it held only a handful of small stones. She shook the contents into her palm. They tumbled out, clear as water, dazzling as starlight, some as large as a shirt button, at least two or three dozen in all.

"Diamonds?"

"Shit," Daniel said. "I thought she threw those damn things down a privy hole years ago."

"Daniel?" Kathryn raised her gaze to his.

John whistled through his teeth. "Those are *some* pretty stones."

"I don't want them," Daniel said.

"Which is, I believe," Libeus put in smoothly, "why she sent them to Kathryn."

"Daniel?" she asked again.

He sighed. "Edward gave them to my mother the day they married, and she took them along when we left him. She always claimed they were part of my inheritance. I *told* her that if she gave them to me, I was going to put them where they belonged."

"There's a note," John said, plucking it from the floor where it had fallen, unnoticed, when it spilled out of the velvet bag with the diamonds. He placed it in her free hand.

The handwriting was even, feminine, easily readable.

"These are mine," it said simply. *"To do with as I choose. I certainly earned them. And I choose to give them to you. I don't imagine Daniel's too happy with me right now, but really, they're just a bunch of pretty*

rocks. Enjoy them, if you'd like. And take care of my son for me."

She looked up at Daniel. His eyes blazed with a furious fire.

He wanted her to give them up.

The diamonds weighed almost nothing in her palm. She poked at them, watching them shatter the light into tiny crystalline rainbows. She'd no idea what they were worth. Hundreds of dollars? *Thousands?* How could so much wealth be concentrated in such tiny chunks of precisely cut mineral?

I'm sorry, Daniel. She curled her fingers over the precious stones.

Chapter 17

❧

It had been late when Kathryn, dressed as a servant, slipped out of the mansion and headed into the night. She'd waited three days for the chance. At last, Daniel had been called away to attend to a problem at his knitting mill outside Denver. She'd pleaded a slight headache as an excuse not to accompany him. It had taken a fair amount of talking to convince him that she simply needed rest and privacy, and that it wasn't necessary for him to stay home, too, and watch over her.

It was later still by the time she made her way to Blake Street. She'd gone to her mother's first, thoroughly enjoying the look on her mother and sister's faces when she'd dropped a single, good-sized diamond into her mother's palm. She'd preferred to have sold it herself; her mother was not nearly as good a bargainer as she was, for she had an inconvenient tendency to stick close to the truth. But Kathryn had not had an opportunity to leave the mansion during the day unquestioned, and the last thing she needed was to be seen trying to sell a diamond in one of the city's

236

fine jewelry stores. Perhaps there was only a slight possibility the story would get back to her husband, but she didn't intend to take even that small a gamble if she could avoid it. The biggest gamble of her life had paid off so well she figured she'd already used up all the luck she'd ever have.

But, even with her mother arranging the sale, that one diamond should be more than enough to get her brother out of the smelter for good, and get the entire family out of those tiny rooms over The Schatz House. It might not fund a luxurious life, but it should support a safe one. And there was more where the first one had came from, hidden in a sock underneath her mattress.

The floating sense of impending freedom had followed her all the way to Blake Street, making even that horrid, dark hallway through Simon Moore's establishment seem far less threatening that it had the last time she traversed it. After settling things with Mr. Moore once and for all, which another diamond—a big, impressive one this time, just to make sure—should take care of nicely, the only thing she'd have left to deal with was the lies she'd told Daniel about her family. And once she created a reasonable story he'd accept, she'd be free to spend the rest of her life making sure Daniel was never the slightest bit sorry he'd married her.

That, she thought happily, was a challenge, and a promise, she looked forward to meeting.

She rubbed her fingertips over the arm of the chair where Albert, Mr. Moore's anonymous clerk, had deposited her. She couldn't identify the wood, but it was dark and exotic, the finish as smooth and shiny as glass. How many scared, desperate young women had given over their bodies to strangers to pay for it? She snatched her hand away and jumped up from the chair as if it had scalded her.

"You don't find it comfortable?"

Damn! How did the man manage to enter a room without making a single sound?

"It's a lovely chair," she said, turning. "I simply prefer to stand."

Simon Moore did not seem any less impressive upon second look. He must top even Big John's height by at least half a head, and, despite his lean frame, he did not seem any less capable of inflicting severe damage to those upon whom he chose to unleash his whipcord strength.

But he no longer struck terror into her heart. Perhaps it was crazy that she wasn't frightened now. However, this time she did not come as a penitent but to fulfill her part of the bargain fully, completely releasing her from her connection with this unholy man. Even here, just the thought of her husband protected her.

"You are a few days early," he murmured. "Shall I assume, then, that you are surrendering a bit sooner than you had anticipated?"

"No."

"Ah, well, you cannot blame me for hoping." He indicated a heavily carved sideboard, where a collection of bottles and decanters twinkled in the soft gaslight. "Would you like a drink?"

"No." It was probably taking her life in her hands, to say "no" to Mr. Moore twice inside of ten seconds.

But she wanted out of there as quickly as possible, and Simon out of her life even faster.

"And how is your lovely sister?"

"She is . . . improving." Kathryn stuck out her closed fist. "I have something for you." She turned her hand over and opened it, exposing the diamond.

His expression was singularly unimpressed. She wondered if any emotion ever pierced that dangerous calm.

He contemplated the brilliant stone for a long moment. "It's a lovely one."

"Take it," she urged. It would not be over until he'd received and accepted his payment.

Finally, he plucked it from her palm and held it up to the light, his long, dark fingers a perfect setting for the clear, dazzlingly white stone.

"This is worth far more than you owe me."

"I don't care. I just want to be paid in full."

"You are." He tossed it in the air, tucked it in his pocket as if it was a worthless pebble. "I guess that new husband of yours is a generous sort."

"My—my husband?" she stuttered, stunned.

"Of course. Daniel Hall. Sellington. Whatever he prefers."

Hearing Daniel's name out of Moore's mouth, in this place, seemed a blasphemy. "I don't have a husband."

His eyes narrowed, and the fear she'd lived with for years and mostly ignored, the fear she thought she'd conquered, roared back redoubled, now that she'd had a brief respite from it. Better that she'd never hoped at all, she thought in despair.

"Please," he said. "Surely you'd expected me to keep a close eye on my investments."

"He has nothing to do with you. With our agreement."

"Beyond providing the means to allow you to fulfill it so handsomely, is that what you mean?"

Her hands fisted, nails digging futilely, painfully, into her palms. There was no answer to that, for he spoke the truth.

Simon strolled to the sideboard and pulled a large, diamond-cut stopper from its decanter. "Are you sure you won't join me?"

"I'm sure," she said stiffly.

Liquid the color of honey splashed into a tall, clear tumbler. "Then these are my further terms—"

"Further terms?" At her outburst, all of his pretense at geniality vanished. One slashing brow rose in clear warning. "But—but—you agreed I was paid in full."

"You are."

"I had always heard—I mean—" She must tread carefully. She already knew how well Mr. Moore took to having his word questioned. "I know that you have always been a man of your word, Mr. Moore, and therefore would not back out of our agreement. I apologize. I must have misunderstood your meaning."

"Our original arrangement *is* complete," he said smoothly. "Your sister is no longer in my employ. Nor will she ever again *be* in my employ, nor anyone else's—at least not in the capacity for which she worked for me previously. Nor will I expect you to join us here anytime soon. Unless, of course, you are seized with a sudden, overwhelming desire to, ah, begin a more venturesome life."

"I will not be," she said darkly.

"I didn't think so." His gaze slid over her slowly, and she had to force herself to remain still under his attentive regard. "A pity."

"I don't understand, then."

He tipped the glass to his mouth, topaz light slanting through the liquor. He savored the mouthful a moment before answering. "It is the price of my silence that is under discussion now."

Her heart dropped into her belly, a cold, hard lump that hit bottom hard and stayed there. "That's blackmail."

"Is it?" His jaw dropped in mock horror. "How thoughtful of you to inform me."

Stupid, she cursed herself. Stupid to have believed, even for one stunned, foolish moment, that Simon Moore might balk at blackmail. On the list of his sins, this one probably didn't even make the front page.

And how utterly foolish of her to think that she could be free of him. That she could build that golden life with Daniel that she yearned for, that she could feel just beyond her reach, tempting her with what she'd never have.

"I don't need to pay for your silence."

"No? You have something else in mind to ensure it? I am not fond of negotiation, as you well know, but I am always willing to entertain intriguing offers."

Lifting her chin, she stared hard into his black, soulless eyes. Confidence, however feigned, was her only weapon now. "I don't need to pay for your silence

because I do not *require* your silence. There is nothing
you can tell my husband that worries me."

"Oh?" He lifted one brow and waited.

"Unless you intend to make up lies about me. And
I have complete faith in my husband's faith in me.
Whyever would he take *your* word over mine?"

He set his glass aside and applauded lightly. "Ah,
that was nicely done, my dear."

"I would prefer that you not call me your dear."

His cold smile flashed. "You know, I do believe that
I rather regret that. Surprising." His grin disappeared.
"However, that will in no way affect our further business. I'm certain your rich, private, wellborn husband
would be very interested in knowing all about your
life . . . and your family's. Purely in the name of en-
hancing his knowledge of his wife, of course."

She kept her face blank. "Daniel knows all about
my family."

"How nice for you both. Then I'm sure you won't
mind at all if I have a little chat with him about it,
would you?"

Her shoulders sagged. She'd known from the start
that her bluff probably wouldn't work, but she'd little
choice but to try. "What do you want?"

He pulled the diamond from his pocket and rolled
it between his fingertips. "One of these every month
or two should suffice. If you're not satisfying my re-
quirements, I'll be sure to let you know."

"I'm certain you will," she said, an immense wear-
iness falling on her like a cloak. What was the use?
Perhaps she should just wander out into the street and
find a carriage to run her down. It was too difficult to

struggle and struggle and have it all fall apart just when she thought she'd finally made it.

But what would happen to her family then? They'd depended on her for so long; she could not knock those props out from under them and leave them to fall, as her father had done.

Hollowed of all hope, she turned for the door. But then a tiny tornado in a blue flannel nightgown burst into the room. "Daddy!" she hollered, and launched herself at Simon. With an ease born of long practice, he swept her up, lifting her to his great height and wrapping his arms around her small body, his hand fisting around his new diamond.

Kathryn would not have been more surprised if he'd suddenly decided to have mercy on her and release her from their agreement. Here was all the emotion and warmth that she'd sworn would never appear on that fearsome visage. He closed his eyes and rested his cheek on top of the girl's braids.

A plump woman, her black hair threaded with gray, appeared through the draperies obscuring the door through which the child had dashed, concern etched on her lined but still handsome face. "I'm sorry, Mr. Moore," she said. "She was determined that you and only you could tuck her in tonight."

"And so I shall." He dropped a kiss on the child's head. "As soon as I'm finished talking to this lady."

"Lady?" The girl twisted around in her father's arms. She was an enchanting child, small-featured, her brown hair shaded with copper, her fine-textured skin a warm, rich brown many shades lighter than Simon's. "Oh," she said, spying Kathryn. "Hello."

"Hello," Kathryn answered, curious despite herself. She'd never heard a whisper of a rumor about Simon having a child.

"You're pretty," the girl said.

Kathryn smiled. "So are you. Very."

The girl dimpled, and Simon laughed. "Now there, don't go filling her head. She already expects the world to bow at her feet."

As her Simon obviously did. Simon leaned down and let her go with some reluctance. "There now, Mollie, go with Mrs. Holmes. I'll be there in just a moment."

"All right," she said brightly, and hugged him tightly around his knees. Simon's eyes closed briefly, his hand coming to rest on her shiny head, as if the love that swamped him was nearly more than he could bear.

His eyes burned with fierce pride as Mollie skipped across the room, tucked her hand in Mrs. Holmes's, and disappeared through the heavy green curtains.

"How old is she?"

He tucked his hands behind his back and tilted his head, contemplating Kathryn seriously but without the threat she'd felt so often, as if trying to decide whether to answer her. "Six," he said at last.

"She's wonderful."

He smiled gently. "Yes," he said softly. "She is that, isn't she?"

Mollie could be his niece, Kathryn supposed. But she didn't think so. "I didn't know you had a daughter," she said boldly.

"I didn't either. For a little while."

She knew she was taking her life in her hands, staying here, pursuing a conversation with Simon Moore rather than bolting out while she still could. But this was a far different Simon, and if she could just find out a bit more about him, maybe . . .

"Where's her mother?"

Wrong question. All the love in his eyes subverted into anger that was just as potent, just as consuming.

"Guess she decided that her father had been right all along. She went back to her nice, pretty life and didn't want any reminders, including our daughter, of just how far she'd fallen."

"I . . . I'm sorry."

"Sorry for what? Sorry for her, sorry for me, sorry you asked?"

"All of the above," she admitted.

She held her breath until his tension eased, a small smile lifting the corners of his wide mouth. "Do not think," he warned her, "to use her against me."

"I would not," she said truthfully. But she knew that she was close to understanding what drove him, and in knowing that, she might find a way to defuse her situation. "I cannot imagine a mother giving up a child like that."

"Well, she did." His mouth thinned. "She doesn't need her mother anyway. She's got me."

She glanced around a room that emanated money and power. Six years old, he'd said. And it had been four or so, perhaps a little more, since he'd made his presence felt in Denver with a vengeance, expanding his small interests into an empire. He'd let nothing stop him since. For Mollie, she realized. For his daughter.

His posture seethed with challenge, daring her to tell him that he wasn't enough for his daughter. "I can't give her the life that should be hers, the life her mother lives. I can't make it possible for her to walk in any door in this town and be accepted, to sit in any restaurant or attend any school. I can't help that most people will only look at her and see that she had a colored father."

He burned with it. Not cruelty, as she'd once thought. Injustice, and fury, and fierce parental love. His hand swept the room, taking in the expensive furnishings, the elegant luxury he'd bought at the price of all those women and men who peddled their bodies and their souls at his behest. "Someday I'll be gone. And money is the only protection I can leave her. The more, the better."

Well, there it was. She not only understood him, she *knew* him. Was what he did so much different than what she'd done? She shied away from the repulsive thought; she'd drawn a line much further up the slope than he had, and, God willing, she'd never slide down further.

But she couldn't blame him anymore.

"You did what you did for your family," she said softly, "and I did what I did for mine."

And that, she thought, was really all there was to say.

Most of the streetlights on Blake Street had been shattered long ago. Two blocks down from where she stood, just outside the door, Kathryn could see a faint puddle of light. But where she was it seemed as if the two buildings on either side of the street listed in, leaving only a thin slice of black sky visible between them, casting the path beneath in menacing gloom.

For a moment she regretted heading out on foot. Maybe she should have taken one of the horses. But she'd never had an opportunity to learn to ride, and mounting a horse would have been taking her life in her hands every bit as much as walking the streets alone. At least she was experienced in surviving the streets.

Head down, handbag clutched in her fists, Kathryn strode off at a clip designed to get her out of there as quickly as possible and discourage any unwelcome overtures along the way. She could hear the bright, brassy spill of music from a saloon a block over; the last thing she wanted to do was make eye contact with a patron who wandered into an alley to take a piss.

" 'Scuse me, ma'am."

The voice oozed from the dark wedge of space between two darkened storefronts. She ignored it and charged on, automatically scanning the route ahead in search of safety. Perhaps it would be better simply to turn around and return to Simon Moore's. And what an odd thought *that* was, that she might find haven there.

She was more annoyed than afraid. She'd grown up on a street not far different from this one and had shed unwelcome attentions on a daily basis. Thieves and thugs and rapists were weak, lazy predators, fond of the easiest mark, and she was very good at convincing them that there was much easier game than she.

But then she heard the thud of heavy footsteps behind her. Without hesitation, she grabbed her skirts in both fists and took off at a dead run. Her heart pounded hard, a heavy thudding in rhythm with the beat of her heels on the hard-packed earth.

The blow came from behind, at the back of her thighs. She hit the ground hard, driving the air from her lungs, the awful weight of a heavy body preventing her from springing to her feet and taking flight again.

A broad fist clamped around her upper arm. The weight released, and she was dragged to her feet.

"That weren't very polite of you to ignore me," he growled. "I said 'ma'am.'"

"Now I don't know why that didn't convince me," she muttered. She twisted, trying to escape, but her attacker's grip only tightened painfully.

"Now, while I ain't opposed to a good chase now 'n' then, we really ain't got the time right now. I'll let you go, if you promise not to run away again."

The moment you let go, idiot. "Of course not."

"Yeah, well, not that your word ain't good 'n' all, but I figure this here revolver might encourage ya to keep your promise."

Damn. He let go. She rubbed her bruised upper arm and turned slowly to face him, her thoughts spinning, searching for and discarding plan after plan.

He wasn't tall, but thick-bodied and short-necked. His small eyes nearly disappeared in the folds of his puffy face, his bald head smooth as a billiard ball.

And the gun was only a foot from her chest.

Her calm surprised her. Perhaps her encounter with Simon Moore used up all her day's allotment of fear. Or perhaps it was simply momentarily quiet, waiting until it could do her some good.

"What do you want?" Slowly, she drew her bag up toward her chest, both hands wrapped around the top. "I've not much worth stealing."

"You'll find out soon enough." He prodded her with the gun. "Let's get goin'."

She didn't move. "Going where?"

"You'll find that out, too."

"No, I won't." She willed him to keep his attention on her face, as she slowly wiggled her thumbs into the opening of her bag, which was loosely fastened. She'd learned her lesson on that one. "I'm not going anywhere. Not with you."

"What?" His doughy face clearly showed his surprise. "But I've got a gun!"

"I noticed."

"I'll shoot you," he warned.

"So shoot." She twisted her thumbs, easing her handbag open slightly. Only a little more . . .

"What?" He blinked slowly at her.

"So go ahead and shoot if you want. I'm not going anywhere with you."

"Aw, come on." He drew a circle in the air with the barrel of the gun. "I'm not kiddin'," he threatened.

"Neither am I," Kathryn replied. Did the guy really think she was dumb and innocent enough to go tripping off into the night with him? She'd much rather take her chances with a gun out in the street than follow meekly into some private place where he could do God only knew what with her . . . and *then* kill her.

Nope, she'd much rather get shot right then and get it over with. Though she'd prefer to avoid that, too, if at all possible.

"But . . . but . . . Just come with me," he said, as if that would be enough to convince her. "You *gotta*."

"I most certainly do not," she said, drawing her bag up before her like a shield. The thug took a couple of steps back, as if he were afraid she would whack him with it, and Kathryn almost smiled. Just a little more . . .

Suddenly he jerked. "Hey!" he hollered, and put a hand up to his temple. His thick fingers came away shiny with dark blood. He swayed like a big bear ready to topple, as if he couldn't stand the sight of his own blood.

"Hey, you!" someone hollered from across the street. A kid stood over by a broken streetlamp, his right arm cocked as if he were ready to let fly with another rock. "Yeah, you! Dumbass!"

"Why, you—" He started across the street.

"That's enough, now," Kathryn said. Her accoster looked back to find that she had a gun aimed directly at him, which surprised him enough that he checked his own hand as if afraid she'd snatched his.

"Now move along," she advised him. "There are easier marks than me."

Thankfully, the man agreed. Kathryn watched her would-be kidnapper thud off down the street. She wouldn't have guessed that round body could move quite so quickly. For an instant she considered turning him in to the police, but what was she going to do? Lie to them about who she was, or risk having Daniel find out? Better she just let him go. A criminal that inept was bound to be out of the business soon enough in any case.

The boy wended his way across the street. "Nice gun."

"It has its uses." It was one of a matching pair of Smith & Wesson Schofields. Pete had given her one as soon as she was old enough to fire it without falling on her butt, keeping the other for himself. "I remember you," she said. "Thank you."

"I remember you, too." The young pickpocket she'd met outside Daniel's gate looked much better, she decided. He'd filled out a little, and his clothes were clean and fit him well. "That's why I thought I'd give ya a hand. Now we're even."

"Yes, we are."

He nodded in the direction the thug had disappeared. "Don't think that he expected a fine lady like you to be carryin' a shooter."

"I don't suppose most do." She was doubly glad that she'd not surrendered her bag when her stage had been held up. She'd hoped to use that same element of surprise to her advantage then, too, but Daniel had saved her the trouble. "But it wouldn't be terribly wise of me to be wandering down here without one, would it?"

"Naw. But I ain't sure it's wise anyways."

"No, probably not. But sometimes things are necessary, even if they're not particularly wise." She tucked the pistol back in its place. "How's business?"

"I retired."

"Retired?"

"Yeah." He scraped a toe in the dirt. "Goin' to school now."

"To school? That's wonderful!"

"Got a scholarship." His shy grin fairly burst with boyish pride.

"So what are you doing down here?"

"Yeah, well . . . not used to bein' shut up so much, ya know? Gets to feeling a little close now and then. And I figure it never hurts to keep in practice. Never know when the old skills might come in handy, ya know?"

"Yes, I know." Oh, but she knew. "Hard to trust the good things, isn't it? To believe that they're not just going to disappear?"

"Yeah." He still had a handful of pebbles. He shook them, the stones clicking against each other. "Better to be prepared, huh?"

She couldn't disagree. It was far wiser to be prepared.

But no matter what she did, no matter how hard she tried, she knew she'd never be prepared to lose Daniel.

Chapter 18

His wife was gone.

Daniel had called his meeting short, even though he knew that his mill manager was vastly amused at this display of newly married impatience, and in spite of the fact that it was a long trip back and he wouldn't return until long after Kathryn was asleep. He hadn't cared. He *was* filled with newly married impatience. And he couldn't wait to slide in bed next to her and tuck his body around hers, to hear her sigh in her sleep. Maybe let her stay asleep, just filling his arms and his dreams with her. Or maybe kiss her awake slowly, watch her passion rise as her eyes drifted open, her body welcoming him even before she was fully alert. It never failed to amaze him, not to mention excite the hell out of him, that her body recognized him and responded to him, before she was awake enough to think.

But when he got home and dashed up the darkened staircase, unbuttoning his shirt as he raced toward her, he discovered that she was gone.

He stared for a moment in disbelief. His little room,

bright with moonlight and memories, was empty. The sheets were tucked firmly beneath the thin mattress, the pillows plumped.

He felt a blow to his chest, palpable and painful as one of Big John's punches. For a moment he feared that maybe she'd been a dream after all, as he'd half convinced himself on his long, lonely ride home that she must be. For she'd just appeared in his life out of nowhere, filled it up and took it over, turning it inside out and making it wonderfully, wildly new. And now it seemed she'd vanished just as abruptly, with as little warning.

But then he thought to check. He dug in the chest at the foot of the bed and found her things, her plain cotton underthings tangled with his knit drawers, a faded old blue nightgown tucked in one corner, and he blew out a relieved breath. Fingering a pair of stockings, thick black knit darned at one toe, he smiled. His wife was frugal by nature, and the revelation of her new husband's wealth had not sent her running to buy a pile of frothy, expensive dainties.

Though he had to admit he rather cherished the idea of seeing her in a lacy bit of thin silk. *Very* thin silk.

He released the lid and it closed with a soft plop. He stood up, resting his hands on his hips. She was real, and she hadn't packed up her things and left him. So where was she?

He checked his grandmother's room first. He'd found her in there more than once, quietly sitting by the bedside, bent over her sewing, or reading aloud from a novel—*The Prince and the Pauper* the last time. Surprisingly, she was nearly as effective at soothing his grandmother's agitation as he.

But not tonight. His grandmother rested quietly, her nurse at her side, who, when asked, said she'd not seen Kathryn since she'd come on duty. He stared down for a moment at the remnants of what had once been a beautiful, strong-willed woman, one who'd failed to acknowledge the value of any person on earth save her son. Odd, that all the anger and hatred toward her that had smoldered inside him for so long, had evaporated as soon as he'd seen her like this. But the fury toward Edward burned just as violently as it always had, undiminished by the past fifteen years. If Edward had lived, would Daniel have found a way to forgive him, too?

Unlikely, he thought. More probably, Edward would have given Daniel a hundred more reasons to hate him.

He quietly slipped from the room. In case she was hungry, he peeked in the kitchen. He searched the library, for she sometimes liked to curl up in the big wing chair with a book. No luck. Should he wake someone, ask if they'd seen her? He was reluctant to disturb anyone's sleep for nothing. And it was more than a little embarrassing to admit he'd misplaced his wife.

Perhaps she was sitting up with someone. Last week, when Joey Gibson, the stableboy she'd taken a liking to, had come down with a sudden, sharp fever, she'd stayed with him throughout the night until his fever broke. Daniel poked his head out the back door. A soft breeze ruffled the sheared lawn between the house and the stables, carrying the scent of fresh-cut grass. All the windows of the rooms over the stables were completely dark.

He slowly retraced his steps through the house, worry spreading and darkening into true fear. He'd have to wake the household after all.

He crossed the wide, empty foyer and began to mount the stairs to the employees' quarters. He heard the snick of a lock, the scrape of the front door opening, and turned with his hand on the polished knob of the newel post.

Moonlight from without lit her hair to silver, etched her fine features into light and shadow. His heart lifted, warmth blooming in his heart, his blood.

She was home.

Quietly, she closed the door behind her. The leaded glass that surrounded the door threw odd, figured patterns of moonlight on the floor, a dark tracery like bare branches over glowing white marble.

"Welcome home, Kathryn," he said quietly.

Her hand flew to her throat and her head snapped toward the sound of his voice. When her gaze settled on him, a wide smile that held all the warmth of the sun lit her face. "Daniel! You're home!"

She flew toward him, and he came off the stairs to meet her halfway, lifting her up into his embrace. She stamped quick, laughing kisses on his jaw, his cheek, his neck, wherever she could reach, so he had to crane his neck and chase her down to capture her mouth.

When he drew back to look at her, to remind himself that yes, he'd not imagined her, she really was as lovely and sweet as he remembered, she said, "I didn't expect you home tonight."

"I've found I've lost the knack of sleeping alone."

She mock-frowned at him. "Then you're not allowed to sleep away from me ever again. Why tempt you?"

"Oh? You're not in the mood to share? Don't you want to impress me with your generosity?"

"I'm not generous at all where you're concerned," she said, and kissed him again, hard, until they both were breathless and their hands had begun to explore. "Mmm. Yes, greedy, I think. Definitely greedy."

"Good," he murmured. "I like you greedy." He nipped at her ear, smiling against her skin when she shivered and leaned against him. "Where were you?"

Her hands, which had been sliding up his back, went still. "Where was I?" she repeated on a high pitch, as if she didn't understand the words.

"Yeah, where were you?" Oh, she smelled good, like starlight and flowers. The scent bloomed strong in the hollow of her neck. He buried his nose there and breathed in. "I was worried."

"I'm sorry," she said quickly. "I didn't mean to worry you."

"I guess you'll just have to make it up to me," he told her.

Her hands began to move again, sliding down his back, lightly over his butt to cup and mold before gliding around his hips, and he sucked in his breath.

"So where were you?" he asked while he could still think.

"Oh." Her hands flattened against his hips. "I just . . . I had to get some air. Don't you get tired of being closed up in this place all the time?"

"I would have taken you, if you'd asked," he said, regretting that he'd asked the question, for her hands had paused in their exploration. "Did you go—"

Her hands came around, found him through the fabric of his pants. With her forefinger and thumb, she traced his length, and he gulped air in a heated rush. "I'll take you out tomorrow."

"I'd like that," she said. Her palm cupped him then, pressing hard.

"Somewhere," he said, trying to figure out how he was going to get his legs to work long enough to hustle her all the way up to their room. Her tongue touched his neck, and he gasped. "Anywhere."

"Good," she murmured. "Take me anywhere."

"Ahh . . ." His blood thundered. "All right."

"Daniel!" The thought shocked Kathryn to her bones. It excited her even more.

"Everyone's fast asleep," he murmured, as his mouth did wicked and wonderful things at her neck. "I know. I wandered all over the damn house looking for you."

"Oh." There was surely a good reason that she couldn't make love with her husband right there in the foyer, but damned if she could think of it. Fire danced beneath the stroke of his fingers, burned beneath his mouth, burst within her belly and threatened to consume her.

Her knees gave way. He caught her, of course— Daniel would never let her fall—and lowered her to the floor. The marble was cold and hard beneath her back, Daniel warm and wonderfully hard at her front. All the worries of this night—Simon Moore's demands, being accosted on the street, the breathless panic when Daniel questioned her whereabouts—they all gave way to his passion as easily as the dawn chased the night.

She was safe. Daniel was home.

It was the most perfect day of her life.

They'd left the house with little incident. A week earlier, weary of the reporters lying in wait for someone of interest to put a toe out of the gate, Daniel had sent a statement to every newspaperman in town.

He'd no further information to give about his father's disappearance, it had said, but the estate's lawyers were convinced of his death. He would not be making any further statements—not then, not ever. Nor would he be making any charitable contributions or investments of any sort, and anyone who came to ask would be discouraged most firmly.

It had taken a few days for the crowds to thin, but finally there was only one man remaining, a thin, narrow-faced fellow still stationed by the side gate when Daniel drove his simple buggy through. He'd raised one hand in question, Daniel had waved him away, and the man had meekly nodded and ambled off to the comfortable spot in the shade of a pretty maple where he'd made himself at home for days, having gathered a chair, a pile of books, and a basket stuffed with assorted nibbles.

"Such a persistent fellow," she commented dryly.

"Wonder what he would have done if I really had stopped?" Daniel asked. "Do you think he could have bestirred himself enough to write it all down?"

"Oh, no. Looks like actually holding a pencil is above and beyond the call of duty for him."

He drove her out of town at first. Mrs. Holmes had packed them a generous lunch, and they shared it in the green, secret room formed by the drooping branches of a willow, accompanied by the merry burble of a tiny stream. Once they'd satisfied one appetite, they turned to sating another one, loving each other in a thick, warm haze of sunshine and laughter.

Although Daniel had grave doubts as to whether his appetite for her would ever be sated. Her strong and immediate response to him never failed to stun him and arouse him, for she always appeared to be as hungry for their loving as he was. At the barest touch of his hand, she turned warm and welcoming. A few kisses, a touch, and that welcome turned to hot and urgent demand.

To all outward appearances, she was a proper and obedient wife. But in bed—and a fair number of other places as well—her passion was as strong as his own, without inhibition or concern for propriety, a wildly tempting mistress in the guise of a perfect wife.

He lay back on the carpet of grass, smiling up through the veiling willow branches at the bright bowl of blue sky, his arms around Kathryn's limp, well-pleasured form, her head pillowed on his shoulder.

Ah, but he was the luckiest man on the face of the earth! He was sure of it.

"What would you like to do next?" he murmured.

"Next?" She yawned. "I think we've covered most of the obvious possibilities. Give me a moment to rest, though, and maybe I'll come up with something."

"As tempting as that idea is," he said, smiling against her hair, "I actually had something a bit less strenuous in mind."

"Like sleeping, I hope." She snuggled more comfortably at his side.

"We could do that." He drew a forefinger over the pure curve of her shoulder and wondered why he was even making the offer. "I thought it was about time to get you a wedding present."

"A wedding present?"

"Yup." He lifted her hand and pressed a kiss to her ring finger. "It's about time to get you a wedding ring, don't you think?"

Kathryn frowned, debating. It was probably not at all wise for her to be wandering around Denver; there was always the chance that she might run into someone who would give her away.

They were hardly likely to be going anywhere near her neighborhood. However, the chances were much better that she would run into one of the women for whom she'd sewed or scrubbed. But would they recognize her, on Daniel's arm, much better dressed, and in a place they'd never thought to see her? Few people, she'd learned, ever paid much attention to their servants, as long as the job was done. The vast majority of the women she'd worked for had probably never looked her directly in the face, much less made note of her.

"You don't have to buy me a ring," she said. "It's not going to make us any more married."

"I know." He ran a thumb over the place on her finger where a ring would rest. "But I'd just as soon that any man who lays eyes on you know immediately that you are taken."

"Oh you would, would you?" Amused, she rolled on top of him, smiling down at his handsome face. "If this is about branding, Daniel, then we'd better get you one as well. I don't exactly want any pretty little things running after *you*, either."

His kiss was flavored with warmth, his mouth curling up into a smile even as it met hers. "It wouldn't matter, whether I wore no rings or a thousand. My heart knows fully well to whom it belongs."

"Oh." And Kathryn, who'd weathered a hundred disappointments without tears, felt the gentle burn of them behind her lids. "Daniel."

"Come on." Unceremoniously, he rolled her off him, dumping her carefully on the ground.

"Hey!" she protested.

"Move, woman!" He rolled easily to his feet and dusted off the rear of his pants before starting to fasten all the buttons and ties she'd been in a such a hurry to undo an hour ago. "If you keep looking at me like that, we're not going anywhere for hours. And I've made up my mind."

"Far be it from me to try to change your mind."

He tried to look severe. "And well you shouldn't."

A ring then, she thought. She'd never been all that interested in jewelry, had never understood how a few sparkling stones and a little shiny metal could be worth more than a decent house. She'd take the house any day.

But if Daniel remained determined to rid himself of his entire fortune, at least the ring would be one more item she had in reserve. Surely she could feed her family for some time on its proceeds.

It was a lovely afternoon, August's heat having gentled into September's warmth. Only the sun's flash interrupted the pure sweep of clear blue sky.

She enjoyed strolling along the street with Daniel, her hand tucked into the crook of his elbow. It was not a district of Denver she'd ever spent much time in, the shops and charming restaurants far too expensive for her even to have dreamed about. But it was good fun to investigate the windows, view the pretty displays, and realize she could, if she really wished to, ask Daniel to buy her one of the elaborate hats or knitted shawls.

She didn't, of course. But she could, and it was a heady thought. People smiled at them as they passed, and she fancied that they commented on the happy, handsome young couple.

At first she'd worried whether she might inadvertently hint that she'd far more familiarity with Denver than Daniel believed. But this was not the same city she knew. This one was clean and bright and welcoming, and her surprise was genuine.

"This is nice," she admitted.

"I'd rather be back under the willow tree," he grumbled.

She poked him in the side. "This was your idea, remember?"

"And isn't it your wifely duty to talk me out of foolish ideas?"

"Oh, is *that* my wifely duty? I was sure you told me that it was—"

"There's more than one," he said gravely, but his eyes were bright with humor.

"Really? How many are there?"

"At least a few hundred or so. *At least*. I'm discovering more every day. For instance—"

They rounded a corner, and he broke off. An old man wearing a threadbare uniform at least twenty-five years old, the navy faded to streaky, pale blue, slumped against the corner of a tobacconist's store. One thin leg was propped out in front of him; the other was gone at mid-thigh. A battered felt hat lay on the ground beside him, a few stray coins glinting in the crown.

"Please, sir. Ma'am." The man held up his hat, shook it so the coins clinked in plea.

The impulse to give caught Kathryn by surprise. She'd never had the circumstances to permit generosity, never even felt the urge. She never expected *to* feel it; the need to hoard protection for her family took priority.

But surely a few coins wouldn't matter, she decided suddenly. "Daniel—"

He grabbed her elbow and half dragged her down the street, until they were a block away from the beggar.

"Daniel?" she asked, bewildered. "Don't you want to—?"

He stopped and turned to face her. His face was tightly set, his eyes dark and guarded. "Of course I want to."

"Then why didn't you give him a few dollars?"

"How much good do you think a few dollars will

do that man?" He jammed a hand through his hair. "I used to do that. Hand out a few dollars to everyone who asked. Two days later, all the same people were back there, in exactly the same shape they were before I tossed them a couple of bucks. And pretty soon I had throngs of people, swarming every time I stepped outside my front door. The reporters that descended on the house last week, multiplied a hundredfold."

"But surely it couldn't hurt, just this once."

"I'll come back," he assured her. "I promise. With more than a few dollars, given in a way that will assure he never knows where it came from. It's better that way, Kathryn. I learned that the hard way."

"Oh." She pondered for a moment. "He might not be there, though. The police won't let him stay on that corner long."

"I'll find him," he said with such confidence that she knew he'd done it a hundred times before.

A niggling memory struck her. "Mrs. Mills?"

He grinned. "Mrs. Mills should have discovered four hundred dollars in her flour barrel soon after we left."

For a moment, she debated the propriety of touching her husband on a city street.

Oh, when had she ever found propriety a useful conceit?

Lifting to her toes, she pressed a kiss to his cheek. "Daniel Hall, you are the most amazing man."

He swallowed hard, and she felt her heart tremble in anticipation. He cared for her, she felt it, in her bones, her heart, where her own feelings for him had taken root and grown. And now he would tell her. "Kathryn, I—"

"Kathryn!" *God, no.* The world, her newly promising world, plummeted from beneath her feet.

"We have to go." She latched on to Daniel's forearm and tried to pull him away. "We have to go *now*—"

His brow wrinkled in bewilderment. "But—"

"Now!" she begged.

"Kathryn!" The shout was closer. Familiar, despised. Too near.

"Please, Daniel." A sob broke through her voice. "Please, take me home."

He was there. She didn't look at him, but she felt him, as one sensed a terrible storm hovering over the horizon. "I knew it was you," he said.

The world pitched and she leaned heavily on her husband's arm. "Obviously you're an old acquaintance of Kathryn's," Daniel said, "but she's not well—"

He laughed, the sound a death knell to all her dreams, her brightly beautiful new life. "Well, I'd say I'm a little more than an *acquaintance*."

"If you'll excuse us—" Daniel began to escort her past the man.

"I suppose I must," he said. "Now that I know you're still in Denver, Kathryn, I'll put a bit more effort into chasing you down."

She felt Daniel's hesitation, and inevitability sliced through her like a guillotine's blade.

"Still in Denver?" Daniel repeated. "Kathryn?"

Her head felt like it weighed a hundred pounds. Wearily, she lifted it to meet his eyes, shadowed with confusion and question. "I'm sorry, Daniel," she whispered. "So sorry."

"Kathryn?"

"You know, Kathryn, I would have thought that you could have done better than *this*," he said with clear disdain.

Forgive me, Daniel. The prayer echoed in her head, again and again, the only thing that mattered. An impossibility. *Forgive me, Daniel.*

She turned to face her executioner. Hatred struggled to take over but instead gave way to the sorrow of what she'd done to Daniel.

Richard Chivington. He looked exactly as he had the last time she'd seen him, looked exactly as he *was*, the smug, indulged son of one of Denver's most prominent families. He was expensively dressed, the stiff collar of his fine lawn shirt digging into his softening jawline.

She wanted to blame it on Richard, to transfer her guilt to his narrow shoulders. He was the reason she'd lost her job, the reason she'd been unable to find another. The reason she'd gone after Daniel in the first place.

But what she'd done was her fault. *Hers*.

His lip curled up in revulsion as he took in their simple attire. "You should have stayed with me," he told her. "I could have kept you much better than this." He tucked his thumbs into his vest pocket, where a gold watch chain swooped over his rounded stomach. "Not that you would have kept my interest for long, of course," he added quickly.

"I don't know who you are." Daniel's voice was

even, unemotional. *Daniel.* "But you are talking about my *wife.*"

"Wife?" Richard's eyes widened, then he started to laugh. "Oh, heavens, that's rich. Kathryn, how did you manage to arrange that?"

"Let's go, Kathryn." Daniel's hand at her elbow no longer supported and guided. His fingers dug tightly, numbing her arm from the elbow down.

Richard stepped in front of them to halt their progress. "I had her, you know." His eyes glittered with triumph. Now why hadn't she realized how much he hated her? That he'd welcome revenge for her rebuff? "Dozens of times, dozens of ways. I'm sure I wasn't the only one. Though I suppose there's some advantage to taking a wife who's spread her thighs for half the town. She's hardly going to have a case of the vapors when you whip out your stick, is she?"

"She is my wife." Daniel released Kathryn's arm and moved her safely aside. His fist flew forward as if shot from a cannon. Richard's head snapped back so far that his chin pointed toward the sky. He dropped to the ground as if all his bones had suddenly dissolved.

Daniel bent over Richard's still form, twisting his fists in the cloth of Richard's shirt, slaughtering the crisp finish, and used it to drag him up to a sitting position. "Wake up, you stupid bastard," he said, a savage undercurrent to his voice making it almost unrecognizable. "Wake up."

Richard's eyelids rolled up.

"I know you did not have her." Spittle mixed with blood dribbled out of Richard's mouth and down his chin. "I know you did not, for she was a virgin when we met. If I hear another lie about my wife pass your mouth, they'll be the last words that will ever leave it. Do you understand me?"

Richard gave one weak nod. Daniel let go, and Richard fell back, his head hitting the ground with a solid *thunk*.

Daniel stood up slowly, like an old man with pain aching in every weary joint.

"Daniel?" She stretched a hand toward him in entreaty, began to move toward him. "Daniel, I—"

He whipped an arm up to stop her, his hand fisted. Involuntarily, she jerked back. He stared at her, and then at his fist, still hovering in the air between them. He opened his hand, his fingers spread wide, and turned it back and forth as if seeing it for the first time before allowing it to fall to his side.

"Daniel," she tried again. There had to be a way, something she could say. Richard *had* lied about her; she could explain that much to Daniel and still be truthful.

"Not here," he told her. "Not now."

Not ever, she heard. *Not ever again.*

Chapter 19

He felt nothing. Not there in the street, as he watched horror and fear and guilt spread themselves over her lovely face. Not when she'd lightly, formally, placed her hand in his so he could assist her into his buggy. And not when they entered the mansion, the foyer filled with memories of her twisting and moaning beneath him. Even then, he still felt nothing at all.

It was like when you sliced a finger, looked down at your hand and saw the blood flowing free and knew there must be a deep cut but the pain hadn't begun yet. You could see it coming, anticipate the possibility, but only wait in dread for it to begin.

He started up the central staircase, leaving her to follow, and paused with his foot on the third riser.

No. He couldn't go to his room. It had become *their* room, and would never be simply his again, even if she never again set foot in it.

His office, then, a room in which Kathryn had not made an imprint. It occupied a distant corner of the first floor, far from the grand space just inside the front entrance that his father had used for his own study.

Libeus was there, hidden behind piles of papers and ledgers on his outsize pine desk. "There you are," he said, rising to peer over the clutter. He took one look at Daniel's face and his broad smile vanished. "Oh." His concerned gaze popped back and forth between Daniel and Kathryn. "If you'll excuse me. I must . . . I've got to . . . go . . . somewhere," he finished as he scuttled from the room.

"So." Daniel walked over to one of the windows and stared out at the carefully tended gardens. They were lush with scent and the end of summer, thick with purple and red flowers he'd never bothered to learn the name of, their big, showy heads bending the stems into a graceful arch. Two men worked on their knees, ruthlessly yanking out whatever weeds dared to invade the immaculate beds.

The gardens seethed with vibrant life. Somehow he'd expected to see blackened stems and withered branches, a ruin that echoed what had become of his marriage.

"Daniel," Kathryn whispered. He hadn't glanced at her, not since standing over Chivington's limp body. Now he stood framed by the tall, narrow, many-paned window, a graceful arch overhead, a thick bar of sunlight falling on him and washing gold into his warm dark hair. "Thank you," she said at last. "For defending me."

He swallowed hard. "You are my wife."

My wife. It gave her courage, and she dared to step

closer to him. "I hadn't realized that you knew. That you noticed the blood that first night, that I was . . ." Heat rushed to her face. At least Daniel had proof that part of Richard's story was a lie.

"That you were a virgin?" His skin had drawn tight, giving an odd, pale sheen to his forehead, his broad cheekbones. "I didn't know."

"But you said—"

"How would I know? It was my first time, too. I wasn't noticing a hell of a lot of the details."

"Your first time?" It was as if someone had taken her life, crushed it, and tossed it up in the air for the shattered pieces to fall around her. She could recognize a scrap here and there, but she couldn't grab hold and fit them into a recognizable whole. He didn't know? "But . . . but . . . you told him, you said that—"

"You are my wife," he repeated, his voice stripped of inflection.

"I *was* a virgin," she insisted.

Though she studied him carefully, he gave no hint of whether he believed her or not. "Daniel, I *was*." She laid a hand on his biceps and he jerked away.

"What you did—or did not do—before we met is not of nearly so much concern to me as what you've done since."

"I suppose not." He couldn't even tolerate her touch, she realized. *Oh God, oh God, oh God.* Was it a prayer, a curse, a cry? All of them.

"Who was he?"

"He was no one. No one that matters."

His shoulders lifted, and he shoved his hands deep into his pockets. "I want to know."

She wanted it over. Dead, buried, forgotten. But he'd earned the right to know. "His name is Richard. Richard Chivington. I worked for his mother, and he assumed . . . he thought I would be interested in another sort of employment entirely. When I was not, he . . . well, I no longer had any sort of employment at all."

"I see." *I should have hit him more than once*, Daniel thought, his hands fisting.

"Daniel, that was *all*, I promise. He never touched me, I never wanted him to, and there was never anyone else. *I promise*," she said, desperation cracking through her voice like deep fissures in parched earth.

"You promise," he repeated, hearing all the other promises she'd made, echoing in the hollow, empty place where his heart had once lived. "You promise he never touched you. When you lived in *Denver*."

"Yes," she admitted. "In Denver."

He looked at her then, his eyes, his face, stripped of emotion. "How long have you known who I am?"

And there it was, laid bare and painfully simple, the one irrevocable question that, once answered, they could not retreat from. He would never forget; he could never forgive.

She owed him everything. But did she owe him the truth, or did she owe him a lie? The words froze in her throat. What would be the greatest kindness? Which would be the smallest wrong, of all she'd done to him already?

"I've known since the beginning," she said at last. "I was on that stage to find you."

He could break the window, Daniel thought. Just

slam his fist through it, imbed a hundred shards of
glass into his flesh. Surely it would hurt less than this.

"Why?" The question tore from somewhere deep in
his soul.

"I—" She could tell him all of it. Explain about his
father and hers, about her brothers and her sister and
the desperation born of too few choices and too much
loss. But there were no excuses, no reasons, for what
she'd done to him. It seemed as if that would be another sin, to try to explain away her actions.

"For this?" His gaze swept the high-ceilinged room,
the cabinets holding records of a hundred profitable
businesses. "For the money? I would have given it to
you, if you'd just asked."

"I know. But I didn't know that then." She hadn't
known anything. Not until she'd known him.

His attention, distant and assessing, settled on her.
"You must think quite highly of yourself, to believe
that you could lure a stranger into marriage."

She didn't answer. Daniel wanted her to answer,
longed for her to say something that would make this
seem reasonable, forgivable, an understandable mistake rather than a betrayal. Yet, she merely stared at
him with her mouth closed and her eyes haunted. But
what could she say?

She'd pretended not to know him and married him
for his money. That was the truth, stark and bitter and
aching.

"But then it worked, didn't it?" he acknowledged.
It worked because he was a gullible fool, a stupid man
who'd seen a dream and believed it wholly, even
though he *knew* better.

"Why me?" he asked. Feeling like a man who could not resist pushing farther into a tangle of thorny brush, even though he knew each time would only drive the barbs deeper into his own flesh.

He had to know.

"Oh, Daniel." She sighed deeply. "My father had a fortune once. What part of this place was built with it, do you suppose? The ballroom, maybe. Or perhaps it bought your grandmother's ruby." She laughed, a bare, pained sound.

How could this be his wife? How could this woman who coldly calculated a marriage, weighed it in gold, be the same one who laughed so generously? Who turned warm and welcoming at his slightest touch? Who looked at him as if he were her whole world? In his pockets, he clenched his fists tighter.

"How did you find me?" he asked. As if it mattered. But he was still probing, trying to find the one thread that would unravel it all, make sense of this snarl. Make it be something other than what it was.

She pressed her lips together and shook her head. "What difference does it make?"

"None." But he needed something, *anything*, to make a difference.

She'd stepped close. He could feel the faint heat from her body, hear the stutter of her breath. "Are you going to divorce me?" she asked baldly.

Those beautiful eyes; he'd once thought that he might fall right into them and drown. Well, he sure as hell had, hadn't he?

Divorce her? The possibility tempted him. He would

never have to see her again. Never again have to face the results of his absurd impulse.

But he'd been raised to believe a man honored his promises and took responsibility for his own choices. He'd clung to his duty because God knew what he'd become if he let go of it. The only influence he'd been under when he took Kathryn to wife was lust. He hadn't been the first to make that blunder either, had he?

"No," he said. "No, I'm not going to divorce you."

"Thank you." Relief shuddered through her. He wasn't going to divorce her. All the rest would sort itself out with time. "I'll make it up to you, you'll see, I'll—"

"No." His voice was calm, detached. Utterly distant. "I won't divorce you, Kathryn, but this is . . . what we had, what I *thought* we might have, that's done with."

"I'm sorry. So sorry." Her hands flexed, grasped empty air. They wanted him, wanted to fill themselves with his heat and life and generosity. "I love you, Daniel."

"Love!" Every muscle in his body spasmed. How could she say that word to him? "I want you to go."

"Go—" She looked wildly around her, as if she would find answers in the jammed bookshelves or overflowing cabinets.

"You can continue to live here," he told her. And how on earth was he going to live with that? "Whatever you need, whatever you *want*, however damn much money it takes to satisfy you, you can have."

But you can't have me. She heard the words more

clearly than any he'd spoken. They burned into her heart as if etched by acid.

"Get out of this room now. Stay the hell out of my way. Now, tomorrow. Forever if I want, until I tell you otherwise."

I'm your wife—she bit back the words before they could burst out. What right did she have to claim that bond? Sobs welled in her throat. Vision blurring, she turned and fled, banging into the corner of a table. A vase crashed to its side, spilling water and blossoms. Unmindful of the pain, the mess, she kept going.

Outside, the gardeners still toiled away as if nothing had changed. A swift swooped low over the fading rose garden. A cat lay beneath a chokecherry bush, mesmerized by a half dozen small white moths fluttering by his nose.

Daniel remained by the window until the bright sunlight bled into scarlet. He pulled his hands from his pockets and spread his fingers wide, noting distantly that he'd curled his fists so hard his nails had sliced his palm. He hadn't felt a thing. Hoped to God he never felt a thing ever again.

He touched the smooth, warm surface of the window. And when he took his hand away, he left a smear of red.

Two weeks. Two weeks of which she felt every second, as if each painful instant had sunk talons in deep, refusing to let go.

Two weeks in which Kathryn was warm and safe and well fed. Two weeks in which she could see her family as often as she wished. Tommy quit the smelter,

Isabelle gained a small amount of weight, and Eudora made plans to move the three of them into an apartment that was slightly larger and slightly better than the one they'd existed in for the last twelve years. And which, happily, was a full seven blocks away from Herman Schatz. Two weeks without the slightest fear of Simon Moore, for what could he do to her now?

Two months ago, she would have thought that to have that much was to have everything in life. She should be grateful. She *was* grateful.

And she woke up every morning and went to bed every night, aching for what she'd lost.

She moved into a small room, spare as a nun's cell, on the second floor. The bed was twice as comfortable as the one she'd slept in for most of her life; she tossed and turned into the wee hours.

She yearned for those few moments she saw Daniel, storing them away in her heart because she never knew if there'd be another. Sometimes she saw him far down one of the endless hallways. Twice he was still at breakfast when she arrived. And once, when she passed the entrance to the ballroom, the great double doors opened and he came out, shirtless, a towel looped around his neck. He was breathing hard, his hair curling damply around his sweat-sheened forehead, and she simply stood there, frozen, and drank in the sight of him.

Her hands, unable to touch him, curled hard around the potted violet she carried. He looked leaner than before, stripped down to hard muscle and bone. His plain cotton pants rode low across his flat belly. There, right there, her kiss had followed the line of hair down his abdomen, and lower still, and he'd moaned and arched into her mouth.

Her lips parted. Her gaze traced up, over the swell of his chest and the strong column of his throat. Ah, she missed the way he smelled, the warm scent his skin held, stronger where his pulse beat beneath his ear.

His eyes darkened. With passion? Or anger? Maybe both. His fists were wrapped in the ends of his towel. Her feet took a tentative half step toward him even as her heart rushed full bore. "Daniel," she whispered.

His nostrils flared, the only hint of expression in his rigid face. "I have to go," he said, and charged past her, his arm banging her shoulder as he went. She watched him leave, the broad, tall set of his shoulders, the slight forward cant to his posture as if he couldn't wait to get away from her. And then she covered her shoulder with her palm, right over the place he'd bumped, as if for as long as she kept her hand there, she could hold the feel of him in place.

Daniel heard crying as he bounded down the staircase on the way to yet another sparring session with Big John. John, who didn't care how hard or how often Daniel tried futilely to pound him into the ground. Who, unlike Libeus, asked no well-intentioned questions and flashed him no pitying glances.

Boxing with John was one of the few times he felt like his old self. The rest of the time he paced this stupid, overblown wreck of a house and felt . . . as little as possible. He didn't want to feel. He'd much rather forget.

It was such a *brief* period in his life. Why couldn't he forget?

Instead, he mourned. Mourned not a person, not a reality. Mourned something he should have known better than to hope for, mourned the bright vision of the future he'd been building since he'd first laid eyes on Kathryn.

He reached the bottom of the stairs. Stuttering, half-formed sobs, as if the person who made them hadn't had much practice at it, pulsed through the air.

Keep going, he told himself. Just keep on walking, running, right into the ballroom where you can pound a bag until your bones break.

He knew it was her. It had to be her; each sob shot a sharp pain into his chest, right in the vicinity of his heart.

Not that she would ever again get anywhere close to his heart, he assured himself.

He made it halfway across the foyer. "Damn!" He wheeled around and headed for the seldom-used parlor, directly across from his father's old office.

He'd given away anything of worth in the room years ago. She was curled up in a big old wing chair, a flap of oxblood leather hanging loose from the back, a wedge of matted stuffing straggling out. A blanket was wrapped snugly around her shoulders, and her hands cradled a cup.

"What's the matter with you?"

She lifted her eyes slowly to meet his. "How kind of you to worry about my health." She smiled sadly. "But you needn't."

With her words, she'd released him from any obligation. But his feet still refused to move.

"Why are you crying, then?"

She sighed, flexing her fingers around the pale blue cup. "I've got my monthlies, all right? That's the only thing that's wrong."

"Oh." He debated with himself for a moment before giving in. Just helping out a woman in pain did *not* mean he was getting drawn back into her deceitful web, did it? He stamped over to a battered cabinet, splashed a healthy portion of brandy into a short glass, and thrust it at her. "Here. This'll help more than whatever it is you've got in that cup."

Her brow arched up. "For a man who claims to have had little traffic with women, you know a remarkable amount about them."

"I'm a quick study." He grabbed the cup out of her hand and replaced it with the brandy he'd poured. "Drink it."

Obligingly, she gulped it down.

"Better?"

"I felt fine before the drink," she told him.

"Sure you did. Which is why you were whimpering like a lost puppy."

"That wasn't why." Tears glistened in her eyes, spilled over her cheeks. "I'm crying because I'm not, *we're* not . . . I was over a week late, and I hoped . . ."

A roundhouse punch he hadn't seen coming would have been a kinder blow. "Because we're not having a child," he supplied flatly.

"Daniel." Kathryn wrapped the blanket closer

around her shoulders and leaned forward in her chair. "Let me do this for you."

"No." He could not consider it. She would have his name, she would have his fortune—while it remained—but he could not give her more of him than that.

"Please." As she moved into the light, the tears on her cheeks glittered like his father's diamonds. "I know that you will never forget what I did. But this is all I can do for you now, Daniel. Let me give you a child."

She stood up, and the blanket pooled around her feet like a queen's robes. She still wore her nightgown. Skin showed pale at the open neck, a warm and tantalizing hint of the flesh beneath. He knew what it tasted like, knew how it heated beneath his touch. How her skin flushed as her passion grew, becoming tinged with pink like the inside of a shell.

"I'm your wife," she told him, her voice spinning a web of memories and promises. "I'm the only one who can give you a child, the only one who can—" Her lids drifted lower, the way they did when he sank into her.

She was his wife, she'd said. If he did not do so with her, he would never sire a child. Never know again the intensely physical pleasure of spilling his seed inside a woman.

He'd survived without it before. He could again. Unless . . .

"That's not strictly true," he said. "That, if not with you, with no one."

Color abandoned her face, leaving her white as death. "No," she whispered.

He wouldn't do that. Kathryn had been so sure; it had been the one thing she'd clung to, with the tenacity of a drowning swimmer seizing a lifeline. He was a young, healthy man. He'd want children. He'd want sex. He was not the sort to seek out an adulterous relationship, to break vows he'd taken willingly, if not entirely freely. And so, inevitably, eventually, he'd turn to her. If that was all she could give him, the only way she had to atone for what she'd done, she'd do so with joy and gratitude and the hope that someday, through their physical connection, he might find a way to forgive her, if never to love her.

"You *can't*," she said, even as she knew that to be a worthless declaration. Why couldn't he?

He shrugged carelessly. "Oh, can't I?" he said and turned to leave.

She bit down on the words of protest that sprang to her lips. Because she knew she hadn't the right to stop him.

Not now. And not ever.

Chapter 20

A block from the Sellington Mansion, Kathryn scuffled slowly down the street, heading for home. *Home.* That fabulous, gloomy place was no more her home than the hovel over the Schatz House had been. The only time she'd had a home in the last fifteen years were those few, precious weeks when she'd first married Daniel.

Autumn was coming, lurking beyond the mountains, sending chill winds down to warn of its approach. A few impatient leaves had turned brown and gold, drifting down to settle in the road. She stepped on one, and it crunched beneath her sole.

She was delaying her return, and she knew it. The house seethed with too many reminders for her comfort. Daniel was everywhere she turned, even though she seldom saw him, and she was in no hurry to confront the memories of her sins again.

A soft murmur of voices trickled through the screening of trees and hedges. She turned the corner, bringing Daniel's house into view. At least two dozen people gathered in the street. For a moment she felt a jolt of recognition, of that first afternoon when she'd met Daniel.

But, unlike that boisterous, disorganized throng, this crowd had formed a neat line. Their voices were low, respectful. Mrs. Hughes, the cook, with two helpers, made their way up and down the queue, handing out cups that steamed into the crisp air and paper-wrapped sandwiches.

"What in the world . . . ?" She hurried forward.

Young and old had gathered there. Most were thin; all were badly dressed. Many were children. And all their faces held a wary mix of suspicion and hope.

"Excuse me," she said, trying to edge by a stout woman of perhaps sixty years of age, her hair a bright copper except for the stripe of steel gray along her militarily straight part.

"End of the line's back there." She pointed over her shoulder with the half-eaten crust of a thick ham sandwich. "You can wait your turn, missy, jes' like ever'body else."

"No, you don't understand. I live here."

The woman eyed her with open skepticism. "Sure you do, honey."

"But I *do*," she said, while a swell of confusion tried to inflate into panic. What could possibly have happened? "Mrs. Hughes!"

Mrs. Hughes was bent over, handing a cookie the size of a dinner plate to a small girl. She straightened, shading her eyes from the sun, and looked in the direction of the shout. When she spied Kathryn, she frowned in resignation and gestured for her to come forward. "Let her by," she said, and the lines parted immediately, allowing her to pass.

"I'm sorry to interrupt," Kathryn said when she gained Mrs. Hughes's side. "Is everything all right? All these people, it's not Daniel—"

"No, he's fine." Her mouth drew a thin, disapproving line. "As fine as he ever is these days, that is."

Relief swamped her. "Oh, thank God." The gate yawned open. A man in gray ushered three people through and clanged it shut. "What are all these people doing here?"

Mrs. Hughes sniffed. "You'll have to be asking that of Mr. Hall himself, I reckon."

She waved over a tall, lean man Kathryn recognized as one of the half dozen who usually worked in the yard and gardens. "Sagendorf, why don't ya escort Mrs. Hall in?"

There were six people in the foyer. A couple wearing ragged clothing and bewildered, hopeful smiles stood in the pattern of light and shadow made by the leaded window. A skinny man, the deep lines in his face etched black with coal dust, huddled with three equally gaunt children by the base of the grand staircase.

Libeus, as dapper as ever in black herringbone and a bright red vest, appeared in the doorway that led to the study, a room which Kathryn had never seen Daniel enter. "You may come in now," he told the young couple, and waved for them to enter.

"Libeus?" she asked.

Libeus pursed his lips and thought for a moment. "Come on." He gestured for her to join him.

The room had clearly been designed to impress, with its soaring ceilings and rich, carved paneling, a massive hearth trimmed in glossy black marble. But the room, like many in the house, had been completely stripped, leaving the rows of bookshelves empty, the big windows draped in faded silk.

A cluster of simple, straight-backed chairs had been dragged into the room since the last time she'd peeked in. The couple Libeus had just admitted took seats near the hearth. Over by the window, Daniel sat holding one hand of an elderly woman, who wept noisily into the handkerchief she clutched in the other.

"What's going on, Libeus?"

"What do you think?" Libeus hooked his thumbs in his bright vest. "He's attempting to dispense with all his money again, in a rather more determined and public manner than he has for some time."

"But I thought . . . I thought this was exactly what he was trying to avoid, having all these people descending on him."

He eyed her askance. "I pointed out that precise thing to him."

Oh, no. "He told me once that he had trouble distinguishing between those who truly needed his aid and those who merely wanted his money."

"He's gotten better at it, over the years." Libeus pursed his mouth. "With a few obvious exceptions, of course."

She'd spent a fair amount of time with harsh emotions churning inside her. With hate, and anger, and terror, and grief. But guilt, her new companion, was different, a sick feeling low in the pit of her belly, as if even her stomach could not stand to reside in a person such as she.

Because this time it was all her own fault. No matter what had happened before, at least it had never been her own fault.

"Besides," he went on, "I'm not sure he particularly cares anymore."

"Oh, Libeus." She sighed.

As if alerted to her presence, Daniel looked up the moment she stepped into the room. For just an instant, one that gave her a brief, glorious spurt of hope, his eyes lit up, his mouth threatening to lift into a smile. Then, as if he suddenly remembered that he wasn't supposed to be pleased to see her, all hints of warmth vanished from his face.

He held her gaze as he deliberately took a pile of bills from the leather-covered box resting on a tiny table beside his chair. He counted out a thick stack of cash and added it to the healthy sum the crying woman already clasped. She promptly dissolved into a fresh fit of weeping.

His chin lifted, eyes blazing with fierce blue, silently daring Kathryn to object to his largesse. *It's not yours,* his expression said. *It'll never be yours, you don't have the right.*

She stifled the reflexive protest, finding her automatic denial weak and faint, easily suppressed.

Sunlight streamed through the window behind him and washed warm golden tints into his hair, delineating the fine, aristocratic lines of his features. His shoulders were broad in their crisp white shirt, his hands gentle as they patted the twisted ones of the stooped woman.

He had such a glorious heart, her Daniel. Strong and generous, fathoms deep.

"He'll never forgive me," she whispered in despair.

"Oh, I don't know about that."

She'd forgotten Libeus still hovered at her side. He'd made no secret of his disapproval of her over the past few weeks. She was not hurt by it, for its source was clear: he owed his loyalty, all and exclusively, to Daniel. In fact, she was glad that Daniel had someone like Libeus in his corner.

"I would not have expected to hear that from you," she said in surprise.

Libeus rocked back on his heels in meditation. "I am forced to acknowledge he is not happy without you, either," he told her. "And a marriage . . . well, it is a very long time, isn't it? And you do not strike me as the sort of person who gives up easily."

Encouraged by his words, the same determination that had gotten her through so much before, the determination that had yet to fail her, surged anew. She smiled gratefully at Libeus.

No right to Daniel's fortune? The thought no longer frightened her, not nearly as much as she would have expected it to. But no right to Daniel?

Well, they'd just have to see about that, wouldn't they?

His grandmother lay sleeping, a small hillock beneath her satin coverlet, the jewels that were her comfort and only familiarity scattered about her as always. In the last few weeks, her grip on reality had fluctuated wildly. Some days she was no different, comfortably lost in her illusions and memories. But, for the first time in Daniel's recollection, she sometimes seemed to realize that he was not, after all, his father. And then she would weep, heartbreaking sobs that threatened to break her decimated body in half.

But now she slept, the coverlet just barely rising and falling over her cadaverous chest. He wondered how long she could continue on as she was.

Or how long he could.

"Oh. I didn't know you were in here."

Kathryn stood uncertainly in the door, a book in her hand, one forefinger wedged between the pages to hold her place. She wore something soft and simple that clung to her hips and revealed the upper curves of her breasts. Her hair, loose and fair, clouded around her shoulders. And his heart, his senseless heart that should have been fully armored against her, leapt at the sight of her.

"I thought perhaps I'd read to her," Kathryn said softly.

"She's sleeping."

"So I see." She held her hands at her waist, her fingers twining together, the only motion she made. Silence seemed a living thing, an awkward intruder neither one knew how to get rid of. Finally, she asked, "Do you want me to stay with her?"

"No." He didn't want to ask anything of her. "Julia's downstairs, taking tea. I'll tell her to come up when I go down."

It seemed a dangerous thing to do, to brush by her in the doorway, to be that near her when he remembered far too well the feel of her close against his body. But she remained in place, and so he walked quickly by her.

"Daniel?" she asked, when he'd just entered the sitting room.

Stiff as though he braced for a blow, he turned to face her. She took one step nearer, the door swinging shut behind her, but said nothing more.

If he stood here with her much longer, her eyes wide and misty, the lithe line of her body visible beneath her dress, he'd do something he'd regret.

Though he was beginning to wonder just how much he'd regret it after all. "Did you want something?" he demanded, unwilling to test his resolve further.

"What would you do?" she asked, gesturing toward the room where his grandmother slept, "if you didn't have to stay here with her?"

He'd hardly let himself fantasize about it. Why long for something that might not happen for years and years? But her words released the half-formed plans that lived in the back of his mind despite his best efforts at evicting them.

"I'd leave, of course. Go anywhere, everywhere." The images tantalized him. Minnesota, the deep green forest and ripe fields and clear waters he missed so much. New Ulm, where they'd known him since he was nine and were far more impressed by the fact that he was the best third baseman the town team had ever seen than that he'd been born a Sellington.

And then, once he felt like his old self again, he'd go to all the wondrous places he'd never seen, or glimpsed briefly on family trips and always longed to return to. The ocean, the desert, the grand cities of Europe.

"Places where nobody's heard of Edward Sellington. Or cares who he is." He swallowed hard. "Places where people can make good use of what I have to give."

"Daniel." She swayed closer to him, until her scent reached him, as heady as his dreams. Her mouth, her eyes, were soft with sympathy. He'd revealed too much, he realized. He did not need her compassion.

"You could go," she said quickly. Kathryn could not believe she was suggesting this to him now. She did not want him to leave her. She would be shattered if he left her. "She is . . . she is good with me, Daniel. If I were here, perhaps she wouldn't be so upset at your absence. You could be free."

Oh, the temptations the woman presented him with! Not just the lure of losing himself in her body but the enticement of shedding a burdensome mantle by leaving here, if only for a while. How was a man to resist?

"No," he said, while deep inside, the selfish part of him screamed in protest. "She is not your responsibility."

"Why is she yours?" She took a step forward, tilting her head back to look up into his face. It exposed her neck, a smooth, warm curve that he'd loved to kiss. "She didn't care for you. She didn't raise you. She didn't protect you. Why is she your responsibility now?"

Her statements were undeniable. But it didn't change a thing. He shrugged. "She's family."

"Then she's my family, too. As much as yours, if that's the only guide you judge by." With each breath she took, the swell of her breast lifted her bodice. He could drag the edge down with one finger, expose the lovely bud of her nipple, and take it in his mouth.

She was a blatant opportunist. Unscrupulous, deceitful, untrustworthy. She'd handed him a dream and snatched it back when he'd dared to believe in it.

And when she smiled at him, his body didn't give a damn.

"I can't," he said finally. *I can't leave. And I can't love you.*

"You don't have to decide now. I'm not going anywhere."

And oh, there was ferocious provocation in that. To know that she would be there. That night, the next day, next week. Only a few steps away so that, anytime he wanted her, she could be his.

She'd come so near that her toes nudged his.

"Your button's going to come off," she said, pointing to one low on his shirt, just above his waistband. She reached over and fiddled with it, twisting it on its loosened threads. Her knuckles brushed his belly, and he sucked in a staggered breath. "I could fix it for you," she murmured.

And the suspicion that had been burgeoning for weeks firmed into conviction. "You're trying to seduce me."

"Hmm?" Her hand flattened against his belly, one fingertip finding its way through the gap in his shirt, a hot stroke against his skin. "Noticed that, did you?"

He'd expected denial. Or at least demure prevarication. But to hear her intent confirmed, unvarnished, blatant, caught him in the gut, blasting what had been a slow, manageable simmer into a powerful, nearly uncontrollable need. "We can't."

"Really?" She pressed a kiss to his jaw, just a quick flutter that turned his knees to jelly. "Why not?"

"Because we—" Her tongue touched him this time, in the hollow of his throat, and the reasons evaporated like flamed alcohol, leaving only the burn. "It's not the same for us now. Not anymore."

"No," she admitted. "But why do all those other things make it wrong to enjoy this? Do you hate me so much? Don't you at least want to take what joy you can from this marriage?"

It sounded so reasonable. So forgivable. Maybe . . .

No. He wouldn't hand himself over to her again. Couldn't open himself up to another blow. For this one would surely destroy him.

"I don't want you."

She stilled, her mouth a hairbreadth from his. He heard her quick, pained intake of air, saw her skin draw tight over her features. "Well." She dropped her hands and stepped back. And he felt her absence as strongly as her presence, a keen and painful desert where the rich, vibrant life of her touch had been. "I guess that's clear enough."

Then her shoulders lifted, her mouth firming in determination. "You can say that all you want, Daniel. Maybe it's even true."

Oh, God. He didn't want to hurt her. Didn't she know that he just wanted to ensure that neither of them started building, believing in, expectations that they couldn't fulfill?

"But a lifetime is a very long time, Daniel," she said softly. "And what we had . . . well, I can't believe that's the kind of thing that's contained that easily. And, when you decide to change your mind, I'll be here. Waiting."

He left then, before it was too late, striding out of the room and down to his office to bury himself in work. But, as his footsteps echoed through barren hallways, his frown kept trying to lift into a smile.

Chapter 21

Daniel quite skillfully eluded Kathryn for the next few days. Kathryn—though it took great effort to convince herself of this—chose to believe that he avoided her because he was on the verge of capitulation, and so he'd turned to the desperate, last-ditch resistance of simply never being alone with her. Some night soon, she thought, she would take her courage into her hands and go to his room, and he would not send her away.

She was not fool enough to believe sex would solve everything. But it would make her feel better. As if she'd given something in return for all she'd stolen from him. And, if he could not love her, there was sweet solace in the idea that he might love their child.

Once, over dinner—meals were their only contact, buffered always by Libeus's presence, usually Big John's, and often by a shifting array of other business acquaintances—she looked up from her pineapple Charlotte to find him contemplating her with palpable intensity. Her dessert lodged in her throat, and she had to swallow hard to clear the lump.

"Daniel?" she asked tentatively.

Seconds ticked into a full minute before he answered. "Come to my study later. Eight o'clock."

Excitement fluttered in her stomach, and she laid her spoon at the edge of her plate.

Just his study, she reminded herself. Not his bedroom. No reason to get too carried away.

But what if it was something else entirely that he wanted to see her about? What if he'd decided to divorce her after all? The delicate fluttering turned into a painful wrench.

"Is that an order?" she asked, trying to keep her voice light. "Or a request?"

The corners of his mouth lifted. It might not have been a smile, but it was definitely, thankfully, not a frown. "It's an order," he told her sternly.

"Then I shall be there."

"As well you should," he said, and the smile that his mouth refused expression shone in his eyes instead. And Kathryn felt as if, after weeks of battering storms, finally she just might glimpse the sun.

The door to Daniel's office, a thick slab of beautiful, inset wood, was closed. From behind it hummed a low murmur of voices. She tried not to be disappointed and failed miserably. He was hardly planning to tear her clothes off and ravish her on his desk if there were others present.

At least she was pretty sure he wasn't.

Perhaps a previous meeting ran longer than he'd expected. She hesitated, wondering if she should wait outside. She didn't want to interrupt.

But maybe he wanted her to come in. Make her once again witness him hand out piles of cash, waiting for her to protest, underscoring his low opinion of her. Well, she wouldn't do it. If she had to bite her own tongue off, she was going to let him do what he would.

Even if he was making a huge and horrible mistake.

A clock gonged somewhere in the depths of the mansion; she counted each bell, one through eight.

She straightened her skirts. She inspected the finish on the floor. With her sleeve, she scrubbed a barely visible smudge off an otherwise impeccable window-pane.

Her patience ran out by the time the clock chimed eight fifteen. She rapped her knuckles on the door, and the buzz of conversation inside stilled immediately.

The door opened a crack. Daniel stuck his head out, blocking her view of the interior.

"You're late," he accused her.

"I was here!" she protested. "I didn't want to in-trude."

"I told you eight o'clock."

"I know. But I heard voices, and . . ." Barely leashed tension simmered around him. His mouth remained firm, unsmiling, but his eyes gleamed. "So are you going to let me in?" she asked.

"Yes. Of course."

But it took a full minute before he complied while her stomach twisted into a knot and her mind burst with all the possibilities of what lay inside that door.

"Hey, sis! Nice place you got here."

"Tommy?" Her eyes saw it all, but her brain refused to register the facts. Tommy, thin and pale, blond fuzz bristling on his bony jaw, draped in Daniel's desk chair, his feet up before him as if he owned the place. Isabelle stood by the cold hearth, a bemused half smile on her face, her fingers tracing the design in the carved-marble mantle. Her mother looked more uncertain. She sat strictly upright, her mouth a severe line.

"What..." Her gaze slid uncertainly from her mother to Daniel and back again. Had they somehow discovered just *whom* she'd married? Had they come to beg him for more money?

She would not allow them to harass Daniel about their finances. The irony of that did not escape her, but there it was just the same. "What are you doing here?"

"He brought us." Tommy folded his hands together and popped knuckles that seemed too big for his fingers.

Kathryn rounded the desk and whacked at his legs. "Get your feet off Daniel's desk," she scolded him.

"Hey," he protested, but swung his outsize feet to the floor just the same. "Daniel doesn't mind. Do you?"

"It is my own favorite position," Daniel said. "There is something about elevating the legs that promotes serious contemplation, I've always found."

Oh, wonderful. As if her brother needed another person to indulge him.

"See there?" Tommy grinned up at her, and she battled equal urges to hug him and reprimand him.

"You will keep them off, anyway, or you will answer to me," she said firmly. "And now you will explain how you came to be here."

"I told you. Daniel, there, came and got us. Said we were his family now and were going to come live with you. Brought along a whole lug of big fellows, too, and had our stuff packed up and us over here before Mum could say a damn thing."

"Thomas!"

"Sorry," he rejoined, unrepentant.

Daniel stood tall and straight by the door, his hands clasped behind his back. "I'm sure you all have much to discuss," he said. "I'll leave you alone." And he plunged out the door as if he couldn't wait to leave.

"Kathryn," her mother snapped, her hands in a death grip on the chair arms. "I cannot believe that you—"

"Excuse me, Mother. It's going to have to wait." Kathryn hurried after Daniel, letting the door swing shut behind her. She glimpsed him far down the hall as he turned a corner.

"Wait!" Afraid he'd disappear before she could catch him, she grabbed her skirts and broke into a run. She pelted down the hallway, skidded around the corner, and crashed headlong into Daniel. "Oh!" she said breathlessly.

Reflexively he'd caught her to keep her from falling, and now his strong hands wrapped around her upper arms. It was the first time he'd touched her in nearly three weeks. She closed her eyes for a moment, savoring it, for she didn't know when—she would not consider *if*, only *when*—she'd feel this again.

"What is it?" he asked her.

"I—" It was a hundred things; she didn't know

where to begin. Or which he wanted to hear. And so she simply took the opportunity to study him, drinking in the sight of each familiar feature.

He cleared his throat, pulled his gaze away from hers. He must have realized he still held her, because he yanked his hands away and dropped them to his sides.

"If it's nothing in particular—" he began.

"No!" she burst out lest he leave before she had a chance to start. "My family, you . . . how did you find them? They've only lived there for a few weeks."

"You, at least, used your real name when we met," he said, a touch of bitter irony in his tone. "I'm very good at finding people, Kathryn, and I figured they had to be here in Denver somewhere. It wasn't difficult."

"But—" She couldn't credit it, kindness when he had so much right to anger. "Why did you do this?"

"It needed doing."

She smiled, tentative, hopeful. "You did this for me?"

He jammed his fists into his pockets, his jaw tightening. "I did it for them," he said flatly. He spun on his heel and strode off down the hall.

This time she let him go. So he could not leave her even that glimmer of hope, of gratitude, could he? Despair settled into her heart, sank deep as if it would never be evicted.

It simply would not do, to be unappreciative for what she had. She had life. She had safety. Her family had the same. And she had his name.

It was enough. It had to be.

Slowly she turned and retraced her steps, propelling

her feet back toward Daniel's office with an effort of
will. She stood outside the door for a moment, gath-
ering her wits and strength around her as if they might
shield her.

At her entrance, Tommy scrambled to remove his
feet from the desk and sit up straight, his face the
picture of innocence.

"Tommy, I thought I told you—"

"Hey, it's not like it's that nice of a desk, anyway."

"I know, but—"

"It's rather strange, now that you mention it," Isabelle said, drifting from the mantel to stare out at the
gardens and stables. "It's a beautiful house, but what
happened to all the furniture? Has he been forced to
sell it all off? Or does the man simply have no taste?"

"I believe," Kathryn said, bristling in defense of her
husband, "that he mostly just gave it away."

"How odd," Isabelle murmured.

"That's enough." Eudora rose from her chair, flags
of color on her cheeks, eyes narrowed to angry slits.
"My God, Kathryn, what have you done? How could
you have—"

"Wait a moment." Kathryn tilted her head in her
brother's direction. Perhaps there was no avoiding this
confrontation with her mother, but the others did not
have to witness it. "Tommy, Joey Gibson works in the
stables. Why don't you go say hello?"

"Aw, come on—"

"Now, Tommy," she said in a voice that brooked
no disobedience. He reluctantly rose and ambled from
the room, his toes scraping the floor as he went.

"Isabelle, have you had a chance to select a room yet? If you ask Hannah, I'm sure that she'll—"

"Oh, no." Isabelle fingered the draperies swooping over the arched window that stretched from the floor to three feet above her head. The curtains showed signs of having once been a rich royal blue. Now they'd faded to a streaky color many shades lighter, but their folds were deep and the fringe wide and luxurious. "You really don't think you can still just send me from the room like a child when you don't want me to hear something, do you?"

"I suppose not." Kathryn inhaled deeply, trying to marshal her reserves but finding only bone-deep exhaustion. "All right, Mother. Say your piece."

"I cannot believe that I even have to *say* it." Eudora's voice trembled. "After everything that Edward Sellington stole from us, how could you align yourself with his son now! How could you have done this to us?"

"I didn't do anything to us," Kathryn said, wondering why she even bothered to explain, doubting that her mother could ever be made to understand. "I did it *for* us."

"How can you say that!" Her hands clenched fistfuls of her skirt, her knuckles whitening. "I will not stay in this house. I will not take a cent from that man."

"Why'd you come, then?" Kathryn asked wearily.

"I didn't know until he brought us to this house who he was. He introduced himself as Daniel Hall. You said you had a rich husband. How was I supposed to know?"

"He *is* Daniel Hall. He *is* rich."

"I don't care if we starve in the streets. I will not be dependent on Edward Sellington's son!" Fury burned in Eudora's eyes. All the anger her mother carried toward her husband, toward Edward, that had never had an outlet before found one now in Daniel and herself.

"Who better?" Kathryn snapped. She'd done her best. Done everything she could to help them. Who was her mother to say it was the wrong choice? Knowing her decision was worth it was the only thing that sustained her; it was all she had left. Kathryn waved her arms widely, encompassing the whole of the house. "What do you suppose we paid for? The marble in that mantel? The chandelier in the foyer? What better way to get some of it back?"

Eudora pursed her lips, seeming to consider Kathryn's words, but anger never bowed easily to logic. "Kathryn, you foolish, stupid girl, what have you done to us?"

"I did what I had to do," Kathryn said. "Tommy is out of the smelter. Isabelle is out of Simon Moore's. And you are all out of the Schatz House."

"You have to give her one thing, Mother," Isabelle drawled, wandering over to join them in the center of the room. "When she finally decided to whore, she did a hell of a lot better job of it than I did."

"Don't talk about your sister like that." The crack of Eudora's palm on Isabelle's lovely cheek resounded wickedly through the study. Eudora gasped, all the anger and hatred deflating from her like air from a balloon.

Isabelle lightly fingered the reddening spot on her

face, the same strange half smile playing about her lips. "Do you feel better now?"

"I—" Eudora flexed her hand as if it pained her. Her shoulders slumped.

Isabelle turned to Kathryn and took her hands. "How are you?" she asked softly. "Truly? He's not—"

"I'm fine."

"You don't sound fine."

"But I am," Kathryn insisted, more firmly this time. So what if *fine* had turned out to be a painful state? Her body healthy and safe, but her heart irreversibly wounded? She'd made her choices. It was up to her to live with the result of them.

"He hasn't hurt you?" Eudora asked. "He—"

"No." She shook her head to emphasize her denial. She wouldn't allow them to believe such a thing of Daniel. "He is nothing like Edward was—or what I believe Edward was, from what you and Daniel have told me. He's a good man, a kind and generous man."

"Are you sure?" Isabelle asked with hard-won skepticism. "Sometimes . . . well, men can take on that facade for a while, to get what they want, when there's something very different underneath, and you don't find that out until it's too late."

"I'm sure." Kathryn gave Isabelle's hands a little shake for emphasis. "He's everything I said, and more. In fact, he—" Her voice wavered, and she swallowed to steady it. The truth was the truth. "—he deserves far better than what I did."

"Oh my God." A look of horror crossed Isabelle's lovely face. "You've gone and fallen in love with him."

"I—" Kathryn stopped, shrugging. What was the point in denying it?

"What are you going to do?"

What *could* she do? Except continue to do her best to make it up to him. And pray that, someday, he might find a way to forgive her? "I don't know."

"Oh dear." Eudora rubbed the top of Kathryn's back, between her shoulder blades, the light, circling touch she'd used to soothe her as a child. "I guess that settles it, then?"

"We have to stay now," Isabelle said.

"Yes," Eudora agreed. "We have to stay now."

Chapter 22

❦

"**M**rs. Hall!"

Kathryn stood in the foyer, tying the ribbons of her bonnet beneath her chin, on her way out to the front gardens. Having grown up in a place where a clump of sword grass and a few struggling daisies were passed as lush vegetation, she'd discovered a strong, surprising affinity for the great expanses of green that surrounded the house.

There, amongst the smells and rich earth and growing things, the depression that lingered over her inside the gloomy confines of the mansion was scoured away by the fresh air. The gardeners tolerated her assistance, as long as she asked them to confirm her identification before she pulled any weeds—they'd lost a dozen fuchsias the first day, before that policy was implemented. And, as they'd patiently informed her, the growing season was soon to come to an end in any case. There was not much permanent damage she could inflict at this time of year.

The only drawback was that her hands weren't in much better condition than when she'd taken such pains to hide them from Daniel. Ah well; obviously she was not meant to be a lady of leisure.

"Mrs. Hall!" A strapping young man hurried toward her—Andrew, she thought, though she'd had less success in figuring out what his duties were. Anything that required a young back, for one thing, but she had a notion that Libeus was training the boy as his assistant.

"Yes, Andrew?"

He lit up, a grin that took up half his lower face and revealed a fine set of teeth. Oh, good; she'd remembered his name correctly. Soon she might know them all . . . in a year or six.

"This came for you this morning, ma'am. The fellow who delivered it—and a big one he were, maybe even went a bit on Big John—well, he said it was urgent, but you were up with Mrs. Sellington, ma'am, and I didn't want to intrude—"

"I'm sure it'll be fine," she interrupted, because she was concerned for his air supply if he continued on as he was. "Thank you kindly."

"You're welcome. Ma'am."

The envelope he dropped in her palm was square, fashioned of thick, stiff paper the color of cream, such lovely stuff she hated to tear it. She slid her finger beneath the flap and slowly worked the seal free.

"I'll leave you now," Andrew said. "So's you can read it in private-like."

He looked so pleased at remembering his manners that she didn't dare tell him it wouldn't have bothered her at all if he remained. "Thank you," she said with a nod of her head. He bobbed, still grinning, and tramped off in the direction of the kitchen.

The sturdy seal resisted her efforts, and, as she worked, she idly wondered what it might contain. Anyone who cared enough to correspond with her already lived under the same roof she did. Perhaps one of the society women who'd failed to gain Daniel's patronage for some charity event or another had decided to approach the matter through an easier route. The quality of the paper certainly substantiated that theory. Kathryn amused herself briefly by imagining herself wandering into a grand affair, surrounded by dresses she'd sewn inch by painstaking inch. Would any of the women dare acknowledge her?

But she was Daniel Sellington's wife now. How could they not?

The seal finally broke free. She slid out a single sheet of once-folded paper and flipped it open. It held only a few lines, black, dark, carefully printed.

Mrs. Hall—

You will come to my office as soon as possible. The matter is urgent, and I am certain you are too intelligent to risk the consequences if you do not comply quickly.

Simon Moore

The man certainly wasn't much on polite requests, was he? She considered for a moment, tapping the paper against her palm. What could he be in such a rush about? Surely he wasn't in dire financial straights and in need of another diamond from her.

Well, it didn't really matter what he wanted, did it? She'd finally discovered the silver lining in this whole mess ... nothing Simon Moore did could hurt her now. Daniel already knew the worst.

The thick paper at first refused to tear. She took a firm grip and gave a good yank. The ripping sound was so satisfying she did it again, and again, until a flurry of tiny white-paper squares drifted down around her feet, as though a snowdrop had decided to shed all its petals at once.

"Well, gee, I guess I don't gotta ask if you enjoyed that. The look on your face is answer enough."

"John!" He was just inside the front door, a small leather satchel swallowed in his big grip. "I didn't hear you come in."

"Oh, yeah, happens all the time. I'm such a quiet, stealthy sort, you know, that people never notice I'm there."

"More like they're much too intimidated to say anything."

"Naw, ya think? By *me?*" He grinned.

"Well, you must admit there aren't many who are privileged to realize that the body of a grizzly carries a heart every bit as big as your shoulders." Her voice softened. "I count myself very lucky to be one."

"Aw, now, don't go squishy on me. You're not the type, for one thing. And if you do, then I'd have to come over there and comfort you—can't help *that*—and then, if Daniel caught us, he'd make me fight 'em for two whole hours today, 'stead of one."

"Do you really think he would?" she said, and immediately cursed the wistful tone of her voice. Now when had she started to wallow in self-pity? It wasn't a particularly attractive trait. Nor a very useful one.

Big John crossed the foyer at a speed that belied his bulk. He patted her shoulder awkwardly, his consoling thumps nearly catapulting her to the floor, murmuring "Now, now" between blows.

"John, really, the next time I'm choking to death, you'll be the first one I'll call, but I'm fine now, really."

Grimacing, he dropped his hand immediately. "Sorry."

"It's all right." And, because she couldn't stand to see him looking so contrite, she smiled, and added, "Besides, I was rather looking forward to a hug or two, and all I get is a whack on the shoulder?"

He grinned, an appealing smile for all that it was missing an incisor or two. "Oh, no, you're not going to trick me into that. I know that you fancy your own private match, but I'd probably squeeze all the air right out of you, and that's a fact."

"I suppose it is a distinct possibility." She'd grown very fond of this big ox of a man, she reflected.

She'd always had family. She'd had little time for friends, but now she counted him one—one more precious thing that Daniel had brought into her life.

She reached up and touched the bridge of John's nose, mishappen as a withered potato. "How many times has this been broken?"

"Stopped countin' at twelve." He scraped his toe through the collection of paper bits on the floor. "So what's this all about, hmm?"

The urge to guard her secrets was well ingrained in

Kathryn. But oh, she was tired of lies and evasion! What could it hurt now? "How much do you know?"

"Some would say not much," he admitted cheerfully. "About you and Daniel, you mean?"

"Yes."

"I know a lot about Daniel's side of the story," he said gently. "Not so much about yours. I'm willing to listen to it, if you want."

"No, knowing Daniel, I imagine you got the gist of it." Daniel was nothing if not fair. The problem was that even a scrupulously honest recitation of the facts put her in the wrong. "I can't imagine why you're still talking to me, all things considered."

He shrugged. "People make mistakes. God knows that's somethin' I proved more than once."

"I wish . . ." She trailed off. What was the use in wishing? She sighed and bent to scoop together the paper fragments. "This note . . . someone thought that they could make a good bit by threatening to inform Daniel of my past."

She collected the scraps and rose with them tucked into her fist.

"Guess they're going to be disappointed, aren't they?"

"Guess so." She smiled thinly. "He's not the type to take well to disappointment, however."

"Oh yeah?" He flexed his arm until his huge biceps threatened to pop his sleeve. "He gives you any trouble, I'd be happy to help convince him."

"You and Simon Moore? Now that'd be something to see."

"Simon Moore!" He stared at her. "Hell, Kathryn,

when you get yourself in a tangle, you don't do it halfway, do you?"

She gave a pained laugh. "No, I guess not."

"What are you going to do?"

"I'm not going to do anything. What difference does it make if he talks to Daniel now?"

"Do you really think Moore'll just leave it go at that?" he asked skeptically.

Kathryn suppressed a frisson of anxiety. "I'll cross that bridge if it comes."

"Are you going to tell Daniel about the letter?"

Now there was a question. What good would it do to tell him now? Remind him of what a mistake he'd made when he married her? "I'm not going to *not* tell him. If it comes up, I will. Or if it seems there's a reason to tell him."

He studied her for a moment before nodding. "All right then." He swung his arms in a wide half circle before clapping his hands in anticipation. "So you wanna come watch me beat the crap out of your husband?"

She winced. "No, I think I'll decline the honor this time."

"Okay." He saluted her before clomping out. "But if you change your mind, you know where to find us."

Fists and sweat and curses flew in the ballroom of the Sellington Mansion.

There was a scrape beneath Daniel's chin, an ugly purpling along his jaw. But a wide assortment of bruises covered Big John's abdomen where Daniel, given his height disadvantage, had chosen to concentrate his attack.

Big John's fist shot toward Daniel's nose. Daniel dodged left and the blow glanced off his right ear. He countered, one hard jab bouncing off John's diaphragm, another thudding low in his belly.

Grunting, John planted his feet and rained a series of quick strikes around Daniel's shoulders. Daniel snarled back, stood his ground, and hurled one great punch upward just as Big John ducked to attack Daniel's body. The blow hit Big John squarely beneath his massive chin, and he dropped both fists and staggered before he decided standing up wasn't worth the effort.

John plopped down. His eyes crossed for a moment before focusing blearily on Daniel, who stood over him, fists still at the ready, his chest heaving from exertion.

"Damn, Daniel, d'ya know how long it's been since somebody dropped me?"

Daniel glared down at him, and John thought that he was going to haul off and slug him again. Then Daniel shook himself, visibly throwing off his threatening intensity. "Sorry," he mumbled, and dropped down next to Big John.

"You are not sorry," John accused him. "You're happy as a hog in shit you were the one to do it."

Daniel's grin was almost like his old self. "At least if it's me, you're not losing any money out of the deal."

"True. Except at this rate, I'm not going to be in any shape to fight Lightning Lyle Donovan next month."

"I'll fill in for you." Daniel yanked at the knotted strings on his gloves.

"I've never heard you anticipate the chance to beat up on an innocent man before. Excepting me, of course."

"Donovan is hardly an innocent man." Daniel tore his gloves off. "Besides, things change."

"That they do." John fell back against the mat, his arms spread wide, and gave a sigh of relief. "Wouldn't do to be stubborn about changes then, would it? Kinda stupid to dig your heels in about something a fella should just up and accept."

"What's that supposed to mean?" Daniel challenged, a gleam in his eye that said he'd be more than happy to retie his gloves. Or fight without them.

"I just wish like hell you'd make peace with your wife, that's all," Big John said mildly.

"Make peace with her." Daniel jerked his gloves off and hurled them to the mat. "You know what she did, John. She—"

"Yeah, I know what she did." He laced his hands comfortably over his belly and commenced contemplating the gold-gilt designs on the ceiling. "But what she *did's* not what she's *doin'*, is it?"

"So I'm just supposed to forget what—"

"Naw, I didn't say forget. Forgettin's not easy. Not usually even right, 'cause if you forget, you don't learn from it." He drummed his fingers against his stomach, hummed a tune along with the rhythm. "Nobody said you had to be the happy little lovebirds. But you can't tell me that you wouldn't be happier poking that gorgeous woman once in a while than you are trying to

316   SUSAN KAY LAW

work off your frustrations by pounding on me instead."

"John!" Daniel didn't know whether to laugh or to hit him.

"Hey, don't be mad at me for telling the truth." He pointed at a figure smack-dab in the middle of the ceiling, encircled by a ring of vines. "Whad'ya think that's s'posed to be? A naked pig with wings?"

"I think it's a cupid."

"A cupid. No shit?"

Daniel shrugged. "Yeah."

"A cupid. Huh. What do you know about that? The nose is more smashed up than mine."

"Kathryn thinks I should keep it," Daniel said suddenly.

"The money, you mean?"

"Yeah. She still wants it."

"You can hardly blame her for that, can you? A person would have to be a bit tetched in the head *not* to want it. Now, don't get all het up." He waved Daniel, who'd sprung into fighting pose, back down. "I meant a regular person. The problem is, you and that wife of yours are just too much alike."

"You've taken a few too many blows to the head if that's your opinion, John. I've suspected it for years, but this proves it."

"Naw, think about it." John wiggled his shoulders against the mat, closing his eyes in satisfaction when he discovered a more comfortable spot. "Both trying to make more of it than it is. She figures that if she just gets enough money, nothing bad'll ever happen again. And you've decided that it's the reason for all the bad things that ever happened to you. And the truth is, it's still just a *thing*, and no one thing can ever do that much, good or bad. For anybody."

His philosophical musings were greeted with dead silence. John wondered if Daniel was going to start swinging at him again, and he cracked an eye open to check. Daniel just gawked at him.

John chuckled. "Didn't think I had it in me, didja?"

Daniel had the grace to look abashed. "Well, I did, sorta, but I—"

"Who's that?" Big John burst out, snapping up to a sitting position.

"Hmm?" Daniel twisted, following John's stare. Isabelle, insubstantial and fragile as a wraith, stood uncertainly in the doorway. "Oh, that's just Isabelle." He raised his voice to call to her. "Can I help you with something?"

"I didn't want to intrude." A layered mist of loosely fitted pale gray fabric floated around her slender body. One hand rested lightly on the doorframe.

"You didn't."

"I was wondering if you'd seen Tommy?"

"Uh-oh. What's missing this time?"

She frowned. "Just my gloves. I can't find them anywhere."

"Try the stables," Daniel advised. "The grooms are his best customers."

"I will," she said, and disappeared as if she'd simply faded through the walls.

"Tom's doing a good business selling bits and pieces of her wardrobe to all the young bucks 'round here," Daniel informed Big John. "I suppose I'm going to have to put a stop to it sooner or later, but it goes against my grain to squash such creative young enterprise."

"If I slip him a hundred, do you think he'd pinch me something *really* good?"

Daniel glanced over at his friend. "Lord, you look more stunned than when I connected with that punch." He was tempted to poke John, to see if he'd just up and topple over.

"But who *is* she?" John said in awe.

"Kathryn's sister, of course. Can't you tell?"

"Yeah, I guess," John mumbled, eyes wide and shining. "She sure is a pretty thing, ain't she?"

"You want to meet her?"

Panic flooded him. "But I *can't*. I mean, I—" He looked wildly down at his bare chest and feet, the ugly collection of bruises and blood smearing what hadn't exactly been a refined view to begin with. "I'm not dressed, I don't have a shirt, I have to—"

"No time like the present." Daniel clapped him companionably on one massive shoulder. "Why would you want to cover up about the only thing you've got to recommend you, anyway? Let's go."

Chapter 23

It was a lovely day in early October, the sky clear and the clouds high. The warm air held a faint, brisk hint of the chill to come in a few hours, once the sun no longer held it back.

Kathryn headed for the back door, anticipating a few hours of blessedly mindless grubbing in the dirt. Her mother was happily ensconced in the library, where she now spent most of her time. Unlike the paintings and statuary that once graced the house, Daniel had never dispersed the book collection, but had instead thrown it open to the use of all his employees. Once she'd discovered it, Eudora, having spent fifteen years without books, had devoted herself to making up for lost time.

Isabelle was . . . well, Kathryn didn't know what she did with her time—beyond flirting shamelessly with Big John whenever he was near. It was taking an enormous effort on Kathryn's part to refrain from investigating how else her sister was entertaining herself. But it was not her responsibility, Kathryn reminded herself regularly; Isabelle had been abundantly clear on that point. And at least Isabelle was not at Simon Moore's. That would have to satisfy Kathryn for the moment.

Tommy was, Kathryn suspected, in the stables. Having spent little time in close contact with horses, he'd fallen madly in love with the creatures. His rudimentary riding skills improved daily. The unabashed excitement in his voice when he talked about a new mare was something to behold. Though Kathryn knew that she would soon have to push the issue of *school*, for the moment she was satisfied. It kept him occupied and safely out of the house. Not to mention his new infatuation with all things equine was distracting him from the fact that a few of the younger maids had most definitely noticed Mr. Hall's new brother-in-law. Kathryn would prefer to delay his discovery of *that* as long as possible.

Kathryn slipped out the door and descended the wide brick staircase, determined to enjoy herself. There was no reason *not* to enjoy herself. So what if there was a great big hole in the middle of her chest where her heart was supposed to be? So what if her husband might never forgive her?

Be careful what you wish for . . . the old saw taunted her, mocked her daily.

The warm, twisted iron of the handrail bumped beneath her palm. She reached the ground and turned toward the wide, grassy expanse between the house and the stables, where a broad path of bricks, soft green moss tufting the spaces between like a reversed quilt, led toward the gardens.

Tommy was not in the stables after all. In the open space, he and Joey tossed a ball to each other. It

dropped into Tommy's glove with a soft plop. He
yanked it out and cocked his arm, ready to let fly.

She heard a shout. *Daniel*. The heart she'd thought
absent made itself known with a decided thump as she
watched him straighten from where he'd been leaning
against a tree, watching, and cross over to Tommy. He
adjusted her brother's fingers around the ball and
mimed a throw, kicking his front leg high and letting
his back one fly up as he leaned forward into the toss.

Tommy watched carefully before mimicking Daniel's motion. The ball shot across the space and
snapped into Joey's glove. Daniel nodded and clapped
Tommy on the shoulder in encouragement before he
resumed his position against the tree.

He wore the simplest of clothes—a loose white shirt
and plain tan trousers. He folded his arms across his
chest, bent one leg to prop his foot against the tree.
The fabric of his pants pulled tight over his thigh, and
her hands flexed of their own accord, tingling with an
abrupt, acutely physical memory of what those muscles had felt like beneath her hands. No give at all to
them, power and strength expressed in living flesh and
bone.

The baseball arced through the air again, a bright
white streak against blue, blue sky. Daniel's gaze followed its path. She knew the instant he saw her standing across the lawn. His body stiffened. All the life
and emotion in his face closed down immediately, like
dropping a curtain across a stage, the color and action
of characters and props hidden behind bland, anonymous cloth.

He would vastly prefer she just keep walking. That

she'd go on to work in the gardens, spend her afternoon ripping out dead and unwanted plants as she'd planned. She knew that. It would be easier for both of them.

But they had a whole long life to endure. If they could not find their way back to a semblance of friendship, could they at least achieve some level of unemotional courtesy? So they could be in the same room for a few minutes without experiencing that acute, sizzling discomfort?

The sooner begun, the sooner done, she decided firmly. But her hands clutched great wads of her skirt, curled tightly around it as if she could take some courage from the fabric.

At least it kept her hands from shaking.

She skirted the area where Tommy and Joey still played and acknowledged Tommy's distracted wave with a quick nod. Daniel pushed away from the tree at her approach, his back snapping straight. But he wouldn't just leave. She knew his pride would not allow him to run simply from the appearance of his wife.

His gaze turned to the boys, intently following the path of the ball as if it mattered. She gained his side, watching in silence as well while she gathered her nerve.

Tommy looked so happy. It was a boyish thing, to play a game of catch on a sunny afternoon. She couldn't recall him ever doing such a thing before. He'd played different games as a child, he and the other boys on their street. Games that didn't require balls or gloves or any other equipment that must be bought and paid for. Instead, they entertained themselves with sticks and rocks and items scrounged from the garbage. And much of what they occupied themselves with had a mercenary bent. Could they find things someone would pay them for? Could they chase down one of the feral dogs the city had placed a bounty on? And they gambled, too, even when they were very little and looked so odd hunched over a game, wrangling over pennies or pieces of cheese and bread filched from nearly barren kitchens.

And soon, too soon, there'd been no more play at all. They'd gone to work, in the smelters, mostly, factories for luckier ones, sweeping or fetching or doing whatever else the young ones were put to first. Sometimes other jobs, for people like Simon Moore, ones that paid better and took a lighter toll on the body but extracted a much higher price from the soul.

Her heart lifted, expanding as if taking in some of the sunlight beaming down on her.

This new life for her brother, more like the one he *should* have had, was because of Daniel.

She sneaked a glance at him out of the corner of her eye. The line of his nose was clean, bold, but there were lines of fatigue bracketing his eyes and mouth. He looked older than when she'd met him. Had *she* done that to him? She was so very sorry for it. But sorry, she'd long ago learned, didn't go very far.

Oh, she was sure he'd much rather she retreat, allowing him his solitude. He *deserved* to have her leave him alone, if that's what he wanted.

But he didn't deserve to have his life continue on this spare, joyless path for years and years. And she had to be the one to stop it.

"I know he's not always easy to have around." She gestured toward Tommy, who'd just jumped high to snatch a ball that appeared ready to sail right over his head. "He's . . ." She sighed. "He was born seven months after my father left. All four of us tried too hard to make it up to him, I think. To be something we couldn't. We couldn't give him much, but he got used to getting whatever there was without even having to ask for it."

"It happens." Daniel shrugged. "My mother—and all the servants—tried everything to make up for Edward to me. She couldn't protect me from him, so she tried her damnedest to protect me from *everything* else. It made me too cautious, too careful. I thought the world was lying in wait to get me. I'm not so sure his way's not better. Took me a while to learn that the rest of the world was far too busy going along, dealing with its own business, to take much notice of me one way or the other. He'll learn that, too."

It was an unexpected gift, a glittering bit of his past, this glimpse at some of what shaped him. She held on to the knowledge for a moment, treasured it. She knew something more of Daniel now than she had that morning.

"I worried about him so," she said. "As dangerous as the smelter was for him, the streets were worse. And I knew he'd go back there sooner or later, looking for an easier way. And then he'd end up lost to us, one way or the other."

"He'll be fine."

"I know." He did not want gratitude. He went to great lengths to avoid receiving it from anyone. It made him uncomfortable, because he didn't think he gave from generosity but obligation.

But still, she had to voice it. "Because of you, he will," she said. "He needed a man in his life. As an example. And as someone who can say 'no' and back it up. He'll fight you on it, but he needs it just the same. And I'm so thankful that you are doing this for him—for *me*—despite everything."

His jaw worked. His lids swept down over his eyes briefly, and he swallowed. She saw the slide of his Adam's apple down his tanned throat, disappearing beneath the edge of his collar, and up again. She wanted to follow the path with her mouth, feel the muscles work and his vivid life beat through his veins.

"They've become good friends," he said, gesturing at the boys.

Ah, he would not acknowledge her indebtedness, then. It didn't really matter. She'd needed to say it anyway.

"They have," she agreed.

"Extremely good for having known each other for such a short time. One would almost think they've been acquainted for years."

Her breath seized. "Oh?" she asked carefully.

His gaze spun to her. There was no accusation in his eyes, but there was knowledge, and that was enough.

"It's not his fault," she said desperately. "He didn't know . . . he'd no idea what he was telling me. He'd known me for years, trusted me, and it was *me*, my fault. I took advantage of him."

His pupils were so dark, she felt like she was looking into a bottomless well. They'd swallowed all emotion, turned flat and blank as the entrance to a fathomless pit.

Her tone pitched higher. "Please don't take it out on him. You can't hold it against him. It was my fault," she repeated. "*Please*."

"Is that really what you think of me?" His voice was tight, wrapped in on itself like machine spooled twine.

It stabbed at her, a physical sensation piercing deep and sharp beneath her breastbone. Once again, she'd underestimated him. Because she'd never known a man like Daniel, she'd automatically ascribed to him the actions of the type of man to whom she was accustomed. Assumed that he'd punish Joey for his disloyal, albeit unintentional, aiding of her plot.

A fierce instant of emotion flashed deep in his eyes, then was quickly snuffed. She held herself rigid, awaiting his response. She wanted his anger, anticipated the hot acid burn of it pouring over her. It was passion of a sort, a strong emotion, one she'd earned, and she needed it. Believed that he needed just as much to spill it.

Instead he spun away. Head down, he crossed the yard, big strides devouring the distance as if it were nothing. Tommy called to him, but Daniel didn't hear, or ignored him if he did, and so Tommy shrugged and returned to his game.

She'd told herself that she would do anything Daniel wanted, everything he asked of her. But she couldn't let him go. The anger he refused to allow release boiled up in *her* instead. If she let this issue lie between them again, they might go on like this forever. Rigid, distant, two married people further apart than any strangers.

She hurried after him, across the yard, up the stairs, into the narrow back hallway. She seemed to be forever chasing after him and that goaded her temper higher. "Daniel!" she shouted at his retreating form. He hunched, as if he could deflect her call with his shoulders, and charged ahead.

"Daniel!"

She dashed around the corner, emerging into a wider corridor. It was as if she no longer existed for him. He didn't respond to her calls. His determined pace never altered, neither slowing nor speeding up. Panic rose, along with the desperate certainty that if she did not get his attention immediately, address this wreck of their marriage, she never would.

A maid popped her head out of a doorway, her face bright with question. She took one look at Daniel and immediately withdrew, flinging the door shut.

Kathryn caught up with him at the entrance to the ballroom. She grabbed his arm and dug in her heels to stop him, forcing him to acknowledge her presence.

"I don't want to do this," he ground out, low and harsh. "Not now, not ever." And he wrenched his arm away with a painful yank.

He pushed open the door and shut it gently behind him. And that made her even more furious. Didn't he even care enough to slam the door? Who was he to be so perfect he didn't even bang a goddamn door when he had every right in the world?

So she yanked it open and slammed it herself, the

loud boom resonating through the high-ceilinged room like cannon fire, and defiantly shot the bolt. He would not be saved by the timely arrival of Libeus or Big John or anybody else. Not this time.

He'd picked up his boxing gloves and was working his hand into one. She snatched them away and hurled them against the wall. He merely looked at her, raising one eyebrow in superior question, like a headmaster faced with a disobedient student.

"Don't you ever get *mad*?" she raged at him. "Don't you ever feel *anything*? It's so much easier for you, isn't it, just to keep everybody at a distance? Have this vague pity for everyone and assuage it by giving them *things*, rather than actually get in there and risk feeling something that might hurt. That might *touch* you."

He was absolutely still. The room was alive with silence, stirred only by the faint sound of their respiration. Then, with a move so quick it blurred, he whirled and rammed his bare fist into the punching bag with such force the heavy bag swung wildly, its rope protesting with a shriek. He watched it sway for a moment before letting loose another blow. And then another, and another, faster, harder, meeting the pendulum swing of the bag with the exact peak of his strike, magnifying the power of the hit.

His punches flew. His breathing came quicker, too, matching the manic flailing of his fists. It was as if every trace of dark emotion he'd ever rejected, all the anger and hatred and wild injustice, now concentrated and was released at the contact of fist on old leather.

The bag burst, splitting open along one seam. Sand poured out of the opening and spilled into a growing cone on the floor. Daniel, fists still clenched and raised in fighting posture, chest heaving, watched the fall of sand slow to a trickle, kept staring until the last grains slid out before he whirled on her.

"Don't get *angry*?" His tone seethed with an undercurrent of savagery, every bit as powerful as the force he'd discharged each time he'd rammed the bag. "Edward got angry. He was angry every time he hit my mother. Angry every time he came after me. *Angry*"— he gulped in air—"angry when he pushed the mother who bore me down the stairs and murdered her."

The world reeled around her. Kathryn reached out a hand, groped for something to support her, found nothing.

She should have known. Somehow, she should have known. He'd hinted at it, she realized now, but she'd refused to hear. Hadn't wanted to believe he'd experienced such misery.

All that money . . . it had no more protected Daniel, *saved* Daniel, than it had her.

He looked down at his hands. The force of the blows had split his knuckles wide open. Blood oozed from them, trickling over his fingers, and he blinked as if surprised at the sight.

"I made John teach me how to box, because I swore I would never again stand by while someone I loved was hit and not be able to *stop* it." He wiped the blood off on his pants, leaving a dark smear across his thighs. "And I've spent every day since then terrified that I was going to use that skill on someone I loved instead."

Oh God! Her foolishness appalled her. She should

have left it alone. Allowed his demons to stay safely buried. And there was so little she could do to help him now except tell him the truth.

"You won't."

"I saw my father die." The words kept coming, torn from some place deep and dark. "Not more than ten feet away from me, shot in the gut by a man with an old grudge. I was just a kid, and you know what I wished?"

Mute, terrified, she shook her head.

"I wished I'd done it first."

Thank God he hadn't had the chance, Kathryn thought. He suffered so much for others' sins; his own, however justified, might have destroyed him. "You're a good man, Daniel."

"I—" His pupils were dilated, as dark and fiery as in passion. "How do you know?"

"I just do." Breath staggered in and out of his chest. Perspiration gleamed on his forehead. His white shirt had gone transparent, clinging to his torso. She could see the outline of his undershirt along his collarbone, around his shoulders, and the ridged plane of his abdomen.

She moved nearer to him. His fists were jammed at his hips, his jaw set at a hard angle. Slowly, she lifted up to her tiptoes, pressed her mouth at the hollow of his throat where a bead of moisture clung. She tasted salt. Smelled the heat of his exertions, the musk of aroused male.

Don't push me away. The plea beat in her heart, softened her mouth against his skin. She almost sobbed with the joy of touching him again, of having Daniel's skin, Daniel's smell, fill up her senses, her dreams.

She drew back. He stared off over her head, every muscle held taut. The cords in his neck stood out starkly, his arms fixed at his sides.

But he hadn't pushed her away.

She dropped to her knees before him, the parqueted wood of the floor hard against her kneecaps. Deliberately, she laid her palms flat against the side of his hips, hardly believing that finally—oh at last!—he was allowing it. She could touch him again, she could show him how much he meant to her. She could return something of what he'd given her.

He was already aroused. The outline of his erection strained the seam of his trousers. She leaned forward, pressed her open mouth hard against it. The texture of fabric was a slight abrasion on her lips, the heat of him burning through the cloth.

A low sound broke from him. He grabbed her upper arms and hauled her up. He brought her to eye level, her toes barely scraping the ground.

"Stop," he said harshly.

"Daniel." She'd been so *close*, he could not stop her now. "I'll do anything, I—"

"I don't want you to do anything," he ground out. "I don't want your gratitude, I don't want your damned wifely duty."

She stared at him, fighting despair, battling the part of her that said it was hopeless, and she should give up now before it hurt even worse.

But instead she leaned forward and placed a chaste, gentle kiss at the corner of his mouth. "What do you want, then?" she whispered, knowing the answer might shatter her heart once and for all.

Or it could save it.

"I want your passion," he told her.

He lowered her feet back to the ground and released her. Then he stepped back and brought his hands to his collar button. "Take off your clothes."

Anticipation and trepidation shivered through her. She rushed to comply, lest he change his mind. But her fingers were clumsy and her clothes more complicated than his. So he was done far before she was and waited, naked and tall, while she hurried to catch up and kept getting distracted by the sight of him.

"Lie down." His order was bald, unsoftened by romantic sentiment or pretty words. But they were Daniel's orders, so she acceded automatically, joyfully.

She glanced wildly around. "Where?" She'd lie on the ceiling if he asked, or on the grainy pile of sand. As long as he was with her.

"The mat will do."

It was formed of heavy canvas, stuffed with a thick layer of batting. She felt his regard heavy on her as she complied, and embarrassment washed over her, something she'd not felt with him before. But he'd barely touched her, done nothing but clip out commands in that low voice. For an instant she wondered if that was his intent after all, if he meant to humiliate her now for what she'd done.

But the thought evaporated almost before it formed. Not Daniel. And if her brain did not know him better than that by now, surely her heart did.

The coarse weave of the canvas scored the skin of

her back. She reached for him, anxious to sate her palms with the feel of his bare skin.

He lowered himself beside her and she brushed his shoulder, the nearest spot within reach.

"Don't touch me."

She drew her hand back as if scalded. "Daniel?" she asked hesitantly.

"I don't want this to be something you do for me, or *to* me." His voice roughened, the words mesmerizing her as surely as he wove a spell within the syllables. "I told you I don't want your gratitude. Or your guilt, or your obligation. If we do this, I want you to do it for no other reason than because you crave the feel of my body deep in yours."

If we—? But then her thoughts scattered completely, as he caught both her wrists and linked them in one big hand, bringing them up over her head and holding them there. The motion made her back arch, her breasts lifting as if to encourage his touch.

"You said you'd do anything I want," he reminded her. "I want your passion. I want to watch you arch into my touch. I want to hear you shout my name when you reach your peak. And I don't want you to touch me yet, not until you are touching me because you think you're going to die if you don't, and for no other reason."

He brushed her face first, drawing one fingertip along her brow, down her nose, following the curve of her lips, edging of her jaw. That was all he used, just the bare tip of one forefinger. He outlined a curve around her ear, skimmed over the line of her throat.

And moved down, to graze beneath each breast, to trace the edge of her aureoles and whisk over the tip.

It was such a light, tiny touch. And it felt as if every nerve ending she owned concentrated in whichever small place he stroked. She bit back a sob, a request for more. She was determined to do this his way.

He bumped his finger over each prominent rib and dipped it into the hollow of her navel. He followed the angle of her hipbone, drew a meandering line across her belly that left a sizzle of heat in its wake.

He watched the path his finger drew. She watched *him*. The elegant set to his mouth and the clean line of his brow never altered. She might have thought that what he did, her naked body and his exploration of it, had no effect on him at all. Except his nostrils flared as he dragged in more air, as he struggled and failed to keep his breath at an even pace.

His finger edged the pale curls shielding her sex, wound one coil around it. She whimpered, her hips lifting toward his hand, seeking a stronger touch. Instead he took his hand away and laid it against her throat, his thumb stroking the sensitive skin beneath her jaw.

"If I could pick the last thing I would ever see," he murmured, "it would be my hand on you."

And after that, she could not look away. She dropped her chin as his hand slid down and found one breast. His hand was deeply tanned, long-fingered, the sinews on the back strongly delineated. His dark skin stood out starkly against her paleness, a contrast keen and erotic. Dark against light. Hard, soft. Male . . . female.

She twisted, trying to free her hands to touch him, but his grip held firm. She could just receive. Only look at him, the beauty of lean muscle and bronze skin and vibrant strength. At the bold, dark jut of his erection against her white thigh. And at his hand, squeezing her nipple between his thumb and his palm so the hard tip just peeked out, slicing sharp pleasure through her body.

He claimed her belly. His hand rippled over her, sensation following his caress like twin waves. He moved steadily on, stroking her hip, opening her legs to his gaze and his touch.

He laid his hand upon her then, cupping her intimately, and she could watch no more. Her head pushed back against the mat, her eyelids fluttered shut.

His touch was light at first, tapping his fingertips against her most sensitive spot, a delicate drumming. Her breath came out in little exclamations of sound, in rhythm with each pat.

"I'm going to watch you," he told her. His voice was velvet, the words pouring over her, raising shivers on her skin. "I want to see every expression on your face as you reach your peak. I want to see what I've made you feel."

Helplessly, she let her head loll to one side. His caresses changed, became more insistent. His fingers slid easily against her, gliding on the slick moisture that anticipated his entrance. Long strokes now, deeper, pushing her so high and so fast she thought she might shatter.

"That's right," he murmured. "I can see the color burst in your cheeks like poppies. Your teeth clench to keep from shouting. Your whole body bowing into my touch. Your nipples dark and tight, waiting for release."

"Oh!"

"I like how you feel, do you know that? All sleek and hot and soft. All plumped up for me."

"*Daniel.*"

"I dreamed of this, every night when I crawled into my empty bed, even though I tried not to. Did you think of me?" Heat suffused her, heat and longing and clenching need.

"Yes," she gasped.

"I want to see it now. Will you come for me now?"

She tried to agree, strangled on the word. He slid two fingers deeply inside her, pressing the heel of his hand against her, and each lick of fire he'd ignited in her all burst at once, roared over her in a glorious wildfire, searing her, branding her, making her his.

She forced her eyelids open, looked up at him through a haze of exhaustion and passion. Her Daniel, his eyes a burning blue, his features taut with intense strain.

"Please," she whispered. "I have to feel you."

He levered his body over her and laid himself full length against her. Both hands linked with hers, high over her head, their arms touching all along their length. Chest to chest, belly to belly, leg to leg. His head pressed against her cheek, his breath washing damp over her ear.

He didn't move. Just lay there, every possible inch of exposed skin touching, their hearts thundering hard as if seeking each other out through their skin.

He'd left her in cinders. But this ignited her again, the simple contact of his beloved body on her nakedness. She felt it all, noticed it in minute detail and hoarded it away. The heavy *thump, thump* of his heart against her breast. The slight abrasion of his chest hair on her nipples. The solid length of his thighs bracketing hers.

And, without motion, without determined provocation, the desire built of its own incitement. It multiplied with every heartbeat, staggered higher with every breath. His sex swelled even further against her. Her blood rushed harder, pounded deep in her belly, roared in her ears.

When the movement came, it was so slow, so gentle, it at first seemed only a natural extension of her thoughts. He nudged her legs open with his knee. And then he slid softly inside her, uncomplicated, easy, their joining just one more place they could touch.

Their stillness made each point of contact vital, gave her time to mark the feeling without the blur and rush of impatient desire. She felt his fullness inside her, the deep pulse of his heartbeat.

He rocked against her ever so slightly. A cry burst from deep inside her. Her body curved against him, seeking more.

The rhythm built as slowly, as inexorably and potent as the passion had. His hands curled around hers, fingers linking tight. His shallow thrusts grew deeper each time, like a stream that began slow and easy but swelled and grew into a turbulent, unstoppable rush.

Oh, she had missed this so much! Perhaps she had told herself it was about gratitude, or a child, or duty.

But it wasn't true.

It was all about the fierce, driving energy of his body in hers. About slick skin and stabbing pleasure and emotions made physical. About Daniel pouring himself into her, and her receiving him, a vow that required no words.

And when the end came, it surprised them both. For somehow they'd both thought, both hoped, that maybe they'd go on forever just as they were. For in this, in the staggering ecstasy they found together, there was no hurt or regret. Here, they were perfectly matched.

But it caught them just the same, even as they tried to hold it back. A shout from Kathryn, a groan from Daniel. And even that peaking bliss held a keen edge of sadness.

He slumped against her, his exhaustion a palpable thing. She welcomed his weight. Maybe, she thought, if she didn't move, didn't whisper a word, he'd fall asleep right there, and she could keep him with her for a while longer. His grip relaxed, fingers going slack, and she had to fight to keep from crying *no, no, don't let go.*

"It doesn't change anything," he told her.

She swallowed hard. "I know."

"It's only sex."

She squeezed her eyes shut. "I know."

But when she tentatively laid her hand on his head, her fingers winnowing deep into the rich waves, he let it stay.

Chapter 24

～○○○～

The front parlor looked very different than it had just a few weeks earlier. Kathryn had neatly stitched up a long, unsightly tear in the chaise. She'd dragged in three chairs from unused bedrooms to join the two already there. She'd thrown back the old drapes, tying them in great swoops with a wide length of bright ribbon. And now a pitcher of dried flowers resided on the mantel, and a bowl of glossy red apples sat on a convenient table between the two most comfortable chairs.

It was far from fancy. But she'd claimed it, both for its beautiful wide windows and for its convenient view of the comings and goings in the house. She took enormous satisfaction in that it now looked more like a cozy home than a place inhabited by nothing more than memories and ghosts.

Kathryn sat curled in her favorite chair, a length of soft yellow wool in her lap, fashioning a tiny nightdress. Sallie, who assisted Mrs. Hughes in the kitchen, was due to deliver any day—and none too soon, according to her constant but cheerful complaints, which Kathryn was pleased to listen to at exhaustive length.

Kathryn's life was far from perfect. She hadn't even moved back into Daniel's bedroom. She'd not wanted to assume, and he hadn't asked. But he spent nearly every night in her bed and her arms.

She reminded herself daily that nothing was settled between them. They never discussed her deception. Never mentioned either the future or the past. Daniel still passed out great sums to the people who came to the door although, for the sake of the smooth running of the household, he issued a firm edict that anyone who came to petition him limit their requests to three afternoons a week. Surprisingly, his appeal was, for the most part, respected. Especially after Libeus had made it abundantly clear to those who dared ignore it that inquiries made at any other times would be summarily rejected, a tactic he confessed to Kathryn but had yet to admit to Daniel.

She knew Daniel did not love her. He'd made that obvious. But hope, she'd discovered, was a persistent seedling. Once its roots had taken hold, it refused to be dislodged despite her best efforts.

Although perhaps she really hadn't tried all that hard after all.

And so while her life was not perfect, it was close enough to content her for now.

She'd selected a bright green silk thread to trim the gown. Her precise blanket stitches marched along the neckline like a miniature picket fence. She held the gown up a moment to admire the sunny effect, imagining a tiny, smiling baby in the garment.

"Ho-ho!" Big John said cheerfully, rapping his knuckles on the door in greeting as he popped into the room. A clump of deep red hothouse roses drooped from one massive fist. He caught sight of her project and stopped in his tracks, a broad grin spreading over his face. "Is that what I think it is?"

"No," she denied hastily. "I mean yes, it is, but it's not mine, at least not yet, it's for Sallie—" She stopped, realizing her discomfiture revealed far more than she'd intended.

"Not *yet*?" Big John pounced on the words like he did reeling opponents. "That means there's finally a possibility again, right?"

Kathryn's cheeks flamed, and she pressed her palms to them, the baby garment still clutched in her hand, the fabric a soft caress against her skin. "I don't know why I'm blushing," she admitted. "It's not as if you haven't said far more embarrassing things to me dozens of times."

"Maybe because you want this one to be true." He perched uncertainly on the edge of an armless chair, as if afraid it would collapse under his weight, and blew out a sigh of relief when it held firm. "I'm just glad Daniel's going to be in a better mood. I was tired of filling in for that punching bag he busted. Especially since you damn near fainted when you caught him climbing up to hang another one."

She had to defend herself on that point. "That ladder was *not* in good repair." And her scream upon seeing Daniel wavering dangerously halfway up it had been uncontainable. "And your shoulder, sturdy as it inarguably is, is *not* an adequate brace for his weight at that height."

"The only danger either one of us was in was when we jumped at your screeching. I never would have let go if you hadn't startled me." Chuckling heartily in memory, he slapped at his knee, mangling his bouquet. He stared glumly at the mashed roses. "Oh, damn. Not again."

"Oh, I don't mind," she said with a teasing smile. "They are for me, aren't they?"

"Ah—" Big John shifted in obvious discomfort. "Well, um, actually . . ."

She decided to put the poor man out of his misery. "I really didn't think they were, John."

"Oh." Lit with eagerness and burgeoning joy, his battered, homely face became very nearly handsome. "Have you seen Isabelle, then? Wanted to ask her if she was coming to the fight next week. We're expecting quite a crowd. Bull Newton is a great big oaf, even if he moves slower'n a drunken turtle. Should go down real good."

Come to think of it, Kathryn hadn't seen Isabelle all day. Which wasn't entirely unusual, but she was almost certain she recalled hearing Isabelle mention that she intended to attempt to wheedle Mrs. Hughes into demonstrating her secret pie-crust technique today.

"Sounds like quite an event," she said. "Aren't I invited too?"

"No," he said without hesitation. "They have strict orders not to let you in. And it's beyond me how you got to be so squeamish, considerin' the neighborhood you grew up in and all. You musta seen heads getting bashed in on a regular basis."

"True. But I wasn't so very fond of those particular heads."

"Oh." His gaze dropped, like a schoolboy who'd just been complimented by the pretty young teacher he'd a crush on. "About Isabelle, do you know where I can find her?"

He didn't bother to try and hide his open anticipation at the thought of seeing her.

"Not really," Kathryn admitted, and his face fell.

Big John's heart was a fair match for his outsize frame. And it was, Kathryn suspected, completely unguarded, and as easily bruised as a ripe tomato.

She did not want to see her sister wound him. "John, about Isabelle," she ventured carefully. "There are a few things you don't know—before you met her, I mean—" Oh, dear. Where did her responsibilities lie in this matter? Her heart was firmly aligned with both of them.

"You can stop right now, Kathryn. She told me already, and it don't matter to me none." He smiled ruefully. "I'm hardly parlor material myself."

Isabelle had told him about her former employment? Kathryn paused, readjusting her perceptions. She'd assumed that it was mostly Big John's money and fame that interested Isabelle. Not to mention his obvious adoration. But if she'd taken the chance of confessing her past to him . . . perhaps, just perhaps, she'd grown wiser after all.

And who was Kathryn to judge who belonged together and who didn't? Certainly Big John and Isabelle were no more unlikely a couple, and had less to over-come, than she and Daniel. And she certainly had not given up on them.

"Well then—"

Sagendorf, one of the gardeners who'd taken her under his wing, appeared in the doorway, a dirty trowel in one hand, his begrimed cap jammed under one arm.

"This just came for you, Mrs. Hall. Some guy tossed it to us through the fence, told us to make sure you got it right away, so I thought I'd better bring it on in." He thrust an envelope at her. Dirt smeared one corner. He rubbed it against his denim pants, succeed-ing only in transferring some more grime to it. "Sorry about that."

"Please don't worry about it." Kathryn rose from her chair and went to take the envelope from him. "Thank you for bringing it in."

"Sure." He dragged his cap back over his shiny pate and bobbed his head in her direction. "You coming out later?"

"I expect I am."

"Good. I'll show you how to lay down the crocus bulbs for next spring," he offered.

"I'd appreciate that very much."

He bobbed again and left.

"Getting more invitations to those fancy balls?" John asked, ambling to her side.

"I suppose so," she murmured. "I don't know why they persist in inviting us. I couldn't drag Daniel to one with a full team of oxen, and it's not like I've got an overwhelming desire to spend hours chatting with women who, just a few months ago, didn't even consider me good enough to patch their hems."

There was no address on the front of the envelope. How odd . . . something about the shape of it, the heavy quality of the paper, stirred her memory.

Vague unease rippled up her spine. She ripped the envelope open, snatched the paper it contained, and skimmed the few lines scribbled upon it.

She slammed the paper against her chest, where panic knocked. "Well, John," she said brightly, "you must excuse me, I've just remembered—"

He squinted at her. "You all right?"

"Of course I'm all right." She forced a bright smile and tried to think. What to do?

Your sister is here, the missive had read. *Come and fetch her right now, or I will expend no further effort in keeping her from the career she insists on. Simon.*

Oh, what could possibly have compelled Isabelle to return there *now?* Perhaps it was all some huge, horrible mistake.

Whatever the reason, there was nothing for it but to go down there and fetch her home.

Did she dare go alone? But what choice did she have? Daniel had gone to a meeting at St. Peter's School. And she could not take her mother. Eudora would be of little assistance anyway, and would likely make things far worse by taking it into her head to attack the evil incarnate she considered Simon Moore to be.

Not Tommy, of course. He was far too young to be exposed to such a place.

"You sure?" John was eyeing her far too closely for her peace of mind.

"Of course," she mouthed automatically while her mind spun. Asking John to accompany her was the most logical solution, his might of the most obvious assistance.

But if he saw Isabelle there, in that place . . . it would hurt him so deeply. And God only knew how he'd react. His most immediate response might well be to start swinging indiscriminately. He might get himself killed trying to save Isabelle.

She'd just have to go alone. What was likely to happen? She'd been there twice before and left without incident. It was broad daylight. No threat had been implied in Mr. Moore's letter. She intended to fetch her sister and get out of there as quickly as possible.

If there was even a remote chance that John and Isabelle might find happiness together, she would not jeopardize it by taking John to Simon's whorehouse.

"Kathryn?"

"Hmm?" The smile felt frozen in place, her lips stiff. "Oh, I'm sorry, John." She gave a meager little laugh and fluttered the piece of paper before her. "It's just an invitation, as you suspected. Except this one is from a former employer of mine, who clearly has no idea just who Daniel's wife is, and for a moment I had a brief fantasy of the shock on her face when I showed up at her party."

"So ask Daniel to take you."

"No, I'm sure it will be a dreadful bore anyway. It was all I could do to stay awake while I took her measurements," she murmured before injecting a note of determined gaiety into her voice. "Now then. I think Tommy's in the ballroom, practicing, and thank you *ever* so much for offering to instruct him, by the way, I'm just so *very* delighted to have another man in my life getting the sense beaten out of his head"—she grimaced—"why don't you go on in and give him another lesson before he manages to knock himself out attacking that new punching bag? If I see Isabelle, I'll tell her that you're here. But right now, there really is something I must attend to."

By day, wear showed around the edges of Simon Moore's brothel. Ruts pocked the empty street in front. Old papers and broken bottles cluttered the walk. Daylight stripped the dark, seductive mystery from the place.

Luther, the massive doorman, seemed surprised to see hcr, but let her in immediately. He was even more surprised when she inquired whether he ever got a break from his station. Apparently, someone asking after his comfort was an entirely new experience for him.

The narrow, windowless hallway was dim even at midday. Some of the doors were open, allowing her glimpses of rooms that, while decorated in a bizarre collection of themes—an overblown version of a desert tent, a stone-walled torture chamber, something that looked disconcertingly like a hospital room—resembled theater sets more than anything else, obviously unreal and thus without threat. Uniformed maids toiled in some of them, cleaning industriously with bored expressions, oblivious to their strange surroundings, no different than ordinary hotel maids set on their mundane tasks.

"I don't know where Mr. Moore is," Luther told her. "But Albert's here, he'll take care of you."

The spare office was as neatly organized as always. Albert, nearly invisible in a tan suit the color of his leather chair, flipped through a stack of correspondence at his desk.

But he sprang up at her entrance, as if she were an honored guest he fully expected. "Ah, there you are!"

"If you could just tell me—"

"Luther, you may return to you post," Albert put in quickly. "The lady has no further need of your assistance."

Luther obediently followed instructions, the loud clomp of his shoes on the stairs punctuating the silence.

Albert came around his desk. She jumped slightly when he took her elbow; she did not particularly want to be touched by anyone or anything in this place.

"If you'll just come this way."

"It's really not necessary to disturb Mr. Moore," she said, while trying subtly to tug her arm from his grasp. "If you'll just point me in Isabelle's direction, we'll all get out of your way. I'm sure you have much better things to do than accompany me."

His grip tightened. "Oh, but it is necessary," the clerk said smoothly. "Mr. Moore would be insulted if you came all the way down here and didn't pay your respects." He guided her toward the door leading to Simon's apartments.

"Do you know where Isabelle is?"

"Hmm?" He didn't knock; the doorknob turned easily in his hand. "Oh, of course I know where she is."

He escorted her inside. Unlike the rest of the building, the room looked just as lovely in the afternoon, with daylight sparkling off polished surfaces, bringing out rich jewel tones in the fabrics.

Neither Simon nor Isabelle was there. Albert clicked the door shut behind them and Kathryn spun, finding Albert uncomfortably close behind her, anxiety prickling at the back of her neck for the first time.

"Where is Mr. Moore? I thought that he—"

"Oh, I've complete confidence that he'll be along momentarily. Would you like me to take your things while you wait? Your coat, your bag?" he asked formally, reaching for her.

"No!" Both hands clutching the top of her handbag, she took a step back.

"I'm afraid I really must insist." He snatched the bag from her in one quick move and yanked it open, digging around in the bottom until he pulled out her gun. He dropped the bag unceremoniously to the floor. "Tsk, tsk." He expertly checked the loading and then pointed it directly at her chest. "I neglected to factor in this little detail the last time, and it caused poor Steck no end of misery. But who would have expected such a lovely lady to be carrying around such a nasty thing?"

Kathryn felt as if she'd stepped onstage, right into the middle of Act Two. The other actors knew their lines to perfection, and she didn't even know what the production was. "Anyone with any sense."

He didn't like that. His eyes narrowed in threat. "But I never make the same mistake twice."

Her brain spun uselessly, unable to find an explanation. She didn't know how to react, what move to make, when she didn't have a clue of the problem.

"Where's Isabelle?" she demanded.

"Isabelle? Still propped in the alley behind the dress shop where we caught up with her, I imagine. Oh, we had to drug her a bit, I'm sorry to say. But she'll be waking up in a few hours with nothing more than a fierce headache, and should have no problems finding her way home. I wouldn't hurt someone for no reason at all," he added with some pride. "I'm sorry we had to involve her at all, but you ignored the previous letter," he chided.

"I'm afraid I don't understand."

"I didn't really expect that you would." Soft footsteps sounded behind her and Albert glanced over her shoulder. "Steck, ah, there you are."

Kathryn chanced taking her gaze from the gun for an instant, catching a quick glimpse of a shining bald head and squat body. "But that's—"

Albert sighed. "Yes, I know. And things would have been ever so much simpler if you just would have toddled along when he asked you to after accosting you in the street. Ah well." He shrugged philosophically. "It was a spur-of-the-moment impulse. I should have known better than to expect it to work. And it stimulated me to plan much more carefully this time."

"But I don't—"

He ignored her. "Is he asleep?"

"Like a babe."

"Excellent." Albert nodded in satisfaction. "Though it took three doses before the man so much as nodded off. It's a good thing he's so fond of my coffee. Wouldn't do to have him be seen wandering around the building when people hear the shot, would it?"

"The shot?" she repeated through numb lips. "For me?"

"Of course for you," he said with impatient disdain. "Why else would I go to so much trouble to get you here?" He stepped back and took aim.

"You said I didn't have to watch," Steck complained.

Albert's posture eased a fraction, and he gestured with the barrel of the gun. "Stand watch outside, then."

Steck hurried from the room as if he couldn't wait to be gone.

"If you killed me with your hands instead of shooting me," Kathryn said, "you wouldn't have to worry about anyone hearing the shot. Surely you don't *need* a gun to kill *me*." Just let him come after me with his hands, she thought. And then they'd see how defenseless she was.

Instead Albert laughed. "Oh, my, but that was a clever gambit. Thankfully, I have never been the sort to allow my male pride to goad me into rash action. The gun will do nicely."

The pieces of the puzzle began to click into place. "What if someone comes to see what happened and finds Simon still unconscious? I doubt anyone's going to believe he killed me then."

"Oh please." He waved away such trivial concerns, mildly insulted that she'd even bothered to raise them.

"This is not the sort of establishment where people rush to investigate gunfire. And certainly not in Mr. Moore's private apartments. You see, Mr. Harrison—perhaps you know him—is concerned about, ah, unsavory elements in this city and wishes to speak to Mr. Moore about it. When he arrives for his four o'clock appointment, we will discover the body together." He smiled, smugly secure in the excellence of his planning.

"At which point, of course, you will reluctantly, heroically, assume management of Simon's ventures." Her instincts for men who posed a danger to her were generally well formed. She'd never felt the slightest threat from Albert, and she cursed her intuition for failing her when she needed it most. Maybe because his intended casualty was Simon. She was an unimportant, if necessary, peripheral to his strategy. "But when Simon comes to, he'll waste no time in saying he didn't do it. And . . . oh." She trailed off at the self-satisfied smirk on Albert's innocuous face. "Let me guess. Simon will be dead, too? I suppose he'll have killed himself, distraught after murdering me in a rage?"

Albert clicked his tongue like a teacher disappointed in a weak student. "I admit I'd originally considered that. But Mr. Moore really didn't seem like the sort to do away with himself over a woman, did he? If he had, he would have done it five years ago."

Five years ago. How could she have forgotten? "Where's Mollie?"

"Oh, don't worry. The dear child's off at the park

with Mrs. Holmes. She won't be harmed. Except for missing her father, of course."

"I don't understand," Kathryn murmured. And she didn't give a damn what brilliant scheme Albert had cooked up in his twisted brain. But as long as she kept him talking, he wouldn't shoot her. All she needed was an instant, one moment of arrogant inattention on his part to pounce. He was going to kill her anyway. She'd much rather it be while she was fighting back.

"It is a delicate matter," he agreed. "It's perfectly obvious that Mollie's blood is mixed, and it's widely rumored that her mother was a gently bred woman. And that Simon hates her for spurning them both. However, I—except for the woman herself, and she's certainly not going to tell—am the only one who knows her true identity. So when you are found dead here—"

"But I only met Simon a few months ago!" Albert took such pride in regaling her with his cleverness. Unfortunately, his alertness had yet to waver. Perhaps she needed to prod him a bit more . . . "I can't believe you think that would work. Anybody who does the slightest bit of investigation—"

"Please." His lip curled. "A white woman, the wife of a prominent and wealthy man, found murdered on Simon Moore's floor? He'll be dead long before anyone bothers to check."

It was true. A colored man suspected of harming a white woman—the indignant citizens of Denver would never wait for justice to have its day. Simon would be strung up before he could say a word in protest. He'd be far from the first to suffer that fate.

Her thoughts scrambled, probed for any flaw in Albert's reasoning. "But the letter—the letter you sent me!" Which was actually in her handbag, but he didn't know that. "They'll know it's not his handwriting—"

"But of course it is," Albert said, supremely confident. "Simon can't scrawl much more than his name, though he'd die before admitting it to anyone else. *All* his correspondence is in the same hand."

"Yours," she said flatly.

"Mine."

She'd run out of objections. Albert's fingers tightened fractionally around the gun, and she tensed. All right, so there's no opening to exploit. She'd just jump at him and hope he was a lousy shot.

There was a heavy thump from the outer office, and Albert's head instinctively swung in that direction. Kathryn aimed low, hurling herself at Albert's knees.

When Daniel heard the shot, he was slamming his shoulder against the door, trying to batter it in. The sound gave him impetus, and the next time he hurled himself at the sturdy panel it gave in with a crash.

He stumbled through the wreckage, saw a man struggling with Kathryn.

He tore the man off his wife, hauling him up by his collar, and smashed his fist into that ugly face. He didn't know who the man was. He didn't care. The bastard had put his hands on Kathryn, and that was all that mattered.

There was an awful, satisfying rhythm to his blows. A swing, a crunch of bone on bone. He bent over, following the man as he slumped to the floor, pounding his limp form unmercifully. The slow rivulet of anger Daniel always battled so hard exploded its dam and erupted through him. It rushed through his veins, the chambers of his heart. It fed his power and blotted out his surroundings. He heard nothing, saw nothing. Felt nothing but the awesome fury.

Until Kathryn laid her hand on his arm.

"Daniel," she said softly.

He paused, fist upraised for another blow. The man had stopped moaning and lay in a slack ball on the floor, eyes swollen shut, blood streaming from a broken nose.

"You'll kill him if you continue."

He swallowed. "So?"

"So perhaps we should leave him to Simon Moore's justice."

Air pumped in and out of his lungs. The red haze hovered at the edge of his brain, threatened to consume him again. Surely he had as much right to his satisfaction as Simon.

"You are *my* wife."

"Please?"

Slowly he straightened. Kathryn stared at him, soft mouth trembling, eyes wide and dark.

But not with fear. He looked deep, searching for any hint of revulsion.

His hands were wet with blood. Red blood, the color of fury, of death. How could he ever touch her with those hands again? He'd released the demon, let it flood him.

And he'd stopped merely because she'd asked him to.

"Kathryn." The hell with blood. He grabbed her by the shoulders and hauled her up against him. He stamped quick, hard kisses everywhere he could reach—her brow, her mouth, her ear, her temple, as if to assure himself she was whole.

"It's all right," she said breathlessly. "All the pieces are there."

"Thank God," he murmured. "I'm rather fond of those parts."

"Uh, not to interrupt or anythin'—" Big John stood in the doorway, towering over the bald foothill of a man groaning at his feet. "Do you—"

"John! Isabelle, they left her behind a dress shop, they gave her something to make her sleep, I don't know where it is—"

"I'll find her," his face hardening into the expression that every fighter from San Francisco to Chicago feared.

"Well." After John thundered down the stairs, Kathryn turned to her husband. The relief, after so much tension, left her limp and drained. If he hadn't still been holding her up, she would have slid right down next to Albert. She laid her head against Daniel's chest, reassured by the solid thump of his heart under her ear. "How did you know where to find me?"

"I, um . . . someone told me," he said evasively.

"Who?" She leaned back in his embrace to look up into his face. He refused to meet her gaze. "Daniel, who?"

He sighed in resignation. "I've had someone following you for a while."

"You had someone *spying* on me?" And she'd never

noticed? Well, she supposed she'd earned his mistrust, hadn't she? "Considering how it turned out, I can hardly complain."

"It was for your protection," he said quickly. "When I started giving money away publicly, I thought maybe someone might take it in their head to kidnap you." His eyes grew haunted. "He should have charged in and rescued you right away, rather than tracking me down to ask me how to proceed. We'll be having a conversation about that, you can be sure."

"Oh." She shivered. Kidnapping had never occurred to her. No wonder Daniel had been so adamant about his seclusion. "Wouldn't do for you to have to turn over huge amounts of money to an unworthy criminal just to get me back, would it?"

He laughed, a blessed release. "No, it wouldn't." His arms tightened around her. "Kathryn, what happened?"

The thought of maneuvering the twists and turns of Albert's plot wearied her. "I'll tell you later," she said. "After we get home."

Home. She'd assumed a lot with that word. But he didn't dispute her, and hope sank its roots a little more firmly into her heart.

"What do we do now, then?" she asked.

"First I intend to hold you for an hour or two."

"Good idea." She sighed deeply. "But can we get out of here first?"

"All right." He released her with clear reluctance. "I'll go get the cops," he said. "Though I'd rather—"

"Oh no." She hurried to stop that plan before it got started. She would not be the reason Daniel had more blood on his hands.

But she didn't want to wait around until Simon woke up, either. "You could just tie them up and leave them. There's a doorman downstairs, we can tell him—" She stopped. "You didn't knock him out, too, did you?"

"That is not my first response to everything." He frowned.

"You mean Big John wouldn't let you do it."

"That too," he admitted. "He figured it would be easier all around if we just pretended to be customers."

"Well, I think Luther can handle things from here."

He glared at Albert's broken form. He hadn't moved. "What do you think they'll do with him?"

"Afraid it won't be bloodthirsty enough to satisfy you?"

"Yes," he said darkly.

She did not want to consider Simon Moore's reaction to Albert's betrayal. "I don't think you have anything to worry about."

"We need to do something with the gun." It still rested where it had fallen a few feet from Albert, a cold gleam of beautifully finished metal on the thick blue-and-burgundy rug. "When I heard it go off, I thought that . . ." Rage flickered deep in his eyes again.

"I'm fine, though I doubt the ceiling will ever be the same." She took his face in her palms and looked deeply into his eyes. "I'm fine, Daniel. I promise."

He bent his head and kissed her softly, a kiss of such sweetness and relief it brought tears to her eyes.

"Besides," she said, when he lifted his head, "we'll take the gun with us. It's mine, anyway, and it's proved its worth more than once."

"Yours?" He glanced at the gun suspiciously. "Did you have it with you on the stagecoach route, when we were attacked?"

"Yes," she admitted.

"Why didn't you use it?"

"I was getting to it. But you were so very efficient that you saved me the trouble."

"Hmm." He didn't sound convinced.

But she had a number of ideas on how to convince him. "Come on." She looped her arms around his neck. "Let's go home."

Chapter 25

Libeus met them the instant they came through the front door, his face grave.

Kathryn groped for Daniel's hand. "Isabelle?"

"No, no." Libeus rushed to reassure her. "I mean, I've heard nothing from them as yet, but there's no reason to believe there's anything wrong."

"Oh." Daniel's voice was flat. "Then it's my grandmother."

It took Mrs. Sellington the rest of the day, and a very long night, to die.

Daniel remained by her side the entire time, as a young, dapper doctor came and went, shaking his head regretfully over his patient. Julia, the nurse, hovered around until Daniel firmly commanded her to go to bed, for there was nothing more she could do, and he was determined to stay.

He had far less success in ordering Kathryn away. He told her she looked tired. He insisted it was silly for them both to hold vigil. He promised that he'd call her if he needed her.

He was not fool enough to tell her it was not her responsibility.

She left only to assure herself of her sister's safe return. Isabelle had no memory of what adventure had befallen her, but she was woozily delighted to be carried in Big John's arms. After that, Kathryn slipped out for a few moments at a time, returning with tea or cups of soup or a thick sandwich for Daniel, which she would absolutely not be satisfied until he had consumed.

Hour after hour Mrs. Sellington lay motionless, face pale, her breathing precariously shallow.

And so, in the quiet, uncertain night, Daniel and Kathryn talked in soft voices of all the things that couples usually learn about each other early in their courtship. Daniel related amusing little stories of the trouble he and his stepbrother had gotten into when they were young men. He explained baseball, and described Minnesota, and advised her never, ever to touch his mother's cooking. He told her all about the twins his parents had adopted when he was thirteen, and how much he missed them after he left.

Kathryn depicted Peter in such vivid, precise detail that Daniel almost felt he'd lost a brother, too, one he would have loved as well as she did. She confessed how badly she felt that she could barely remember her father, and how angry she remained at him for abandoning them. She made him laugh with her tale of a customer who kept insisting Kathryn fit her dress tighter and tighter until finally the seams burst wide.

An hour past midnight, the room was as dark and

warm as black velvet. They'd lit only a single candle, an elegant flicker that did little to dispel the darkness.

In a lull in the conversation, she reached over to touch his hair, one thick wave that gleamed in the candlelight. "The first time I met you," she murmured, "all I wanted to do was see the rest of your hair. I was terribly disappointed when you didn't take off your hat."

"My hat? Was I really that impolite, to wear it inside the stage?"

"Oh, that wasn't the first time we met," she said lightly.

He gave her a puzzled frown. "I'm sure I would have remembered—"

Kathryn pressed the back of her hand to her forehead in dramatic fashion. "I am here," she whimpered, "to *beg* him to support his children!"

"That was *you*?"

"That was me," she admitted. "You must have thought I was completely insane."

"I thought you had an extraordinary imagination and a wonderful flair for the dramatic." At her skeptical look, he added, "*And* you were completely insane."

"I'm not quite sure what got into me that day," she said. "At the time I was none too fond of reporters, *or* Daniel Sellington. You were the recipient of both."

He could barely make out her features in the darkness. Just a gleam of teeth, the shimmer of candlelight on a high cheekbone, the shadowy depths of her eyes.

It didn't matter. He knew her in precise detail, the way she held her head, the way her hands reached for something to grasp when she was nervous. He knew the tenor and rhythm of her speech, the tiny hitch in her breath when he touched her.

She could be swaddled in black canvas from head to toe and he would recognize her now.

"I looked for you after you left."

"Really?" Her eyes flashed as she turned her head to stare at him. "Why?"

"I don't know. You interested me, I suppose."

"If you had found me then, things would be very different now."

His fingers linked with hers. "Yes, they would," he agreed, but she couldn't tell if he was happy or sad about that.

Just before sunrise, as the blackness lightened to tentative gray, Daniel's grandmother awoke. She cried the moment her eyes opened, until Daniel sprang up from his seat and leaned over where she could see his face.

She relaxed, sinking into her bed until it seemed as if there was nothing left of her. "There you are," she said with a wavering smile. "I thought I'd lost you."

And just that quickly she lapsed back into unconsciousness. Ten minutes later, they realized the almost imperceptible rise and fall of her chest had stopped. The motion had been so slight they hadn't detected the exact moment it ceased.

Daniel expelled a huge sigh. He stood looking down at the bed as the dawning light picked out every weary line on his face, the deep shadows under his eyes.

Kathryn touched his arm. "She's at peace now."

"People always say that," he murmured. "Do you think it's true?"

"I don't know," she allowed. "But it seems to me she'd be happier in hell with her son than anyplace else without him."

A tired, rueful smile touched his mouth. "Well, that's true enough."

"And now you're free," she said, caught between satisfaction at his release, which he'd earned long ago, and the sudden, sharp fear she could not contain. She'd believed she'd have plenty of time. But her time may have just died, too.

"Free," he repeated, as if repeating a syllable from another language, as though the word held no meaning for him.

Free to leave here. Free to leave me.

Would he go? Of course he would. But could she let him?

"I suppose we should go get someone. We have to take care of—" She gestured awkwardly. *The body* seemed an insensitive word, but that wasn't Mrs. Sellington lying there anymore, either.

Daniel rubbed the back of his neck as if it pained him. "We'll get Libeus. He likes arranging things."

Libeus took over with his usual efficiency. The instant he saw the two of them, he proclaimed them of no use to him whatsoever and propelled them off in the direction of their beds with much greater success than either had accomplished with each other the previous night.

The long corridors seemed to go on forever. They trudged through the halls, heads bowed, never touching. Finally, they paused outside Kathryn's door.

"Well . . ."

Daniel captured her hand, tucked it safely in his. "Come upstairs and stay with me."

They fell asleep the instant their heads hit the pillows, Daniel's body curled protectively around Kathryn's in the narrow bed that only fit two when they were very, very close. They didn't stir when bright sunlight speared through the small window. The clamor and bustle of a busy, awakening household didn't disturb them a whit.

But when Kathryn awoke six hours later, Daniel was gone.

It was all Daniel could do to keep from whipping his horses into a pace completely unsuited for the streets of a busy city. But he had a gift for Kathryn, and he couldn't wait to see her face when he gave it to her. He kept patting his jacket pocket, making sure it was still there, imagining exactly what she might do to show her appreciation.

He careened around the last corner and nearly ran down a half dozen women scurrying across the road. He hauled back on the reins, anticipation riding him hard. The women, of various ages but all dressed in flashy clothes the likes of which were seldom seen in this part of town, giggled up at him. He politely touched his fingers to the brim of his hat. As soon as they passed, he called to his team, who jolted forward immediately, causing the last woman to yelp and dash the last few feet to the safety of the sidewalk.

The women were heading for his house, he realized with a start. Along with at least a dozen other people making their way toward the front gate.

In his excitement, had he forgotten that it was his afternoon to receive requests? But no, he'd given away twelve thousand dollars just yesterday. He was certain of it.

He turned for the side gate, his curiosity now almost as strong as his impatience. A boy—and, try as he might, he could not remember hiring this one—jumped to his feet from his station beside the gate and tugged it open before Daniel could issue a request.

He pulled into the yard, tossed the reins to a hovering groom, and vaulted from the seat. Were they having a party someone had forgotten to tell him about? A mob of adolescent boys were playing baseball in the side yard, home plate perilously near the rosebushes. A few older men leaned against the stable wall, puffing on pipes and chatting with several of his grooms. Two of the gardeners were on their knees in the vegetable garden, three young children he'd never seen before peering over their shoulders at something of interest.

He dashed for the back stairs and into the house. A hubbub of noise greeted him, shouts of bright laughter and the steady buzz of conversation. From somewhere deep inside, he could swear he heard a perfectly harmonized version of "I'll Take You Home Again, Kathleen."

Down the hallway, he could see workers scampering back and forth, their arms full of linens and clothing and, in one case, a huge brass washtub.

He would never find his wife in this madness.

Looking for sanity, he poked his head in the kitchen and found only more chaos. Every stove was lit.

Lengths of toweling covered neat rows of bread pans, gentle curves nudging up dunes of fabric where the dough was rising nicely. Three women chopped carrots on a wood-block table, sacks of potatoes and parsnips at their feet. Sallie, with her feet up, a dish towel draped over her huge belly, was issuing orders from a corner by the hearth.

Mrs. Hughes, wisps of gray hair and steam wreathing her red face, straightened next to the stove she'd been checking, closed the oven door with a bang, and caught sight of him. "Don't come in! We've no room. Not unless you're willing to work."

"I was just looking for my wife."

A secret smile flirted with Mrs. Hughes's lips. "Oh, she's in the front parlor. Of course."

In the hallway, he nearly collided with one of the gardeners carrying a lug of onions. The man nodded in acknowledgment and rushed past without a word. In the foyer, he was beaned by a small leather ball, tossed from the upstairs landing by a towheaded youngster to another one who had to be his twin at the bottom of the stairs.

If madness had overtaken his house, the front parlor was the center of the asylum. At least thirty people were there, on benches dragged in from the garden and blankets stolen from guest rooms. There was the source of the singing, three lean young men standing by the window, now swinging into "My Darling Clementine" in rich full voices that just managed to be heard over the din of conversation. On the other side of the room a handful of young boys threw dice against the wall, bursting into wild shouts when one of them came up with an especially good toss. There were even dogs, two skinny, mangy creatures by the fireplace, intent on cleaning a little girl from head to toe with their tongues.

And right in the middle of the pandemonium stood his wife. She had a babe in her arms, its sticky hands clutching great handfuls of her hair on either side of her head, and she was grinning at the child as if she— he? Who could tell?—had just done the most amazing thing in the world.

"Kathryn," he hollered, but his words got swallowed into the clamor. He gulped a huge breath and tried again. *"Kathryn!"*

She looked up immediately, her eyes searching the room, and when her gaze found him she lit up like a child on Christmas morning. Though he couldn't hear, he saw her mouth form his name. She gently disengaged the child and handed him to Libeus, earning her a startled look.

Kathryn had always been a beautiful woman. But as she wended her way through the crowds, she was radiant, sunshine and happiness spinning a beaming halo around her.

"Oh, Daniel, you're home." Her gesture encompassed the entire room. "Isn't it wonderful? They all helped, Mother and Isabelle and Tommy and Joey. Even Big John and Libeus—"

"Who *are* all these people?"

"From our old neighborhood, mostly," she said, as if the answer was obvious. "Though John found quite a few more, I'm afraid to ask where. And I've made up my mind to send a message to Simon Moore, I'm sure that he knows lots of people who—"

"But Kathryn, what are you *doing*?"

"I'm helping you get rid of your money, of course. I'm not sure how much so far, it was twenty thousand at last count, you'll have to ask Libeus to be more precise, but oh, I've lots more ideas—" She grinned at him, gave his hands a firm squeeze. "Oh, Daniel, isn't it *wonderful*?"

If he didn't get the woman out of there immediately, he was going to do something that Denver would talk about for years to come. "Kathryn, I must speak with you."

"Oh." Her smile dimmed. "Of course, Daniel, I—"

"Alone."

"That might be a bit of a problem."

"Are there people *everywhere*?"

"Well yes, almost, you see—"

He couldn't wait any longer. He grabbed her hand and towed her through the mansion, his grip firm so she wouldn't slip away, his impatient stride forcing her to skip every third step to keep up with him. Twice someone came forward to ask her for something, and he waved them away. "Later," he growled. "She's mine for now."

In his little room beneath the eaves, he kicked the door shut behind them with a resounding slam and turned to her. "What are you doing?"

"I—" A bit nervous now that the moment had come, she pleated her fingers together. "I've given this a lot of thought, Daniel. You are my husband. You are going to leave here now that you are released. And it is my duty as your wife to support you in all things."

"Kathryn," he whispered through a voice suddenly gone hoarse.

"Let me finish. Or I might never get it all out." Her mouth firmed into a beautiful, stubborn line. "But I've decided it is *not* my duty to allow you to go off by yourself. So I'm going with you, and you have no say whatsoever in the matter."

"I don't?"

"No. I love you, Daniel." All the infinite colors of the ocean swirled together in her eyes. "Whether you like it or not, whether you want it or not, whether you *believe* it or not, it's the truth. I love you."

"Kathryn." It was difficult to talk, he discovered, when your heart was jumping up and down in your chest. "What about your family?"

"They'll manage." She paused before continuing softly, "You're my family now, too, Daniel."

He'd taken a thousand mighty punches from Big John. He'd never been more stunned. And then he remembered what he carried in his breast pocket.

Without regard for his pocket seams, he shoved his hand inside and hauled out the tiny, leather-bound book. "Here," he said, thrusting it at her. "It's for you."

Uncertainly, Kathryn took the book and opened it up. Her mouth popped open as she stared down at the figures written in it. Slowly, she lifted her gaze to his. "A million dollars?"

"It's yours," he told her. "I arranged it at the bank this afternoon. Now you never have to worry, ever again. You'll always be safe."

"I don't want it," she said flatly, and shoved it back at him.

"Kathryn . . ."

"All right, maybe I can't say I don't *want* it," she admitted begrudgingly. "But I don't *need* it." Love and faith and happiness beamed from her smile.

He folded her fingers gently around the bankbook. "It's not a test, Kathryn."

"I'm not going to keep it," she insisted.

"So put it away for our children. Or stick it in the back of a drawer and forget about it. I don't care."

"But . . . why?"

"I love you."

"Daniel." Tears stung her eyes. She longed to believe him. She was utterly terrified to believe him.

"I can't pretend that when I met you, when I married you, it wasn't just because you were the prettiest thing I'd ever seen, and because I thought you wanted me without knowing who I was." He touched her cheek. "But the truth is when we're a hundred years old, wrinkled as dried apples, and you'll still be the most beautiful woman I've ever laid eyes on. And it has nothing to do with your face."

She blinked hard. "How can you—"

"I finally figured out I had a choice. If I trusted you, and you—" Daniel paused, for just the thought of that possibility was too much to bear, even now. And then he put it behind him forever. "Then I would be miserable for the rest of my life. But if I didn't trust you, if we went on as we were, I'd be miserable for the rest of my life anyway." He smiled. "I'm not a stupid man, Kathryn, though you might choose to argue that on a few points. So I choose to trust. In you, in us." He brought his hands up to cradle her face. "But I never, ever had a choice about loving you."

She threw her arms around him, held on tight, and believed.

Epilogue

Minnesota
Eight years later

The trim brick house, perched high on the bluffs of the Mississippi near St. Paul, was not large. But in summer its gardens bloomed with flowers, and in winter its hearth crackled with bright flames. The snug rooms rang with a few tears and a lot of laughter. The kitchen always had plenty of luscious food, there were hugs to be had for the asking—and often without asking—at any time of the day or night. The house stretched regularly to accommodate a surprising number of visitors, and no one who ever wandered by saw the place without thinking, *Now, that looks like a home.*

Its owners had built the place four years ago, when they discovered that the continuous travel possible with one daughter was far more difficult with two. They didn't mind a bit. The world could wait, but babies didn't.

It was nearing midnight on a warm September evening. The air smelled of leaves and apples, and vi-

brated with the call of the owl who lived in the big
oak in the backyard.

Kathryn tucked six-month-old Peter, who still insisted on one late feeding to get through the night, into
his cradle, pulling the light quilt her mother had made
snugly over his sturdy little shoulders. She brushed a
finger down the smooth round curve of his cheek,
wondered if a person's heart could possibly be any
more full than hers was, and went down to tempt her
husband away from his work.

The room Daniel used as his office was scarcely
larger than a closet. It was just off the parlor where
their children usually played, and the door always remained open. It was how Daniel wanted it, but it
meant that he didn't accomplish much real work except when the children were sleeping.

She leaned against the doorway, admiring her husband. The single lamp on his desk cast a golden oval
over three piles of paper, two empty coffee cups, a
plate with the remains of a slice of apple pie, and him.
He'd gained a few gray strands in his dark waves over
the years, ones he always claimed he'd earned by
having to assist her when she'd gone into labor in a
jungle camp on the shores of South America, where
they where waiting for a steamship to fetch them back
to the States. She supposed that hadn't been the wisest
decision she'd ever made, insisting that they could
travel a few more miles up the river before heading
home, but how was she to know Sarah would be a
month early? And the child certainly hadn't slowed
down since.

But despite the gray, and a few extra pounds—

which she'd acquired as well—he was still a very fine figure of a man. At that moment, however, he was staring glumly at the letter in his hand.

"What's the matter?"

He looked up at her and smiled. If, over the years, she had ever doubted whether Daniel loved her, it was dispelled each time he smiled at her like that. His chair squeaked as he pushed back from the desk, making room. She plopped down in his lap with a contented sigh, pillowing her head on his shoulder.

"So what happened?" she asked.

"You remember Josiah Benton? The busted old-timer who came by six months ago?"

"No teeth, no hair, no gold?"

"That's the one." He tossed the letter onto his desk in disgust. "He just made the biggest strike in Montana in twenty years."

She chuckled at his dismay.

"Hey!" He gave her a light squeeze. "You're supposed to be properly sympathetic."

"I am," she said. "I've finally received permission from the city to open that orphanage and school in San Francisco. Got a nice big old hotel picked out for the place, too. But I'm afraid it's in terrible need of renovation."

"Oh?" He perked up immediately. "Will it be expensive?"

"Extremely," she told him gravely.

"You are such an excellent wife." One hand stroked her arm softly, shoulder to elbow and back again. He could never get enough of touching her. "Will we need to go out there?"

"Only if we want to. Tommy's ready to handle this one on his own, I think. John and Isabelle can manage to hold down the fort in Denver, especially now that the twins are getting older—and before the next one arrives."

"*The next one?* I'm going to have to have a talk with that fellow."

"Oh, not that I know of, not yet. But it's been almost a year, and you know those two."

Daniel's hand slid down to her belly. "We're falling behind."

Lifting her head, she looped her arms around his neck, her eyes shining. "I have every faith you'll do your best to catch up."

And, as Daniel Hall lowered his head to kiss his wife, he knew he was a very rich man indeed.